PRAISE FOR *THE REVELATORS*

"Raucous [and] unflinching."　　　—*Tampa Bay Times*

"Atkins delivers an action-forward homage, complete with a cordite-smelling finale (blood-spattered, yes, but cleansing, too)."　　　—*Booklist*

PRAISE FOR *THE SHAMELESS*

"Atkins' signature blend of country noir and Southern humor remains on display here, though this time the focus is on the personal traumas in the Colson family's closets. Another strong outing in a consistently fine series."

　　　—*Booklist*

"Atkins makes the thrilling plot accessible for first-timers, while further deepening both main and secondary characters. Series fans will be eager to see what's next in store for Quinn."　　　—*Publishers Weekly*

PRAISE FOR *THE SINNERS*
A *NEW YORK TIMES BOOK REVIEW* EDITORS' CHOICE

"Mississippi's rural Tibbehah County—the evocative setting for Ace Atkins' superior series about Quinn Colson, a former Army Ranger turned sheriff—is the crossroads of all things good and evil. . . . Action-packed . . . Tibbehah County and the town of Jericho are small areas with big-city problems as Atkins maintains the sense of community that flows through the region."　　　—Associated Press

"[A] boisterous series."
　　　—Marilyn Stasio, *The New York Times Book Review*

"With its Elmore Leonard–feel and a cast of unforgettable characters, this is noir with a Deep South edge."

—*Parkersburg News and Sentinel*

PRAISE FOR *THE FALLEN*

"Beneath the down-home Southern trappings, fans will find Atkins' customary mixture of political corruption, true-blue policing, intimate betrayals, and wholesale violence. . . . Puts a whole new spin on catharsis."

—*Kirkus Reviews*

"As in recent books, Atkins lightens the mood with some humor, presenting a warts-and-all portrayal of a Southern community."

—*Publishers Weekly*

"Action-packed and engrossing . . . A superb novel about corruption, politics, crime, dirty deals, and people trying to lead honest lives. Atkins delivers stronger tales with each outing."

—Associated Press

"*The Fallen* stands as an example of crime fiction's ability to reflect society while completely entertaining the reader. . . . It is Michael Mann's *Heat* filtered though both Faulkner and *Smokey and the Bandit*, with Atkins fully engaged in every trope he loves as well as the time he is writing in."

—MysteryPeople.com

PRAISE FOR *THE INNOCENTS*

"Scorching . . . Quinn Colson and his ornery sidekick Lillie Virgil embark on a tense search for answers that may rip the community apart." —*The Atlanta Journal-Constitution*

"Atkins delivers another rousing thriller. *The Innocents* moves at a brisk pace through Mississippi backroads to diners and cigar bars where deals are made but not always carried out. Atkins allows Quinn to make mistakes and have foibles, making him an even more complex character."
—Associated Press

PRAISE FOR *THE FORSAKEN*

"Articulate characters [and] a densely layered stack of stories. Atkins finds his natural-born storytellers everywhere. It's all music to these ears."
—Marilyn Stasio, *The New York Times Book Review*

"Atkins excels in solid pacing, effective dialogue and compelling characters. . . . [He] shapes Quinn not as a superman, but as a flawed man who wants to do the right thing for his hometown. . . . The excellent Quinn Colson novels, as illustrated in *The Forsaken*, are the true showcase for Atkins' storytelling skills."
—Associated Press

"A darkly exciting thrill ride."
—*Tampa Bay Times*

PRAISE FOR *THE REDEEMERS*

"Gripping . . . Atkins's Quinn series has been twice nominated for an Edgar Award, and *The Redeemers* continues those high standards. Atkins delves deeply into each character's motives [and] a thrilling chase through the woods shows the beauty and ferocity of nature."
—Associated Press

"Adventure writing of a high order . . . Richly packed with colorful characters and expert writing. An exciting, fast-moving portrait of a formidable hero doing battle with an all-too-believable onslaught [of corruption, violence, and rampant ignorance] that threatens the little hometown he loves."
—*The Washington Post*

PRAISE FOR *THE BROKEN PLACES*

"Ace Atkins's killing honesty sets a new standard for Southern crime novels."
—Marilyn Stasio, *The New York Times Book Review*

"The action is stark and gripping, the Southern locale suitably atmospheric and the bevy of characters convincing."
—*Houston Chronicle*

PRAISE FOR *THE LOST ONES*
NOMINATED FOR THE EDGAR AWARD FOR BEST NOVEL

"Masterful . . . The novel offers fast-paced action, believable dialogue—it's clear that Atkins has long lived among the kind of folks populating his work."
—*The Commercial Appeal* (Memphis, TN)

"Quinn has a quick wit, a strong code of honor, and radiates sex appeal, but more importantly he knows the difference between law and order."
—*Milwaukee Journal Sentinel*

ALSO BY ACE ATKINS

QUINN COLSON NOVELS
The Ranger
The Lost Ones
The Broken Places
The Forsaken
The Redeemers
The Innocents
The Fallen
The Sinners
The Shameless

ROBERT B. PARKER'S SPENSER NOVELS
Robert B. Parker's Lullaby
Robert B. Parker's Wonderland
Robert B. Parker's Cheap Shot
Robert B. Parker's Kickback
Robert B. Parker's Slow Burn
Robert B. Parker's Little White Lies
Robert B. Parker's Old Black Magic
Robert B. Parker's Angel Eyes
Robert B. Parker's Someone to Watch Over Me

NICK TRAVERS NOVELS
Crossroad Blues
Leavin' Trunk Blues
Dark End of the Street
Dirty South

TRUE CRIME NOVELS
White Shadow
Wicked City
Devil's Garden
Infamous

THE
REVELATORS

ACE ATKINS

G. P. PUTNAM'S SONS · NEW YORK

PUTNAM
— EST. 1838 —

G. P. PUTNAM'S SONS
Publishers Since 1838
An imprint of Penguin Random House LLC
penguinrandomhouse.com

The Library of Congress has catalogued the G. P. Putnam's Sons hardcover edition as follows:

LIBRARY OF CONGRESS CATALOGING-IN-PUBLICATION DATA

Names: Atkins, Ace, author.
Title: The revelators / Ace Atkins.
Description: New York: G. P. Putnam's Sons, [2020] |
Series: A Quinn Colson novel
Identifiers: LCCN 2020017668 (print) | LCCN 2020017669 (ebook) |
ISBN 9780525539490 (hardcover) | ISBN 9780525539513 (ebook)
Subjects: GSAFD: Suspense fiction. | Mystery fiction.
Classification: LCC PS3551.T49 R49 2020 (print) |
LCC PS3551.T49 (ebook) | DDC 813/.54—dc23
LC record available at https://lccn.loc.gov/2020017668
LC ebook record available at https://lccn.loc.gov/2020017669

First G. P. Putnam's Sons hardcover edition / July 2020
First G. P. Putnam's Sons premium edition / June 2021
G. P. Putnam's Sons premium edition ISBN: 9780525539506

Printed in the United States of America
1   3   5   7   9   10   8   6   4   2

For Charles Portis

Some things you must never stop refusing to bear. Injustice and outrage and dishonor and shame. No matter how young you are or how old you have got.

—William Faulkner, *Intruder in the Dust*

Let the enemy come till he's almost close enough to touch, then let him have it and jump out and finish him up with your hatchet.

—Rogers' Rangers Standing Order No. 19

THE
REVELATORS

Quinn. *Quinn*. Goddamn you."

Sheriff Quinn Colson knew it was Boom Kimbrough but couldn't focus on his best friend's face. Rain hammered the creek bed where he lay on his back, knowing he was bleeding out but not feeling much of anything. The sky above him was half-covered in fast-moving gray-black clouds over a hazy yellow harvest moon. It was Halloween night out on Perfect Circle Road in Tibbehah County, Mississippi, and damn if the shit hadn't hit the fan.

"Quinn, man," Boom said. "Stay with me, brother. Can you hear me? We got folks coming."

Boom pulled Quinn from the creek bed onto a sandy shoal. His GMC truck lay on its side, engine still running with one headlight shining down the length of the crooked creek. Holy hell, it was tough to breathe, a raspy hollow pain with each breath letting Quinn know he'd collapsed a lung. He'd been shot twice, maybe a few more times for good measure.

Those militia boys had ambushed Quinn as soon as he rolled up. One stuck a gun to his spine while they took his deputy Kenny and locked him up inside the trunk of his own cruiser. Kenny kicking and yelling while the Watchmen went to work on Quinn with their fists, boots, and stocks of their rifles. Quinn thought he'd be protecting a stripper named Dana Ray from her shitbird boyfriend but instead walked right into a trap.

Boom held Quinn's head in his lap, pressing his old hunting jacket to Quinn's back and side, again promising help was on its way. All Quinn had to do was breathe, stay awake and alive, and with him. Boom used the hook of his prosthetic hand to tear Quinn's bloody shirt loose from his chest, rain falling in curtains all around them. Cold water running down Boom's black face and down his curly black beard.

"She set me up," Quinn said. His mouth was so damn dry, tasting the rainwater on his lips.

"I know."

"Fannie Hathcock," Quinn said. "She got 'em out here."

"Who shot you?" Boom asked.

Quinn couldn't answer, feeling a searing pain in his back and deep into his chest, eyes closing and not opening until he was in the white-hot light of the hospital being wheeled down a long hallway. No longer his best friend Boom, but his wife Maggie, a registered nurse in street clothes, talking to him, telling him everything was OK. He was going to be OK. She smelled like clean laundry and sunshine, a silver cross ticking from around her neck. Maggie's calm, pleasant freckled face flushed red and worried. Her long, lean fingers on his face telling him how much she loved him.

"Why?"

"Because you don't know what it's like to quit, Ranger."

Her face so perfect and interesting, the clearness of her green eyes and the intensity of all those little freckles on her cheeks. Her mouth a red pout, eyes radiating heat and electricity and warmth and goodness. He reached up to touch her face, all that soft white light enveloping him in a bright explosion. And then it was hours or several days later when he saw his wife again, this time with Boom standing over her shoulder. She said Quinn was on the other side of two surgeries, his body healing up and getting stronger every day. Boom looking down and smiling, promising they now had the bastards on the run, the real fun just about to start. Quinn seemed to stay in that hospital bed forever. Lillie Virgil sitting up with him on long nights, updating him on what she knew from the Marshals Service. His mother Jean praying and offering daily inspirational quotes from Jesus Christ and Elvis Presley. His nephew Jason and his adopted son Brandon stopping by each morning, looking awkward and nervous, not sure what to make of Quinn lying flat on his back with all those tubes and wires. Quinn would wink at them and tell them they'd be back out hunting turkey and fishing for bass real soon.

It was weeks later, or maybe a full month, when Quinn woke up to see the familiar shape of a man sitting in the shadows, reclining in a chair in his hospital room. It was very late or very early, full dark outside the window. The shadow man noticed Quinn's movement and turned on a lamp beside him, illuminating his bald head and clean-shaven face. He wore a black polo shirt, both arms covered in a labyrinth of colorful tattoos.

"Shit, that was close," the man said.

"Missed my heart by a quarter-inch," Quinn said. "That's either good luck or bad aim."

"You see who did this?" Jon Holliday, federal agent, asked. "Which one of them?"

"One of the Watchmen tried to stop him," Quinn said. "The shooter was an Indian. Son of a bitch looked just like Jay Silverheels."

"Midnight Special from the Rez," Holliday said. "Same one who busted in the jail for Wes Taggart."

"That's the way I see it."

"Could you ID him?"

"Pretty dark night out on Perfect Circle Road," Quinn said, lips cracked and dry. "But I could try."

"You know who sent him?"

"You bet," Quinn said. "Fannie Hathcock."

"Yes, sir," Holliday said, leaning forward in the chair. His face moving deep into shadow. "Only we can't get close to her or any of her new friends in Jackson. Governor Vardaman signed a special order to lock down Tibbehah County. Says the lawlessness has gone on too long."

"He can't do that."

"Too late," Holliday said. "Already has."

Quinn tried to push himself up off his back, the pain coming on now, something fierce and sharp hitting him in his spine and deep down into his lungs. His eyes watered as Holliday got to his feet and helped Quinn lower back into a soft pillow. Quinn let out a long and ragged breath, his wind raspy and uneven.

"We've got to play Vardaman's game for a while."

"No way," Quinn said.

"Don't have much choice," Holliday said. "You're going to have to trust me. *Again*."

Quinn didn't answer, trying to steady his breath, adjust his eyes into the shadows across Holliday's face and body as the man stood over his hospital bed. On his forearm, a tattoo of a skull in a beret grinned under the banner DEATH BEFORE DISHONOR.

"I trust you," Quinn said. "But I can't hang back. As soon as I'm back on my feet—"

"I'll need help," Holliday said. "But you won't be alone. Even if you don't see 'em, we got this whole county wired to take down Fannie Hathcock and the Syndicate. OK?"

"Are we under martial law?"

"Vardaman's version of it," Holliday said. "He's set up some kind of committee in Jackson to scrutinize the criminal element in Tibbehah County."

"Son of a damn bitch."

Holliday stuck out his hand. Quinn reached up slow and steady to take it. His grip weaker than he would've liked.

"Good to see you back with the living," Holliday said.

"How long?"

"Patience and perseverance," Holliday said, grinning. "We're baiting the field now."

1

Ten months after the shooting out on Perfect Circle Road, a twelve-year-old girl named Ana Gabriel walked in the ninety-five-degree August heat with her little brother Sancho. Sancho was only nine and knew nothing about politics or corruption in Tibbehah County, only that their mother hadn't shown up to drive them home on their first day of school and he was upset. It frustrated him even further that Ana Gabriel had decided they'd better walk than wait, Sancho questioning all that was good and holy, a full four miles back to the Frog Pond Trailer Park, where so many of the Mexican and Guatemalan families had settled. They were very tired and sweaty, cutting through a thicket of pines and down through a kudzu ravine that hugged the highway.

"I knew this day would come," Sancho said. "The Rapture. Just like the movies from church. Angels blowing trumpets. People being whisked into the clouds to

meet Jesus, even those in airplanes or sitting on toilets.
He has taken all the good people and left the sullen and
the wicked behind. Every story must end, Ana Gabriel.
We know as much. Now it is time for the human race."

"Would you please shut up?" Ana Gabriel Hernandez-
Ramirez said, walking beside her little brother. "Mamá
has a reason. She is still at work. Maybe she had to go to
the market to buy eggs, cheese, and milk. Perhaps even
had engine trouble. Her car. You know that car. So many
troubles."

"Then why won't she answer her phone?" Sancho
asked, wide face shining with sweat, trudging alongside
her, short legs trying to keep up. "We have called her
twenty times."

An odd August stillness fell over the Frog Pond
Trailer Park on the outskirts of Jericho, Mississippi. Ana
Gabriel had never heard it so quiet or seen it so empty,
draped in an odd dusky gold light, the heat radiating up
from the ground. Sancho followed her into the little
maze that took them to the far corner of the park to the
white single-wide they rented by the week.

"Our family left us," Sancho said. "Again."

"They would never leave us," Ana Gabriel said. "They
love us very much. Take that back or I will punch you
very hard in the head."

"Then it is the Rapture," he said, excited. "We have to
find the others, start deciding who is in charge. I would
like to be the mayor of the city. Or perhaps the president
of the United States. I would also like my own very large
truck. One with big silver wheels and a winch. I like

GMC but would settle for a Chevy if we find one with the keys in it."

"You're only nine."

"Does it matter now?" he said. "Now that we are the only ones left? All of it so very sad. The bad children who didn't mind their parents or eat all their dinner. Ana Gabriel, we haven't been to church in at least three Sundays. Think of the shame."

"This is something else," she said. "Two girls I know were brought to the principal's office and never returned. You yourself said you saw Tomas in the lunchroom, crying along with his uncle. I don't like where any of this is headed."

"Mamá forgot us."

"Mamá never forgets," Ana Gabriel said. Her mind already turning over a hundred different possibilities of what might have happened. All of them bad. "She works hard. She works late. You know this. It's a new job. She has responsibilities. So many chickens to clean and pull out their insides. Why do you always worry? Why do you always think the worst?"

"That's my job," Sancho said. "I am the man. The head of the household. Our uncle Chuy told me as much over the summer. *C'mon*. We need to start gathering wood for the fire."

"It's ninety-five degrees," Ana Gabriel said. "Why would we need a fire?"

"Anytime anyone is lost or left behind, they build a fire. Don't you pay attention to what we've seen on *The Walking Dead*?"

The journey to the Frog Pond hadn't been so bad, pushing through the woods, rows and rows of skinny pine trees planted as neatly as crops of corn, the August sun shining down through the branches and onto the copper-colored needles at their feet. Sancho was as wide as he was tall, hoisting his heavy Spider-Man backpack across his shoulders. His face round, with black hair cut still and straight with their mother's scissors. Ana Gabriel stood a head taller but didn't let her mother touch her hair, letting it grow straight, long, shiny, and black down to her backside.

Today, she'd tied it in a neat purple ribbon, freshly combed for the first day of school. If only she hadn't had to sweat through her new linen shirt embroidered with red roses or dirtied her jeans from Walmart, covered full of brambles and cockleburs.

"If you're so smart," Sancho said, "you tell me where is everyone? Where has everyone gone?"

Sancho was right. The Frog Pond park was filled with a quiet so complete, she could hear the wind cutting through the spaces between the old rusted trailers. A loose door slamming over and over against the jamb. She looked down at her new Reeboks, bright white and perfect this morning, now covered in a fine brown dust.

"I bet everyone is on the Square, getting ice cream and milk shakes at Sonic," she said. "Or buying new shoes."

"My shoes are old," Sancho said. "They have the name *Bobby* written inside with marker and smell like sweaty socks. Who was this Bobby? Why did he smell so bad?"

"We are grateful for what we have."

"You are grateful for that silver bracelet," he said. "The one your boyfriend gave you."

She felt her face flush. "He's not my boyfriend."

"Then why do you sit with him at church and walk with him for Sunday dinner?" Sancho said. "I even saw you holding his hand maybe six times this summer. The boy with the light brown skin and bright blue eyes. *Jason Colson*. I know his name. You've already written it in pink marker."

Ana Gabriel moved her hands over her backpack, biting her lower lip. "Shut up," she said. "Shut up. Shut up. Shut up."

"Saying it so many times only proves what I say," Sancho said. "I hope he was a bad kid, maybe one who cheats and steals, for your sake, and that he wasn't taken up to heaven in a golden light. That way you and him might kiss and warm yourself by the fire."

She was about to whack Sancho on the back of his head with her book bag when they spotted the other children gathering in the center of the trailer park. Maybe eight, nine of them, some of them crying. One boy sitting on the wooden steps of his trailer, his head in his hands. They were all *The Others*, the new ones to Tibbehah County. The Mexicans. The Guatemalans. The Hondurans. All different, although most of the children had been born here. They were supposed to be Americans, but few seemed to agree.

After ten different schools in twelve years, Ana Gabriel had moved across much of Texas and Alabama and then Georgia. Their last home had been in a very old apartment complex on Buford Highway in Atlanta, barely seeing their father, who worked every day in construction, doing the jobs that no sane person would want. Lathering tar on roofs, connecting tubes under old houses. He was still there, or so she thought, sending them money every few weeks even though he had a new wife and family. Their mother had taken a job at a poultry processing plant in Tibbehah.

A place that smelled so horrible, her mother would strip and shower after work every day, letting her clothes soak in bleach.

Little dust devils turned and kicked up in a hot summer wind between Ana Gabriel and her brother. She looked over at Sancho, and he gave her a smug, self-knowing smile.

"What?" Ana Gabriel said, approaching the other children. "What is it?"

"They've taken them," a boy about her age said. She'd seen him only once, maybe twice, at The River, getting supplies. His name was Armando and his father had been the one who'd offered the processing plant job to her mother. Hector, his father, acting as a go-between, often gathered workers at the trailer park, telling them what he'd heard from the plant owners, letting them know their rights when there was trouble.

"Who?"

"Our parents," Armando said. "They are all gone."

Although it hadn't quite been a year since the shooting, Quinn felt like his recovery had gone on forever. Draining and bandaging the wounds, getting up slow and easy to his feet, learning to walk again, taking weeks and months off from the Tibbehah County Sheriff's Office. If it hadn't been for his wife Maggie, he'd probably still be in the hospital or gone insane. She made him walk, drove him to rehab, looked after his medication and nutrition. No fatty foods. Almost no alcohol and limited coffee. Damn, how Quinn loved coffee.

"Maggie sees you smoking that cigar, she's gonna have your ass," Boom said.

"You gonna tell her?" Quinn said.

"Nope."

"Wasn't I told to resume normal activities?"

"Is drinking and smoking at four in the afternoon normal?"

Quinn shrugged and blew a smoke ring. "Is now."

Quinn and Maggie and his adopted son Brandon lived on a fifty-acre parcel of land near a hamlet called Fate. The house was white and tin-roofed, a classic old L-shaped farmhouse built more than a hundred twenty years ago by his great-grandfather, an austere, big-bearded Methodist preacher by the name of William "Big Bill" Beckett. Quinn had barely left the land the last few months, taking walks on the trails in and around the property, at first moving slowly up to the pond, taking nearly thirty minutes for what used to be a five-minute trip. Over the summer he'd taken to fishing, welcoming his old deputy Lillie Virgil and Special Agent Jon Holliday. Boom came over nearly every day, sitting with Quinn until the sun went down.

Quinn was a tall white man, thinner than normal, with a sharp profile and close-cropped dark hair. Some folks told him he had "flinty eyes" and he wasn't sure whether that was a compliment or an insult. His best friend Boom was black and much larger, six-six and two-sixty, with only one arm. His right arm had been blown off while delivering a tanker of water to Fallujah. Boom had been in the Mississippi National Guard and Quinn in the 3rd Battalion of the 75th Ranger Regiment. They'd known each other since they were five years old.

"What bothers me most about this new sheriff is his attitude," Boom said. "Man's cocky as hell. Sure loves telling folks that he'd gone to Vanderbilt and served as a captain in Afghanistan."

"Even wrote a book about it," Quinn said. "I heard they're selling it at the Jericho Farm and Ranch for nineteen ninety-five. *Honor and Duty.*"

"I wouldn't wipe my ass with that shit," Boom said. "Most folks saw more action playing *Call of Duty.*"

Quinn shrugged. "Governor Vardaman calls him an American hero," he said. "Just the kind of man Tibbehah County needs to clean up the filth and corruption of such a wicked county."

"You trying to get me to start drinking again?"

The sun hadn't even thought about setting yet. Quinn reached for the bottle and refilled his coffee mug. Boom didn't touch the bottle, again on a long period of abstinence from booze. Booze and Boom never mixed well.

"No, sir."

"Then let's not talk about Vardaman," Boom said. "Not now. Not after all that man's done."

"You don't believe he wants to see a clean and corruption-free state?" Quinn said.

"No more than a hog wants to see his crib free of mud and slop," Boom said. "You want to see exactly what's going on? How about me and you go riding tonight and I'll show you just how much that son of a bitch has cleaned up."

Quinn drank some whiskey, feeling the hot bourbon slide down his throat. Cicadas chattered high in the pines, a hot wind blowing through the big oak that shadowed his tin-roof porch. As Quinn took another pull of the Liga Privada, he spotted Maggie's green Subaru cross the old wooden bridge, kicking up dust and grit and pulling into the front yard.

"She gonna get your ass," Boom said.

"That woman loves me."

"I know she do," Boom said. "That's why she wants you whole."

Quinn set down the cigar on the edge of an empty coffee can. He would've stood up if he could, still exhausted from his mile walk that morning. Hondo raised his head and got to his feet and stretched before running out to meet Maggie and Brandon. Maggie, still dressed in navy scrubs and carrying cloth grocery sacks, made her way up onto the porch. Boom met her, hooked a few bags with his prosthetic arm, and headed into the old house. Brandon, towheaded and skinny in khaki shorts and an *Adventure Time* T-shirt, had run off into the back field with Hondo, tossing a stick toward the pecan trees.

"Lousy job getting rid of evidence," Maggie said, waving her hand through the dissipating smoke cloud.

"Would it have made any difference?" Quinn asked.

"Nope," Maggie said. "You've been sneaking cigars for the last month."

"Never smoke around you."

Quinn grinned, tapped the ash of the cigar, and carefully edged out the burn. Maggie took a seat on the old porch swing and stretched out her long legs, hair wrapped up in a messy bun on top of her head. She lay her hands over her expanding stomach and looked down to it, cutting her eyes over at Quinn.

"She's been active today," she said. "Kicking and punching my ribs."

"She's going to be tough."

"Damn straight, Ranger."

"Gets it from both sides."

Maggie nodded, lifting her eyes to Quinn. She tilted her head and pushed some stray hair off the nape of her neck. "You think you might slow down a little tonight?"

"Boom wants to get me out tonight, go low riding on some country roads like we used to," Quinn said. "Cool out. Take in some sights."

"I know what he wants to show you," Maggie said. "You really think that's a good idea?"

Quinn didn't answer, reaching for the coffee mug and finishing what was left, not sure if Maggie knew it wasn't coffee. He stretched his legs out and looked out into the cow pasture across the road, dozens of cattle huddled under a well-worn oak, seeking shade from the heat. They were beautiful to watch. Red Angus, brought over from Texas by his father back when he'd been living in a trailer in the back field. Quinn hadn't heard from Jason

Colson now for almost three years. Even after he'd been shot and it had made national news.

"I guess Boom told you all about the trouble in town today."

Quinn shook his head.

"New sheriff and his deputies met up with ICE," Maggie said. "Arrested most everyone out at the chicken plant. I figured you knew all about it. The news was all over town."

"Heard from Caddy?"

Maggie shook her head. "Nope," she said. "But I figured she's right in the middle of it. You know your sister."

"Son of a bitch." Quinn gripped the rails of the old metal chair and pushed himself to his feet. "Where's my phone?"

Ana Gabriel sat on the steps to her trailer watching the sun set through the gathering of pines near the road. They'd scrounged for an early dinner, fried eggs with sweet plantains and warm tortillas. There was a little coffee left in the pot and she halved it with milk, adding four teaspoons of sugar and heated in the microwave. Sancho was inside, half asleep and watching television. Her phone showed she'd called her mother a total of forty-nine times.

If what the boy Armando said was true, she'd need to find her father in Atlanta. Or her uncle in Houston. She'd found only ninety dollars hidden in her mother's room, tucked into the insides of a ceramic pig in a makeshift bookshelf. How long that would last, she didn't know. She promised herself that she would try her best to make it as routine as possible for Sancho. Ana Gabriel could wake him in the morning, make their breakfast, and get out to the highway to meet the bus. They would go to school and say nothing about what had happened. It was always a possibility. Her mother had always promised this day would come. *Protect Sancho. Protect your brother.* But never said anything about protecting herself. Just as the sun had about disappeared, she began to cry.

"Don't cry," a voice said. "Come with me."

She looked up, seeing Jason Colson. He was out of breath and sweating, offering his hand to her. The last light illuminating his blue eyes and bright white smile. She bit her upper lip, nodded, and took his hand, standing.

"My mother's here," Jason said. "We'll drive y'all to the plant. Maybe there is something that can be done. My mom has called lawyers and powerful people she knows to kick everyone free."

Jason was tall and lean, his skin the color of milk and coffee. She'd been at his birthday party the month before when he turned twelve and she'd given him the braided bracelet he still had on his wrist. They'd had the party at the place called The River that his mother ran, a church and outreach she'd started in an old wooden barn that offered Sunday services in English and Spanish. Miss Colson was spoken about with reverence all over Frog Pond.

"Let me get my brother."

"Bring everyone you can find," Jason said. "Momma

has a van. Anyone who can't find their parents can come with us. We're here to help."

Quinn and Boom got out to the Johnny T. Stagg Industrial Center right outside Jericho a little after six. Boom parked his jacked-up Chevy on a slanted hill, the road clogged with cars and news trucks, law enforcement and big black buses. Boom limped alongside Quinn as they both saw Caddy screaming at two men in black tactical gear wearing ICE vests, M4s slung over their shoulders. It had been some time since he'd heard his little sister curse. But tonight, she worked out a damn symphony of profanity on the men who smirked at her behind mirrored sunglasses.

"You chickenshit sonsabitches," Caddy said. "You don't have any right to come to our town and steal these people. These are good people. I have two babies not a year old who are still breastfeeding, and you took their mommas from them. What about that? What the hell are you going to do about that?"

The men didn't answer. Quinn walked up to his sister, lightly touching her elbow. She hadn't seen him and turned around fast and hard. Caddy's face was sunburned, her blonde hair turned almost white from working outdoors all summer.

"Let's take a walk," Quinn said.

"I don't want to walk," Caddy said. "I want you to do something. Did you know about this? Aren't they supposed to tell the sheriff when they invade his county?"

"My current status is complicated," he said. "But I can find out."

A tall fence topped with concertina wire encircled the property and the four large white sheet metal buildings where they slaughtered and processed thousands of chickens a day. Even at this distance, the smell was overwhelming, like rotten flesh and a well-used latrine. Boom had gone over to a white church van adorned with a winding purple cursive with the words THE RIVER on the side. He leaned into the open doors of the van, speaking with some kids. Boom always had a way with kids.

"I have thirty-two children missing their parents," Caddy said. "Today was the first day of school. If these assholes wanted to pull that shit, why today? Why would they want to snatch these parents who've been working here for months, some of them for years? Did I mention that I have two babies still nursing? We're doing all we can. But still."

"Roger that."

"Do something," she said. "They won't talk to me."

"Maybe it's the way you're speaking to them?"

"Don't you think I tried nice?" she said. "I'm not Lillie Virgil. I tried both logic and compassion."

"And?"

"No one will tell me a damn thing," she said. "Sometimes a kick in the nuts is the only way to start a conversation."

Quinn nodded and headed toward the front gate, seeing more immigration agents and a few deputies from the sheriff's office. He didn't recognize a single one of them but the interim sheriff, a skinny, dark-haired man with a narrow face, black eyes, and jug ears. His two meetings with Brock Tanner hadn't been pleasant. The man was doing his best to keep Quinn away from returning to his job, protected by the governor's investigation into corruption in Tibbehah County after Quinn was shot. Quinn had challenged the shaky legal grounds at nearly every level, waiting for the latest hearing with his personal attorney, W. D. "Sonny" Stevens. A good lawyer when sober and even better when drunk.

Quinn nodded to Brock.

The man was dressed as if he was about to be dropped deep in a war zone, complete with fatigues, combat boots, and an M4 rifle. His hair had been shaved short across the nape of his neck and around his gigantic ears.

"Can I help you?" Brock said.

"You can start by telling me what's going on."

"What's it look like, Quinn?" Brock said, snorting. "We're rounding up a mess of illegals who've thrived in this county too long. Tried running. But we got 'em. Got 'em all."

"You were supposed to keep me posted on any and all operations within the county."

Brock shook his head. "This wasn't the type of thing ICE wanted to broadcast," he said. "This crackdown has been a long time coming."

"You saying I'd broadcast the information?"

Brock didn't answer, taking a call on the radio microphone attached to his tac vest. He turned to a few of the deputies he'd brought along with him from Jackson with limited experience in law enforcement. "I'd be glad to sit down with you and discuss specifics tomorrow," he said.

"But I have a job today. I wasn't brought up here by the governor to sit around the office and drink coffee."

"You're doing a heck of a job," Quinn said. "Looks like some real tough hombres down there."

Quinn lifted his chin to a group of portly brown women dressed in blue uniforms, heads covered in protective plastic caps. Their hands locked behind them with plastic handcuffs.

"They tried to run," Brock said, grinning. "But we filled up every damn hole on the fence line with rocks."

"Damn, Brock," Quinn said, giving him a sloppy salute. "I can see how you made captain before you ever deployed. Real smart thinking."

"I don't need any pushback with this, Quinn," Brock said. "We've been working on this operation since I got here."

"Where are you taking them?"

Brock stared hard at Quinn and shook his head. "What the hell does it matter?"

Ana Gabriel spotted her mother behind the chain-link fence down the harsh slope of the hill. She had her wrists cinched behind her back, still dressed in the blue work clothes from the plant. Her mother, Luisa, looked sad and ashamed, absently nodding at a fat man in a navy uniform, who stood without speaking, flipping through a stack of papers. When her mother turned, Ana Gabriel saw the blood that covered her coat, a breathing mask loose around her neck. She jumped up and down and waved, shouting, "Mamá. Mamá!"

Luisa Ramirez looked up the hill, lifting her chin and smiling at her daughter. She yelled something but Ana Gabriel couldn't hear her words with all the other sounds. The motors of the buses rumbled, the men with guns shouted, and their radios chirped with beeps and static.

"Mamá!" she said, yelling again.

Sancho joined her at the barrier, both of them reaching into the chain link and rattling the fence. It was night now, the gravel lot pooled in the bright lights above. She did her best not to cry, only to let her mother know she was there and that she knew what was going on. She was safe. She and Sancho were safe and would look out for each other.

She watched as the officers pushed her mother toward the others who'd been arrested, forming a line onto the bus. Many of them she knew from the Frog Pond, mostly women, but a few men. There was Armando's father, his hands unbound, holding a plastic bag full of papers, speaking with a dark-skinned woman wearing a vest that said HSI. The conversation seemed hot, although she looked as if she could have been one of them with her dark hair and eyes. But she had a badge and wore a gun and it seemed nothing Armando's dad said made a difference. Ana Gabriel watched as the line continued to push forward, her mother nearing the door. A bald man with a head like a thumb forced them forward like cattle with the flat of his hand.

Te quiero, Mamá. Te quiero, Mamá.

Luisa Ramirez turned before taking a step on the bus and mouthed that she loved them both. Sancho started to cry, his round little face in his hands. Ana Gabriel screamed and rattled the metal fence topped with razor wire.

"Come on," Caddy Colson said. "Come with me. We all need to get out of here now. People are asking me questions I don't like."

"Where is she going?" Sancho said. "Where are they taking our mother?"

"I don't know," Caddy Colson said, wrapping her arm around them both. "But I promise you, we will find out."

2

The son of a bitch was late. Fannie Hathcock had been waiting for Buster White to show for more than two hours and still no sign of his private plane. She stood there, stiletto heels wobbly in the gravel near the airfield and Quonset huts, staring up into the starry sky, checking the narrow gold watch on her wrist while burning through three cigarillos. "That fat cocksucker does this shit on purpose," Fannie said, spewing smoke from the side of her mouth. "Pissing me off must make his little Twinkie hard."

Midnight Man didn't answer. He was a half-ton black man who'd worked for her since she first came from Tibbehah County, promoting his big ass from barbecue pit master at the Rebel Truck Stop to running security at Vienna's Place, an all-nude bar that operated right off Highway 45. In all the years she'd known him, he rarely spoke, mainly nodding or saying "Yes, ma'am." Tonight, he was dressed in a black silk shirt, black pants, and black leather shoes to run the show at her new place out on the lake.

"Are the girls ready?"

Midnight Man nodded.

"Is the barbecue and chicken ready to be served?"

"Yes, ma'am."

"Those dealers in from Tunica yet?" she asked. "They should've gotten to the club three hours ago. I promised the deluxe poker room would be primed and ready for Buster and whoever the fuck he's flying up with him."

Midnight Man nodded.

"He came to inspect the goods, see what kind of show we're floating up on Choctaw Lake," she said. "He's worried as hell that once we open up some high-dollar gambling in north Mississippi, it's gonna chip away at the swinging dickwads who come down to Biloxi for his potato chip and dip parties at the Grand. Probably thinking, *Oh shit, this bitch's gonna poach all my big dogs from the back room* and he's gonna be stuck with gallon tubs of caviar from China and teenage Mexican cooze that can't speak a lick of English."

Midnight Man grunted and pointed up to the red flashing lights in the sky. She heard the high whine of the jet engine and fished out the cell from her purse. Within a few seconds, the freshly paved tarmac glowed with pulsing blue lights, a roving beam of white light circling the narrow valley and over the pine trees and kudzu-choked ravines. The crickets and cicadas started to go silent as the plane started its descent.

"And Midnight Man?" Fannie asked. "Don't trust

any of these bastards. They'd just as soon shoot you in the back of your big head as pat you on the back."

"Yes, ma'am."

The small white jet landed quick and hard, skidding to a stop just a few feet shy from the barricades at the end of the tarmac. It was flat-ass dark, nothing but the pulsing lights in the valley. The pilot turned and began to double back, jets cooling, engines at a high whine.

"The bastard's got a big set of balls on him," she said. "Not many folks would have the guts to fly into my damn world, wanting to get a grand tour of a place they're no longer welcome. You know what he's gonna say? He'll want to sweet-talk me about the old times, twenty years back, when I was a knobby-kneed piece of country trash with long red hair and teeth spread out like a rake. He'll say that he made me, saw promise in my intelligence and sizable attributes, and say something about friendship and a shared history. He still wants to be a part of a good ole boy club that doesn't have a fucking thing to do with boys at all. Does it, now?"

Midnight Man stood still, a dark shape cut from onyx. Fannie spewed out more smoke, waiting, hand on one hip, the other ashing the tip of her cigarillo. She tapped her right foot fast as a piston, already sweating through her thousand-dollar silk dress from Neiman Marcus.

The plane door opened with a hiss and the stairs unfolded down to the landing strip. She watched as two older white men walked down the steps. They both wore blue blazers and khaki pants, pistols bold on their hips. One was chubby with a graying goatee, and the other seemed a decade or two older, someone she'd seen be-

fore, Irv or Merv or some shit. Ole Merv had been working for Buster since before Buster got his cherry popped
in Angola doing a ten-year stretch for racketeering and
mail fraud.

Buster White walked out of the plane last, waddling
down the steps in long blue shorts and a gigantic Hawaiian shirt with palm trees and parrots. He looked like
Jimmy Buffett had wasted away on too many margaritas
and fucked a killer whale.

"Fannie Hath-cock," Buster White said, opening his
arms. "Baby. My sweet, sweet baby girl."

She stood rigid for the embrace, feeling it linger like a
wayward preacher, his whopping stomach against her,
smallish hands brushing across her ass. Fannie tried not
to think about acts she'd done for that man when she was
younger, happy, and eager to rise in the favor of the Syndicate, up the damn food chain of morons, and learn the
business from the dirt up.

"You can let go of my ass now," she said, pushing him
away.

"Gimme a while to take it all in," he said, licking his
lips, looking her up and down, and stifling a belch with
his fist. His breath smelled like dead shrimp and onions.
"They don't make women like you anymore. So many
curves and bumps, a man could get lost in the topogra-
phy."

"Did you forget the party?" Fannie asked.

"Just me and Merv," he said. "And Frank. You know
Frank? Used to work the blackjack table at the Beau
Rivage. Don't you worry. They're just here so we can
have a proper visit, sit down nice and easy over fine whis-

key and catch up on old times. And maybe, just maybe, conduct a little business."

"We don't have business," she said. "Not anymore. I made that damn clear."

"I know what you said on that telephone," Buster said. "And I know how you felt about me since ole Ray kicked the bucket. But fuck me five times in the ass, we got things that need to be hashed out. We don't have no Ray to sit down in his white linen suits and fine New Orleans manners to work out the details. We got to come to the fact that it's just me, you, and the savages down on the Rez now. It's best for everyone we play safe, baby. Besides, I missed your sweet fine ass. I could bounce a half-dollar off it from here to the moon. I'll be god-damned if you didn't dab those tatas with a little Chanel Number Five."

"Chanel Gardénia is what I wear," she said. "You must've sent me a dozen bottles. Or don't you recall?"

"Did I now?" Buster said. "How about you tell me more about this place you set up on Choctaw Lake? I heard it's a hell of a step up from selling flat champagne and lap dances for twenty bucks a throw on the highway."

"You know it," she said. "It's a real class joint."

"A class joint?" Buster said. "Well, shit. Can't wait to see it. Might just redneck up the place a little. I'll even let you sit in big daddy's lap on the ride over. How would you like that, Miss Fannie? Just like old times with you and me."

Fannie felt the heat in her neck and face as she ditched the last of her cigarillo onto the gravel, watching it spark into the night. The pulsing blue lights and rotating white light on the airfield fell fast and dark, and it was hot and dry out in the north part of the county. She could hear the brittle leaves in the trees, starved of moisture and burned up in the heat of a summer drought. The cicadas started again as two SUVs flicked on their headlights and rolled to where Buster and his men waited. As one of the white Escalades slowed to a stop, Midnight Man reached out and held the door open for their guests.

"Sure is good to see you, Miss Fannie," Buster said. "Feels like an ole-time family reunion."

Fannie watched as Buster and his men disappeared into the SUV and it rolled off the gravel and away from the landing strip.

"Call Vienna's," Fannie said, hands shaking as she lit a new cigarillo. "Let 'em know we're headed out to the lake. And Midnight Man?"

The big man turned, eyes dark and leveled at her.

"Chill the beer," she said. "But lose the dealers and the fucking girls. Looks like this is gonna be a goddamn private show."

Quinn stood with Boom in the hills overlooking the landing strip. When he'd been a kid, he and Boom used to wander all over the old airfield, shut off from the main highway with concrete barricades and NO TRESPASSING signs and barbed wire and all those good things that made boys have to know what it's like inside. But the airstrip and old outbuildings had been updated in the last few years. The busted old tarmac had been recoated with slick black asphalt, brand-new equipment set up along the strip. Most recently, five new Quonset huts shuffled between the old relics, painted a flat green. He and Boom had been visiting the airfield a lot lately, noting the traffic in and out, logging tail numbers and photographing new visitors in Tibbehah County.

They were both dressed for hunting, dark green T-shirts, camo pants, and armed with shotguns and rifles. Quinn carried his Beretta M9 that had accompanied him on thirteen tours to Iraq and Afghanistan. The walk in from the road hadn't been easy, tough as hell on his back and lungs. But Quinn liked being back in the quiet woods, doing work he'd been trained to do and spent half of his life doing. He lifted his night vision goggles to the airfield just as the two white Escalades pulled away toward the highway.

"You recognize the fat man?" Boom said.

"Maybe."

"That man's shirt bigger than a circus tent," Boom said. "But if he's standing toe to toe with Queen Fannie, he must be important."

"Fannie wants everyone to know Tibbehah County is open for business."

"Sure am glad the new sheriff is keeping a lid on the corruption since you did such a horseshit job of it."

"Maybe I should read his damn book," Quinn said. "Pick up a few things about honor and duty."

"You know Maggie knows what we're up to?" Boom said. "She don't believe for a damn second that we're running the back roads for the hell of it. She knows even shot up, you can't just sit on your ass and do nothing."

"Ain't that the reason I came home?"

Boom nodded, sliding the shotgun onto his back with the sling, his metal hook glinting in the soft glow of the moon. Quinn caught something in the corner of his eye and headed a few meters down the hill, through a thicket of pines. He got on his haunches and pulled out a penlight from his ruck. He looked up at Boom, who saw just what he was seeing.

"Trip wire."

"Yep."

"I didn't get my ass patched up at Walter Reed just to get it blown up in the hills of Tibbehah County," Boom said. "Just what all is Miss Fannie moving through north Mississippi?"

Quinn scanned the trees for cameras, the ground for more wires. He looked down at the big collection of new Quonset huts and back up at his friend. "Everything."

"Where is everybody?" Buster White said. "I thought you said y'all were open for business."

"We are," Fannie said. "I just figured you and I might have a little privacy before the party started. You can't get a lot done once we truck those girls in from Vienna's Place. Never met a man in my life who could think with his pants down around his ankles."

"Don't know about that, doll," he said. "That's how I study on things best."

Buster followed her through the brand-new sprawling cabin out on the northeastern tip of Choctaw Lake. Fannie had secured fifty acres of privacy around the parcel, setting the main cabin so far into the tree line that passing boaters couldn't see it. She'd built a dock from stone trucked in from Tupelo and a large kidney-shaped pool out back of the gaming house where special guests could drink cheap champagne and make small talk with topless women. Fannie taught her girls to make 'em feel special. Always look the man in the eye, give him a reassuring touch on the forearm, toss the hair, lick the lips, and smile. Don't ever stop smiling through whatever kind of bullshit he was telling you. His goddamn bitch of a wife. His bad luck at golf. They all had busted egos and walnut-sized brains and would put their peckers into a ring of fire to get laid by some young tail.

"Damn, this place is sharp," Buster said, strolling through the expansive house, letting his fat little fingers trail on the green felt of the craps table. "Y'all sure went all out."

Buster White eyed the big mahogany tables for late-night poker games for the high rollers and a billiard table up by the bar where you could challenge a girl in short shorts or lingerie to play a game of straight pool or foosball. He stopped when he saw the tall wooden Indian by a glass cigar humidor. He patted the big Indian on his chest and turned back to Fannie.

"I bet you call this ole chief Kaw-Liga," Buster White said. "If it were mine, that's what I would do. *Fell in love with that ole Choctaw maid at the Georgia store.* So tell me this, Fannie. Just what are you expecting as a monthly take in a place like this, going with the seasons as they are, up and down. Just what do you hope to average?"

Fannie rested a hand on her hip, the sweat drying

across her neck and her chest in the cool refrigerated air, and looked Buster up and down. They were alone. Midnight Man stood outside with Merv and Frank, showing them the big stone pool filled with salt water that would be heated in the cooler months, and maybe on out to the special dock they planned to build next year. "You wouldn't believe me if I told you."

"Come on now, baby," Buster said. "Ain't no secrets between me and you."

Fannie told him. Didn't seem to make much of a difference now. Buster made a low whistle and shook his head.

"Honey, hush your mouth."

Fannie shrugged. The gaming room smelled of heart pine and fresh leather and the faint trace of cigar smoke from the weekend before when she had folks flying in from damn near everywhere. Fannie stopped by the bar to open up a bottle of Johnnie Walker Blue, knowing it was Buster's favorite and that he liked to see a fresh bottle opened just for him. Buster would never forget the SOB who put paint thinner in some Jim Beam nearly thirty years ago and took out a good chunk of his throat and stomach.

She clinked in a few ice cubes in a crystal glass, poured in three full fingers, and walked slow and easy back over to him. His pig eyes full on her tall, long-legged strut, the slit in her black silk dress running damn near up to her coot. The room was so silent and shadowed that it hummed.

Buster accepted the whiskey and put his big nose to the edge of the glass, sniffing. "Did you expect me to wish you all the damn luck in the world with my thumb jacked up my ass?"

"I don't recall asking permission to run my fucking business," Fannie said.

Buster swallowed down nearly half that brown water and rested his hands on the edge of a pool table. He picked up a cue ball and absently sent it barreling through the other balls arranged on the green felt. The balls cracked and spun, wheeling out in chaos from the center. Buster set down the drink and stared down at the table, hands resting on the edge.

"Ray's dead," Fannie said. "I do as I please."

"I am truly sorry about Ray," he said. "But you and me was tight, too. Good ole times back in the day."

Fannie didn't answer.

"You sure did know how to please a man," Buster White said, his upper lip wet from the scotch. "You were so damn strong, too. Like some kind of wild woman loose from the swamps. So damn eager. Yes, ma'am. I always asked for you personal. *Send that redheaded country girl. She knows how to work that ole gear shifter. She doesn't just dally around. No, sir.*"

Fannie's hands shook as she lit a cigarillo and gritted her teeth. "I'm sorry you came all this way," she said. "For nothing."

Buster grinned and shrugged, strolling through the wide-open space of cabin built for gaming and entertaining, his fat ass making the heartwood pine floors creak as he walked. He headed over to the wall and selected a pool cue, testing its weight and size in his hands. He held it tight in his right hand and tapped it lightly into his left.

Something in his pig eyes had changed, giving them a flat coldness that Fannie had only seen a handful of times. Only half the house lights were on, leaving most of the floor in shadow.

"Sorry, baby," Buster White said. "Ain't no way 'round this. How about we talk this over like a couple of civilized white folks?"

"You trying to intimidate me?"

Buster White seemed to relax, his hand holding the pool cue falling to his side. His eyes met hers and he slowly nodded. He handed her the crystal glass. "Oh," he said. "I think we're long past that. How about we just skip ahead to the good part."

"And what's that?"

"A drink to seal the damn deal."

Boom cruised by the dozen diesel pumps at the Rebel Truck Stop, turning down toward the diner's plate-glass windows. Truckers and old folks huddled over steaming plates of the best chicken-fried steak in the state and the worst catfish in the county. Boom had a Charley Pride album in the tape deck, playing "Just Between You and Me." The neon lights blazed along the roof of the truck stop and the titty bar behind it, Vienna's Place. Quinn thought back on the time when a crew of bank robbers had holed up inside and later blew up his favorite truck. Damn, he sure did miss the Big Green Machine.

"Did you hear anything about a party out at the lake?" Quinn said. His arm hung out the window, fingers touching the top of the truck cab.

"Nope," Boom said. "Not a damn word."

"Don't see those Escalades from the airstrip here," Quinn said. "Not many other destinations in Jericho for them."

"Maybe they went for Taco Tuesday at the El Dorado," Boom said. "A side of those margaritas Javier mixes up with grain alcohol. The kind that make Miss Jean recall all those nights at Graceland with your daddy and Elvis."

"Half that shit never even happened."

"Does it matter?" Boom said. "Your daddy always said to never let the truth get in the way of a good story."

Boom rolled on into the parking lot that separated the truck stop from the strip club and drove through the empty spaces by the front entrance. A few of the working girls stood outside with the thick bouncer with a shaved head, smoking cigarettes in short black robes, tall in knee-high boots and plastic platform heels, craning their heads to see just who was passing by. Boom wasn't shy, lifting his good hand and giving them a salute. Neon and flashing white lights shone off the hood of the jacked-up Chevy.

"Fannie now runs those big rigs right through the garage out back of the Rebel," Boom said. "There was a time that she'd take 'em out to the airstrip to tear them apart and divvy up the goods. Now it's all out in the open. Me and you park here for a few hours and we'll see two, maybe three hot trucks run up into that double bay. They'll be chopped up and out of state by sunup."

Quinn nodded. He reached into the glove box for a pint bottle of Jack Daniel's and unscrewed the top. "How close do you think we can get to the gambling house?"

"You really need more of that?" Boom asked, looking down at the bottle.

"Coming from you?" Quinn asked, hearing more edge than he meant.

"Just asking, is all," Boom said. "We can't get far at all to Fannie's new place. Best we can do is by boat. And last time me and you did that, they started shooting at our ass."

"She's got even more girls working?"

"Oh, hell," Boom said, turning the wheel with his prosthetic hand and taking them back onto the main highway, past the Golden Cherry Motel and its flashing sign with yellow neon fruit dangling and empty concrete swimming pool. "Don't even have to walk across the street no more for action. Fannie got cribs set up in the back of Vienna's. Men get their crank worked free and easy out in the open. That damn county ordinance Skinner wanted enforced? About pasties and G-strings? *Shit.* They buck-ass naked all in that place now. You want pillow talk and a girl will meet you over at the Cherry. Run you about five hundred bucks. Better-looking women can score about eight hundred, maybe a thousand if they're known."

"And how do they get known?"

"Internet," Boom said. "Fannie's got girls in the Cherry right now hooked up to the web, doing all kind of wild shit for tokens. They'd park a damn rocket ship in their privates for a hundred bucks. Way I heard it, Fannie is making more money on that shit than any damn lap dances at Vienna's. She's gone high tech and worldwide. Seems men just can't get enough of that hot Southern action."

Quinn turned up the pint bottle of whiskey. He felt

the heat spread down his throat and across his chest, offering him a little relief from the pain in his back and legs. It had been a long while since the shooting, but his breath still felt ragged and heavy. He missed running the hills. Running is what had kept him sane.

"You think she's dialed back on the weed and shit rolling in from Houston?"

"My friend can't get close to that," Boom said, punching the accelerator and taking them toward the Jericho Square. "She sees the women and the internet shit running twenty-four/seven but can't find out where, when, and how much shit Miss Fannie's been running out of Tibbehah."

"The drugs and the guns are what Fannie's always done best," Quinn said. "The skin trade, out in the open, has never been much more than a money wash for her buddies."

"Place kinda looks like when you came home ten years back?"

"Nope," Quinn said, placing the small bottle back in the glove box. "It's a lot worse."

Buster White finished his second helping of Johnnie Walker Blue and set the glass aside. He flattened his hands onto his big stomach and leaned back into the comfortable leather chair. "I don't care if you slit that seal yourself. That damn whiskey's been watered down."

"You know it," Fannie said, smiling. "Learned from the best."

"I am truly sorry about ole Ray," he said. "Fine, fine

man. Ray kept this whole world straight. From New Orleans up to Chicago. I never for one second believed the
lies they spread about what happened."

"That I fucked him to death?" Fannie said, blowing
out some smoke.

Buster nodded. He ran his fat tongue over his front
teeth and turned his head to cough.

"Oh, that's true," she said. "The lie is that I meant to
do it."

She heard feet clatter and gather up on the wooden
porch facing the lake. Merv and Frank, casino-issued
blue ties pulled loose in the heat, walked into the room
and looked at their boss, nodding in his direction. Buster
seemed to relax a little, crossing his little fat leg over the
other and rattling the ice in his glass.

Midnight Man stood big and thick outside the front
windows, looking out into the darkness of Choctaw
Lake. Merv and Frank stood near Fannie as she relit a
cigarillo and leaned back into the couch, smiling at the
security guards. The older one, Merv, nodded back,
sucking in his stomach and straightening the lapels on
his navy sport coat. Frank smoothed down his goatee,
looking to Buster White and then back around the room.
He seemed to notice something he didn't like, staring at
the cool air blowing through the vents. The workers had
left little plastic strings on the registers, flapping hard
and strong. It must've been sixty degrees inside.

Fannie refilled Buster's glass, reaching for the leather
strap of her Birkin bag. She took a slow walk behind his
chair, setting the bag at her feet, reaching her hands
down around his thick neck, noticing the fat rolls under

his buzz-cut white hair. She started to massage Buster's shoulders, feeling her fingers work into the thick folds of skin and fat, flabby muscle.

Buster craned his head to stare up at her and winked. "Fine place," he said. "Shame I'll have to burn the motherfucker down unless we come to some kind of terms."

"You got me, Buster," Fannie said. "I tried to run. I tried to hide."

Fannie massaged the skin folds harder, looking to Midnight Man standing outside the French doors. He was nothing but a shadow but saw that she nodded in his direction. Merv and Frank leaned against the bar, Merv checking his watch and looking toward the front door. He should've looked toward the back. The side door opened without either of them knowing it, Fannie feeling the hot summer air blow through the cold room. The men just starting to turn as the big Indian passed by ole Kaw-Liga, standing nearly as tall and straight, with high cheekbones, black eyes, and his black hair threaded into a ponytail. He raised a .357 toward the bar and shot through the two men, splattering glass, blood, and whiskey all over the marble.

Fannie was already onto Buster, pulling out her sixteen-ounce framing hammer and whacking it into the side of his thick skull. His fat head lolled forward and then back, teeing himself up for another solid whack, this time misting her hands with fine bits of blood. She recalled that man's hairless flabby body crawling on top of her so long ago, when she was little more than a kid, pushing nearly all her breath away, twice cracking her rib trying to make something happen out of nothing.

His hands reached out and gripped her forearms. But damn, he was so fucking old and weak. She hit him again. And again. And again. Didn't take but about thirty seconds and it was all over.

He let out a final raspy cough and then settled into stillness. Fannie's lithe hands and fine dress covered in Buster White's blood.

Fannie caught her breath, swallowed, and dropped the hammer to the floor. Sam Frye, right-hand man of Chief Robbie of the Mississippi Choctaws, came into her view and placed a steady hand on her shoulder.

"It's done," Sam Frye said. "What about their plane?"

"That plane belongs to me," Fannie said. "I'd been planning on a night like this for more than twenty years."

Quinn and Boom pulled into the Sonic and killed the engine. They ordered burgers and shakes and sat in the old truck with the windows down. The drive-in was full of light and action, high schoolers sitting at little round tables by the take-out window. A sky blue '69 Camaro with a white racing stripe cruised past. A red El Camino with a rebel flag license plate followed, moving in a slow parade around downtown Jericho. Boom popped out the Charley Pride and plugged in some N.W.A "Alwayz into Somethin'."

The music reminded Quinn of being twelve and hanging out at Boom's house after church, playing the music through headphones so his preacher daddy didn't hear what was going on. Boom's father called rap "the

devil's music." Somehow knowing the music was dangerous and evil made it all the better.

Quinn watched as a Tibbehah County Sheriff's Office
patrol car rolled into the lot, a white man Quinn had
never seen behind the wheel. He wore sunglasses at
night, a blue ball cap down in his eyes.

"You know these motherfuckers?" Boom asked.

"Nope."

"But you know why they're here?"

"You know it."

"What they're saying about you, about me, about the
whole damn county that allowed a woman like Fannie
Hathcock to roam free?"

"Sure do."

"Goddamn Brock Tanner," Boom said. "We seen this
dirty game before."

The patrol car circled around again, the white man
behind the wheel wanting to make sure he'd made his
point, established his territory. He slowed for a moment
before Boom's canary yellow Silverado and then scratched
off quick from the Sonic, flashing his light bar and heading out into the darkness.

"You scared?" Boom said.

"Damn well terrified," Quinn said. He lifted the bottle of whiskey and finished it off.

Boom studied his friend's face for a long moment but
didn't say a word.

3

When Donnie Varner came home from a federal prison in Texas two months ago, his father had thrown him a party out at the Jericho VFW Hall. His daddy Luther had tried his best, offering a catfish and hushpuppy spread, all the sweet tea and Mountain Dew you could drink, and even a special cake made of dozens of Moon Pies. His cousin Randy had brought a nice Bluetooth boom box to play Donnie's hit list: Guns N' Roses, David Allan Coe, Marshall Tucker Band, and Confederate Railroad. He sure did love him some "Trashy Women."

But the damn party had been a bust. Besides Randy and a few cousins that he didn't give two shits about, no one really showed. Donnie had gotten drunk anyway, slipping out to his daddy's prized gold '68 GTO to fill up a red Solo cup with the Jim Beam he'd stashed. At one point, he wasn't too damn sure, but he felt like he'd had a pretty good time dancing with his big Aunt Hollis, who weighed in at maybe two-fifty and some change and sure could move that big ass across the floor. He thought they'd done some fine work on "Boot Scootin' Boogie" although he sure as hell always hated Brooks & Dunn. He and his friend Quinn Colson had always been sure those ole boys about dropped the damn atom bomb on real country music, along with the true anti-Hank, Garth Brooks.

Donnie Varner never figured on a ticker tape parade but didn't expect to come home as a fucking pariah to the place where he'd been born and raised. It wasn't like he'd killed no one. Or ran buck-ass naked through the Jericho Square. All he'd done was try and work out a business deal between himself, a local crook named Johnny Stagg, and a crew of fucked-up Cartel boys for ninety-seven M4 rifles. All he cared to remember about that time was a woman named Luz who had been—in Donnie's true and less than humble opinion—the most gorgeous creature God had ever put on this earth. He would've eaten glass and walked through fire to have one more last kiss with her.

He thought about Luz, praying as he did every night that she was still alive and safe down in Old Mexico, while he watched the sun rise over the Confederate cemetery outside town. He'd borrowed Luther's GTO that morning, not asking permission but not trying to hide it, either, and had driven out for a quick meet with Mr. Coldfield. Since he'd been out, he'd tried to gain the old man's trust, coming out to his furniture store in the late afternoons when the whole warehouse was empty and listening to Coldfield's grand retelling of how Nathan Bedford Forrest had outsmarted a thousand Yankees under the command of William T. Sherman himself, the motherfucker who'd burned up most of a grand and noble society. Or at least that was the way the old man told it.

The furniture store, Zeke's Value City, sat right next to the cemetery, a red sheet metal building with a sloping white roof that promised two football fields full of discounts and deals. Donnie sat in his dad's GTO studying the old headstones of all those boys in gray, bracing himself for another history lesson from goddamn old man Zeke himself as if he'd been there back in the winter of '64 for the Second Battle of Jericho.

Donnie fired up an American Spirit cigarette just as he saw Zeke Coldfield's maroon Cadillac wheel into the gravel lot, always right on time at seven a.m. Donnie got out of the GTO and stretched, feeling a little hungover from drinking the night before. Not shit to do around Jericho for a single man but go to Bible study or get drunk. Last night, he'd done both. Donnie stood a little more than six feet, with sandy-blond hair and a little stubble on his face. Most women thought he was handsome as hell. But who was he to judge? Donnie was just a simple fella in jeans and boots and an old black T-shirt. Much better than that stiff prison orange.

"Mr. Coldfield," said Donnie, shutting the GTO's door. "You are better than a Swiss clock. I sure hope I have your energy when I get to be your age."

Donnie wasn't sure how old Coldfield was but suspected somewhere between eighty and a hundred and fifty. On second thought, maybe the pruned-up son of a bitch really had been around since the Civil War. Coldfield stood and pressed LOCK on his key fob, the old man complaining of "colored children" who'd been using the nearby cemetery to frolic and play.

He walked with the old man, who hobbled up to the front door, unlocked it, and moved to the security panel. Donnie found a square metal box nearby and started to flick on a half-dozen switches in the big store that had probably seen better days back in the 1970s. Some of the dinette sets he sold were so damn old they were actually in style again, straight out of the fucking *Brady Bunch*. The sprawling warehouse was a patchwork of bright white light shining down from high above.

"Mr. Varner," Zeke Coldfield said, his head looking exactly like a rotting apple with eyes like blue marbles. "How about you make us some coffee while we wait for the others?"

"Others?" Donnie said.

"Yes, sir," Coldfield said. "I told you my friends were mighty interested in meeting you."

"Oh, yeah," Donnie said. "Nearly forgot all about that."

"Make a big ole pot," Coldfield said. "I think there's a box of Little Debbie snack cakes in the refrigerator. Bring 'em up to my office where we can talk some business. I have the feeling this is your lucky day. I believe I've found exactly what you've been searching for since you came home."

"Appreciate that, Mr. Zeke," Donnie said. "You are a gentleman and a fine American."

"Two Sweet'N Lows please," Zeke said, hobbling off through the little dining rooms and big-ass family rooms, lit up with detail and drama like a fucking Showcase Showdown on *The Price Is Right*. "And a spot of that hazelnut Coffee mate."

Hot damn. Donnie Varner knew he was finally about to get front and center with the good ole boys from the Watchmen Society.

"Please don't go," Jason Colson said.

He held Ana Gabriel's hand in the darkness of the big barn at The River. Ana Gabriel had stayed there last night, his mother feeding all those left behind and bringing cots to the barn where she'd held Sunday services since he could remember. The girl smelled like fresh laundry, her hand smooth and soft, a purple ribbon wrapping a ponytail. The young girl's hair was so black and shiny, her eyes so large and brown. Jason could feel his young heart hammering in his chest just being next to her.

"My father will come for us," she said. "I sent word through our uncle. Everything we own is back at the Frog Pond. Sancho has to get back to school. He is so thickheaded and stubborn, I shudder to think what he'd be like without an education."

"Y'all can stay here," he said. "You can ride to school with me. My mother is here every morning. We get up at first light, take care of chores and help feed folks, and then go on to school."

"But if my father comes for us, he won't know where

to go," Ana Gabriel said, shaking her head. "He might think we're lost. Or that the government got us, too."

"My mother said they bused everyone to Louisiana," Jason said. The barn was dark and warm, large metal fans like contractors used blew from up on the stage. Didn't seem to be making a lick of difference. Jason was sweating, worried that Ana Gabriel would get swept up by her father and never come back to Jericho. "Please wait for me until after football practice. Come here after school. We're having hamburgers and hot dogs tonight. Momma says Señor Hector wants to speak. He'll know more about your mother. He'll know more about everything."

"Señor Hector is a good man," Ana Gabriel said. "My mother trusted him."

"See?" Jason said, squeezing her fingers. "Everything will be OK. You'll be safe here. I promise. Momma always has enough for everyone."

Jason could barely remember a time before The River. There were patches of his memory, living with Grandma Jean and brief moments of his mother Caddy looking worn and ragged, smelling smoky, coming to see him. She'd bring him toys and gifts from Memphis, sometimes Krispy Kreme donuts and little wooden trains, and promise she'd come for him soon. Everything would be fine. There was always talk about them having a real home somewhere away from Jericho. When he was young, his mother made good on the promise, finding that little house near the town square, cutting her hair short and meeting a kind man named Jamey Dixon. She and Dixon had started all this. Then Jamey Dixon died and that little house got torn to shreds by the tornado.

Everything Jason owned was lost, his mother disappeared before returning to him and The River, not doing much else but helping folks since then, stocking food at the pantry and used clothes in the old barn, bringing together visiting preachers, musicians, and volunteers to keep the place alive. Jason always had a fear that if his mother stopped moving, she would die. The thought often woke him up at night.

"Your mother will be OK," Jason said. "I promise."

Ana Gabriel didn't speak, pulling her hand away and tucking it into her lap. Her school backpack propped beside the hay bales where they sat. Jason watched her cry, hating to see it, wrapping his arm across her back. Ana Gabriel rested her head on his shoulder and he could smell the sweet shampoo and sunshine in her hair. They'd been here in the barn on his birthday over the summer. She'd been one of a handful of special friends he wanted with him. There was a cake and Ana Gabriel's momma brought a piñata. Mr. Boom had played some old-school music from the big speakers in his new yellow truck. Later, Jason had wandered off with Ana Gabriel into the barn church. She'd kissed him on the mouth right under the altar. Jason knew it was the greatest day of all his twelve years.

Jason and Ana Gabriel sat there for a long time in silence until he heard some vehicles pull up outside. Jason turned to the open door of the barn to see two men crawl out of a truck. They wore stiff tan uniforms and mirrored sunglasses. Jason stood up, squinting into the harsh morning light. None of the men speaking or smiling, just staring down at him.

"*Habla inglés*, kid?"

"Damn straight." Jason gritted his teeth.

"And what's your name?" the man said.

"My name is Jason Colson, mister. My uncle is the county sheriff and his uncle before him. This is my momma Caddy's place. Yeah, I speak English."

The man smiled and shook his head. He had big jug ears and wore the silver star of the sheriff like his Uncle Quinn. "That's good," the man said. "How about you run and go find your momma. We got some business to talk to her about this hotel she's been running for all these illegals."

Besides the corny and outright shitty commercials Zeke Coldfield made for Zeke's Value City, what really made the store famous was the history museum in back. Donnie had to pass through the glass cases and barrister bookshelves full of bayonets, swords, bullets, and belt buckles on the way back to the office. Dozens and dozens of Civil War–era rifles hung on the wall and in the hands of mannequins in gray uniforms wearing kepi caps. A large sign proclaimed the Battle of Jericho the last stand of a great and noble fight. Donnie bit into a Little Debbie snack cake and stared down into a long glass case like you'd find in an old drugstore. Only instead of shampoo, cheap wallets, and pills, Mr. Zeke had arranged a tattered battle flag along with cannonballs and buttons stamped CSA.

"Hits you right in the gut, don't it?" Mr. Zeke said, the old man nearly scaring the shit out of him. A man who looks like the fucking Crypt Keeper should know better than to skulk around in the dark.

"Oh, yes, sir."

"My daddy started this museum out of nothing but his own personal collection," he said. "He dug most of it out of the hills as a boy. Back then, you didn't have to go that deep into the soil to see the scars and the blood that spilled that day. *Lord Almighty*. Just thinking about it. I mean the sacrifice."

The old man was crying, or at least he was shaking. No tears fell or anything, probably because ole Mr. Coldfield had to have been dried up for years.

"Would you like a snack cake?" Donnie asked. "Looks like y'all had some Cocoa Cremes, Nutty Buddies, and Swiss Rolls. Those Swiss Rolls are something else. My daddy used to send 'em to me in Texas with the latest *Playboy* when he could. Couldn't have made it through without those nekkid women and snack cakes."

Mr. Zeke dried his face of the nonexistent tears and stepped out of the shadow and into the light of the display cases. "That's one of the things my friends wanted to know," he said. "Have you been rehabilitated?"

"Oh, yes, sir," Donnie said, having the conversation down pat since he'd come home. "Me and Jesus are thick as thieves."

Mr. Zeke didn't laugh. He nodded, mouth hanging open slightly. His blue suit draped off his bony ass like a scarecrow at Halloween. He accepted a Nutty Buddy and hobbled toward his office, the door open, with light shining from it. The old man slid down into a thick, highbacked leather chair and placed his skeletal hands across his desk. "I guess what I need to understand is just why in God's green earth you would want to sell weapons to a crew of dirty Mexicans?"

Donnie wanted to say *Because they offered a lot of money.* Instead he said, "Oh, sir. I didn't know who the buyer was. I was just trying to unload a few rifles. I was deceived in thinking they were for some hardworking Americans restricted by all them federal gun laws. You know I ran a range and gun shop when I got out of the service? Like I told my lawyer, what those Feds did to me was pure and simple entrapment. They had this red-headed woman with a body like a brick shithouse running that operation. Tatas like a couple of German turrets. She was obsessed with getting my ass in jail. *Me.* A hardworking American. Just because I was in the gun business."

"It's our God-given right," Mr. Zeke said.

"Damn straight."

"You know there some folks in California who'd like to take all our guns, melt them all down into a hot soup and build statues of flowers and fairies," Zeke said. "Makes the bile rise up in the back of my throat."

"Well, sir, I can promise you that once I'm back in business, I'll only sell weapons to upstanding white Americans."

Zeke grinned at that, hands not moving from the top of his desk. His eyes shifted just off Donnie's shoulder to three men who'd entered the room, all of them dressed like they'd just finished a Secret Squirrel mission in

Trashcanistan. Military-style clothes, black ball caps with sunglasses resting on the brims, and knives and guns on their belts.

"Gentlemen," Zeke said, making great effort to stand. "This is Mr. Varner. His daddy is one of the finest men in this county, a Marine sniper with more than thirty confirmed kills. Donnie here served in the Guard over in—where was it, again?"

"Oh, just a few pleasure trips over to Afghanistan."

"Not the way I heard it," Zeke said. "Man doesn't get a Purple Heart that way."

Telling the men he'd gotten his ass blown up while touring around a bazaar looking for some primo hash wasn't what they wanted to hear. He just looked at the three men, leveled his eyes, and nodded. Donnie Varner. Warrior. Patriot. Hero. Jailbird.

The trio stood like this: an older white man with a goatee, mustache, and one eye; a skinny middle-aged dude with a long ginger beard; and a strange little fat man with small pig eyes. All of them wearing tactical pants and black T-shirts adorned with some kind of gold watch symbol. Donnie found it odd that the older guy with the goatee wore both an eye patch and a pair of gold glasses at the same time. But Donnie figured it would be hard to find eyeglasses with only one lens.

"Heard you got some weapons we need to see," One Eye said.

"Working on it," Donnie said. "Just trying to put my toe in the north Mississippi market. I'd like to know my demand before I start trucking in my supply."

The one-eyed man looked over to old man Coldfield.

Coldfield reached down for his cup of coffee and Nutty Buddy, slick and brown as a cat turd, and bit into the end. He nodded back to ole One-Eyed Willie.

The man grinned, showing more spaces than teeth, stroking his white chin. "We aren't looking for no chickenshit deals," he said. "We heard you deal in the big time."

"I can definitely get my hands on whatever y'all need," Donnie said. "My resources are far and wide."

"We need a hell of a lot."

"I sure like the sound of that," Donnie said. "Y'all got some kind of little ole grocery list you can share with me?"

The men didn't say anything, One Eye reaching into his pocket and handing over two sheets of ruled notebook paper like Donnie used in high school. Zeke Coldfield mawed up his Nutty Buddy and then licked his cracked old lips as Donnie went through it line by line. When he finished, he gave a low serious whistle.

"Son, you messin' with me?" Donnie asked. "Looks like y'all gonna invade some foreign country I never heard of."

"Our business ain't no fucking business of yours," One Eye said. "You even think about cornholing us and there won't be no mercy."

"Damn, son," Donnie said. "Let's hold hands first. There won't be no cornholing on the first date if I have anything to do with it."

"Can you deliver?" Zeke Coldfield said.

"Yes, sir." Donnie grinned. "Does the damn pope shit in the woods?"

* * *

Jason and the other kids headed up onto the porch of The River's main office behind the barn. His mother was on the steps, speaking down at two men, telling them they had no right to be here unless one of them could produce a warrant. She had her hands on her hips, wearing a man's undershirt and light Western shirt popping in the wind. Her hair was white blonde and short as a boy's.

"This is a friendly visit, Miss Colson," the main guy said. He had dark brown hair and big jug ears. He stood tall and straight, wearing the tan uniform with a patch on the shoulder that read SHERIFF. "My name's Brock Tanner."

"I know who you are," she said. "Every child out here is an American citizen. They were born here."

"So you say," Brock Tanner said.

"I have birth certificates on record in my office," she said. "Given the upheaval you people created yesterday, I'm working to make sure they are cared for and understand their legal rights. As well as the rights of their parents you people ambushed."

Brock grinned a wide, picket-fence smile. He wasn't a handsome man. He had a long, narrow face and a damn honker of a nose. Every word that came out of his mouth sounded like he was talking to someone not too bright. Jason knew his mother wouldn't be standing for any of that shit. His momma, Caddy Colson, never suffered a fool in her life. At least that's what Grandma Jean said.

"Can I come inside?" Brock said. "You can show me documentation for all these kids. Go and get it over with. We're trying to make some sense of this for the schools. The superintendent isn't sure if they should be allowed back."

"These kids are going to school," Caddy said. "If you hadn't blocked the damn road, we'd be on our way now. In fact, I'd appreciate if y'all headed back the way you came. We're already late."

Brock had his hands on his hips, leaning up onto his toes as he spoke. He craned his neck around as if seeing all the shacks and metal outbuildings for the first time.

"Quite a place y'all got out here," Brock said, turning his head to spit. "What are you building down the road? I saw you got the concrete poured and beams already set. Some kind of rec center? That must cost a bundle. Seems like y'all have a lot going on."

"We're late for school," Caddy said. "Please move your vehicles."

A few dozen brown kids wandered on and off the wide porch. Some of them sat on the picnic tables in the shade of the old barn, finishing up sausage biscuits and bowls of cereal that his mother had provided. They had on tattered T-shirts and secondhand pants and sneakers. On a few kids, Jason recognized clothes he'd worn just last year. On the steps, his mom stared down at the men. She didn't look scared in the least. In fact, she looked tough and pretty in jeans and boots, her old snap-button Western shirt that once belonged to Reverend Dixon.

"I don't have to welcome you here," Caddy said. "And

I don't have to show you a thing. You do have to clear the road and get off my property. If you try and come back, I'll introduce you to my lawyers, who work for the biggest firm in Memphis."

"I'm not trying to make trouble," he said. "As sheriff of Tibbehah County—"

"Pretend sheriff," Caddy said. "My brother Quinn Colson is the damn sheriff. You and Vardaman's people are just putting on some kind of morality play for the sake of the weak-minded. It won't last. Y'all are about done. There's not a single person in this county who believes my brother was a thing but the most honest man to wear that star."

"Well," Brock said, a big smile on that long, dopey face. "I guess we'll have to agree to disagree."

"Do as you damn well please, Brock," Caddy said, heading down the steps and standing right in the man's face. Brock Tanner standing a good head higher than her but having to jerk his weak chin back to make room. "But clear the road as you do it. I got a school bus to fill."

4

"What a fine and glorious morning," Skinner said, standing over Quinn's back booth at the Fillin' Station as if expecting an invitation to sit. "Every day is a blessed day. I even think I smelled rain in the air. Lord knows we could use it. This heat's burning up half this county."

Quinn was alone, Boom just leaving to run over to the Farm & Ranch, and eating the Working Man's Platter of two eggs, country ham, grits, and two biscuits. About the best thing about getting shot was having to regain all the weight he'd lost. He buttered his second biscuit with a steak knife while looking up at Skinner and wondering what in the hell the old man wanted.

"You mind if I take a moment of your time?" Skinner said. He removed his pearl-gray LBJ Stetson off his liver-spotted head and took a seat before Quinn could respond. "I don't think you and I have seen much of each other since the shooting last year. A real tragedy. Horrible thing to get shot in the back like that. And on Halloween, too. Has anyone been able to piece together just who could do that to you?"

Quinn sliced some country ham and made a sandwich from the biscuit. He took a mouthful and started to chew. He couldn't think of anyone he'd want to see any less than Skinner. The old man ran the Tibbehah County Board of Supervisors, a crooked bunch, less one honest man, who made their careers out of funneling off state and federal tax dollars. It had been that way for more than a hundred years. They looked at graft as their birthright, a sacred and dutiful part of the good ole boy system.

"I have to say you're looking a heck of a lot better than when I ran into you and your sweet wife, Miss Maggie, at the Piggly Wiggly," he said. "I said to my wonderful Merva Joy, married more than fifty years now, that the sheriff sure didn't seem like himself. You got a little testy with me there in the frozen food aisle. Saying something about making me eat my ole Stetson."

Quinn leveled his eyes at Skinner and swallowed. He reached for a napkin and wiped his mouth. "You gonna tell me what you want, Skinner, or you want me to start guessing?"

"Now that's the old sheriff that I know," Skinner said, hee-hawing. "Yes, sir. That's the Quinn Colson who speaks his mind. We may not have gotten along, but I always knew where I stood with you. Yes, sir. You are one straight shooter."

"Well," Quinn said, picking up a thick ceramic mug

and taking a sip of coffee. "Get on with it." Miss Mary sauntered by and refilled his cup. She left without saying a word to Skinner. Most folks didn't like Skinner. And those who did called him an acquired taste. Like sardines. Or the music of Jim Nabors.

"I guess you know what happened out at the plant yesterday," Skinner said. "I stand with our government and do not support folks slipping across our borders. But I don't like being run roughshod over without warning. I think even you would have let the supervisors know just what was going on."

"Never did," Quinn said. "Unless I was presenting my budget."

Skinner laughed, looking a lot older than he remembered the ancient bastard. His skin looked thin as parchment paper to the point he could see the veins in the man's temples. His eyes so clear and blue they almost seemed transparent. When he called out to Miss Mary for a cup of decaf, his outstretched hand quivered and shook. Small dots of perspiration had popped out on his forehead.

"I'm on leave," Quinn said. "Go talk to the interim sheriff."

Skinner widened his eyes and coughed into his shaking fist. He looked up at Quinn, the skin at his throat fluttering like a turkey's. "I did," he said. "I tried to speak to him yesterday. And first thing this morning. It seems that old boy thinks he's big news for little old Tibbehah County on account of him attending Vanderbilt before heading overseas. I even read the man's book, *Honor and Duty*. I pegged him for a different kind of individual than the one who's sitting in your gosh-darn seat."

Miss Mary plunked a cup of coffee in front of Skinner and handed him a menu, a slight as the man had been coming here since before Quinn was born. There were rumors Skinner had been part of the original sixteen men who'd packed the back room when the diner closed on Monday night to hold a Klan meeting, although no one had ever offered any real proof.

"Brock Tanner won't give you the time of day," Quinn said, reaching for the Tabasco for his eggs. "And so you come complaining to me? Sorry, sir. Since you threw in with Vardaman and his Watchmen people, I really don't give a damn. Those folks wanted me dead."

"Now hold on," Skinner said, raising his voice to the point that a young couple by the front door turned around. "Hold it one gosh-dang second. I never said I was a Watchman. And from what I read in the newspaper, one of those men tried to save your life."

Quinn nodded, taking a bite, chewing slow. He looked across the table at the vein pulsing in Skinner's temple. Skinner wiped the sweat from his forehead. "Not having the guts to shoot me and trying to save me are two different things," Quinn said. "That big Indian is the one who shot me in the back. I don't suppose your Watchmen friends have any information on where he came from or who he is?"

Quinn lifted his coffee to his lips and stared across at an old man that he'd learned to despise over the years. The man exuded a complexity of weakness, piety, entitlement, and greed that had pushed him into wanting to lick the boots of every politico, crooked businessman, and shady preacher in north Mississippi. The combo had served him well. Skinner was a very rich man for Tibbehah County, maybe the richest one in two counties, although Quinn had no idea what he did outside running the supervisors.

"I want to help you get your job back," Skinner said. "I want to facilitate whatever cockamamie process there is to get you back in the sheriff's office and get these folks from Jackson the hell out of Tibbehah."

Quinn looked up, not expecting anything like this from Skinner. The man had run interference on him since he'd taken over the county Board of Supervisors after Johnny Stagg went to prison.

"I didn't sign up for this," Skinner said, pointing down at the table. "The whole damn state has gone crazy. What I've seen with my own two eyes is hard to even contemplate. That nasty woman Fannie Hathcock has run buck wild. Did you know she even put some kind of laser light show up on the Tibbehah Cross? Instead of seeing a simple declaration of faith, the lights read 'Party Tonight. Repent Sunday.' What kind of sick person does something like that?"

"Sorry, Skinner," Quinn said. "I've already been shot in the back four times. I've grown a little cautious."

"I know you don't trust me," Skinner said. "But I don't trust these new people."

"You sure trusted Governor Vardaman," Quinn said. "Go talk to him."

Skinner nodded, pursing his purple lips, and looked down at his folded hands. He didn't say a word.

"I want to make amends," he said. "I want to do what's right. I already spoke with folks down at the County Barn to get your friend Mr. Kimbrough back on as mechanic. Our vehicles haven't been running right since he left."

"That's between you and Boom."

"And then I want to get you back," Skinner said. "Supervisors will make a motion on it tonight."

"And how do you know you'll get enough votes?" Quinn said.

"This old fella can still work a miracle or two," Skinner said.

He reached his withered hand out to the middle of the table, arm shaking, waiting to see if Quinn would accept. "What do you say, son?"

The old ways were dead.

Sam Frye knew it but preferred not to live in that world. The young people always laughed at him when he spoke in the native tongue or talked of spirits, most of the tribe now Methodist or Baptist. But he watched for signs, paid attention to dreams. He might not have ever come back from Oklahoma if his dead son Mingo hadn't appeared to him. He had pennies over his eyes and cried out that he was lost and wandering, unable to see or find his way home from a broad, wide-open pasture where there were no trees and only a brightly lit moon.

"Did he speak?" Chief Robbie asked, being one of the few who still believed in such things.

"No," Sam Frye said. "He cried. He pleaded. This was

two weeks ago and I still can't clean it from my head. The mist covered both of us. I couldn't reach him."

"That's what causes you pain," Chief Robbie said. "Because with Buster White dead, too, there will be no answers. Fannie Hathcock had promised you that you'd be able to speak to him before she killed him."

Sam Frye nodded as he stood in an empty ballroom on the second floor of the main casino on the Rez. Chief Robbie had been holding talks for investors into his latest plan, an outlet mall and theme park right outside Gulfport called *Takali*, meaning "lodge." He had artist renderings and small models of a giant roller coaster and large indoor water park. To hear Chief Robbie say it, the whole plan was to educate outsiders on Choctaw ways. The mascot of the lodge was a mischievous raccoon named Oka, who would adorn thousands of T-shirts and signs across Takali, pointing the way to river rapids and perhaps, if they were lucky, a Wahlburgers.

"You told me that White's people had my son killed."

Chief Robbie nodded. "We sent Mingo to work with Fannie Hathcock to watch the Syndicate. Buster White didn't like this. He was very upset."

"Fannie told me if I would assist her, she'd give me time with White," Sam Frye said. "She lied. She denied me this."

"What did she say?"

"She says she didn't mean to kill White," Sam Frye said. "She said she only meant to knock him unconscious. That's why she didn't use a gun."

"But she hit him more than once."

"She hit him as though she was hammering a nail into

a very old piece of hardwood. His brains and blood splattered across her."

"She wanted him to stay quiet."

Sam Frye nodded again. They left the banquet room and moved out of the great hall and onto the main casino floor, the tables empty in the middle of the day, only a few elderly people bused in from the Coast playing the slot machines, pinging and whirring in the neon-lit space.

"You shouldn't have come back from Oklahoma," Chief Robbie said. "It's too soon. There has been a woman looking for you. A U.S. Marshal from Memphis who wants to find out what happened in Tibbehah County last year."

"There is no description, no details," Sam Frye said. "The sheriff was in no shape to remember. To him, I'm nothing but a shadow. A bad dream. That part is over."

"Perhaps," Chief Robbie said. "But is it worth the risk? Come back when we start building Takali. Everything will change then. We will be bigger than the old Rez where you and I grew up, playing stickball and living off government handouts and that bad cheese. We are in charge now. We have everything."

"I want to stay close to the woman," Sam Frye said. "I must know."

"You can no more trust that woman than a hissing snake," Chief Robbie said. "She speaks from the side of her mouth and tells falsehoods that will get friends to wrestle each other to the death. If you stay with her, she will intoxicate you, turn you. I promise you. She did it to me. She is a sorceress. A poisonous flower."

"No one knows who I am," Sam Frye said. "Only those Watchmen people. And some of them are dead."

Chief Robbie patted Sam Frye on his back, walking toward the exit door and the bright hot light from the outside world. Sam could smell the casino already permeating his clothes, the sweat and stink, the alcohol and cigarettes. He already felt that he needed another shower.

"Now you have two women to watch out for," Chief Robbie said. "This Marshal may not know your face but is hunting you all the same. If she gets close, you'll have to leave Mississippi. You can't come back here. Not for a while anyway."

"Takali?" Sam Frye said, smiling.

"It's a fun word," Chief Robbie said. "The marketing people like it, too. They agree it's something white people can pronounce."

Quinn knew Donnie Varner was back in town but hadn't laid eyes on him since the sentencing in Oxford. But there he was, Donnie himself, making small talk with a young woman in a tight yellow dress walking a bulldog on the Jericho Square. Donnie looked unchanged in the eight years he'd been away, left hand on his hip and his right hand plucking the long cigarette from the corner of his mouth. Something he said made the young woman laugh and she and the bulldog headed across the street toward the new Chinese restaurant, the Golden Dragon. Quinn left his truck and headed out to meet him, Donnie not recognizing Quinn until he crossed under the big oak and into the sunshine.

"Do my eyes deceive me?" Donnie said, squinting.

Quinn smiled and held out his hand.

Donnie looked at it, shook his head, and then out-stretched his arms, wrapping Quinn in a bear hug. Quinn feeling relieved, as he'd had to testify against Donnie in federal court, detailing what he knew about the man doing business with the Zetas in Tibbehah County.

"How you feeling, brother?" Donnie said.

"Might ask you the same."

"Nobody's been shooting at me," Donnie said. "Not in a long while."

"Those Cartel boys got you pretty good," Quinn said. "You're lucky they didn't kill you."

"Takes a lot more to kill ole Donnie Varner," he said, grinning. "You see that woman I was just talking to? That's damn Rita Wright, Pat Wright's little sister. She wasn't nothing but a kid when I left. But damn, she ain't a kid no more. That little yellow dress about busting at the seams."

"You're too old for Rita Wright," Quinn said. "You forget we're the exact same age."

"Nope," Donnie said. "I'm six months older. And six months smarter. I rode a bike, drove a car, and got nekkid with a woman long before you and Boom. Y'all can deny it all you want. But those are some braggin' rights, son."

"And got arrested."

"Before you and Boom?" he said. "Oh, hell no. Y'all might not recall my daddy not allowing me to hang out with either of y'all junior year. He said you two were ju-venile delinquents on a highway to hell."

"That doesn't sound like Luther."

"Sorry," Donnie said. "He said you two were a pair of serious fuckups that were going to get your damn nuts caught in a bonfire of shit."

"Better," Quinn said.

"How's your daddy Jason doing?"

"Haven't heard from him in three years."

The two walked together down the busted concrete path toward the gazebo and fallen soldier memorial. They knew or were related to at least twenty men on the plaque, one of them Donnie's uncle who never made it back from Vietnam, dying at Hamburger Hill. Four boys Quinn and Donnie knew from high school. Three dead in Iraq. One in Afghanistan two years after Quinn returned from the service.

"Listen," Donnie said, blowing smoke away from Quinn but the hot wind bringing it into his face. "I'm sorry for not reaching out when you got hurt. Luther told me about it almost straight off. I wanted to write you a letter, send flowers, or some shit. But I was embarrassed about where I was and knew I couldn't do a damn thing for you. I apologize for that."

Quinn shook his head. "Meant to come see you in Texas," he said. "I should've found the time."

"You been a little busy," Donnie said, punching Quinn in the shoulder. "You know we do get the goddamn internet in jail. A tornado takes out half the town. Johnny Stagg's sorry ass finally gets arrested. And you go and get married. Signs and fucking wonders."

Quinn pulled an unfinished Liga Privada from his T-shirt pocket. He tugged his dark green sheriff's cap down in his eyes, making sure that even out of uniform, his presence was known and contested the status quo. The grass across the Square had yellowed and withered over the summer, leaves already dropping from the big oaks in the heat. The burned-up leaves spinning and twirling across the lawn and into the street. They needed a hard rain bad.

"And now you got a son?" Donnie asked.

"Brandon," Quinn said. "He's eight. And Maggie's pregnant now with a little girl."

"Damn, son," Donnie. "You have been busy."

Quinn nodded, not really sure what to say. Donnie had been frozen on ice for the last eight years. He could never go back to his profession running a gun range and the shop. The best his buddy could hope for was Luther letting him run the register at the Quick Mart, maybe making him full-time manager until Luther wanted to retire. Quinn knew Donnie wasn't the type to find a lot of enjoyment in selling hot sausage biscuits and live bait for the rest of his life.

Donnie sat down beside him on the park bench. Quinn was hit with the sudden image of he and Donnie as much older men running the Memorial Day festivities. White hair and humped backs, looking over the better parts of their lives in the rearview. Quinn took a puff of the Liga Privada and let the smoke out, scattering out in the still air.

"You know Daddy sold the gun range to the Bundrens?" Donnie asked.

"Heard that," Quinn said.

"They plan to build the new funeral home outside

town and sell their land to some folks wanting to start up a Popeyes chicken."

"Progress."

"Yep."

"Square looks good," Donnie said. "Coffee shop and tanning salon. Candlemaker and gift shop. A new florist and three new restaurants. How's the Golden Dragon?"

Quinn made the so-so gesture with his right hand.

"Been bunking out at Daddy's," Donnie said. "He kept my Airstream. I spent the last few days getting rid of the damp smell and plugging those bullet holes. Thinking about pulling it on out to where they used to have the old drive-in theater. Remember that place?"

"My dad used to take me there when he'd visit from Hollywood," Quinn said. "When I was seven, he took me to see *Malone*. I remember him walking back to the projection shed and telling them to run it back and show the stunts he performed. Strange thing watching your dad blown up, set on fire, and shot at. Jason always thought the whole thing was funny as hell. A real joke."

"Ain't nothing funny about getting shot at."

"Never is."

"You ever figure that's the reason you got into the Army?" he said. "On account of you thinking crazy was the same thing as being brave."

"I went into the Army because my Uncle Hamp didn't give me much choice."

The men didn't talk for a while, just watched the cars and trucks slowly circle the Square. A man gunned the motor on his Harley before turning off on Jericho Road on toward Highway 45. The smell of burnt oil and exhaust hanging in the air. A beat-up red truck with the windows down blasting Big & Rich. *An' this town ain't never gonna be the same.* Donnie heard it and spit his disdain onto the gazebo floor.

"Can't wait to get me a little space," Donnie said, turning to look at Quinn. Donnie had on worn jeans and a black Sun Records tee, blond hair grown long and shaggy. "I love my daddy, but damn, how he can snore. I can also do without the morning roust and Bible study. Luther sure has grown devout and humorless in his old age."

Quinn nodded.

"Don't you worry," Donnie said. "I don't plan to stay long. I got a little business to tend to and then plan to boogie on down the road. Maybe Florida. Maybe back to Texas. Eight years gives a man a long time to think on things."

"That OK with your probation officer?"

"Yes, sir," Donnie said. "She finds me charming as hell."

"You know you can be and do anything you want, Donnie," Quinn said, offering his hand. "Don't let the shitbirds drag you down."

"Don't you worry, Sergeant." Donnie stood up and stretched. He ground the spent cigarette under a pointy-toed boot and winked at Quinn. "I'm doing my dead-level best to keep on the straight and narrow. See you around."

5

Fannie Hathcock hadn't been sure what to do with Buster White's body. There were plenty of ways to discard the tub of lard without it ever being seen. But she wanted something more, a shameful tribute to the former crime boss of the Gulf Coast, a disrespectful epitaph to his fetid breath, horrible hygiene, and nasty-ass legacy. She finally decided to have her boys run him on back to the Coast in four Hefty trash bags salted with lime. They tossed them into a dumpster behind an Olive Garden off I-10, not ten miles from the big casino castle he once ruled. A phone call was placed to the cops, and by the next night, Buster White's face was all over television. There was talk of ties to organized crime and hints of a battle with a notorious family in New Jersey. The whole damn thing just tickled Fannie pink. She had the new bartender Nat fix her a third Dirty Shirley, half grenadine and half gin, and settled in for a slow night at Vienna's

Place, counting her money and enjoying the goddamn beauty of being the last bitch standing.

She plucked a cigarillo into her mouth. Nat, a beautiful green-eyed black girl with an enormous afro, reached across and lit it without being asked. Her arms long, lean, and muscular in a sleeveless red top.

"What's on the schedule tonight?" she asked.

"Bus of frat boys coming up from State," Nat said, chewing gum. "Might have some visitors from that family values convention up in Tupelo. You know how much those youth pastors love them some titties."

Fannie lifted her cocktail glass in Nat's direction. Nat was a fine new addition to the club who did not smoke or drink and declared she would never take the stage or work a back room. She could stock the bar and run the kitchen with the best of them. Her references in Memphis and New Orleans so damn good, Fannie wondered why in the hell a woman like that would want to work at a truck stop titty bar. But when she and Fannie got into the matter of salary, it made sense. Someone like Nat, no matter how good she could pour a drink, could never make coin like this at some hipster joint up in Cooper-Young.

"Midnight Man coming back?" Nat asked.

"Not tonight," Fannie said. "Still tending to some business for me."

"Getting some trouble from that girl Brandy," Nat said. "She told me that I wasn't her boss and that she could dance to any damn shit she wanted to. I told that bitch she better not play that 'Old Town Road' one more time, Billy Ray Cyrus remix or not. And there she came in today, strapping on that ugly-ass leather cowboy hat and red sparkly G-string and telling me that I could kiss her motherfucking white ass. I'll tell you what, Miss Fannie. You need to fire that girl. She's rude to customers, don't tip out, and the kind of woman who's gonna soak this place in gasoline one day and drop a match."

"She's been going through a bad breakup," Fannie said, ashing her cigarillo. "Give her some time."

"Some time?" Nat said, crossing her arms over her chest, going as sexy as she got with a small Vienna's tee over her big tatas. "Shit. That just don't sound like you."

Fannie gave Nat a look that meant no more questions and the black girl walked down the length of the old onyx bar she'd had shipped in from Kansas City special, bought for nearly ten grand at an antique auction. The kind of detail that her grandmother, the late great grand madame Vienna, would appreciate.

Fannie had to smile at the events of the last few days, only having some remorse for her favorite hammer. She'd taken it out to the dock at Choctaw Lake and flung it far and wide into black water. Now she'd make do with the little derringer she kept, another gift from sweet old Vienna.

Fannie finished her cigarillo and then the Dirty Shirley and stood, turning only to check her reflection in the old mirror. She looked especially good tonight in a black Valentino dress, knee-length with a plunging neckline. Her ruby heart-shaped necklace dropping into her massive cleavage, red hair styled high on top of her head. Fannie Hathcock had come a long way, baby, and was in top fucking form.

As she turned to head up to her catwalk office above the stages, she nearly ran right into a scruffy, shaggy-haired man with a handsome face and clear blue eyes. He had on a black Sun Records T-shirt, faded jeans, and pointy-toed boots.

"Don't leave on my account," the man said.

"Excuse me?"

"Buy you a drink?"

"I don't work here," Fannie said. "I own here."

"Damn," he said. "Do you believe in love at first sight? Or should I walk past you again?"

"How about you try the hired help," she said. "Lap dances are two for one. And all domestics half off. You look like a man who sucks down Budweiser."

"I don't pay for no woman to ride my rail."

Fannie widened her eyes and took in the entire club as if seeing it for the first time. She cocked her head and studied the face of the handsome man. "Are you trying to find the Rotary Club?"

"No, ma'am," he said. "I like to look at hot women while I drink cold beer. Where I've been that's in short supply."

"And am I supposed to ask you where the fuck you've been?"

"FCI Beaumont for the last eight years," the man said. "In case you don't know, it's a medium-security federal prison. No one ever took me for a hard case. I go down smooth and easy."

"Did someone send you?"

"No, ma'am."

"Did you come to scare me?"

"No, ma'am," he said, offering his hand. "But I sure wanted to meet you. Fannie Hathcock, right? I'm Donnie Varner."

"Is that supposed to mean something?"

"No, ma'am," he said. "But I hope it does someday. I sure do respect the way you operate, Miss Hathcock. I'd really like it if you and me might become friends."

Fannie blew some more smoke into his face.

Quinn brought Maggie and Brandon for dinner over at his momma's house, Jean promising to make fried chicken with field peas and the last of the summer tomatoes on the side. Fried chicken was Quinn's favorite, having a big advantage over her meat loaf, a meal that no one in the family seemed to be able to get behind. Quinn never understood why Jean Colson took such pride in that bland hunk of meat.

His mother wanted them to have supper on her back patio, lighting citronella candles to keep the mosquitoes away, and played *The Best of Glen Campbell* on the stereo. "Rhinestone Cowboy" played loud and proud in the family room while Jean flipped the chicken in a sizzling iron skillet. Quinn kissed his mother on the cheek and walked to the refrigerator for the beer. Jean always kept a cold six-pack for her son just like she'd done for his father decades ago.

"No Elvis tonight?" Quinn asked.

"I'm giving Elvis a rest," Jean Colson said. "I start listening to Elvis and that'll make me start reminiscing on the past, thinking back to your daddy and me up at

Graceland. Shooting guns and riding horses with the Memphis Mafia. And Lord God, you know how the thought of your daddy drives me to drink."

"Jason has that effect on most people."

"Funny," Jean said, removing a piece of chicken and placing it on a paper towel to soak off the grease. "You've been calling your daddy by his first name since you were twelve."

"Uncle Hamp advised me to think of him as a flesh and blood person and not just my daddy," Quinn said. "He figured maybe I wouldn't be so angry all the time."

Jean walked to the big sink to wash her hands, an apron tied over the back of her sizable rump. She'd regained a little of the weight she'd lost last year, her reddish hair now returned to blonde thanks to the stylists at Peggy Raye's boutique. "And how'd that work out?"

"You know exactly how that worked out," Quinn said. He cracked open the can of Coors and found a seat looking into the backyard. Outside, Maggie set the table with Brandon's help, moving around clockwise, Brandon straightening knives and forks, reaching across the table to add a rose he'd picked in Jean's garden for a centerpiece.

Jean caught him watching his family as Quinn placed a hand on his mother's shoulder. She reached up and touched his hand. "He's a fine boy," she said. "Reminds me a lot of you when you were that age."

"He fights about as much," Quinn said. "He's already gotten in two fights this week. And it's only the first week of school."

"Tends to happen," Jean said, checking on the chicken

again. Glen Campbell moving on to "Gentle on My Mind." *Not shackled by forgotten words and bonds.*

"Can't say I blame him," Quinn said. "One of 'em was Gerry Byrd's kid and you know what a damn turd Gerry was."

"Afraid I do," Jean said. "I don't want to say anything bad. But those are some nasty folks."

"All Brandon did was explain to some kids that the universe was created by a big space explosion," Quinn said. "Maggie had just taken him to a presentation about the Big Bang at the Pink Palace up in Memphis and the boy was just relaying what he'd heard. And Gerry's kid got all hot under the collar, telling Brandon that he didn't know what he was talking about, explaining how everything was created by the living God in seven days."

"Brandon didn't buy it?"

"Nope," Quinn said. "He called the boy a damn moron. Said, and I am quoting him, 'You're living a lie.' And you can guess how it all went from there."

"Those Byrds aren't the brightest folks," Jean said. "But maybe Brandon could be more accepting on how most people think about things."

"That dinosaurs aren't real and that science is a bunch of hocus-pocus?" Quinn said. "I love me some Jesus. But come on. No reason Jesus and science can't coexist."

Jean nodded at that and pointed her fork at Quinn's chest. "How many pieces of chicken you want?"

Quinn held up two fingers and grabbed the platter of sliced tomatoes, pushing out the storm door and onto the back porch. The light was an off-shade of gold, a gathering of pine trees marking their property line, an old fort still standing where he and Caddy had once played. Brandon looked up, already working on a biscuit from a wicker basket. The biscuits came from the freezer, not a rolling pin, but it didn't seem to matter a bit to Brandon. After he finished, he reached for another along with a knife heavy with butter.

"I can promise you nothing on this table is organic," Quinn said, taking a seat on the bench next to Maggie.

"The tomatoes are organic," Maggie said. "They came from our farm."

"And the chicken?"

"Piggly Wiggly," Maggie said, smiling. "I didn't have time to butcher one of ours."

"You hate killing our chickens," Quinn said. "You should've never named them."

"I don't name them all," Maggie said. "Only the cute ones."

Maggie faced forward and Quinn sat backward, looking up at the old tree fort. He recalled Caddy sometimes stole his *Dukes of Hazzard* figures and let the Duke boys go on some wild adventures with Barbie and her sister Skipper. He didn't know exactly what Caddy had in mind, but more than once he'd found Malibu Christie passed out in the back of the *General Lee* buck-ass naked.

Brandon was balancing on the edge of the porch and then jumped off to come see Quinn. Quinn held out his hand and Brandon high-fived him. "I did good today," he said. "No fights."

"That's good."

"I came close to kicking that Byrd boy right in the

nuts," he said. "But I did like you said. I imagined him as a big pile of crap. That sort of made me laugh."

Brandon looked very proud. Quinn turned his head back to Maggie and nodded at her.

"Did you really say that?" she asked.

Quinn shrugged as Brandon jumped into Quinn's lap, sending a shooting pain down his spine and into his left leg, the pain so sharp it brought water to his eyes, and he turned his head so Maggie wouldn't see him. He patted Brandon on the back while the boy reached for the last of his biscuit. Quinn got up slowly and made his way to the back door, trying not to limp or slow his walk.

"You OK?" Maggie asked.

"Right as rain," he said. "Let me get that chicken."

He passed the kitchen, his mother asking if they needed more biscuits, and headed on back to the hallway bathroom. Turning on the faucet, he reached into his pocket for two white pills he'd wadded up in some Kleenex. He popped one and scooped water to his mouth from his right hand. He swallowed and steadied himself with the sink, feeling the pain start to slip away as he raised his eyes to the mirror.

He didn't like what he saw in his reflection.

"So let me get this straight," Fannie Hathcock said, stretching her legs at a little table by the round stage and giving Donnie Varner the good once-over. "You didn't come here for the titties. You came here to meet me, maybe charm the goddamn panties off me, and then hope I gave you some kind of job?"

"Yes, ma'am," Donnie said, grinning. "That's about the tall and short of it. Only not just any job. I'm not looking to Febreze the VIP sofas or scrub down the toilets that frat boys piss all over. I hoped you might need a man with a special set of talents."

"You look nice in a pair of Levi's," Fannie said. "But I'll warn you about something. I'm not into boys."

"That's OK," Donnie said. "Always figured my sister for a switch-hitter on account of her five-dollar haircuts and taste in music. Last Christmas all she wanted was two tickets to see the Indigo Girls at the Ryman. She might as well have written what was going on up in the sky."

Miss Hathcock looked as if she was about to spit out that pink cocktail she was sipping on. Instead, she swallowed hard and shook her head, making a face like she'd just been caught sucking on some diesel fuel. "I like men," Fannie said. "Not boys."

"Ah," he said. "OK. Well, last time I checked, my old ding-dong was still hanging loose and free down there. I'm trying to tell you that I'm not just some local yokel fucknuts. It took the damn FBI and ATF to take my ass down eight years ago. And I'd already managed to outsmart and outmaneuver a big-cat hombre from down south of the border folks called Tony El Tigre."

"If you can fit all that bullshit on a résumé, drop it in the trash can by the bar," she said. "I got all the help I need around here. Unless you know how to spin some damn records. My fucking DJ called in sick tonight although I know damn well he hooked up with my girl

Chardonnay last night and they bolted over to Tunica to play blackjack until they lose every last dime."

"You got a woman working for you named Chardonnay?"

"Her real name is Becky but that shit won't cut it out on the floor," Fannie said, waving her hand into smoke and red-tinted light. "All men want fantasy. Any bitch can be Becky. Who would you rather give you a hand job?"

"I never really thought about it," Donnie said. "Doesn't seem like a name would make it even better. That's like asking me if I'd like vanilla ice cream more if they called it a Fun Sundae."

"Matters later on," Fannie said. "When you check your wallet and say to yourself, how many times in your life do you have a woman crawling in your lap that smells like cherry perfume and has an exotic name. We have a Trinity, a Sapphire, two Jades, a Nokia, and even a Ramen, named after the girl's favorite noodles. I help them like that. Come up with names that are personal."

"Why Trinity?"

"What's that?"

"Why'd that girl want to be Trinity?"

"Said she couldn't help herself from getting into three-ways with her boyfriend," Fannie said. "Said that's how they met and it was his favorite activity outside racing dirt bikes down in Louisiana."

Donnie nodded, taking all the information in as if this might be an important part of his job one day. He tried to make himself seem attentive and interested in about everything that came out of that woman's mouth. Although it didn't take much to pay attention to a woman like Fannie Hathcock. She was a walking, talking erotic dynamo. A damn Venus de Milo with both her arms and a bigger set of tits. She knew he was looking, too, the way her long, delicate hands with those sharp red nails would play with the silver necklace and dip down to the ruby locket set right in her cleavage.

"Is there somewhere more private we can talk?" Donnie asked.

"What's wrong with right here?"

"Figured you didn't care to talk business out in the open."

"You see anyone around?"

"Damn sure never know who's listening."

"You think I'm so goddamn stupid, I don't know when the Feds have bugged my own home?"

"No, ma'am," Donnie said.

"Then come out and say it," Fannie said, touching his knee like you would a bad boy who wouldn't come forward for teacher. *Who put that tack in my chair, Johnny?* "What's on your mind, Donnie Varner?"

"Guns," Donnie said, throwing up his hands. "Got some folks who need a whole bunch in a real bad way. They got plenty of money and I know you, Miss Hathcock, know where I can get them."

"I don't know you."

"You will."

"I don't like men who come on strong."

"Try me, Miss Hathcock," Donnie said. "Kick my

tires, take me for a spin around the block. I'm here and don't plan on going nowhere for a good long while. How about me and you play a little house together?"

Fannie held her cigarillo high and stared at Donnie for a while. "I'll do some checking," she said. "And will be in touch if I like what I find out."

"And if you don't?"

"Mr. Varner, you better do some checking of your god-damn own," she said. "Nobody fucks this bitch over."

"Ana Gabriel," Sancho said. "Are you asleep?"

"I was asleep until you woke me," she said. "And now you will try and keep me awake with your constant talk and worrying."

"How can I not be worried?" Sancho said. "Here we are in the middle of a foreign land in someone else's home with no idea where to find our father. Or where the police took our mother."

"This isn't a foreign land," Ana Gabriel said, pulling the soft white linens up to her chin. They were both in a small cabin at The River, a nice woman with the church helping them move their things over from the Frog Pond before they were evicted. "It's Mississippi."

"It feels like a foreign land to me," Sancho said.

"And this isn't someone else's home," she said. "This is our church. And Miss Caddy is a friend."

"Your boyfriend's mother," he said. "Do you think that perhaps you like to stay here because it keeps you closer to Jason Colson?"

"Please shut up," Ana Gabriel said. "And go to sleep. School will come early."

"I can't," Sancho said. "I can't keep thinking about that mean man's face and his crazy big ears. Like Dumbo, the flying elephant. Did you see the way he looked at the children? Like someone on the hunt. Someone who would like to catch us all in a net and take us far away."

"You have a large imagination, Sancho," Ana Gabriel said. "Please. Good night."

"You know I am not normal."

"Yes," Ana Gabriel said. "I most certainly do."

"I have premonitions," he said. "Dreams. Didn't I tell you I awoke on Christmas Day, crying? I had dreamed that our mother fell into a hole that had no bottom. Like the one we visited at Tamaulipas with Grandfather. The great blue lake, water like a jewel. The place that he told us had no bottom, that went all the way through the core of the earth."

"Grandfather was a great liar," she said. "He liked to tease you."

"I miss him," Sancho said.

"I know." Ana Gabriel felt a rock form deep in her throat. The air conditioner humming and rattling under a window to the big barn.

"I miss Mother, too," Sancho said. "When can we see her? Where will we find her? Will she ever be able to come home?"

Too many questions that Ana Gabriel didn't want to answer. She turned on her side, her eyes facing away from Sancho. She could not let him see her cry.

* * *

Boom had let Quinn borrow a '76 Ford Highboy 4×4. It was royal blue with a decent lift and good tires. The engine needed some coaxing from time to time, but with his sheriff's vehicle still in impound, he didn't have much choice. He drove the blue Highboy up and around the winding fire road, zigzagging toward the airfield he'd been watching for months. It was late, Maggie getting Brandon to bed when he left, and now he headed down a narrow dirt road with the windows down listening to Merle Haggard. "I'm a Lonesome Fugitive" seemed just about perfect on a night like tonight. The moon was high and silver, coating the valley in a soft white glow. He had a Liga Privada going, orange tip glowing in his right hand, tapping in the truck's ashtray as he slowed and stopped by a black SUV pointed in the opposite direction.

A dark figure stood at the edge of the road, looking down into the valley. He wore dark clothes and a dark ball cap. Quinn got out and walked toward him, the truck's engine knocking a few times like an old dog shaking its coat.

"A classic," Jon Holliday said, stretching out his hand. Quinn shook it.

"A loaner," Quinn said. "Until I get my badge and keys back."

"Patience," Holliday said. "Tell me again what you guys saw."

"Three men," Quinn said. "Plus the pilot who never left the plane."

"And one of those men might've been Buster White?"

"I'd never seen White in person," Quinn said. "But whoever it was sure looked like the mug shots. A face even a momma couldn't love."

Holliday nodded. Quinn reached into the front pocket of his T-shirt and handed him a cigar. Holliday snipped off the end with a pocketknife and Quinn pitched him his old Zippo. After a few moments, the cigar kicked to life and they stood looking down at the compound Fannie Hathcock owned. At the moment, it was still and quiet, no lights at all, the moon shining off the metal of the Quonset huts.

"Police in Biloxi just pulled a dismembered body from a dumpster," he said. "Once they found a hand, they were able to match prints to Buster White. They said the face wasn't much to look at. It had been beaten past any recognition."

"Y'all know what time he headed back to Biloxi?"

"Never did," Holliday said. "That plane never made a return trip. Buster White never came back from Tibbehah."

"What about his people?" Quinn said.

"You think they're gonna talk to the Feds?" Holliday said. "Most of White's people have hightailed it back to New Orleans. Got a few people on the inside that said they saw it coming a long way off. They said ole Buster had gotten soft in his old age. Miss Hathcock has been edging his fat ass further and further out into the Gulf."

"From what I read about Buster White, that couldn't have been easy," Quinn said. "I read that he hosted a barbecue for the family of a man who had crossed him, using him as the main course. After, they told police it had been the best damn brisket they'd ever eaten. Sweet and juicy."

"All these folks, Miss Hathcock included, have brains that would send a psychiatrist screaming from their office," Holliday said, staring at the glowing end of the cigar. "Just how the hell do you afford smokes like these?"

"One of the men in my unit lives in Miami," Quinn said. "Sends me a box from time to time."

"You save his life or something like that?"

"Nope," Quinn said. "I ran his ass ragged at Benning. Tried to make him wash out and quit and I never could do it. He was too damn tough. A real Ranger. The cigars are more of a fuck-you than a thank-you."

"Look, man," Holliday said. "I know this process is long and slow as hell. I can't imagine you having to put up with the slights from Vardaman's people. But I promise you, Quinn, we are damn close."

"How much more do y'all need?" Quinn said. "Fannie does most of her business in the wide open now. Y'all could raid this place almost any night of the week and come up with a dozen different charges against her and her people."

"Yeah," Holliday said, puffing on the cigar. "But don't you want it all? Wouldn't you love to scoop up damn near all these folks that've been giving both of us hell for all these years, going way back to Johnny Stagg and Bobby Campo? Buster White doesn't end things. It's only the beginning. Fannie Hathcock and Jimmy Vardaman is a match made in Hades. They won't rest until they loot and burn every inch of Mississippi."

Quinn crossed his arms and leaned against the old truck, the hood feeling warm against his scarred back. In the darkness, he tapped at the cigar and looked at Holliday. "You're asking a lot of me."

"You're not alone," Holliday said. "You know that?"

"How many y'all got?"

Holliday clasped him on the shoulder and winked. "I prefer to keep all these nasty little stories separate until the end."

6

Donnie was having a hell of a dream about being trapped on an island full of half-naked women, a few of them taking him to a secluded waterfall to wash his parts, when he heard the grumbling pipes of his daddy Luther's GTO. The man left him a message that he'd be by at 0700, but Donnie didn't even have to look at the damn clock to know he'd arrived early. It was still dark outside, the shades down, and he nearly broke his damn neck trying to turn on the light in the Airstream. Donnie pulled on a T-shirt and blue jeans and walked to the tiny kitchen counter to find his pack of smokes. He lit one up and just had time to inhale before Luther was knocking.

Donnie opened the door, trying to look like he'd been up for hours. The old Marine already gave Donnie a ton of shit at the Quick Mart for being a first-rate joker and smoker. That old man had a million lines like that.

"See you got the power hooked up."

"Last week," Donnie said. "Don't you recall me bringing you back that generator? You think I'm living out here with a flashlight and my pecker in my hand?"

"You paying for it?"

"Hell yes, I'm paying for it, Dad," Donnie said. "You think I'm going to hook up to the damn power association myself? I'd rather not get my ass flambéed into no crispy critter."

"How about some coffee?" Luther said. The old man's hair cut even higher and tighter than Quinn Colson's. Luther only left a little silver on top, the rest shaved down to damn near nothing.

Donnie got to work making the coffee in an old percolator his momma used to use. Luther wandered back outside, leaving the door wide-ass open, the cold air from the trailer blowing out into the hot summer morning. It had been a week since Donnie had gone to see Fannie Hathcock at Vienna's and not so much as a fucking greeting card. For the first time in his life, Donnie began to doubt his Southern charm.

"Damn, old man," Donnie said, closing the door. He wandered out of the Airstream as he scratched his ass, finding Luther sitting on an old-fashioned metal chair. "You trying to bankrupt me before I even find a job?"

"Figured we might talk over Saul on the road to Damascus today."

"You didn't tell me we were talking Scripture so early," Donnie said. "I figured you just wanted to see where I was living."

"You remember that's when Saul come across Jesus,"

Luther said, the battered leather Bible splayed open to Acts on his lap. "The light was so bright and overwhelming it blinded him. He couldn't see for days. Didn't eat or drink until he made it to Damascus and found Ananias to restore his sight and baptize him."

"How about some coffee before Saul?" Donnie said. "I need a couple smokes and a shot of caffeine if you and me are going to jump right back into Biblical times."

Luther didn't answer. Donnie grinned at the old man, feeling like he did when he was a young kid and had accidentally lit the back forty acres on fire. Luther would never let him live that one down, although all it did was burn down an acre of old cornstalks and worthless pines, lighting those sonsabitches up like Roman candles.

Donnie found an old Dallas Cowboys Super Bowl Champs mug and filled it with hot black coffee, bringing it out to his father. The old man sitting in half-darkness and watching the creeping pink and blue light begin to shine from behind the old drive-in movie screen. The lot of the theater was busted and cracked, covered by weeds, with crooked metal posts where they once hung little speakers. Donnie had found a box of them all rusted and loose in what had been the concession stand. The owner told Donnie he could stay out there as long as he liked if he took care of the rat problem. And by god, that joker wasn't kidding. Just two nights ago he'd seen a gray rat up in the rafters as big as a lapdog, eyes glowing red in Donnie's flashlight.

"Do you want to start reading?" Luther asked. "Or would you like me to begin?"

"I'd rather you tell me why you needed to wake me up

so damn early," Donnie said. "You got me working three nights this week at the Quick Mart."

"You call this early?"

"Yes, sir," Donnie said. "I sure as hell do."

"The way I figure it," Luther said, "seeing the sun rise every morning is a gift. It puts everything into perspective. You're up and at 'em and got the world by the nutsack. Or do you plan on working at the Quick Mart until I finally go and kick the bucket?"

"You doing that anytime soon, old man?" Donnie said.

"Don't be picking out flowers just yet," Luther said. "Before I drove out here, I did a hundred push-ups and sit-ups."

"Good on you, Daddy."

Luther studied the end of his extra-long cigarette and then turned his hard blue eyes at Donnie.

"This place looks like shit," Luther said from behind him. "I remember when this was the hot spot of Jericho. When I was boy, I saw *Rio Bravo* here five times. Your grandfather made two of us hide in the damn trunk of his Buick to save a nickel. Used to be a beautiful sign out on the road. Magnolia Drive-In. Hell of a place. Can't figure why a man would want to live out here now."

"Well," Donnie said, pinching the cigarette between his thumb and forefinger. "You sold the gun range while I was in prison. My finances continue to be limited."

"You left me with a few bills."

"I do appreciate you keeping the Airstream," Donnie said. "And making sure it didn't rust and turn to shit."

Luther nodded, still transfixed by the light spreading

behind the old metal movie screen, sheets of tin hanging askew from the metal skeleton. His mouth hung open as if experiencing a miracle. "I know it ain't easy finding a job after you been out of circulation."

"Damn, Dad," Donnie said. "You make me sound like a fucking library book. We can just all admit I was in prison. I fucked up. I did my time. I'm good with it. I bet even Jesus is good with it, although He didn't shine no blinding light out of the sky when I got walked out of those chained gates."

"You don't believe in signs?"

"Oh, hell."

"Have you lost your faith?"

"I don't know," Donnie said. "I still pray if that's what you're asking. But I hadn't seen or experienced anything in my life that I felt was divine intervention."

"Those Mex boys should've taken your ass out," Luther said. "I prayed and prayed that He would keep you safe. That's something. Ain't it?"

"I figure," Donnie said, taking a seat beside his father and resting his feet on a section of an old log he'd dragged back from the woods. He knew come fall, this would be a nice little spot for a campfire, a place he could watch the stars. The stars were a spectacle he could behold that didn't require setting no damn alarm clock. The sun started to touch the streaks of white clouds crossing the sky, turning everything a bright hot-pink and -blue.

"I am grateful to be free," Donnie said.

"Five years knocked off," Luther said. "I'd call that a fucking gift."

"I might argue that point."

"You want to enlighten me a bit?"

"How about we just sit here?" Donnie said. "I appreciate your company."

Luther looked down at the Bible, using his long bony finger to find his lost place. He peered up at Donnie before he turned the page. "Now that you're home, maybe you should go down and visit The River sometime."

"Caddy Colson's place?" Donnie said. "Sure. Don't see why not."

"Good," Luther said. "I told Caddy I'd send you her way. She said she sure would like to see you. I don't believe you've been to church since you got back."

Donnie shook his head. Luther Varner didn't take a shit without a damn action plan. And it looked like The River was going to be ground zero to save his wicked soul. Donnie didn't speak, cigarette burning between his fingers as Luther's gravelly voice started into *"Saul, Saul, why do you persecute me?"*

"These people will stop at nothing to shut us up and get what they want," Hector Herrera said. "It infuriates me."

"How many has ICE let go?" Caddy asked.

"Fifty-three," Hector said. "The ones with papers. They were in this country working legally and still suffered such humiliation. One woman, Adrian Calderón, left five children at home. No one notified her children or informed her of her rights."

She stood with Hector outside the big old wooden barn a little before noon, the sun high and hot on the hard-packed dirt road. Hector's white cargo van idled next to them, coated in a fine brown dust. He was a medium-sized man with a round stomach and a shaved head, big black eyebrows, and black mustache and goatee. He had on a red V-neck T-shirt and wore a large braided gold chain and cross, complete with a crucified Jesus. His face and bald head were shiny with sweat.

"And where are the rest now?"

"Still in north Louisiana," he said. "An ICE facility in Pine Prairie."

"Pine Prairie?"

"I know," Hector said. "Sounds nice. But it's anything but lovely. They are not officially prisoners but are forced to wear orange jumpsuits and are shackled while moved."

"Lawyers?"

"We are working on it," he said. "Most do not speak English. And we are told the government is under no obligation to provide counsel. These people are the voiceless. Those in power want to see them disappeared."

"We're overloaded here," Caddy said. "We've gotten some local support but not much. I can offer as many as fifty beds. But I could use some help. The children get restless. They are scared for their parents. I give us maybe four days before we run out of food. But I have faith. He always comes through when we need Him."

Hector nodded, placing a strong hand on Caddy's shoulder and looking her in the eye the way he did when he was serious, when it was a matter of honor. "Thank you," he said. "We all thank you. If this place wasn't here, the children would have nowhere to go. That whore of a trailer park has kicked everyone out who can't make their weekly payment. They didn't care if they were legal. They didn't care if they were children. Everything is about money."

"What I don't understand is how the money people allowed this to happen," Caddy said. "The processing plant is the biggest money in the county. You'd think they'd have some friends in Jackson to make sure no one gives them trouble. They run more than fifty thousand chickens a day."

"More like eighty thousand," Hector said. "What they do is not sanitary and is not legal. The foremen are brutal and mean. Few speak Spanish. They make insults and use their hands on the women."

"Why didn't you say anything?"

Hector shook his head and spit. "You do not get it, Miss Colson," he said. "This raid was not about stopping that business—they helped it. It was about shutting me up and shutting the mouths of anyone who spoke up against the plant. Did you not know about the lawsuit?"

Caddy shook her head. She had her hands on her hips, her Carhartt work pants cut off into shorts, high rubber boots covering her calves. Dirt and sweat stained the front of her white T-shirt. She'd spent the morning in the field, gathering the very last of the corn that hadn't been completely destroyed in the heat. She was tired and hungry, and within two hours, the school bus would return with nearly fifty kids that she could barely house or afford to feed.

"I helped many women at the plant with a class-action lawsuit," he said. "One woman that had moved too slowly was hit with a broom handle. Another woman, this one at a plant outside Jackson, was accused of stealing and forced to a strip search. There are so many humiliations. And so many things the plant doesn't want known. All I can say is don't eat the chicken from that place. If you knew all the practices, it would turn your stomach."

"Why didn't they get you?" Caddy asked.

"They would like nothing more," Hector said, reaching down and absently touching the large cross on his neck. "And have tried in other ways. Legally, they can't touch me. I was born and raised in Houston. I am an American. I have a voice and can speak loud."

"And the children?"

"Feed them," he said. "Protect them. They are safe here. And the schools will offer help and support. I will get you assistance when I can."

"The children want to speak to their parents."

"I'm working on that."

"Doesn't seem right," Caddy said. "Doesn't seem human."

"There is nothing human about this," Hector Herrera said. "Or decent. This is about money and power and doing all they can to flush these people down the toilet."

"And then what?"

"Find more to take their place," Hector said. "Who will know better than to ever raise their voice again."

Quinn had just finished running a round of hay over to the cows when Maggie pulled up and hefted herself out of her Subaru. She looked huge and beautiful, dressed in blue scrubs, pregnant enough now to be on half-days at the hospital. Quinn crawled off the tractor, removed his leather gloves and stuck them in his back jeans pocket. He was careful on the dismount, mindful of his doctor warning him a dozen times to avoid sudden movements or jostling. His old International Harvester tractor was nothing but sudden movements, jostling, and thick black smoke. It had belonged to his Uncle Hamp, his grandfather before that, and had sat for twenty years in an old barn before he and Boom got it running again. Both Brandon and Jason really loved the tractor and named it Otis after a favorite children's book.

"You're home early," Quinn said.

"Nope," Maggie said. "Right on time."

"And Brandon?"

"Your mom got him today," she said. "Don't you remember?"

Quinn nodded.

"He got into another fight today," she said. "Fourth one in two weeks."

Quinn nodded again, following her up to the house, knowing that look on Maggie's face and not being thrilled with what was coming next. They'd had a few arguments about dealing with Brandon's anger, finding some kind of common ground to help him control it. Maggie wanted him to meditate. Quinn wanted him to ignore the bullies or take them on. And Jean just wanted everyone to pray on it, although Maggie made it clear she didn't have a vote.

Quinn walked into the kitchen and filled an old Mason jar with cold water. Maggie took a seat, looking worn out and exhausted, carrying around fifty more pounds than normal. Quinn figured it was worse than carrying a rucksack everywhere you went. The rucksack didn't kick your ribs and keep you running to the bathroom.

"Remember the advice you gave Brandon?" Maggie asked. "You told him to imagine those boys are living, breathing piles of shit."

"I actually said sacks of crap," Quinn said. "I figured it'd give him a visual to laugh at."

Maggie clenched her jaw and began to absently sort through the mail, separating the bills from the junk. Judging from the pile, it looked to be mainly junk. "Well, today he went one further and called them a couple of dumbass shitbags," she said. "One of the boys jumped him and the other punched him in the stomach."

"How is he?" Quinn said.

"Brandon is fine," Maggie said. "But he gave that Byrd kid a bloody nose."

Quinn drank some water and grinned down at the jar.

"It's not funny."

"I didn't laugh."

"But you're smiling," she said. "Don't think I can't see that little grin on your face? You think he did the right thing. That he did good trying to take both those boys on. But he can't talk like that. He's only eight years old, Quinn. He's just a little boy. He shouldn't be calling kids shitbags and pussies."

"Who'd he call a pussy?"

"Different kid," she said. "Same idea. Kid was making fun of what Brandon was having for lunch. Said the curry smelled funny like old farts."

Quinn took a seat at the table and took another long drink from the glass. Everything in the old kitchen was damn near perfect. Before Maggie, Quinn had gotten by with four plates and four place settings, a few coffee mugs and Mason jars. After Maggie, the kitchen walls were filled with her photographs and art she and Brandon had made. It was all color and light, the curtains pulled back with views out onto the back field and down into the apple and pecan orchards.

"Brandon is different," he said. "Kids know he's not from around here and resent it. None of them have ever left Tibbehah County and many never will. They see Brandon has nice clothes, brings a nice lunch, has a father and mother who love him. That's something that's in short supply."

"Can't be that simple," Maggie said.

"I know these people. I grew up with them. Most of them are fine, hardworking people. But some folks, like the damn Byrds, are just mean-spirited. They hate what Brandon has because they know that whatever they do, they'll never find it."

Maggie had her arms crossed over her stomach, feet stretched out in front of her. Her wonderful freckled face flushed with a ruddy glow, green eyes wide and suspicious. She looked mad at Quinn but he hoped she was just mad about the situation. It had been tough to ease Brandon into Tibbehah County, at first because he was new and then—even worse—because his real father had been an infamous bank robber.

"I don't like the advice you're giving."

"Sorry," Quinn said. "This is all new to me."

"You're treating him the way your Uncle Hamp treated you."

"Probably."

"And you know better than anyone how much it means to have someone to look up to when you don't have a father."

Quinn nodded. He stood up and walked to refill the glass. He'd been out in the field working for a few hours. His back hurt and his forearms and face were sunburned. At the sink, he turned and leaned against the counter, waiting for whatever else Maggie wanted to say.

"This isn't you, Quinn."

"You just said it was."

"I said you're acting like your Uncle Hamp," she said. "Not you."

Quinn felt his face flush. He never liked to hear Maggie running down a man that she'd never known. Everyone knew that it had been a long, hard fall for his Uncle Hamp, but he was still the man who helped raise Quinn and Caddy.

The back field was freshly cut and looked clean and neat, big rounds of hay neatly aligned every twenty meters or so. It felt orderly and straight.

"I'll do better."

"Not just on Brandon," she said. "I mean everything."

Quinn set down the glass and turned back to Maggie. She reached up and let down her reddish-brown hair from the bun and let it spill across her face and down her neck. Maggie didn't look mad anymore. She looked hurt and confused. Quinn watched her face.

"I see you got a new supply of pills," she said. "You want to tell me where?"

"I've had some more pain," Quinn said. "Didn't want to worry you."

"Didn't come from your doctor here," she said. "Where'd you go?"

"Memphis."

"When?"

"A few weeks back," Quinn said. "Like I said, I didn't want to worry you."

"Part of your recovery is detox," she said. "You don't need that crap anymore. If you're having problems with your injuries, we need to get you back in for more X-rays. Everything should be healed by now."

Quinn nodded.

"You know that," she said. "Don't you?"

Donnie had stopped off for a plate lunch at the Piggly Wiggly when he spotted Caddy Colson across the blazing hot parking lot. He'd gotten the meat and three—hamburger steak, turnip greens, fried okra, and mac and cheese—and was well onto washing it all down with a cold Mountain Dew as Caddy started to have what looked like a goddamn breakdown. She was yelling out some choice words and kicking at the tires of a busted-ass truck.

He had the plate set up on the trunk of his dad's GTO, parked closer to the old Hollywood Video store than the Pig. Caddy was way across the lot, up close to the front of the grocery store, stooping down to pick up cans that had torn loose from a brown sack and began to roll all over the place. Being a true and good man, Donnie put down his spork and jogged across the lot to find a rolling can of SpaghettiOs, picking it up and setting it in the back of the old truck.

"Thanks," Caddy said, standing up and wiping the sweat off her brow and nose with her hand. Her long blonde hair had been chopped off as short as a boy's, cheap white sunglasses covering those beautiful blue eyes.

"Woman hadn't seen me in eight years and all she says is thanks for picking up a can of SpaghettiOs. I think she just might come over here and hug a man's neck."

"Damn, Donnie," she said, taking off her sunglasses. "I'm sorry. I didn't even recognize you."

"Prison just made me even more handsome," he said. "Just the other day, two elderly women at the El Dorado buffet mistook me for Matthew McConaughey."

"You're a hell of a lot smarter than Matthew McConaughey."

"Damn, girl," Donnie said, opening up his arms. "Come on over here. What the hell's got you down in the mouth?"

Caddy reached out and hugged him back, pressing her face into his shoulder. Donnie tried to recall a time that he didn't know Caddy Colson but couldn't come up with a minute he didn't know that blonde hair and bright blue eyes. Damn if she didn't still smell like strawberries and sunshine, but he knew he'd only get a sock in the jaw if he said it.

"When did you get back?" she said.

"Couple months ago."

"And you didn't come see me?"

"Didn't you hear?" Donnie said. "My daddy threw me a welcome home party at the VFW. Hell of a night. Should have been there. I got to line dance with Aunt Hollis."

"I thought she was down with diabetes."

"Hell," Donnie said. "Can't keep that woman from cutting a rug. You know that."

Donnie noticed a dozen or so more cans spread across the hot parking lot. He started picking them up and holding them in his arms, and Caddy began to pile boxes of cereal, crackers, and loaves of Wonder Bread into the back of the truck.

"Sorry I didn't make the party," she said. "I hope it was fun."

"So damn crowded, you couldn't even breathe."

Caddy squinted an eye at Donnie, always knowing when he was full of shit. She looked at him and smiled. "Matthew McConaughey?"

"Maybe it was Robert Redford," he said. "I can never be too sure. What's all this shit for? You having a party of your own?"

"I forget how long you've been gone."

"Looks like you're feeding a damn army."

Caddy told him a little bit about a place she was running out on some logged-out property called The River. His daddy had already told him most of it, but he liked to hear Caddy talk. She'd been in a rough spot last time they'd crossed paths. He heard she'd been working the fucking pole in Memphis, drinking and drugging like there was no tomorrow. It broke his damn heart to hear it. They'd spent a night together, maybe fifteen, sixteen years ago, long before her kid, and from his point of view had a hell of a time. Only thing, Caddy had been the one who'd scooped up her panties off his trailer floor and hauled ass in tears. They hadn't seen much of each other since.

"Given that I am a recently released convict with few job opportunities besides selling hot biscuits and shit coffee at the Quick Mart, what if I stopped by sometime to help?"

"I'm good," she said. "But thank you."

"Oh, hell no, you're not," Donnie said, readjusting the cans and boxes in the back of the bed so they didn't blow out. He placed all the boxes up toward the cab and moved the heavier stuff toward the tailgate. Caddy watched him from the other side of the truck, her white sunglasses back down in her eyes. A hot wind blew across the lot and ruffled her short hair.

"You afraid I'll ruin your reputation?"

"It's a lot of work," Caddy said. "I don't wish it on anybody."

"And you think I'm still too selfish?" Donnie said. "One thing I can promise you is that prison does indeed change a man."

"I've heard that."

"Every damn day is a Happy Meal delight of surprises and little gifts."

"Like picking up cans in the Piggly Wiggly parking lot?"

"Exactly."

"I have about fifty kids and a few adults needing some assistance," she said. "I need to make supper for them in a couple hours."

"I am the goddamn master chef of microwaving SpaghettiOs."

"A little bit more involved than that."

Donnie leaned on the back of the old truck, finding a solid dent in the metal to rest his forearms. He looked across at Caddy Colson and couldn't keep from smiling. He felt like his damn face might break, so he turned his head to pop an American Spirit into the side of his mouth. The Bic clicked in his hand and he cocked his head the way he'd once seen Robert Mitchum do it in *Thunder Road*.

"I ain't got shit to do, Caddy Colson," Donnie said. "How about you give me a little something?"

7

The buffet breakfast at the Hampton Inn in downtown Jackson had been a sumptuous feast. Skinner enjoyed a rare four biscuits and gravy with his wife of fifty-two years, Merva Joy, before his ten o'clock meeting with the governor. The meeting hadn't been easy to wrangle; the testy woman working for Vardaman had been slow about returning his calls or assigning a date or time. Skinner wasn't used to such nonsense. When Vardaman had been serving on the state senate or running for governor, he'd always been quick to pick up Skinner's speed dial. Now the man acted as if he couldn't even find Tibbehah County on a gosh-durn map.

He tried not to take it personally, but the latest debacle, the mess out at the chicken plant, had been the final insult. The county needed that plant up and running. It had been the cornerstone of bringing back the economy that had been on a slow decline since that polyester slacks factory from up in New York City had shuttered its doors.

Skinner had dressed that morning in a brand-new pinstripe suit, a clean white dress shirt, and a baby blue tie with little white dots. Merva Joy had gotten him the tie for Christmas, saying it brought out the color of his beautiful eyes. His wife seemed excited to be on the adventure out of Jericho. The last trip they'd taken had been to Gatlinburg for the Spring Christian Jubilee, featuring three noted Southern pastors, the uplifting music of Exalt!, and a comedian who specialized in telling clean, wholesome jokes guaranteed to tickle the ole funny bone. He and Merva Joy had laughed and laughed at the one bit he'd done about not being able to get even an inch of a pew on Easter Sunday. Another howler was about that fella drinking too much espresso and not shutting up for a dang hour!

The thought of it tickled Skinner as he rode up the elevator with a real nice colored man to the third floor of the Gartin building. The old gent commented on the dry spell they'd been having and wondered out loud when they'd ever see a drop of rain. Skinner said he wasn't sure as he removed his Stetson and dabbed at his bald head with a show hankie that matched his special tie.

Not five minutes later, after perusing a two-year-old copy of *Field & Stream*, a young woman with blonde hair and more makeup than a circus clown brought him before Vardaman's desk. The governor was on the phone, the woman smiling and asking if Skinner would maybe like a cup of coffee or some water. Skinner curtly dismissed her, as he was pretty durn sure she'd been the holdup for the meeting all along.

"Sorry about that," Vardaman said, reaching his hand across the desk without standing. Skinner got up and greeted him, knocking his Stetson down onto the big Oriental rug and sending it rolling like a lost quarter. As he picked it up, Skinner was pleased to see facsimiles of the Ten Commandments had been set up before the Mississippi and American flags.

"You're not an easy man to get holt of," Skinner said.

"Been a busy time, sir," Vardaman said. "How are all my friends in Tibbehah County? Y'all making it through this drought?"

"Creek bed's dry as a bone," he said. "Hitting our farmers hard. How y'all been doing? How's that wonderful family of yours?"

"Youngest son off to Ole Miss, plans on pledging KA like his daddy and older brother." The governor was dressed in a flat black suit with his white dress shirt starched and open at the collar. "Little ole Madison's heading into tenth grade. I just can't believe it."

Vardaman had swept back his long silver hair from a face that looked like it should be stamped on an old coin, soft around the jaw but regal, tanned to the color of a leather belt. Vardaman had a bemused look in his eye as he let a little silence hang in the air. Skinner just nodded and mopped his face some more. He didn't know why he was so dang nervous.

"Something on your mind, Clarence?"

"Well," Skinner said, not being used to anyone addressing him by his first name. "I came to talk to you about what happened at the chicken plant. That sure cut hard and deep in my county. If that plant shuts down, I can see Jericho looking like it did ten years back. Shuttered doors and For Sale signs."

Vardaman stared down at some papers on his desk as if not paying attention, finding interest elsewhere. But he finally looked up and shook his head as if Skinner had gone simple. "Can't have a bunch of goddamn illegals running amok in my state. You know how many good hardworking rednecks would cut their damn throats to work in that plant?"

"Sir, I'd appreciate if you didn't take the Lord's name in vain," he said.

"Let me tell you something, Skinner," Vardaman said. "I don't have a problem telling the federal government to stay the hell out of our business. But if they want to do some housecleaning in Mississippi, that's fine by me. Those Mexicans remind me of goddamn armadillos infesting the state. You see one, got to be twenty of 'em right behind."

"Might've tipped me off those ole boys were headed our way," Skinner said, swallowing a bit. "I don't care to be awoken at first light with news from the sheriff."

"How's the new one working out for you?"

"I figured the boy to be an ideal prospect," Skinner said.

"And?"

"Well," Skinner said. "I'd like to see him doing his gosh-dang job. That redheaded woman's barnyard act out by the highway seems to be having a banner year. She's even building some kind of pleasure palace out on Choc-taw Lake. Members only and that kind of thing. Lord knows the kind of immoral activities she has planned."

"You may not like her methods," Vardaman said. "But she brings in more money than those Mexicans cutting up dead chickens."

Skinner pursed his lips and nodded, feeling the crown on his Stetson. The last few weeks had made the sweat ring even more pronounced. "Almost sounds like you support that kind of activity, sir?"

"I don't make the laws in your county," he said. "You do."

"And you told me—"

Governor Vardaman held up the flat of his hand and shook his head, letting him know that previous discussions and private deals were not to be discussed. Skinner nodded, being a longtime player in the political arena, and knowing that sometimes you took a loss on the road for a win later at home. Skinner bit at his cheek, feeling that tic jumping under his left eye. He swallowed again, hands starting to shake on his prized cowboy hat.

"For how long?" Skinner asked.

"We'll let you know."

"Those workers spent a lot of money in Jericho," he said. "And that plant has stabilized our little old town. What are we supposed to do now?"

"Last I heard, there wasn't a shortage of Mexicans," Vardaman said.

"But what about the plant?"

"It'll be open before Christmas."

"Got your word on that?"

Vardaman didn't answer. Only stared back.

"Let me ask you something, sir," Skinner said, lifting his eyes to the governor. "I heard you may have called in some favors with old friends up in Washington to make this here raid happen. Any truth in that?"

"Oh, I don't know," Vardaman said, grinning. "Maybe a little."

"Ain't no white man gonna take those jobs for what they're paying," Skinner said. "Even the durn blacks turn up their noses at that low pay."

"And why wouldn't they?" Vardaman said. "With government handouts and vouchers, they'll never be hungry enough to hitch up their damn britches and put in an honest day's work."

"Lots of folks been asking me just who owns that plant," Skinner said. "And how come they trucked in those folks from all over the South and Texas if they didn't have papers."

"And what do you tell them?"

"I tell them the plant's owned by a big holding company down here and I'm not really sure who's on the board."

"And that's all they need to know," Vardaman said. "We straight on all this?"

Skinner stood up tall and looked down at Vardaman. He placed the Stetson on his bald, liver-spotted head. "I do a heck of a lot for the good of my county," Skinner said. "But I'm getting sick and tired of telling my own people lies."

"Skinner, you been licking boots for as long as I've

been alive," Vardaman said. "Don't tell me you never got a little shit on your tongue."

Vardaman scratched at the edge of his leathery cheek just as the side door opened. Miss Smarty Pants ducked her nose into the office and told the governor about a meeting he had over in the Capitol in ten minutes. Vardaman stood from his desk and pointed to the door. "Mr. Skinner was just on his way out."

Quinn met up with Deputy Reggie Caruthers out on County Road 412, taking the long, winding road through Blackjack and Burnt Oak not far from the sheriff's office gun range. There was an old general store with a gas pump, long abandoned and left to rot, with a small white house down a short dirt drive that had alternately been both a karaoke bar and a Pentecostal church. A sign for the church placed out along the roadside had been made from plywood and bright green spray paint.

"When'd they go back to being a church?" Quinn asked.

"Family had to close down the karaoke place," Reggie said. "They were serving moonshine on Monday nights."

"We never stopped them before."

"Brock Tanner wants all the moonshine out of the county," he said. "Didn't you see him on the news last week?"

"There's not enough moonshine in this county to fill a bathtub," Quinn said. "Trust me. The production all but stopped when my uncle shut down my grandfather for good."

"Gives Brock something to do," he said. "Makes him look good shutting down the juke joints. You saw they closed down the Club Disco 3000?"

"No, sir," Quinn said. "I didn't."

"Brock locked the doors in June," Reggie said.

"All these businesses black-owned?"

"What do you think, Sheriff?"

Reggie was a compactly built black man in his mid-thirties with a neatly trimmed afro, thick biceps, and a winning smile with dimples that drove the women at the courthouse wild. He had a cool, easygoing way about him but could turn hard fast. Quinn had seen many prisoners try and one-up Reggie and be shut down with a mean look or a hard word. Since Brock Tanner had been sent up from Jackson, Reggie was one of only two deputies who'd remained. Their dispatcher Cleotha had walked off the job when she heard Quinn had been placed on temporary leave.

"What's he say about Vienna's Place?"

"Official word is to keep clear unless there's trouble," Reggie said. "Last time I got called out to Vienna's was with two dancers fighting over tips from a big spender who'd come down from Jackson."

"Who won?" Quinn said.

"Big fat corn-fed girl from Starkville who worked under the name Sunshine. She beat that other woman senseless with the heel of one of those big old stripper shoes. Took me a week to get all the blood out of my vehicle."

"You're doing God's work, Reggie," Quinn said. "Don't you ever forget it."

"When you coming back, Sheriff?" Reggie said. "I mean, damn. I don't know how much longer I can take this shit. From the first day, Brock's been talking like he's the man in charge and sent by Jesus Himself to clean up the vice of this county. But that's all it is. Talk."

Quinn leaned against his truck. A white minivan sped by the old general store, kicking up grit and dirt, sending a Styrofoam cup twirling in its wake. A logging truck rambled by, strapped down with shorn pine logs, jostling on the long stretch of bad road.

"Who's Tanner been meeting with?"

"Mainly keeps to himself," he said. "Closes the door when he talks with those boys who followed him up from down south. To be honest, Sheriff, he doesn't really do much of nothing. Only thing I can recall is he got into some kind of fight with Ole Man Skinner two weeks back. I could hear them yelling from outside your office and tried to listen. Don't know what was being said, only saw Skinner leave the office and slam the door behind him."

"That tracks."

"On what?"

"Skinner came to see me a week ago," Quinn said. "Hat in hand and wanting to be my friend."

"Shit," Reggie said. "Something's messed up about that picture."

"Yep," Quinn said.

"They can't shut you out forever," he said. "Folks here elected you to serve. This state investigation is bullshit. Like I told you, some folks interviewed me about you and connections to folks on the Coast. I gave them a piece of my mind and hadn't heard from them since."

"Be patient," Quinn said, clasping a hand on Reggie's shoulder.

"Want to tell me more?" Reggie said, grinning. His dimples wide and deep, smile big and bright.

"You really want to know more?"

"Not sure," Reggie said. "Maybe I don't want you spoiling the surprise."

"What about Fannie and Tanner?" Quinn said. "Has he said anything about that new place out on the lake?"

"No, sir."

"Or the trucks they've been cutting up behind the Rebel?"

"Everyone in town knows about that shit," Reggie said. " 'Cept him."

"Is he a bad cop?" Quinn said. "Or a dirty one?"

"You mean is he stupid or crooked?"

"Yep."

"I'd figure he's a little bit of both."

Quinn looked up beyond Reggie's shoulder as one of the new Tibbehah County Sheriff SUVs sped past and then came to a slow stop past the church. The SUV made a sweeping U-turn and headed back to the old general store, bucking up from the asphalt onto the gravel and moving past the old pumps. The window came down slow to reveal a sleepy-eyed man with pouches under his eyes. His hair looked like the kind you'd see on a third grader, bangs cut in an even line across his forehead. He wore a tan county uniform and silver star, but Quinn had never seen him before.

"Y'all doing all right?"

"Just fine," Reggie said.

"Figured you might be having some car trouble, Deputy," the man said. "Given that you was supposed to be patrolling down in Sugar Ditch."

"Oh, no, sir," he said. "Doing just fine here. About to head that way."

The sleepy-eyed man looked Quinn up and down and nodded. He lifted a Styrofoam cup to his lips and spit. "Oh, hell," he said. "Didn't you used to be Sheriff Colson?"

He hiccuped up a laugh, raised the window, and turned back toward the road, accelerating back toward town.

"Who's the shitbird?" Quinn asked.

"Mitchell Danbury," Reggie said. "Chief deputy. Spends most of his day tending to Tanner's business. Must've been Tanner sent him out to follow me."

"They know we're friends."

"Danbury's been looking for an excuse to let me go," he said. "Been riding my ass all summer long."

"Where's he from?"

"Hattiesburg," Reggie said. "Says he served in the Army with Tanner. But when he got down to specifics, his story didn't make much sense. I looked him up and saw he'd been let go from a police department in Louisiana. No charges, but I found a story where a teenage girl had accused him of rape."

"I've been doing some digging on Brock Tanner, too," Quinn said. "Made some calls to some buddies that are still active."

"And?"

Quinn shrugged. "Doesn't look like Captain Tanner

spent much time off the base," he said. "The one time he went out on patrol, he nearly got killed in a friendly fire incident. The report I read indicated that two of his own men may have tried to shoot him."

Reggie laughed, nearly doubling over. "Where the hell do they find these folks?" he said. "True honor and duty."

"How much time do you spend talking about what you did over in the Sandbox?"

"None," Reggie said, holding out a fist. "Please tell me y'all at least got some hooks on the line?"

Quinn bumped fists with the deputy. "A whole mess of 'em."

Jason met Ana Gabriel after third period under the bleachers of the football stadium. She looked scared and worried they'd get caught as she stepped under the support beams, the aluminum seats throwing slatted shadows across the ground. The girl had on a white shirt with lace at the neck and the sleeves, her black hair in twin braids, and a purple backpack over her shoulder.

"What's the matter?" Jason said.

"I'm leaving tomorrow," she said. "I don't know when I'll see you again."

Jason felt a rock form in his throat. He looked at Ana Gabriel and nodded, the neatly folded note she'd slipped into his locker still in hand.

"There is an older boy named Angel."

Jason looked away from her face. He nodded. "I understand."

She reached for his right hand, placing it in both of hers. She looked into his eyes. "No, you don't," she said. "You need to listen. And whatever you do, you must promise to tell no one. Not even your mother."

The girl's hands felt steady and warm. The underside of the bleachers looked like a garbage dump with paper cups, empty popcorn sacks, beer cans, weeds, and trash of all kind. A place too ugly for a girl like Ana Gabriel. The only people who seemed to use this place were the boys from the middle school to play war games or the older kids who liked to hide and smoke weed before school.

"Angel is driving some of us to Louisiana to try to see our parents," she said. "We are leaving after school. Sancho can't go. He's too young. I need you to look out for my little brother. Would you do that for me?"

"He'll be safe at The River," Jason said. "Lots of good folks will be watching him."

"But I need you to watch Sancho," she said. "He's such a funny little boy. His mouth gets him in trouble with the other kids. He might cause trouble. Or worse yet, he may try to run away and follow me. You have to keep him safe. I will come back for him when I can."

She hadn't let go of Jason's hand. He didn't want her to let go. Her eyes were so large and black, looking at him as if he were an adult and pleading for his help. Jason would never tell Ana Gabriel's secrets. And he'd share all of his. Anything she wanted to know. Anything she wanted to do. His momma always said to help the less fortunate, people in need. If this wasn't that kind of situation, he didn't know what was.

"I'll come with you," Jason said.

"No," Ana Gabriel said. "There's no room. And I need you here. To look out for Sancho."

"I've made up my mind, Ana Gabriel," Jason said, pulling his hand free. "And there's nothing you can do about it. I'll just say I'm going to walk over to my grand-momma's house. No one will even notice I'm gone."

"The drive will take us seven hours," Ana Gabriel said. "We plan to sleep in the truck overnight and ask to see our parents in the morning. I can't promise when we'll be back. I can't risk people looking for you, think-ing that we've done a bad thing. We're already not wanted in this town."

"That ain't true."

"You hear things," Ana Gabriel said. "Even more than me."

The air seemed even hotter in the shade, under all that silver metal. Jason looked away behind the bleachers and into the teachers' parking lot to make sure no one had seen them. He turned back, tasting the grit from the wind on his tongue, and slid his hands down into his Wranglers and toed at the spinning trash with his work boot.

"When do we leave?" Jason asked.

"That is a very bad idea," Ana Gabriel said.

Jason shrugged.

Quinn felt like he knew every inch of the county, from high up north and into the Big Woods to down in the soggy, flat bottomland of the Sugar Ditch. He drove with little purpose and no direction in Boom's secondhand Ford, heading out past the old Confederate cemetery where the dead from the Battle of Jericho were buried, headstones tall and skinny and lined up like busted teeth. Most old folks still called it the Second Battle of Jericho, having to give credit to the fight from the Old Testament. The whole county, no matter how many people turned their backs to him, still seemed like a wild, mythic place. He recalled his grandfather, his daddy Jason's daddy, telling him stories of buried treasure from a train robbery still hidden in the hills around Carthage. But when he and Boom went out there digging as little kids, they found only remnants of the Confederate holdouts who camped there for months after Appomattox: bullets, buckles, and buttons buried deep in the hard-packed earth.

If you looked even closer along the creek beds or down into the upturned soil of the field, there were shells and sharks' teeth from when all of Mississippi had been covered by an ancient sea. Forests had been logged out, new ones had started to grow, old homes had been razed and plowed under, entire stretches of farmland covered in spindly pine trees that were planted and cut down like cornstalks. Somehow Tibbehah didn't give up. It was so wild and fertile, you couldn't kill it. Tibbehah was too damn strong.

Quinn kept moving, driving back into JERICHO, POPULATION 1,280, the city limits sign pocked with bullet holes no matter how many times they replaced it. The Square still and quiet in the heat of the day, Quinn circling and passing the old movie theater where he'd once seen *Fievel Goes West* with Caddy and years later a militia leader had crucified a gold-toothed preacher named Brother Davis. He headed on past the old Jericho Dry Goods store, now a logging museum, and by the *Tibbehah Monitor,* where old Betty Jo Mize still put out two editions a week, covering everything from the county supervisor meetings to the winners of the latest recipe contests. Beauty queens and football stars, births, weddings, and all those who had gone on to "enter the gates of heaven."

He drove south again from the Square, toward the bottomland, passing the VFW Hall with the old Patton tank parked outside, the Tibbehah County Farm Supply, Annie's Soul Kitchen, and then knocked the truck in a higher gear and shot up County Road 121 past the Traveler's Rest Motel, still advertising heat and cool AC, Wi-Fi, and bass fishing at their private pond. Quinn had stayed there for a few nights when he'd first come back after his Uncle Hamp killed himself. And just last year, two journalists from New York City had made it their home as they looked into the cold case death of Brandon Taylor. Only fifteen but murdered for peeping into windows of J. K. Vardaman's hunt lodge and taking pictures of gray-headed men with their trousers around their ankles.

Quinn could turn and head home, but something kept on drawing him south toward Perfect Circle Road and the trailer of Miss Dana Ray. The night he'd been shot, Quinn had responded to a domestic at the woman's home. She'd told dispatch that her sometimes boyfriend Bradley Wayne threatened her and was coming for his damn shit. Only Quinn didn't find Bradley Wayne, but a gathering of part-time militia men in tactical gear and military-grade weapons lying in wait. They'd surrounded Quinn and beaten the hell out of him, the night ending with four slugs shattering two ribs, a shoulder blade, and puncturing his lung. If it hadn't been for Boom scattering those boys and scaring off the shooter, Quinn would have bled out in a shallow creek.

Quinn had to see it. He had to go back.

The state folks had charged three of the men with attempted murder. They'd lawyered up with a high-powered firm in Jackson and were out on bond. But the shooter, the one who'd actually shot Quinn in the back, was still somewhere out there. About all he could recall was a face that seemed like a photo from a book on the Old West, a weathered and worn Native American, god-damn Geronimo, coming from the afterlife to call Quinn home. The Watchmen had tried to teach him a damn lesson and had left him for dead. The Indian didn't fit that crew, falling more in line with a description of the man who'd killed Wes Taggart and E. J. Royce for the Syndicate. Taggart was about to flip on Fannie Hathcock after his arrest, and Royce, a racist old deputy, had tried to shake down Governor Vardaman. Before all that, Quinn had never figured the Syndicate and the Watchmen played on the same team.

Quinn stopped in front of the trailer. It was a single-wide up on blocks, with the frayed curtains drawn and no vehicle in sight.

He knew Dana Ray was long gone. She'd disappeared after that night. No one had been able to find her. But Quinn damn well knew who'd told her to make that call.

Didn't take too much to draw a direct line between her and her employer, Miss Fannie Hathcock. Quinn was still not sure why Fannie would've wanted him dead, as they'd pretty much settled on a direct relationship over the years.

Quinn walked toward the gaping gash of the creek, the cottonwoods barely clinging to the eroded earth, the creek bed completely dry. Nothing but sand and tiny smooth rocks. The night they'd come for him, the water had flowed, cold and gray and ankle-deep. He'd hidden right around the bend under a large root ball and taken out two of the Watchmen. There were still ruts at the hard turn of the creek where Boom had sacrificed himself and his old GMC to save Quinn's ass.

He headed toward the edge, looking for something. Trying to make sense of what happened. Maybe some brass casings, some kind of relic of that night. Nothing. There was no wind, only the goddamn heat on his back, neck, and ears. Everything that had been collected had already been processed, including the .22 slugs taken out of his back. The Watchmen admitted they'd been there but agreed there had been another shooter that had killed one of their own men and then tried to kill Quinn. Quinn wasn't really sure what to believe.

He walked back toward Dana Ray's trailer. The cicadas whirred into the tree line up behind the clearing. He tried the door, but it was locked. Quinn stepped back and kicked it in, moving into the dark, dank space. The air hot and moist, the rooms filled with overturned furniture, bare mattresses, and empty chests with open drawers. Quinn went from room to room, checking and rechecking, but found only clothes, empty beer cans, and

ashtrays full of cigarette butts. A pair of thong underwear reading IT AIN'T GONNA LICK ITSELF hung from a
ceiling fan.

He left and closed the door behind him.

Quinn wandered down to the road and found Dana
Ray's old blue mailbox overflowing with bills and junk.
He tossed everything onto the passenger seat of the
truck, got behind the wheel, and sifted through the mail.
Plenty of unpaid electric and water bills, but what interested him most was a whole mess of statements from a
Discover card. He worked through several statements
until he found one that ended last month. Dana Ray was
still using the card, the last batch of charges from several
places around Corinth.

Son of a bitch. Nobody was looking for the best wit-
ness they knew about. No one gave a damn if they found
her or knew who the hell had shot Quinn that night. He
stuffed the bills into the console and wadded up the
junk, tossing it into an empty oil barrel by the roadside
before heading back to the farm.

On the highway, speeding north, he picked up his cell
and dialed the number of Lillie Virgil, U.S. Marshal.

"Lil," he said. "Got something for you."

8

Donnie had spent most of the day at The River helping Caddy Colson sort and bag supplies for all those homeless Mexicans. *Damn.* He'd never known a woman or man more determined to get a job done. Caddy was like some kind of cross between Loretta Lynn and Mother Teresa. Ready to take the hand of some flaky leper or go straight to Fist City. Quinn's little sister always had a smart little mouth and plenty of attitude, the kind of girl whose smile would light up your soul while she kicked you right in the damn nuts. But this new woman made you step back and take notice. Not just on account of her looks, although it was hard not to admire those sunburned shoulders and cute upturned nose, but more with her sense of purpose.

Caddy didn't just study on these things. She damn well lived it. *Jesus on the mainline down in Tibbehah.*

As he drove back to the Magnolia Drive-In, Luther's

CCR in the tape deck, he thought back on their conversation before he'd headed home. "How about I buy you the deluxe carne asada burrito over at the El Dorado tonight?" Donnie had said. "Bring along Jason. We can down a few margaritas and talk about days gone by."

Caddy had informed him that she didn't drink anymore but would consider the offer.

He'd smiled back and said, "Caddy, don't believe everything you hear about me. I'm just a simple man making my way in complex times."

She'd laughed and smiled, sort of noncommittal, but there was something there. *Damn*, Donnie thought, as he thumped at the wheel of the GTO to "Up Around the Bend." *Purpose. Truth. Jesus. Helping folks.* Hell yeah. If Caddy Colson was there, Donnie Varner was in for all that shit.

At the turn to the Magnolia Drive-In, he slowed to unlock the swinging gate by what had been the ticket office. He stepped out, fished a joint from his dusty T-shirt pocket, and started to light up. Midway from flicking his Bic, he noticed the lock dangling loose and free on the gate. His first thought was maybe the son of a bitch who'd rented him the land was nosing around his trailer or maybe ole Luther was waiting around for a brand-new Bible lesson. But then he started recalling that high-dollar attitude of Miss Fannie Hathcock as he got back behind the wheel, the pipes of his solid gold GTO growling like a jaguar across the sunbaked asphalt. *Son of a damn bitch.*

Down into the expanse of the Drive-In lot, he spotted an old Crown Vic, green as a Martian's ass with tall,

fancy silver rims and windows tinted as black as midnight, sporting a big whip antenna and Tennessee plates.
Donnie reached into his glove box, snatched the .38, and
spun loose the cylinder to make sure it was loaded. He
got out and moved low under the trailer windows, hearing cicadas up in the trees and laughter and clapping on
the TV. He saw the back of a man reclining in a La-Z-Boy
watching the fucking *Price Is Right* on Donnie's brand-
new 4K Vizio, Drew Carey making some small talk with
a busty blonde in a sequined dress about an all-expense-
paid trip to Cozumel.

Didn't take Donnie but two seconds to rush inside
and point his pistol right at the son of a bitch in his daddy's old chair.

Some big black dude, looking about Donnie's age,
although it was hard to tell age with black folks, looked
up at him. He had on a white sleeveless Nike T-shirt,
long white workout pants, and white athletic socks and
shower shoes. The man wore sunglasses, head still turned
to Drew Carey and the woman with big tatas, as he pet-
ted a gray French bulldog on his lap. The little dog, still
a puppy, growled up at Donnie.

"Don't worry, dude," the man said. "That's just Lola.
You scared her, bustin' in the door like that."

"Oh, I'm so fucking sorry," Donnie said. "You want
me to leave my own domicile and let y'all continue
watching *The Price Is Right*? Let me tell you something,
that show hasn't been worth a shit since Bob Barker retired."

"Ain't it the truth," the man said, smiling up at Donnie. He had copper-colored skin and a precision trimmed

afro and clipped mustache. "Bob Barker was one smooth motherfucker. He was still in his damn eighties with that white hair and cool California attitude, hopping in the sack with his models, showing them that long microphone he carried."

Donnie stepped back and studied the man's profile, pistol lowering to his side. The man's neck was thick, his biceps huge and swollen like the weightlifters back at FCI Beaumont. "Hey, man," Donnie said. "I know you. Right?"

"Maybe," the man said, grinning.

"You played ball?" Donnie said. "Big time. Right? A few years back?"

The man shrugged and put the little gray bulldog down on the green carpet. The dog wandered off between Donnie's legs and toward the kitchen. Donnie watched as the man stood up, looking fit and muscular in his spotless white workout gear. The man nodded, reaching up and fingering at the big diamond stud in his ear. "Akeem Triplett."

"Goddamn," he said. "I knew it. You was on the cover of *Sports Illustrated* back in the day. I recall some kind of special issue of you making that catch in the 'Bama game. My daddy used to sell a shit ton of 'em along with *Juggs* and *Barely Legal*."

Triplett shrugged.

"What the hell happened to you?"

"Oh, you know," he said. "Did a little bit of time in the pros. Up in Seattle and in Atlanta. Shattered my right ankle in a million pieces. You heard that story all before."

"Akeem Fucking Triplett in my goddamn trailer,"

Donnie said. "I don't mean to be rude, but you're not on drugs or something? Maybe hitting hard times after the pros, looking around to score a big-screen TV or some shit? 'Cause if you are, that's cool. You can take the TV. It'd be a fucking honor."

Triplett didn't look like he was paying attention, staring at the pocket on Donnie's T-shirt. Donnie looked down and spotted the end of the joint sticking out.

"Say man," Triplett said. "You gonna smoke that shit or what?"

Donnie reached down and passed him the joint, turning to see the little gray dog wander from the kitchen and squat to pee. Both of them saw it, Donnie knowing there wasn't time to stop all that piss soaking into his green carpet. He just shook his head as Triplett lit up the joint and took a big hit.

"I know," Donnie said, snapping his fingers. "My daddy sent you. You're doing some kind of motivational shit to talk to me about Jesus and getting up with people and all that. Don't worry about it, man. I got all that covered. I just got in with the best-looking preacher woman you ever seen in your life. She's got the damn road map to Jesus."

Triplett stared at him from behind the sunglasses, letting out the smoke slow and easy. He didn't speak for a moment, waiting for the dog to come back, and then scooped her up into his waiting arms.

"Mr. Sledge sent me."

"OK," Donnie said. "Does that mean something?"

"Are you fucking with me?" Triplett said. "Mr. Sledge runs Memphis."

"Used to be Craig Houston until some Cartel boys put his head in the back of Johnny Stagg's Cadillac."

"Long time since Craig Houston got taken out," Triplett said. "Mr. Sledge and his nephews the Bohannons cleaned house with those folks long time ago. Been a while since Mexican folks think they can run things the Memphis way."

"God bless the USA," Donnie said.

Triplett looked hard at Donnie, from his head down to his old pointy-toed boots. His T-shirt dusty and dirty, Wranglers faded and worn.

"Say, man," Triplett said. "Are you, or are you not, Donnie Varner?"

"Yes, sir," Donnie said. "I am the one and only. Tibbehah County's great folk hero."

"The big-time gun dealer?" Triplett asked.

"Used to be," Donnie said. "But not no more. I'm straighter than a Mormon's pecker."

"Hmm," Triplett said. "That's too damn bad. Guess me and Lola drove all the way from Memphis for nothin'. I heard you were looking to resupply your load."

"You in the gun business?"

Triplett fingered at that diamond stud again and shrugged, moving toward the door. Donnie, standing in the way of him and his dog, reached out and plucked the blunt from Akeem Triplett's hand and took a deep hit.

"OK," Donnie said. "OK. I'll bite. Tell me what's on your mind, Mr. Triplett. And maybe later you tell me about that damn 'Bama game. I can't stand those sorry bastards over in Tuscaloosa."

Triplett grinned. "Cool."

* * *

Quinn headed back to Tibbehah General hoping to catch Maggie on break. She'd been working the day shift since June, planning on taking off a long while when the baby came. There was talk about her starting back at the first of the year, with some help from Quinn's mother, but they still weren't sure how that would all work out. Most of it depended on if and when Quinn would be back in the saddle as sheriff, so much going on that he hadn't been able to share with his own wife.

He parked the old blue Ford in the visitors' lot and headed in through admissions toward the cafeteria. The county hospital bustling as always. Old folks in wheelchairs and walkers, a weathered woman named Janet Hobbs moving down the hallway in her flowered gown and paper shoes, dragging an IV drip behind her. Quinn stopped to hear about the agony of her hemorrhoid surgery until he got relieved by Raven Yancy, one of Maggie's best friends, who ran the ER. Raven said she'd let Maggie know Quinn was here when she finished up with a patient.

"Tell her not to rush," Quinn said. "I'll get some coffee."

"Take your life in your own hands with that bad coffee, Sheriff," Raven said. "Looks worse than what we drain out of those bedpans."

Quinn grabbed a cup anyway and found a quiet corner to wait for Maggie. He wasn't sure how much he could tell her now. Maggie was tough as hell, but her workload, the baby coming, and the stress of dealing with legal shit from her ex-husband was enough. Her ex had sent Maggie a batch of insane letters from prison when he'd heard she was pregnant, letting her know that now it was truly over for them. He even threatened to write a song about their breakup and put it on YouTube. Rick Wilcox, besides being a felon, also fancied himself as the next country music sensation. Quinn called him Garth Crooks.

Quinn felt an arm wrap around his neck and Maggie's soft lips on his cheek. Her skin felt warm to the touch and she smelled of fresh laundry.

"Howdy, stranger."

"Better be careful," Quinn said. "This is how folks start talking."

"I won't tell your wife if you won't."

"I think the whole town already knows."

"Let 'em talk," Maggie said. "Anyone who sees this belly knows we've been up to no good."

The thought of the time they'd spent together over the winter made him smile. It hadn't been easy. He hadn't been able to walk for more than a month. Maggie had gently gotten him moving again, changing his bandages, getting him his pills, trying to reward each little goal in her own way. She'd promised to lie with him naked at night if he walked from the bedroom to the kitchen and back. He accomplished the goal on the first try. Each goal more intense with the next, the rewards more wonderful and heated. Maggie Powers had brought him back full and intact and in the process they'd created a daughter.

"How's she doing?"

Maggie sat down and let out a long breath. She stared

downward and started to run her hands all around her stomach. Tilting her head, Maggie closed her eyes in thought and said, "Knocking on the door. I think she's gonna be early."

"How early?"

"A week or two," Maggie said. "Brandon was two weeks early. Of course, you never know until it's time."

"I once helped a teenage girl give birth out at a trailer in Hell Creek," Quinn said. "I have a healthy respect for the process."

"This is coming from a man who's been shot several times."

"I don't think you can compare the two."

"Ever shot a watermelon out of your pecker?"

"No, ma'am," Quinn said. "I don't believe I have."

"As a registered nurse, I'd have to say it would probably be a similar sensation."

"And no epidural."

"Nope."

"No painkillers?"

"Not a one."

Quinn nodded, thinking on how he needed two pills and a shot of whiskey just to get moving this morning. He'd washed the glass and placed it back where he'd found it. The pill bottle he'd taken out to his truck and hidden under the seat. He was damn ashamed about the whole thing. Quinn knew he'd get through it; the pain couldn't last forever. All that mattered was keeping on his feet and moving forward. No one kept you on your back. You pressed on. You fought back or it would kill you.

"Hey," Maggie said. "Where'd you go?"

"I'm right here." Quinn turned back to her and smiled.

"Can you still pick up Brandon at school?"

"You bet," Quinn said. "Gonna hitch up the bass boat. I promised to take him fishing."

Maggie smiled back at him. Maggie had the most wonderful, sly little grin as her hand rested on her jaw. Her pale green eyes lit up with love and intelligence, a little playful heat in her face. The freckles across her skin and her nose even more prominent with her cheeks scrubbed of makeup and reddish-brown hair twisted up high into a tight bun. Quinn knew that in a select little piece of real estate under her left arm was a simple scrawled tattoo that read BE HERE NOW.

Quinn reached out and held her hand. He looked around the small cafeteria and spotted a large woman emptying out stainless steel trays filled with steaming water. The steam lifted and dissipated in big clouds under the fluorescent lights.

"What you see right now, with me, isn't everything," he said. "I only need you to trust that I'm doing right."

"You and Boom."

"It's more than just me and Boom," Quinn said. "We've got help."

"I hope so," Maggie said. "That new sheriff and his people are some bad seeds."

Quinn nodded. "I was just down at Perfect Circle Road, looking for something that Dana Ray might've left. I found a whole mess of bills, unpaid credit cards. No one had even gone out there to check on her. No one was even looking."

"Can you find her?"

"Maybe," Quinn said. "Lillie's gonna help."

"Lillie will find that sorry little bitch."

"You bet."

"And then what?" Maggie said. "You, Boom, and Lillie. Just like the old days. You're gonna hook up that busted-ass pickup truck to the establishment and bring it all down like a rotten old building? I'm not so sure that's gonna work anymore."

"It's more surgical than that."

A light flashed in Maggie's eyes. Her black-painted fingernails cut down to the quick as she put her finger to her lips and smiled. "Holliday."

"Maybe."

"And others."

"This is it," Quinn said. "The reason I came home. But if it gets rough, you and Brandon and the baby might have to head back south for a while. Can you stay with your momma in Mobile?"

"Nope," Maggie said. "No way in hell."

"Come on, now."

"Nope."

Quinn didn't say anything. Maggie leaned back in her chair, hands on her stomach, watching Quinn. Their connection had been intense and personal from the first moment they'd come across each other, Maggie returning to Jericho trying to escape a bad marriage and find a semblance of normalcy in Tibbehah County. He reached out and cupped his right hand across her face, Maggie holding the look, her eyes so pale they seemed translucent.

"I'm tired of running, Quinn," she said. "I was too

young to pack up my life and follow Rick's sorry ass from base to base and across the country. This is my home, same as yours. We're sticking tight through all of this. There's no way in hell I'm leaving you. Not for one damn second."

"I wish you'd think on that."

"I know you do," Maggie said. "But you always finish what you start. I just feel sorry for that dumb bastard Brock Tanner. Does he have any idea on how all this is going to turn out?"

"Not yet," Quinn said. "But he's fixing to find out."

"You really live out here?" Akeem Triplett asked.

"Yes, sir," Donnie said. "High living and high style down in Jericho, Mississippi. This used to be the primo spot to watch John Wayne kill the bad folks while getting your pecker tugged. Long before they opened up that titty bar behind the Rebel."

"I used to go to the movies at the drive-in on Summer Avenue when I was a kid," Triplett said, kicking back outside on an old metal lawn chair, that bug-eyed Lola up in his lap. "I saw *I'm Gonna Git You Sucka* there twice with my momma and auntie. Both of them laughing like hell when that dude puts on those glass pimp shoes filled with goldfish."

"This place shut down when I was in high school," Donnie said. "Only folks who came out here were old folks reliving old times and burnouts flying high on acid and weed."

"Ain't that a damn shame," Triplett said, dragging on that joint. "You hiding from folks out here?"

"Naw, man," Donnie said. "Just a cheap piece of real estate to rent while I get my affairs in order."

"If you're hiding from something, Donnie Varner, you sure as shit are an easy man to find."

"Who told you where to find me?"

"Mr. Sledge."

"And who told this Mr. Sledge?"

"Don't know," Triplett said. "Don't care. Your name just came up is all. In regard to unloading a big ole mess of guns. I'm a businessman. Me and Lola was just checking on your ass to see if you'd like to do a little business."

Donnie nodded, burning down the last of his last joint. He handed it back to Triplett, the .38 now slid back on his Western belt and under his T-shirt spattered with mud and dust from working at The River. Thinking on it, he knew it had to be Fannie Hathcock who made the connection to this fella Marquis Sledge up in Memphis. She'd want to do a little business but keep herself clear of the whole situation besides getting a little cut.

"OK," Donnie said. "Ain't no harm in me seeing what y'all got."

Triplett burned down the joint and flicked the last bit of it down into Donnie's barbecue grill. He had his big hands stretched onto his thighs, nodding to himself as if just coming to some kind of decision. "See, it ain't that simple," Triplett said. "You got to go all in for this shit. I mean total and complete participation in a grand fucking adventure."

"A grand fucking what?" Donnie said. "So let me get this shit straight. Y'all don't have any guns yet?"

"No," Triplett said. "But we will. Real soon."

"How many are we talking here?"

"Oh," Triplett said. "It's a real mixed bag. Some AR-15-style weaponry. Automatic pistols. You know, forty-fives, nine-millimeters. All that shit. I'd have to check the grocery list but we're looking at about four hundred fifty guns."

"Damn," Donnie said, giving a low whistle. "That is a shit ton of guns, Akeem. Where does an old ballplayer like you acquire such an impressive stash?"

"Are you in?"

"In for what?"

"That grand fucking adventure."

"Come on, man," Donnie said. "Quit pulling my pecker and tell me what you're thinking. If I can't make the deal, I can help you make a few connections."

"Maybe you aren't the man I'd hoped to find," Triplett said, rubbing Lola's pricked little ears. "The Donnie Varner I heard about was some kind of Southern wild man who'd do anything anytime and wouldn't think twice about the volume of what I'm offering."

"I can't make an offer on something sight unseen," Donnie said. "The volume doesn't bother me. I'm more concerned about quality."

"But can you move that much?" Triplett said. "Because when that shit hits, we got to move it fast and hard. Hit that honey hole like a black man."

"Oh, come on now," Donnie said. "You're planning to steal a bunch of guns and then you want me to fence that shit down in Mississippi?"

"No," Triplett said, taking off his sunglasses for the first time and looking right at Donnie. "I'm asking you to put a little skin in the game. I need you to help us steal them guns and then move 'em down to Mississippi."

"Son of a damn bitch," Donnie said. "You're kidding me? Right?"

"What you think, country boy?"

"*OK, OK,*" Donnie said. "Slow down. Just exactly who is *us*?"

Quinn picked up Brandon from school and drove him to the launch at Choctaw Lake to hunt for some fat lazy bass. Down at the landing, the boy helped loosen the straps on the trailer and then floated out with a paddle as Quinn jumped off from the shore and onto the jon boat. He started the little Evinrude motor and soon the two sat facing each other as Quinn worked a drop shot hook onto his line. The lake was big and wide, spread out like a misshapen pancake, more than seventy thousand acres built as a WPA project in the thirties.

Quinn had grown up fishing the lake, as had his father and Uncle Hamp. It was a big part of life down in Tib-behah County. There were a half-dozen fish camps back onshore, along with two bait and tackle shops and a run-down old restaurant that hadn't been open in more than a decade.

Brandon was quiet and serious as he cast his line with deft and precision on the opposite side of the boat. He had a light, delicate touch that wasn't common with most kids his age. The trick was going to be finding some deep cool water on a hot afternoon, but with a little pa-tience and some time, Quinn figured they might have a little luck. Last week, he'd helped Brandon reel in a bass that weighed almost six pounds. As he worked, the boy looked almost afraid to breathe, worried he might spook the fish.

"They can't hear you all the way up here," Quinn said.

"I don't want to take any chances," Brandon said.

"Sound doesn't travel too good between air and water," Quinn said. "Talk as much as you want. Just don't jump around too much in the boat or drop anything. That ping will resonate down below."

Brandon nodded, serious. He had on Quinn's old Auburn University ball cap, a worn-out trucker that he'd bought not long after he'd arrived at Fort Benning.

"Everything all right at school?"

"Uh-huh."

"Having any more trouble with that Byrd boy?"

"No, sir," Brandon said. "Not after I punched him right in the nose."

"Not sure that's the best tactic."

"Isn't that what you told me to do?"

"Well, yeah," Quinn said. "But your momma and me discussed it. May not be the best approach for the future unless you want to be heading to the principal's office."

Brandon nodded again, his hair as light and blond as Caddy's. At first glance, some folks figured him for a Colson. Maggie was more fair with her pale Irish skin, dark reddish hair, and freckles. A hot wind blew across the large lake, shuffling the trees and scattering ripples across the surface. The motor was turned off and the jon boat glided in a quarter circle. The sun high and hot over them as Quinn scanned the shore for pockets of darkness where the bass would be waiting.

"What if he tries and gets me in trouble?" Brandon said. "He's a real butthole."

"Someone like that will get himself in trouble," Quinn said. "You can just stand back and enjoy it. I went to school with that boy's uncle. None of those folks are right in the head."

Quinn pulled the brim of his ball cap down in his eyes, reeling in the line and casting it back to the same spot. He'd always found that if he repeated the same cast ten or fifteen times, that bass would finally take note.

"I just get so mad sometimes," Brandon said. "I don't know why. I just can't help it."

"I used to feel the same way," Quinn said.

Brandon was quiet for a long while, reeling in the line and recasting back in the same spot as Quinn had taught him. On the last cast, he had a little nibble but nothing solid and brought the rubber worm back to the surface, skimming the water.

"What used to make you mad?"

"Lots of things."

"Like what?"

"Oh, I don't know," Quinn said. "Usual stuff. Trying to make myself known, that I was better or different than my father."

"Your daddy was famous."

"He used to be," Quinn said. "He was good at some stuff but didn't much resolve with his family. He couldn't make a decision on whether to stay with us or head back to California."

"Why didn't y'all just go with him?"

Quinn thought about it, removed his cap, and wiped his brow. He readjusted the hat on his head, working the bill to shade his eyes. "I guess 'cause he never asked."

"My daddy is a bad man."

Quinn didn't answer. He didn't have much of a reply.

"He robbed banks," Brandon said. "He shot folks. Even killed a couple people."

All true. And a lot more of it, too. Quinn wanted to add that the son of a bitch had also blown up his favorite pickup truck. Something that he'd never be able to forgive.

"Do you get mad at him?" Quinn asked.

The boy thought on it, making a perfect cast big, wide, and deep into the expanse of Choctaw Lake, the boat slightly turning clockwise, drifting back toward shore. The air was dry and light, the sky an eggshell blue without a cloud in sight.

"It's not his fault," Brandon said. "It was in his blood. His daddy was bad, too. At least that's what he tells me. I guess I'll be the same way."

"That's not true."

"That's why my mom wanted to have another baby with you," Brandon said. "A baby with a good daddy so that she'll get a good kid."

Quinn reeled in his line again. He scanned the shore for a large section of cypress trees and a wedge of darkness and shadow. The bass loved to hide in the darkness among the stumps and fallen logs. Quinn knew it could be a hell of a place to snag your lures, but if you could drag a line through it, you just might annoy the hell out of some big fish.

Quinn moved over to start the little motor. He waited for a moment, trying to gather his thoughts, find some words that would make sense to Brandon.

"You are not or ever could be a bad kid, Brandon," Quinn said. "And I promise, no one would ever replace you. I love you and your mother so much, I just want our family to grow. You guys are home now and nothing is going to change. I'm not going away. Neither is your momma. Your daddy is exactly where he needs to be. And you and me are pals. Everything I got is yours. Everything I know I want to pass on to you."

Brandon stared at Quinn and nodded, the fishing pole held tight in his hand, the rubber frog lure bouncing over the edge of the boat.

"I know what it's like to be lost," Quinn said. "If it hadn't been for my uncle, I might have ended up like your daddy."

"Don't call him that," Brandon said. "Not anymore."

"You sure?"

"Yep," Brandon said. "I like this place. I don't want to leave. I like the farm and this lake. I like having supper with your momma."

"That won't end."

"Promise?"

Quinn winked and started the little motor, seeking out a better spot to find those big bass that would fight like hell and bend your pole, making a young boy smile and laugh and forget adult problems and troubles that ruined the fun.

9

Fannie Hathcock had been less than impressed with the couple dozen girls they'd routed up from Biloxi via Houston. She didn't know their ages, nor wanted to ask. Besides, she didn't speak Spanish and didn't have any intention to learn it. That's why she had Nat be the go-between once they got the girls off those trucks and showered and cleaned up. It was their damn problem that they wanted to live in America so bad that they'd sign on for a tour of duty on the flat of their backs. But they were eager and worked cheap and after she got a good bit of use out of them, Fannie would send them on up to Memphis or on to Chicago. No shortage of folks who like some nice young tail from south of the border or from over in Vietnam. Fannie could arrange work visas, some hard cash, and a decent place to live. All the peanut butter sandwiches and lube they needed.

She had to give herself credit for expanding into the

internet market. She made more damn money from dip-
shits sending tokens to her girls online than a month of
Sundays over at Vienna's Place. She'd actually contem-
plated shutting down the bar for a while and building
some cribs out on Choctaw Lake or somewhere out in
the county to keep up with the demand. That electronic
click and whir of tokens coming through online was
sweet music to Fannie's ears. All she had to supply was a
laptop and an internet connection. At that very moment,
she had all twenty-five rooms at the Golden Cherry
livestreaming out on the worldwide internet to every
hairy-backed, sweaty jerkwad with his pecker in his
hand. Cash. Cash. Cash. Livestreaming peep shows for
lonely men.

Want me to take off my bra? That'll be fifty bucks.

Take off my G-string? How about a hundred?

*Dance around nekkid while slow-eating a banana?
Now that, sir, is a special request for the discerning freak.
How about an even thousand damn bucks?*

Fannie had to explain all this to Sam Frye in her office
above Vienna's Place in hopes that Chief Robbie might
want to sign on for a franchise opportunity. He provided
the space and she provided the girls. No johns. No
drunken fights. No crotch rot. It was a fucking win-win-
win. Sam Frye looked like an iron statue in the shadow
on her office. Seated in a leather chair, legs crossed, and
dressed in a funeral-black suit and skinny black tie.

"No," Sam Frye said.

"What do you mean *no*?" Fannie said, tapping an un-
lit cigarillo against her sterling silver case. "Aren't you
even gonna think about it?"

"These girls I just saw are too young," Sam Frye said. "They don't speak English. The Chief would not approve."

"What kind of language skills do you need to stick a cucumber up your twat?"

Sam Frye shook his head. "These girls aren't happy," he said. "You keep them in that old motel like rabbits in a hutch. When do they eat? When do they use the bathroom?"

"That's the beauty of it all, Tonto," Fannie said, winking. "They do it all on camera and get paid for every filthy moment."

"No," he said. "I came here to discuss Takali."

"I know you boys think a carnival for fat fucks on the Coast is a brilliant moneymaker," she said. "But there's a better chance y'all are gonna fail. Too much competition. Too much overhead. I heard y'all were even thinking of bringing in that crazy bitch Paula Deen to fry up some fried chicken and fatback for those turds when they get through puking on a Tilt-A-Whirl or roller coaster. It all sounds like some kind of Country Bear Jamboree gone wild."

"And what you do is better?" Sam Frye said. "Keep women in cages. Making them eat and urinate on camera?"

"Hold on," Fannie said. "Hold on one goddamn moment. Let me tell you about the big goddamn picture you're missing. There are men out there with very specific and very focused needs. We can supply that for them. There's this one son of a bitch who lives up in New York City somewhere that pays one of my girls to rub her nekkid body all over with Jergens lotion. No other kind of lotion will do. She has to open up a fresh bottle each time and show him the label. Something about that shea butter formula really gets that old boy off. He pays nine hundred dollars for a twenty-minute session. That, my native friend, is absolute growth potential."

Sam Frye didn't react. He sat across from Fannie's desk with those cool, sleepy Indian eyes wanting to know why she wouldn't toss in a few million for big momma's redneck shopping and funnel cake extravaganza on the Gulf Coast. That kind of bullshit wasn't only a big risk, it wasn't exactly Fannie Hathcock's style. Fannie hadn't shopped at a goddamn outlet mall in twenty years.

Fannie fired up her cigarillo and fanned away the smoke. Looking across her great glass-top desk, she studied Sam Frye's hard, craggy face.

"Chief could've called me up about this Takali bullshit," Fannie said. "He's been peddling that goddamn time-share show for two years now. What's really on your mind?"

Sam Frye didn't flinch. He was a damn mountain of a man, hard and chiseled as if cut from granite. Under the black suit, he wore a nice white shirt with a wide silk collar, his black hair pulled back and tied with a leather strap. She'd find him somewhat handsome if he wasn't so goddamn old and didn't have a reputation of making folks disappear.

"Buster White," he said.

"What about Buster White?"

"I wanted time with him," Sam Frye said. "You whacked him with that hammer before I could."

"Oh, shit," Fannie said, grinning, pursing that cute

little red mouth of hers. "Damn, I'm sorry about that. I just had a hell of a lot of pent-up aggression for that fat tub of shit. When I got to hammering his skull, it just gave me so much pleasure I couldn't stop."

"He knew what happened to my son."

"Probably," Fannie said. "That's why I gave him an extra few whacks. Like I told you, I loved that boy more than I could ever love a real-life son. That boy did everything for me. He ran the girls, the liquor, the shit coming out the truck stop. I was grooming him to take over some little piece of the business. God only knows what Buster and his people did to him. Damn, I'm sorry. Mingo was a good kid with a big heart and lots of brains."

"Why him?" he said. "Why Mingo?"

Fannie sucked on the cigarillo and tapped off an ash. She shrugged and pushed back on her leather chair's rollers. "I'll give it to you straight," she said. "Your boy was skimming off Buster's take. Mingo put some serious miles on his truck between Jericho and Biloxi. Somewhere along the ride, he pocketed a little cash. A little at first, but then he got cocky."

Sam Frye nodded. "How did Buster White find out?"

"You never short-changed that tub of shit," Fannie said. "When Buster found out, I tried like hell to protect your boy. And I thought I had until one trip when he never rolled on back to the sweet sanctity of Vienna's Place. I'm sorry, Sam. I truly am."

Fannie could play poker with the damn best of them. Her face didn't flush or color. She didn't even damn blink.

"Do you know how it was done?"

Fannie shook her head. She ran her tongue over her teeth to clear off a stray bit of tobacco and gave an empathic, yet sad, smile.

"I want his body returned," Sam Frye said. "This is important to me."

"Make him one with the spirit world and fly high with the eagles?" Fannie said, nodding.

"Can you find out?" he asked. "Can you talk to the people who worked with Buster White?"

"For you, Sam Frye?" Fannie said. "Sure. Of course. Anything."

Nat came up from the staircase, holding two bottles of Veuve Clicquot, wanting to know which year Miss Fannie wanted her to chill for the guests coming down from Oxford. She was wearing a man's white tank top over her dark skin, her wild, tall afro bouncing as she walked on some six-inch heels. She was a roller-skating, funkytown lover's wet dream.

"Those shitbirds don't know Veuve Clicquot from mule piss," Fannie said. "Pour the good stuff for the girls and cut some Barefoot Brut with grain alcohol. Those fuckers will be throwing their wallets up onstage within an hour."

"Yes, ma'am."

As she turned to go, Sam Frye studied the black girl's face and curvy body as if he'd seen her before. Their eyes met and she smiled before excusing herself, bouncing along and whistling out the door and down the spiral staircase. Her big booty jostling and dancing in those short shorts.

"Sorry," Fannie said. "She's not on the menu, Tonto."

Sam Frye nodded but something in his face had shifted and changed. He stood up fast and headed straight for the door. Fannie propped her heels up on the edge of her desk and pointed the end of the cigarillo right at the bulge in that big Indian's pants.

"Tell Chief Robbie sorry about Takali," Fannie said. "He gets a Bed Bath and Beyond and maybe a Bubba Gump Shrimp Company and we'll talk. Redneck women eat that shit up with a goddamn spoon."

"You'll be hearing from the Chief."

"I'm grateful," Caddy said.

"There are good people in this world," Hector Herrera said. "We can't forget that. We must never forget that."

Caddy leaned against the tailgate of her old GMC truck, the sun just going down over the flat, cleared land near the uncompleted all-purpose building of The River. Herrera stood across from her, his gold crucifix swinging from around his neck. His head freshly shaved and his black mustache drooping down his lips like an old-time bandit. As they spoke, the sky turned a bright red and gold across the skinny pines and over the meandering dry creek bed.

"This will keep you going?"

Caddy nodded and patted the pocket of her Western shirt where she'd slipped in the folded check. Thousands of dollars had been donated to Herrera's foundation since the raid and he'd shared some of what he'd been given with Caddy, to keep the kids safe and fed.

"This lawsuit will embarrass some rich people in Jackson," Herrera said. "They believed they could keep us quiet. And when that didn't work, they thought they could make threats, intimidations of more roundups. Let them do it. Our voices will only grow louder. We will unite against this injustice."

Caddy turned her head to see twin boys playing soccer in the dirt, both parents arrested in the raids. They'd been born and raised in Tibbehah County and spoke with thick country accents. That young girl that Jason was so crazy about, Ana Gabriel, sat on a bench made of a stump and barn wood. She seemed far off and sad, staring off at the sunset over the dry creek.

"The rich don't get punished," Caddy said. "Not in Mississippi."

"Why haven't the companies been fined?" he said. "Why haven't any of those men who profit from illegal labor been charged? Instead they punish the voiceless. They didn't make this situation."

"This crap has been going on forever," Caddy said. "When black workers refused the low pay and nasty conditions, the plant started trucking in labor from Florida and then Texas. They not only knew these people were undocumented, they cultivated this whole system. The chicken business isn't much different from cotton picking in the old days. I'm sorry, Hector, but you'll never touch the owners of these companies. They've been around for decades and will cut you off at the knees if you give them trouble."

Hector smiled. "Do I look scared?" he said, a gold incisor shining. "I have been speaking to a reporter at the

Free Press in Jackson. She's searching through records to find the real owners. We thought the companies were headquartered somewhere up North, but she says it all circles back to Mississippi."

"Of course it does."

"But the truth means something," Herrera said. "Those who profited from using illegal labor and exploited poor people have to be exposed. The owners are very rich and very powerful and have the ear of your governor."

"Vardaman isn't my governor," Caddy said. "I wish I could say he's an aberration, but that would be a damn lie."

Herrera pulled out a blue bandanna from his back pocket and mopped his head and face. He looked very tired, eyes dark rimmed and bloodshot. His portly body sagged against Caddy's tailgate. "I didn't want to cause trouble," he said. "But I have heard you were friends with a man named Bentley Vandeven."

Caddy took a deep breath and swallowed. She looked across at Herrera. "What about him?"

"I don't know if he's connected," he said. "But his father is. His father sat on the board of these shell companies. We're hoping you might be able to speak with him. Perhaps relieve the pressure on these people?"

"I don't know."

"This man, Bentley?" Herrera said. "Vandeven. Vardaman. All these V families make my head spin. Is he a good man? Does he have a heart?"

Caddy didn't answer. She'd broken it off with that spoiled kid last year when she'd found out how deep his connections ran with the good ole boys in Jackson. Damn, how could she have ever let her guard down and thought a boy six years her junior hadn't wanted something from her? He'd been sent up to Tibbehah County to make the calls on the local yokels and probably play bagman for his father, a wretched old son of a bitch who normally wouldn't let a man like Vardaman cut his lawn. But it turned out he was a hell of a greedy realist when it got down to election time.

Caddy looked over at Herrera, who was checking his phone. His face seemed to deflate, drained of color.

"Is everything OK?"

"Yes," he said. "Yes. I am fine."

"Do not be overcome with evil," Caddy said. "But overcome evil with good."

"These men," he said. "These people. I feel they walk with the devil."

Caddy nodded. "Hand in hand."

Herrera pushed off the truck and started to walk back down the dirt road to his car. He opened the door and smiled back at Caddy. "I see your son and that girl Ana Gabriel," he said. "They are good friends. They enjoy each other's company."

"She's very beautiful," Caddy said. "He's very taken with her."

"Your boy is a good kid," Hector said, winking. "He has a big heart. Like his mother. He wants to fight injustice. Help people make a life here."

She thanked him and then watched his car make a big turn and head out toward the front gate, dust kicking up behind the tires in the last light.

* * *

Jason was alone inside the little bungalow on Stovall Street, a few blocks away from the Jericho Square. The house used to belong to Aunt Maggie and to her grandmother before the old woman died. It reminded him a lot of the house they'd lived in before that tornado when he was a little boy, leveling damn near half the town. Aunt Maggie said this old place was safe and strong, so solid it would probably just keep in one piece and roll down the street. That night, heat lightning cracking far to the north and his momma at The River working, he went ahead and packed his backpack with everything he thought he might need: laptop, clean T-shirt, toothbrush and toothpaste, and that new Buck knife Uncle Quinn gave him for Christmas. A real pretty knife that his uncle said a lot of Rangers carried with them.

He finished stuffing his backpack and slid it under his bed just in case his mother noticed it had doubled in weight. Jason sat on his bed and looked around his small room. WWE posters covered the walls. The Rock. John Cena, Sasha Banks, and his all-time favorite, the Undertaker. There was a small handmade bookshelf with too many children's books and a few that Uncle Quinn had brought him. *Huck Finn*, all five Leatherstocking Tales, *Northwest Passage*, and *Shane*. He thought about taking one of them with him, maybe reading it on the way to Louisiana. But his mind was too busy, too worried about what would be waiting when he got back home.

If he left with Ana Gabriel tomorrow, skipping Thursday practice, Jason knew he'd catch hell from his coach as well as his mother and Grandma Jean. But there was no way he was going to allow Ana Gabriel to get in that van with some older kids she didn't know. He thought about maybe talking to his momma about it but knew what she'd say, even though he was just shy of being a teenager. Sometimes it was easier to ask for forgiveness than permission.

Jason walked into the living room and then the kitchen, opening the screen door and walking out into the hot August night. Everything was still so dry that it felt like Mississippi was on another planet.

Once they got good and clear of Tibbehah County, Jason would message his momma that he was safe. He couldn't tell her where they were headed or she'd be there to meet him and embarrass him in front of Ana Gabriel and those teenagers. Jason wanted Ana Gabriel to know she could trust him and he was there for her. He didn't need his momma holding his hand. Besides, he'd heard stories about his own mother and Uncle Quinn running away when they were kids. Although that wasn't the story that most folks knew. Most folks believed that Uncle Quinn had just gotten lost in the Big Woods and survived by just being a tough country boy who knew how to take care of himself. Jason knew better. There was a worse, darker story that he'd never been able to completely piece together. Maybe his momma could find some forgiveness in her heart for him when he'd come back home.

He pulled out his phone from his back pocket and texted Ana Gabriel: *You reckon we'll be home before supper?*

Of course, she texted back. Then after a few minutes, *I love you, Jason*.

Jason pulled the Buck knife from his jeans. He would protect her. He would make sure Ana Gabriel was safe.

Nat Wilkins lied and told Miss Fannie that she thought she was coming down with something, her plumbing out of order. Nat said she needed to take off from Vienna's early, after the bachelor party headed back to Columbus but before those medical sales folks flew in from Birmingham. Fannie didn't even glance up from her desk, trusting and appreciating Nat, and knowing that she'd never leave her on a busy night unless she'd come down with something real bad. Nat headed back to the locker room to change out of her uniform, a damn ridiculous tank top and hot pants, and back into jeans and a simple black blouse. Out of those four-inch slingbacks and into a pair of Nikes. She swung her purse over her shoulder and waved to DJ Gemini on her way out. He gave her a salute and soon she was back in her Pathfinder, headed out of Jericho and sliding up onto the Natchez Trace.

She'd been working at Vienna's since the start of the year, doing everything that woman asked of her except working the pole. She tended bar, stocked the frozen chicken wings, and once or twice even cleaned the toilets. She made runs for Fannie's dry cleaning once a week and took her Lexus in for a tune-up down in Jackson. Each time she left that big metal cave that was Vienna's she made damn sure she wasn't being followed. You never got comfortable. You always watched your back, played the part, or else you'd end up dead. One thing she knew: nobody played with Fannie Hathcock.

She never carried her real cell, real ID, or anything that might link her back to the DEA, where she'd been a special agent for seven years now. Nat Wilkins knew what she'd signed up for long ago, lucky to be working in her own backyard, close to Memphis, and not out in Phoenix, where she'd first started her career. Nat had been married once but had no kids. No way a normal person could keep up this kind of life.

Two years ago, she'd been working an operation in north Mississippi with the Tibbehah County sheriff and a friend of his named Boom Kimbrough. They'd brought down a couple of bad dudes named Wes Taggart and J. B. Hood, who'd run an illegal trucking operation out of Tupelo. That mess had only brought her further into the circle, getting closer and closer to Fannie Hathcock, the queen hellcat of north Mississippi. Both Taggart and Hood were dead and there wasn't anyone close to Hathcock who could possibly ID Nat until tonight. But when she'd walked into Miss Fannie's office and seen Sam Frye, personal leg breaker to Chief Robbie, she nearly had a goddamn heart attack on the spot.

She'd arrested Frye's big ass four years ago for running cocaine down to the Rez from a Mexican club in South Memphis. She wasn't sure he'd made her. But it was enough to give her a damn start.

Nat headed fifteen, twenty miles up on the Trace, with few lights and no buildings, that old original road that stretched from New Orleans to Nashville. A place populated by Indian mounds and the sites of old trading posts.

She checked her rearview every few minutes, once pulling into a secluded little cove to see if anyone saw her. Damn if Jon Holliday didn't love this little stretch of road for meets, but she'd told him no less than fifteen times, they better start changing up their routine. DEA, FBI, some folks from the ATF, and the Marshals Service had been covering Tibbehah County like fire ants since Quinn Colson had been shot. They called it Operation Deliverance, the joint task force headed by Holliday that he'd said in meetings would be bringing ole Dixie down real soon. Not soon enough for Nat. She'd had enough of Fannie Hathcock and the sweaty, stinky, grinding naked bodies at Vienna's. Enough of the 18-wheeler chop shops, the warehouses filled with stolen electronics and appliances, the variety of drugs rolling in from Mexico via Houston and worse, the endless line of teenage girls being trucked in from God knows where who didn't speak English and went to work in Fannie's internet cribs.

These folks were bold and arrogant. Between Nat and several other well-placed agents, they'd be locking down this shit tight as hell.

She slowed and turned off at a historical marker, a grand Indian mound where the Choctaws had buried their dead and valued treasure. There was a black government-issue sedan and an old-school blue pickup truck sitting high on big tires, a VOTE FOR COLSON sticker on the rear bumper.

Nat walked out to the viewing area under a portico to see Jon Holliday dressed in a black suit and Quinn Colson with Boom Kimbrough. She smiled at the boys club but she smiled a little longer at Boom Kimbrough.

They'd had a little thing going on for a few months after the shit went down at Sutpen's Trucking. Too bad it didn't work out. No way she could keep a steady in the life she'd chose.

"Is this a cigar social?" she asked.

Quinn Colson held out the cigar burning in his fingers.

"Not now," she said. "Not ever, Sheriff."

Quinn grinned and plugged the cigar into his lips. Boom sat on the edge of a cinder-block wall. He had a cigarette in his fingers, light glowing against his handsome bearded face as he inhaled. Boom Kimbrough was big and country, quiet and good-looking, straight cool and as dependable as a badass truck. Hmm. She sometimes really missed that man.

"Figured we should all meet," Holliday said. "Got some trouble?"

"Maybe," Nat said. "Fannie was meeting tonight with a man I busted a few years ago. A big-ass Indian named Sam Frye. One mean motherfucker that does most of Chief Robbie's dirty work."

Holliday and Colson looked at each other. No one said anything for a while.

"That's the man you mentioned," Quinn said. "The one I couldn't ID."

"Yep," Holliday said. "Probably the same one who killed Wes Taggart last year."

"First time we've seen him with Hathcock?" Quinn asked.

Holliday nodded. He turned to Nat Wilkins and asked her what she wanted to do.

"Thing is, I'm not so sure he remembered me," Nat

said. "I was just one of the agents and we never went to court. He got out on bond and disappeared. We had the Marshals looking for him somewhere out in Oklahoma."

"He's still wanted?" Quinn said.

"Yep."

"I'd get your ass out of there," Boom said, tapping the ash of his cigarette on the sole of his work boot. "If this is the same son of a bitch who shot Taggart and Quinn, he won't think twice about taking you out."

"Then again," Nat said, "I take off and disappear and Fannie gets nervous. She starts shutting things down, not keeping the same routine. Damn, boys. We're so goddamn close. Let's not fuck this party up."

Another car rolled in from the Trace, high beams shining on the crew of them and then shutting off cold. The door opened and then slammed, boots clicking around the walkway into the viewing area to the Indian mounds. No one said a word until a woman walked into the grouping and set her hand along her hip.

"Goddamn," Lillie Virgil said. "Why don't you just build a fucking bonfire and let everyone know we're here?"

Quinn again lifted the cigar, and this time U.S. Marshal Lillie Virgil accepted it and took a long pull.

"Got something for you, Lil," Quinn Colson said.

"More than just that little skank that set your ass up?" Lillie said. "Because I got Dana Ray locked up tight in Memphis earlier today."

"Someone y'all have been looking for," Holliday said. "Man named Sam Frye."

"And who the fuck is he?"

"Fits the description of the man who shot me in the back," Quinn said.

"Big Indian."

"Big Indian who works directly for Chief Robbie and who Nat saw with Fannie Hathcock tonight at Vienna's Place."

Lillie nodded. She was a tall woman, in her cowboy boots standing nearly the same height as Quinn Colson. She had on jeans and a black blouse with sleeves rolled to the elbows. A U.S. Marshal's badge dangled from her neck and she carried a chrome-plated Sig Sauer on her hip. Lillie Virgil was known in law enforcement circles as one of the best shots in the South, a star shooter on the Ole Miss rifle team. She'd more than once embarrassed some military vets at the shooting range with her accuracy and smart-ass attitude. Nat Wilkins had worked with her before and respected her.

"OK," Lillie Virgil said, taking another puff of Quinn's cigar and handing it back to him. "Mean motherfuckers just happen to be my specialty."

10

Donnie headed to Memphis the next morning, catching 78 out of Tupelo on up to Airways Boulevard and a crummy little strip mall diner called the Take Off Grill. A jet flew low overhead, the engines making a big racket, as he got out of the GTO and walked across the empty parking lot. Half of the strip mall was burned out, nothing left but the brick and busted windows, leaving the Take Off Grill as the lone tenant boasting the BEST BURGERS IN SOUTH MEMPHIS, SMOKED TURKEY LEGS, FRIED CATFISH, and the HOME OF THE HOT WING CHALLENGE. The building had wide plate-glass windows looking out onto Airways, where Donnie saw Akeem Triplett sitting in a booth along with a fat white man in a flat-billed Grizzlies cap. When he walked in and sat down, Triplett introduced the white boy as Rerun.

"Rerun?" Donnie asked. "That's funny as hell. Re-

member him doing that dance on *What's Happening!!?*
Cracked me up every damn time."

The fat white boy just stared across the booth at Donnie and then picked up a chicken wing drizzled in blood-
red sauce and started chewing meat off the bone. Triplett
looked to have on the same white satin Nike workout
clothes and nice white shoes as he did when he visited
Donnie in Jericho. Donnie wondered if he'd stay away
from those wings. He knew Triplett probably couldn't
handle stains on that satin.

"I thought there was three of you," Donnie said.

"Tyrell's running late," Akeem said. "Had some shit
to do for Mr. Sledge. Big-ass funeral this morning down
in Olive Branch. I got to get back for when they put that
motherfucker in the ground. We got to feed something
like three hundred people."

Donnie listened and reached across for a drumstick.
He'd gotten up early and hadn't had breakfast yet. The
wing wasn't so spicy, more sweet, like that red sauce on
moo shu pork. Donnie licked his fingers.

"Not bad."

"You need to check out my big place off Hacks Cross
Road," Triplett said. "Right by the Krispy Kreme. Buffet-
style dining and all that shit. Chinese soul food. Come on
by anytime. I'll set your ass up."

"Chinese soul food?" Donnie said. "What the hell's
that?"

Triplett tilted his head and placed a toothpick in the
corner of his mouth, eyes damn near serious. "Wait until
you try some barbecue egg rolls, General Tso's fried

chicken, and dirty-ass rice. You'll see what I'm talking about."

"Your wings ain't too bad," Donnie said, gnawing on that damn bone. "But they ain't got no heat. What's up with that? You black folks like your wings sweet."

"Oh, hell naw," Rerun said. "I know he didn't just say that."

Rerun, trying to act all cool and hip like Triplett, looked more like a country fella who'd overcharge him to snake his toilet. Triplett looked at him, grinning, switching the toothpick to the opposite side of his mouth.

"You think so?" Triplett said. "You want to put some money down on that shit?"

Donnie shrugged. Triplett looked over his shoulder at an older black woman working the counter, gray haired and hump-backed, wearing a blue apron. He nodded over to her and raised a finger. Another jet flew overhead, rattling the plate-glass windows.

"You game for a little hot wing challenge?" Triplett said.

"Why the hell not?" Donnie said. "I once ate a whole fried habanero pepper at the Neshoba County Fair. Not bad going down but sure was hell coming out. Real fire in the hole. What do I get if I win this challenge?"

"A Take Off Grill T-shirt and a crisp hundred-dollar bill," Triplett said. "But if you lose, you got to work this job for free."

"This job?" Donnie said. "Shit. You still ain't told me what the hell you want me to do."

"What is it?" Rerun said. "You scared, Tibbehah County?"

"Just don't seem worth the effort, Rerun," Donnie said, looking over at the fat man, not liking his beady little black eyes and sad little soul patch on his fat chin. "But fuck it. Yeah, I'll try some of them wings with a cold Mountain Dew on the side."

"Nope," Akeem said. "Nothing to drink. And you got five minutes to eat five wings."

Donnie nodded and Rerun wiggled out of the booth and waddled on up to the counter, his big chunky blue jeans falling down below his ass crack. A few minutes later, he wandered back with five wings aligned nice and neat on a Styrofoam plate. A bright red sauce coated the wings and three pieces of celery had been set along the side. The sauce glowed like nuclear waste.

"Five in five minutes?" Donnie asked.

"Yes, sir," Triplett said.

"And then we get down to business?"

"Depends on how you do with them wings," Triplett said. "We looking for a wild man, goddamn country-ass crazy, to join our little all-star team."

Triplett and Rerun smiled, watching as Donnie picked up a warm chicken wing, smelled it, put his tongue to it, and then took a small bite. Wasn't bad at first, but then Donnie felt the heat up into his head and through his nose. Had he been a damn cartoon character, smoke would've come out his ears. *Goddamn it all to hell.* Akeem Triplett had cornholed him down deep.

"Come on, now," Triplett said. "What's a little ghost pepper sauce to you? Show us what you got."

Donnie's eyes filled with water and he took another bite.

* * *

Fannie was early for work, down from Memphis and parked crossways in the lot at Vienna's Place, sitting in her brand-new white Lexus texting with two dancers from New Orleans she wanted to bring up for a special show. They did an act with whips and chains and a bucket of canola oil that was within an inch or two of breaking five different laws in all fifty states. But she put down her phone when she spotted the car pull in behind her, some kind of sporty little silver coupe, the kind of thing that a frat boy from Jackson like Bentley Vandeven would choose to drive. She unlocked her doors and waited for the lumbering boy to crawl inside and try to stretch out his long legs, all khaki and polo, sporty tan brown loafers and a shaggy-ass haircut.

"Buttons on the side, baby," Fannie said. "Go on and get comfortable. Me and you got some talking to do."

"Yes, ma'am," Bentley said, falling in line with his infuriating Southern manners and bullshit. She recalled a time when he'd come up from Jackson and put his feet up on her furniture, trying to get her to play by those old rules they had for Johnny Stagg. She let those nameless, faceless fuckwads from the cigar bars and steakhouses know she was her own woman, thank you very much. Back then, she had Buster White's fat ass to back her up.

"Don't call me ma'am," she said. "Ever. Ever. Do I look like your goddamn momma?"

"No, ma'am," he said. "Not at all."

"I hope your momma is a hell of a lot older than Miss

Fannie," she said. "Unless she was some kind of damn Mississippi child bride."

"No, ma'am," Bentley said. "She's regular age. She had me a few years out of Ole Miss. I have a little sister and a brother, too. He's older. Lives over in Atlanta."

"Bentley?"

"Yes, ma'am?"

"Do I look like I give two fucks?"

"No, ma'am."

"And again, please stop with the *Blue and the Gray* Southern fried manners shit," she said. "You learn that up at Ole Miss? Damn it. What the hell?"

Bentley didn't answer and swallowed. He looked down and checked his phone and then back at his sporty little car. "Should we really be sitting here out in the open? What if someone found out how it all worked?"

"You ever been blindsided in Tibbehah?" she asked.

Bentley started to say *Yes, ma'am* but then just shook his head.

"That's right, baby," Fannie said, reaching down and squeezing Bentley's khaki-covered knee. "That's because you're in my county. Nothing's gonna go wrong right here. Safe as in your momma's lap. You pull into the truck wash when I say, open your goddamn trunk, and Midnight Man will fill you up. Your daddy and all his good ole boys can uncork that fine old scotch and jerk each other off, the money train is coming southbound and down."

Bentley nodded, looking a lot skinnier and more ragged than when she saw him last. His face was sallow and sweaty, more pockmarked with acne. Blondish stubble lined his jaw where he'd missed a few spots shaving. That crazy-ass woman Caddy Colson sure did do a number on this kid. He looked as if his head was all kinds of fucked up.

"You look like you need some company," Fannie said. "Want me to send you down the highway with a smile? Got this new girl from Guadalajara who can tongue tie a love knot with baling wire."

"No thank you," Bentley said.

"You do realize that Colson girl wasn't worth your time," she said. "She's crazy with Jesus. Have a girl working for me now who says that woman would sometimes talk to her dead boyfriend, that convict preacher Jamey Dixon, just as if he was standing right there with her."

"My personal life is none of your concern," Bentley said. "And I'd rather you not talk about Caddy."

Silence hung around for a good long while, so long that Fannie wanted to see just how long it might go on. She looked down at her cell again, those two girls from NOLA naming their price, skills, and availability. Somehow they needed extra for some midget woman they'd met while on tour. Fannie cut them down by a thousand and waited for them to reply. She lifted her eyes up at Bentley, his hands tucked in his lap and his head down.

"Go ahead," Fannie said. "What's on your mind, Bentley Vandeven?"

"My daddy needs a favor."

Fannie looked in her rearview and saw a Tibbehah County patrol car glide past, the deputy behind the wheel giving her a salute. Bentley didn't speak until the patrol car hit the gas and sped out of the lot.

"Damn, that was close," he said.

"Nope," she said. "Not even a little."

Bentley took a deep breath. "There's some man named Hector Herrera up here. Do you know him?"

"Nope," she said. "Should I?"

"Herrera is causing us a whole mess of trouble," he said. "Daddy's damn near to having his fourth heart attack."

"OK, baby," she said. "Tell Miss Fannie all about it."

Boom was right, Sutpen's Trucking was back in business. The chain-link fence that had closed off the property had been removed, workers roamed the loading dock, and eighteen-wheelers came and went from an entrance that had been padlocked for nearly two years. Quinn sat behind the wheel of Boom's ancient Ford in the shadow of one of the dozens of warehouses in the Tupelo Industrial Park north of Tibbehah and straight off Highway 45. He'd been there since sunup watching the action with field glasses and noting the license tag numbers when he could. He took a few breaks over at a truck stop a half klick away. He drank black coffee from a metal thermos and ate cold sausage biscuits wrapped in tinfoil. As the day grew longer, he fired up a cigar, far enough away that no one would notice the smoke streaming from a window.

The waiting was easy. He'd more than a few times had to nestle himself among the boulders in Afghanistan without eating or taking a leak. You had to go and you had to do it right there and then in your fatigues or risk getting exposed and having a shitstorm fall upon your unit. The damn hard part now was the pain in his lower back that felt like needles shooting into his spine every time he stood up and tried to move. It had been a little more than ten months since the shooting. Two surgeries and a long time with rehab, getting back on his feet, healing up after being shot in the stomach, spleen, and lungs. The shooter had missed Quinn's heart by less than a quarter-inch.

Sometime after ten, he got out of the truck and noted a lot of commotion up on the Sutpen's loading dock, five or six men moving large boxes into the rear of a full-size trailer. For a moment, he thought maybe they hadn't changed the signs and that this warehouse was under new and legal management. He'd wait for the rig to pull out and note the tag anyway, hoping to head on back to Tibbehah and meet up with Lillie Virgil as promised.

Quinn tapped the ash of the cigar against the door-frame and reached for his field glasses. A nice pair made by Steiner, even better than the pair he'd carried with him overseas. What caught his attention most were two men who stood off from the loading dock and seemed to be engaged in some kind of argument. There appeared to be a lot of yelling and gesturing between a skinny little fella who had his back to Quinn and a muscular older guy with a gray goatee and a shaved head. The skinny fella had on a straw cowboy hat and jumped down from the dock onto the asphalt, marching his way to the truck cab.

Quinn couldn't be sure until the man moved from the shadow out into the sunlight, but then he knew Sutpen's was really back in business. He watched as Curtis Creekmore, infamous north Mississippi fence, crawled up into the Peterbilt. Quinn shook his head and tried calling Boom, not getting an answer.

He fired up the cigar again, waiting for the Peterbilt to pull out so he might follow Creekmore to wherever he was headed.

Quinn was about to open the truck door when three men walked around the corner. All of them holding long pieces of metal pipe.

"He'p you with something?" asked the man in the center.

"Damn," Akeem Triplett said. "I didn't see that comin'."

"You need to turn up the heat on them wings," Donnie said, wiping his mouth with a fistful of napkins and downing his third bottle of water. "That wasn't shit."

"Oh, come on now," Triplett said. "You cryin' like a baby on that last one."

"Bullshit."

"I seen it," Triplett said. "What do you say, Rerun?"

"Yeah, I seen that shit, too," Rerun said. "You one crazy son of a bitch, Mr. Varner. Ain't never seen a white man win that challenge. I tried myself no less than fifteen times."

"I'll take that T-shirt in a large and the hundred in all twenties if you don't mind."

Triplett laughed as he headed behind the counter and retrieved a shirt and some cash from the till. He sat back down and crossed his arms over his chest. He placed his sunglasses back on and looked direct at Donnie. "OK, then," he said. "Rerun?"

Rerun studied Donnie's face with his little beady brown eyes. He nodded both chins and then turned back to Triplett. "I like him," Rerun said. "I think he'll work out just fine."

"You mind standing up and placing your arms over your head?" Triplett asked.

"Why?"

"Cell phone, too," Rerun said. "Make sure you ain't recording nothing."

Donnie stood and laid down his phone, raising his hands. Triplett patted him down, making him empty out his pockets, hold up his shirt, and take off his boots. As he raised his shirt, Triplett took note of the .38 on a holster clip but didn't pay it any mind.

"Clean?"

Rerun nodded and slid the cell phone across the table and Donnie caught it before it landed on the floor. "Feds got microphones these days smaller than a mouse's pecker hole."

"When can I see the guns?"

"Might be this Saturday," Triplett said. "Might be the next. Got to be flexible, man. Depends on what we hear from Tyrell's people. We heard you can drive an eighteen-wheeler."

"From Fannie Hathcock?"

Triplett shrugged.

"Damn straight," Donnie said. "Drove trucks all across this country and even over in Trashcanistan."

"Can you get us one?"

"Maybe," Donnie said. "How many guns you moving?"

"Don't you worry about that," Triplett said. "All you got to do is drive us in, help us load up, and drive out."

"Nothing's that easy."

"Oh, yeah?" he asked. "How about you and me take a little ride?"

Donnie and Triplett left Rerun at the Take Off Grill and headed on down toward Winchester and the airport. They drove past the signs for the terminal when Triplett made a U-turn and headed back in the opposite direction. He slowed at the gate of a big compound south of the airport and let his Crown Vic idle. He pointed up to a sign and the several big warehouses connected to the tarmac.

"You've got to be shitting me, man," Donnie said. "You're going to rob the fucking UPS warehouse?"

Triplett grinned. "I bet you look sharp in brown, Donnie Varner."

Quinn had his arms raised and told the man to let him reach for his badge.

"Badge?" a new man said, walking out from the side of the warehouse. "You ain't no more sheriff than I am, Quinn Colson. How 'bout you tell us what the fuck you're doing over here in Lee County."

Curtis Creekmore joined the three men holding the sections of pipe. He had on a T-shirt that read WALK BY FAITH and ragged jean shorts held up by a Western belt with a rodeo buckle. On his skinny left arm he showed off the tattoo of his recently departed cat wearing a cowboy hat and smoking a corncob pipe.

"Glad to see you've found the Lord, Curtis," Quinn said.

"Damn straight," Creekmore said, spitting onto the ground. "Working for the good folks at Petco delivering supplies all over the state. Dog food. Collars. Squeaky balls. All that shit. You trying to make trouble for me? Because this here is private property and these boys don't care for you making trouble."

"Can I grab my badge?"

"Do as you please," Creekmore said. "But I already told them you ain't the law no more. Not here. Not in Tibbehah. Not nowhere."

Quinn lowered his hands. "How about you call up Sheriff Johnson and see if he can explain it all to you? I'm sure he'd be happy to sort out any confusion."

Creekmore turned to spit and exchanged looks with the trio holding the pipes, trying to be tough. One of them palming the end of the metal every few seconds. "Your head's got to be made out of fucking concrete, Colson. You ain't being paid for all the trouble you're causing."

Two of the men walked up on Quinn, one of them swinging the pipe toward Quinn's stomach. He caught the pipe, twisted it from the man's hands, and punched him right in the throat. The man fell back as his friend came for Quinn, wildly swinging the pipe. Quinn ducked one of the swings and tackled the man's legs out from under him, knocking him in the back and twisting his head into a choke hold. Quinn squeezed tight, the man smelling like the inside of a petting zoo, flailing in the dirt. Quinn trying to catch his breath, heart racing with sharp pains shooting up his back and down his legs.

"Come on, now," Curtis Creekmore said. "Knock that shit off or I'm gonna have to shoot your ass."

He pulled out a little pistol and aimed it at Quinn. Quinn slowly let go of the man's throat as they all heard the distinctive *snick-snick* of a shotgun racking.

Lillie Virgil walked out past Quinn's truck, pressing the barrel of her gun against the base of Curtis Creekmore's head. "U.S. Marshal," Lillie said. "Enough of this bullshit. Drop that pistol, Curtis. Or you're about to meet your long-lost pussy, Mr. Whiskers, up in the sweet by-and-by."

"Goddamn it, woman," Creekmore said. "Why you always got to make this shit personal?"

Creekmore dropped the pistol. All the men raised their hands.

11

Clarence Skinner met Brock Tanner for lunch over at the El Dorado for what he'd told the acting sheriff was a matter of great and immediate importance. Skinner ordered the Speedy Gonzales, a beef taco and enchilada with a side of rice and beans, and a tall sweet tea to wash it down. He offered to treat Sheriff Tanner, but the man didn't seem interested in the hospitality, saying he couldn't stay long, looking down at his phone while Skinner chewed on some refried beans and patted his mouth with a napkin.

"My wife and I took a trip down to Ole Mexico on our honeymoon," he said. "Lord, that was fifty-two years ago, back when you could drive down there. Before all those cartels and drug dealers and that mess. I recall drinking a cold Coca-Cola at a little cantina, all those brown little kids pestering you for a nickel, trying to sell you tickets to a bullfight. Bought me the fanciest sombrero you've ever seen. I think I still got it somewhere in my machine shop."

Tanner was typing something on his cell phone. Skinner didn't care for all that modern technology, people paying more attention to that little TV screen than what was going on in the world around them. He tried like heck not to get one of those new phones, finding a nice simple one that just made phone calls, with big old buttons so he didn't need to reach for his glasses.

"Mr. Skinner, I don't have a lot of time today," Tanner said. "You said you've got an emergency?"

"Well, sir," Skinner said. "To be real honest, I've heard from some folks around town that your deputies have been spending an inordinate amount of time protecting and serving Miss Hathcock's establishment on the highway. I know that woman is full of all kinds of wiles and charms, but I wanted to assure you, that isn't part of your duties."

"I don't see how that's any concern of yours," Tanner said. "My job is to look out for the safety of all the businesses in the county. It just so happens that Vienna's Place is the main draw off Highway 45. In my experience, at any place with liquor and music there's bound to be some fights and trouble. Just doing the job that Governor Vardaman appointed me to do."

Skinner cut off a little enchilada and forked a bite into his mouth. He chewed on it, letting a silence befall the table, making sure the young man knew the importance of his company. Skinner's trademark pearl-white Stetson hung from a hook along the booth.

"I figured you and the governor would have discussed

your job here," he said. "You're temporary until the state finishes its investigation into the lawlessness in the county."

"That's correct," Tanner said, leveling his eyes at Skinner in a manner Skinner didn't appreciate. His face swarthy and tanned, ears as large as that flying cartoon elephant, Dumbo. "But that investigation could last well into next year. Until then, I'll do my job as I've been trained to do. If you have a problem with the way I conduct my business, we can discuss that at the next supervisor's meeting."

Skinner nodded and took a long sip of sweet tea. His hands shook a bit around the big plastic cup. He looked up to see ole Wade Spratlin and his wife Tammy walk into the El Dorado and greet Javier, making small talk about his float for this year's Big Redneck Christmas Parade. Spratlin, who'd bought out the Cobb family lumber mill, had just been given the honor of being the grand marshal. Skinner made himself smile and wave at the couple.

"This is just a temporary thing," Skinner said. "You do know that?"

"No, sir," Tanner said. His face as flat and impassive as a poker player over in Tunica. "I thought I might stick around for the next election."

Skinner smiled and nodded, trying to keep his voice low and even. "Well then, sir. How about you let me give you some friendly advice about Tibbehah County. Folks sure do love to talk around here, and if you plan on sticking around, I'd be right careful about the company you keep. Miss Hathcock ain't from around here, nor does she have the best interests of this county in mind. In fact, I don't 'spect to see that business keeping its doors open into the next year. We're currently working on an ordinance that would ban and prohibit the kind of services she's offering to truckers fresh off the road."

For the first time, Brock Tanner grinned like a man holding all the cards, laying his long fingers flat on the table, about to rise, still looking Skinner dead in the eye. He clenched his teeth as he spoke. "If I were you, Skinner, I'd keep my old head down and start paving these shitty roads and let me take care of whatever Governor Vardaman wants doing."

Without much thinking, Skinner just blurted out, "Quinn Colson is coming back. I have it on authority you and your thugs will be gone before Thanksgiving. Fill your damn pockets fast, Brock Tanner, because a reckoning is headed your way."

Brock Tanner smirked and stood up in his pressed county uniform, gun on his hip and star on his chest. "Guess we'll just have to wait and find out," he said, before leaning into Skinner's ear. "In the meantime, stay the fuck out of my business, old man."

Before they could hitch Curtis Creekmore to a D-ring in the patrol car, Lillie asked the Lee County deputies to take his pals but leave him. "I'll drop him by the fun house a little later," Lillie said. "Curtis and I have a little catching up to do."

"This woman's crazy," Creekmore said. "She's gonna knock me in the goddamn head with that shotgun of hers. She's done it before. I swear to Christ I'll call up the folks at Morgan and Morgan if you don't let me go. Pain and distress. Pain and distress!"

Quinn stood with Curtis Creekmore, hands shackled behind him, as they watched the deputies pull off and head down the road through the industrial park.

"They got your buddies on assault," Lillie said. "But we didn't mention a damn thing about all that shit inside your truck."

"No," Creekmore said. "I guess you didn't. But holy fuck, Miss Virgil. Why do you have to be so damn mean? Why can't you just call me up on the telephone and discuss matters like a couple of civilized white folks?"

"Damn, Curtis," Quinn said. "I'd expect you to be a little more grateful. Be a real shame for a whole truck-load of TVs to get lost on the way down to the Rez."

"Yeah," Lillie said, still holding her Remington pump. "Chief Robbie might just decide to turn your nutsack into a dream catcher."

"That shit ain't funny," Creekmore said. "Let me tell y'all something. I ain't your problem. I'm just plying my fucking trade. Y'all need to be worried about your own backyard down in Tibbehah County. That place makes Dodge City seem like goddamn Disney World. Fannie Hathcock does as she pleases with no one holding her leash. Did you know they found ole Buster White cut up like a damn Kenny Rogers rotisserie chicken and throwed into an Olive Garden dumpster?"

"No shit, Curtis," Lillie said.

"You know all them new cops the governor sent to keep order are crooks, too?"

"Yep," Quinn said.

"And y'all ain't trying to do nothing about it?" Curtis asked.

"One asshole at a time," Lillie said.

Curtis Creekmore looked from Lillie back to Quinn, shaking his head. He spit out the rest of his snuff, licking the tobacco off his teeth. He shook his head again as if he'd just witnessed the sorriest thing he'd ever seen in his whole rotten life. Quinn leaned against the truck, crossing his arms over his chest, waiting for Lillie to get down to it.

"When y'all used to harass my ass, I figured that meanness you inflicted on me was all about some kind of pent-up sexual energy," Creekmore said. "Now that Sheriff Colson done got himself married and you moved on to become a big swinging-dick Marshal, that leaves me in a real tight position."

"You sure did nail it," Lillie said. "You glad that's out in the open, Quinn?"

"It's a relief," Quinn said. "I've been praying on it."

"Let me ask you something," Lillie said, turning back to Curtis. "Who owns this operation?"

Creekmore snorted. "Who the hell do you think?"

"Might cause a real problem for you if we were to get a warrant to look inside on account of that shit you and your boys just pulled," Lillie said. "Fannie just might blow her top."

Creekmore didn't answer. He did his best to look tough and indignant in handcuffs. Lillie walked up on him as Quinn continued to lean against the truck. Quinn having to grin a little bit, enjoying watching Lillie at work again, turning each little screw on Curtis Creekmore's tiny brain.

"You know what?" Lillie said. "You might just be able to help us out a little."

"How's that?"

"We're looking for a big mean Indian goes by the name of Sam Frye," Lillie said, lowering the shotgun. Holding it in her right hand. "You think you might be able to point us in his direction?"

"Shit no," he said. "I ain't fuckin' with that fella. He's a goddamn red-skinned assassin."

"No one has to know."

"Go ask Chief Robbie."

"We're asking you, Curtis," Lillie said. "For old time's sake. And for us leaving you and your truck to head on down the highway."

"Damn," Creekmore said. "You really would enjoy seeing my nutsack turned into a dream catcher. Probably hang it from the rearview in your Dodge Charger over there."

"Probably."

Creekmore swallowed and looked across the street over at the Sutpen's Trucking Co. and then back to Lillie and Quinn. "Y'all know about Fannie's new place out on Choctaw Lake? Where rich men drink fine old whiskey and get themselves a high-dollar pecker pull?"

Quinn nodded. The face of Sam Frye just starting to reassemble in his mind. He could still hear the fast *pop-pop-pop-pop* of the pistol, bullets flying into his back.

"Heard he might be layin' low somewhere out there."

Football practice was about to start and Jason was still in street clothes, hiding like some kind of criminal under the bleachers and carrying his heavy backpack. His heart thudded in his chest as he watched his teammates take the field, lining up to stretch while he waited for Ana

Gabriel. She said that kid Angel would be driving up real soon and they didn't have much time to jump in and hitch a ride down to Pine Prairie, Louisiana. Ana Gabriel not sure how or if they'd let her see her mother, but she had to at least try. Thinking on it, Jason knew he'd do the same thing if someone took his mother. He'd climb a fence or dig a tunnel to get her out.

"All of this trouble, all of this pain, caused by chickens," Ana Gabriel said, dropping her purple backpack by Jason's feet. "I was thinking about that. It's all so silly."

"My momma says there's a lot of money in chickens," Jason said. "Eggs. Meat. We eat chicken at least two times a day. Three if you count the eggs."

"Señor Herrera spoke to us last night," she said. "He says he has a lawyer who can get our families free of this. He says the blame is on the men who own the plant and wanted workers who wouldn't earn a living wage. He says we were used by a broken, corrupt system."

In the fading light of day, Jason smiled at Ana Gabriel. Her light brown skin and hair as dark as a raven's wing. Her little ears were pierced with small gold hoops and she wore a purple tank top and blue jeans. Her white tennis shoes were spotless.

"Welcome to Mississippi," Jason said.

"Then why do you live here?"

"My family's lived here since before the Civil War."

"You know you can leave."

"Not when you have family," Jason said. "My grand-momma needs us. And my momma has work here. It's her calling. She said everyone has a purpose and hers is to look out for the unfortunate folks who land in Tib-behah County."

"Your mother is a saint."

"Yep," Jason said, taking Ana Gabriel's hand. "She's something special. I just hope she doesn't hate me for going."

"You didn't tell her?"

"Of course not," Jason said. "Why would I? She'd never let me go."

"I'm fine," she said, letting go of his hand. "I'll be back tomorrow. This boy Angel is the cousin of my friend Alejandro. He said he is a very good driver. A very good boy. We packed plenty of food. We all found enough money to pay for the gas."

"I don't know this Angel," he said. "He doesn't go to school here. I never heard a damn word about him."

Ana Gabriel didn't say anything, turning her head as a white van pulled into the parking lot and curved toward the stadium ticket stand. Smoke poured from the exhaust and the front windshield was cracked. It sat idling for several moments, the front windows tinted nearly black.

"May I kiss you?" Ana Gabriel asked.

Jason nodded. "Sure."

She kissed him on the cheek and as she reached for her backpack, Jason reached down for his. He slung its heavy weight up onto his shoulder.

"It's only one night," Jason said. "Momma can't ground me past Christmas. Everyone gets forgiven at Christmas. It's the law."

The van's side door slid open, revealing a skinny teenager

with a thin little mustache and long black hair. He smiled at them both, showing off a row of bright gold teeth.

"Oh, hell," Jason said.

"Get in," Angel said. "There is little time."

Caddy wasn't exactly sure how she and Donnie started dancing in the barn at The River but it had a little to do with her weakness for George Strait. Donnie knew it, had known it forever, and started playing "One Step at a Time" from the tape deck in his daddy's gold GTO. He'd driven the car on into the dusty space where they held service on Sunday, bringing in two big boxes of chicken wings he said he was donating to the cause. They'd loaded them into the freezers, and then Donnie leaned in the open window and started the song, grabbing Caddy by the hand and leading her round and round in a Texas two-step. His blue eyes clear and focused, stubble against her face as he held her close, the tape moving on to the song "Maria," his hands clasping at the base of her spine until they heard a couple of the children giggling, that boy Sancho and his friend, Abel, watching them.

Caddy let go of Donnie's waist, heading back to close one of the great barn doors, already thinking about suppertime and wondering how many families might show up tonight. Her mother had promised to pick up Jason from football practice and she'd bring him home later. Until then, there was a lot to get done. The kids had run off and Donnie was back with her, reaching for her hand again, laughing and grinning, telling her that even Jesus would want her to have a little fun once in a while.

The afternoon light bled in through the cracks in the barn walls and shone onto the dirty floor. The song stopped and it was quiet, Caddy's hands filled with a great big sack of masa that a local woman needed to make fresh tortillas. Donnie reached his arms around her, pulling her back to his chest. He set his face down on her shoulder and said, "Won a hundred dollars eating hot wings today. How about me and you head to the town square and have us a big nice meal."

"Not tonight," she said. "Tonight's Thursday."

"What's Thursday?"

"Open house," she said. "And we have to set out the tables and chairs for the kids."

"How about tomorrow?"

Caddy turned and pushed him away. "I'll think about it."

"Don't think too long," Donnie said. "That money's burning a hole in my pocket. I'll even drive you up to Big Creek for a T-bone steak."

Caddy laughed and Donnie bent down to kiss her on the lips. She closed her eyes but didn't move. She didn't kiss him back but she didn't stop it, either. It felt damn familiar, him being there, the smell of drugstore aftershave, the funny comments and light touch with the hands. She finally opened her eyes as Donnie backed off, staring toward the barn doors and saying, "Can I help you out, friend?"

"Looks like I'm interrupting something," the man said. "Sorry about that. I can come back later."

Caddy turned and squinted into the light. It was Bentley.

12

Excuse the mess," Chief Robbie said, moving through the casino floor with Sam Frye. Lights, cables, and cameras were set up around the blackjack tables and roulette wheels, the air thick with smoke and the stench of the working people burning through minimum wage. "We're announcing the expansion for Christmas. Double capacity in two years. Not to mention the Legends Theater. Have I told you about the Legends Show?"

"Many times," said Sam Frye.

"It's like having all these famous people, most of them long dead, up onstage without having to pay full price," he said. "I have a Dolly Parton who looks more like Dolly Parton than she does anymore. Her voice, the same. Her breasts even larger, more magnificent. We have a young Garth Brooks, an old Whitney Houston. A Las Vegas Elvis, of course, and this young man from Branson who can put on a whole Bruno Mars act. The dancing, the splits. All of it. It's going to be amazing, brother. Fantastic."

Sam Frye nodded, walking beside the Chief, trying to keep up as Chief Robbie went from subject to subject, one grand plan to the next, never slowing down to enjoy all they'd accomplished in the last thirty years. Robbie wore a lot of makeup, the blemished parts of his face showing at the edges of his ears and forehead. Somewhere between busting heads and keeping order on the Rez, his old friend had become an entertainer. A Native American Wayne Newton, only in turquoise and denim instead of a tux, with a closet full of alligator boots that cost two thousand dollars a pair.

"It pains me that we can't go ahead and break ground on Takali," Chief Robbie said, walking in the big ring around the casino floor. "But this expansion is long, long overdue. Our third pool. Think of it. Three grand pools and the tiki bar. With Tunica being what it has become, we will be a beacon of light for families. Waterslides and games for the children, shopping and spas for the women, and gambling and golf for the men. White men love golf so very much. It's almost a religion. And now we will be unrivaled entertainment. I have not forgotten about the REO Speedwagon incident. No more of that. Never."

Sam Frye nodded to two men in green blazers standing by the big metal doors back to security and the counting room, heading in with the Chief, the Chief stopping to say hello and shake hands or pat the backs of everyone he passed. He moved through the shuffling money counters and the jingling of the token and change counters on the way up the staircase into his office. The

Chief launched up the steps like a much younger man and headed down a dark, narrow hallway. More hand-shakes, a few jokes, talk of the new commercial they were shooting with members of the tribe excited about the expansion. The biggest the casino had made since the late nineties. Big, thick Choctaw women squealed with delight.

"What would you think about a Tanya Tucker?" Chief Robbie asked.

"For what?"

"The Legends Show," Chief Robbie said. "I've always liked her music a great deal. I recall when she was all but thirteen and singing 'Delta Dawn.' She sang it so true and deep that it broke my heart. But she is very expen-sive. Her people won't return our phone calls. So what do we do? We find a replacement, a teenager who looks and can sing just like she could."

"Yes," Sam Frye said. "Of course."

"You are so far away, Sam Frye," Chief Robbie said, stepping over to the broad window and staring down on the casino floor, spread out with the glowing slot ma-chine displays, the green felt of the tables, the wild hand-blown glass lights and cheap and durable patterned carpet. "Are you leaving us again? I told you that's what's best. But then you return and return again. This place calls to you."

"It's not this place," Sam Frye said. "I have other rea-sons."

"Do you want a different car? Perhaps a Mercedes this time."

"I don't need a new car," he said. "The one I have is

fine. I had Pinti put on new plates. No one knows this car. It's big, has leather, good gas mileage. Thank you."

Chief Robbie rested the flat of his hands across his grand cypress desk with eagle-claw feet. He stared at his old friend. "I know what is bothering you."

Sam Frye didn't answer.

"It's the makeup," he said. "You know my hair has gone gray. I have added color to it for almost ten years now. The color that comes in the box for smiling white men. You believe I've gone soft? That I am no longer Robbie who would dive into an alligator pit in Houma and come out with two gators in each hand, gripped by the throat, wiggling and snapping?"

Sam Frye didn't know what to say, but was spared as the back door opened and Pinti walked in. The young man had been a close friend of Toby's, a kid Sam had been grooming before he got shot and killed up in Tibbehah County. Toby had wanted to become a famous rapper someday, throwing away a good and profitable life his late father and Sam Frye had offered. He hoped Pinti had more of a commitment to his people.

"Yes?" Chief Robbie asked.

"There's a white man on the Rez who says he must see you."

"I am too busy."

"He's out at the gin," Pinti said. "Dropped off some TVs and computers for us."

"Was he not paid?" Chief Robbie said.

"He was paid," Pinti said. "But he says he has personal business with you."

"Hah," Chief Robbie said, pushing off the desk and

rolling up the denim sleeves of his shirt. "Tell him to speak with Jackie Jim."

"Jackie Jim is on the Coast."

"Too bad."

"He says his name is Curtis Creekmore," Pinti said. "Says he has news of Sam Frye. A warning."

Sam Frye lifted his eyes up to Robbie. Robbie looked across to Pinti and told him that they would drive out to the gin and listen to what this man had to say.

There were eleven of them, mostly kids, sitting on the dirty van floor, packed behind the driver and that boy Angel in the front passenger seat. The driver was a wiry guy, older, maybe in his twenties with head shaved nearly bald, a skinny little mustache and goatee with tattoos all over. Jason tried to ignore the men up front, resting with his back to the sliding door and touching feet with Ana Gabriel.

Jason recognized two, maybe three, kids from school, mostly girls his age or a little older. They all carried backpacks or cheap suitcases, none of them speaking for the first hour on the road as the radio pumped out some Mexican-sounding music, lots of accordions and a big brass band. It sounded big and heroic as they cut across the state, heading on over to Meridian and then down to Jackson. Ana Gabriel saying they'd be across the state line by nightfall. That's when Jason would call his momma and let her know everything was OK.

There was little, in fact zero, doubt he'd be getting an ass-whipping when he got home. His momma still believed that sparing those willow branches might spoil the child. But looking across at Ana Gabriel, her flushed and nervous face when Angel turned back to joke with her, he knew he'd done the right thing. He didn't know what Angel was saying, but Jason sure as hell didn't like the way the older boy was eyeing Ana Gabriel's bare legs.

"What'd that boy say?" Jason asked, whispering as the van cruised along.

"Nothing."

"Well, he said something."

Angel turned back to look at Jason again, giving him a hard, black-eyed stare, and then traded some words with the driver. The driver didn't answer, Jason focusing on the back of the man's neck and the black ink that read MS-13. He knew what the letters and numbers meant, but pointing them out to Ana Gabriel would only worry her more. Jason stood up, bending over not to hit his head, and stepped around all the legs and backpacks, some of the girls already falling asleep in the jostling van. It was hot and humid inside, smelling of sweat and rancid breath. He wished to God someone would open up a window.

Jason poked his head up between the driver and Angel, catching sight of the road ahead. They weren't on Highway 45 or even I-20 but riding up far north of Jackson, a sign saying they weren't but eight miles from Batesville. *What the hell?*

"Hey," Jason said, pointing. "You're going the wrong damn way."

"*Siéntate, chico,*" the driver said. His voice was low and mean, eyes on the road ahead.

Jason looked to Ana Gabriel, who was up on her knees

now, sweeping her hands toward him, telling him to please come back. "Please," she said. "Please."

"*Siéntate*," Angel said, pushing Jason hard with the flat of his hand and knocking him on his back right on top of all those young girls. Jason tried to get up to hit that smartass but Ana Gabriel and three other girls held his arms, begging him no.

"They're going the wrong way," Jason said. "They don't know what the hell they're doing. Bunch of damn idiots. We're headed north up to Memphis."

"He's taking a shortcut," she said. "They will get us there. I promise."

"My grandmomma calls it going around your ass to get to your elbow," he said. "Ain't no damn way we're getting down to south Louisiana like this. Who the hell are these people anyway?"

"*Chico*," Angel said, turning down the music. "I said sit the fuck down and shut up. Or else we throw you from the van."

Jason started to sweat, heart racing and adrenaline pumping through his body like it did before kickoff. He wanted to launch himself through that van and tackle that son of a bitch right to the ground. He locked eyes with Angel, ugly as sin with a buzz cut, flat nose, and gold teeth. The boy might be older, but he wasn't nothing special. If it wasn't for that man behind the wheel, Jason could take him down real easy.

Jason slowly lowered his back to the sliding door. Without any windows, he kept his focus on Ana Gabriel. She tapped at his foot with hers and smiled.

"Everything is fine," she said. "We will all be OK."

*   *   *

"I don't see how that situation has anything to do with you," Caddy said, standing in the shade of the metal roof off the single-wide she used as an office. "I haven't heard from you for nearly a year and you drive up in a slick little sports car, wanting me to back off this current shitstorm in Tibbehah County."

"I didn't say that," Bentley said, his navy polo shirt untucked and hanging loose from his wrinkled khakis. "I only said for you not to worry so much. I know your main focus is taking care of folks in this county. Right?"

"You know it is."

"That plant will be open next week and the jobs will be filled with actual locals," Bentley said. "Not migrant workers. We're going to make sure the jobs are taken by hardworking Americans right here in Mississippi."

Caddy narrowed her eyes as Bentley grinned, acting as if he'd just brought her the best news in the world. A hot wind crossed over the flat and dusty land of The River, wind chimes on the porch tinkling.

"That's awfully nice of you and your daddy," Caddy said. "How come y'all didn't come up with this idea years ago? Would've saved this town and all these people a whole lot of trouble."

"Wait a second," Bentley said, holding up the flat of his hand. "Wait one damn second. Don't do me that way, Caddy Colson. Last year, I may have deserved it, but here I'm just trying to do the right thing. Sure, some folks were trying to cut corners, not wanting to pay minimum wage. When my daddy caught wind of that he was furious. I promise you. That's why I came up here, trying to right things, make sure that plant is up and running with good labor from this county."

"I'll believe it when I see it," Caddy said, placing her hands on her hips. "But that still doesn't fix the mess y'all caused. You people brought these workers here from all over the South. Now they're locked up in Louisiana with their children left behind. What are you asking me to do? Tell them to hit the highway? That we're done using them up and they're on their own?"

"I'm saying help who you can," Bentley said. "I respect what you're trying to do. I just don't want you to go and get in too far and deep with the whole political mess of it. I wanted to assure you I'm handling it. You have my word, all that's going to get done. Your foundation, The River, all of it will continue to be funded."

"Continue?" Caddy asked, stepping up one foot from Bentley's face. His face lean and handsome but looking more worn and drawn. His usually clear blue eyes, something she always found attractive, were bloodshot. "Have you been too busy to notice that I haven't cashed a single check since last year? I don't want or need your family's money."

Bentley swallowed and caught a four-by-four post holding up the roof, spinning himself halfway around. He looked out over the expanse of the treeless land, the old church barn, and on up the hill, the unfinished metal skeleton of the all-purpose building his family had promised to fund.

"You'll get everything," Bentley said. "Don't you see? Money to help these illegals, money to finish construction, and hardworking folks, locals, back to work. Just let me handle the politics."

"Politics?" Caddy said, catching Bentley by the wrist. "What are you talking about? This isn't about politics. This is about decency."

Bentley's face tightened, his left eye twitching a bit. He gritted his teeth and turned his head back toward the unfinished building. Last year it had been a dream of theirs, a joint project that Caddy figured would be up and working by now. There was going to be a community center for after-school programs and continuing education for adults. A new place that would help them expand outside the shadow of that old Southern barn. "I heard you were seeing some Mexican fella named Herrera," he said. "Before you say anything, you might want to check into that man's background. He was arrested dozens of times in Georgia and Texas. He's not just some crazy socialist, he's more like a communist. He's a radical."

Caddy let go of his wrist and stepped back. She looked at gangly Bentley Vandeven, all wrinkled and haggard at not even thirty years old, coming to her not with hat in hand for forgiveness but with a bunch of busted-up, half-hearted promises.

"Hector Herrera is a good man," Caddy said. "Not that it's any of your damn business. But no. I'm not seeing him. I'm working with him. Can't a woman be in the company of a man, on the side of the same damn cause, without people talking?"

Bentley, face split in shadow and light, turned his head away from the skeletal frame on the hill and back to Caddy. His face flushed and sweaty, trying to calm himself without much success. The wind chimes tinkled again for a second and then settled in the still, unmoving heat. "Just promise me that you'll keep away from him for a while," he said. "He's a bad dude that's in with some bad folks. I just don't want to see anything happen to you. That's all."

Caddy watched Bentley step back away and turn toward the stairs, his head down and sulky, running smack-dab into Donnie, who was headed up from the barn.

"Interrupting something?" Donnie asked.

Bentley shook his head and tried to walk around Donnie. Donnie stuck out his hand and introduced himself.

Bentley looked away and then back at Caddy before shaking his head. "Another damn convict?" he asked. "Well, no one can say you don't have a type."

Donnie placed his hand on Bentley's shoulder and looked him right in the eye. "Kid, if you don't want to leave Jericho with your teeth in your front pocket, I'd say it's best to get your ass back in that slick little car of yours and pedal it back to Oxford or Jackson or whatever little monogrammed world you live in. You ain't welcome down here."

Bentley knocked Donnie's hand off his shoulder and headed back to his sports car, Donnie walking up on the porch to stand shoulder to shoulder with Caddy. They watched Bentley pull on a pair of sunglasses hanging from his rearview and fishtail out from The River.

"What did ole junior want with you?" Donnie asked.

"He wanted to warn me about the company I keep."

"Huh," Donnie said, grinning. "Are you listening?"

"Nope," Caddy said, turning and heading back into the office. "Not one damn bit."

* * *

Sam Frye drove the Chief from the casino way the hell out in the Rez to an old cotton gin they used to unload trucks from Memphis and New Orleans, sometimes sending the repackaged goods on over to Atlanta. Three eighteen-wheelers were parked outside the big silver metal building, where a white man in a straw cowboy hat hopped down from a cab and approached Frye's big black car. He had on a bright yellow T-shirt and shorts with cowboy boots that came up to his knees, his lower lip thick with snuff.

"That's him?" Sam Frye said.

"Yes," Chief Robbie said. "Creekmore. He's a true and authentic idiot."

It was late in the day but still hot, the back of his dress shirt damp with sweat. Chief Robbie walked ahead to greet and shake hands with Creekmore. The man grinning like a moron, pumping their hands, and saying that it was hotter than Hades up in that truck cab. He kept rambling on about the deal he'd just made on the televisions and how the Chief wouldn't be so lucky next time. "Yes, sir," Creekmore said. "If my warehouse wasn't so damn filled, I might've kept them around until Christmas. That's when you make your real money, people with no credit getting real desperate for that big-screen experience. Bowl games and such."

"What is it you wished to say?" Chief Robbie said.

Creekmore closed his left eye and nodded. "Sure do like you, Chief," he said. "You always getting right to the point. And is this Mr. Sam Frye with you? The man I've been hearing so much about. Damn, he sure is a big ole boy."

"You told Pinti that you had news for us."

Creekmore nodded and nodded, and then turned his head and spit. "Yes, sir," he said. "Yes, sir. I sure do."

The men waited. Sam Frye standing, arms across his large chest, sweating through the white shirt, listening to the cicadas buzzing far out in the trees. He could feel the sun on the back of his neck as no one spoke for a long while.

"Figured what I know might be worth something to y'all."

Chief Robbie stood still. He said nothing.

"I mean, we're friends and all, but a man's got to eat," Creekmore said. "You know I didn't make a penny on this here deal with the televisions. Bought them from some blacks up in Memphis, sold 'em to you for what I got 'em for. They was headed for some Walmarts over in Nashville. Sweet-looking picture on 'em. I set one up last night in my tool shed and watched two nekkid women going at it like there wasn't no tomorrow. Good Lord, it was like they was standing there right with you. They called that picture *Russian Invasion Three*. Yes, sir. That's what they called it."

Sam Frye said nothing.

"What I done is worth something," Creekmore said. "Come on now, fellas. Mr. Sam Frye, I know you don't know me from Adam's house cat, but the Big Chief can vouch for me that I'm a man of honor and integrity. I've been doing business down here on the Rez with you folks since I was a teenager. Used to haul moonshine this way in a '63 Coupe de Ville with a ragtop and whitewall tires. You could fit a damn swimming pool in that trunk, and Lord knows you people sure do like to drink."

The comment was ridiculous and offensive. Neither Sam Frye or the Chief cared to reply.

"OK," Creekmore said. "OK. How about this? I'll tell you what I heard and what I done and then maybe you make a little offering to the Curtis Creekmore Society. I stuck my dang neck out going against one of the meanest, craziest damn women in the South. Done it for y'all on account of you being such good customers."

Sam Frye shifted on one foot to another. A fly buzzed across Chief Robbie's forearm and he swatted at it.

"See, Mr. Sam Frye, you got a U.S. Marshal bird-dogging your ass," he said. "She says you not only killed my dearly departed pal Wes Taggart but also shot Quinn Colson four times in the back. If she wasn't a woman, I'd say she had herself a big old throbbing hard-on to bring you in. You get what I'm saying to y'all?"

Sam Frye looked to the Chief. He shrugged. He rubbed his hand across the back of his neck, feeling the baking heat out in front of the cotton gin. The afternoon sun glinting off all that bright silver metal. The words CHOCTAW PROUD faded and worn on the corrugated tin out by the loading docks.

"But y'all listen to what I done," Creekmore said, putting a little hand over his mouth to giggle. "I done told them you'd thrown in with Miss Fannie Hathcock and that you was staying out at her brand-spanking-new pussy palace up on the lake. See, the way I figured is, I'd give you a head start and good old warning about watching your back. Ain't nobody wants to see you strung up for taking on Quinn Colson. That smart-mouth bastard had it coming, you ask me."

Chief Robbie nodded and toed at the ground with his alligator boots. "OK," he said.

"That's it?" Creekmore said. "Y'all sure are cheap. Damn, I wish I was still working with that boy Mingo. He was a good kid. Always looked out for me and treated me fair and square. Damn shame. Boy never saw it coming."

Sam Frye reached out and grabbed Curtis Creekmore by the upper arm. "Hey," Creekmore said. "Hey, now. What the damn hell?"

Sam Frye shook him like a wild dog with a squirrel. "Where did you hear this?"

"Goddamn son of a bitch," Creekmore said. "What are y'all doing?"

Sam Frye slapped Curtis Creekmore hard across the face, knocking the tobacco from his mouth. Spit and blood ran across his cheek. "Where did you hear this?"

"Everybody knows them good ole boys took him out," Creekmore said. "Wadn't me. Shit. I didn't have a damn thing to do with it."

Chief Robbie reached out and grabbed the man by the front of his yellow T-shirt and lifted him off the ground and tossed him far into the weeds. Sam Frye reached him first, kicking and punching Creekmore. Chief Robbie kicked at the man's ribs with the pointy toes of his boots. They worked on him until he was bloody and cowering like a little child in a ball, protecting his head and his private parts. The man breathing heavy, waiting for the next blow. It felt good, both of them working together again as a team. They hadn't lost a step.

"What do you know about Mingo?" Sam Frye said.

"I heard it from an old boy who worked direct for

Buster White," Creekmore said, trying to catch a breath and wiping his lip with the back of his hand. "Said they took that kid somewhere down near Kosciusko, shot him in the back of the head. Used a backhoe to bury him up under a levee of some sort. Y'all didn't know about that? Hell, you didn't have to mess me up to get to it. I think you cracked two of my damn ribs."

"Why?" Sam Frye said. "Why did they do this?"

Creekmore got on all fours, spitting blood and snuff onto the ground, looking like an animal, crawling around and searching for his straw cowboy hat. He finally stood, placing it on his head, his face bloody and puffy, one eye nearly closed. He seemed to seek dignity in the situation but failed.

"I don't know, man," Creekmore said. "I swear to Christ, I don't know. I sure liked that kid."

Chief Robbie reached into his wallet, pulled out several hundred-dollar bills and tossed them at the man's feet. Sam Frye walked back to the car, started the engine, and turned the AC to full blast. He could feel the vein throbbing in his temple.

"You deserved answers," Chief Robbie said. "Now you'll never know why they killed your boy. I am sorry."

Sam Frye didn't answer as he yanked the wheel and U-turned the car back to the casino.

"Hold still," Maggie said.

Quinn was on the front porch of the farmhouse, seated in an old metal chair as Maggie sewed up a gash on his head. She had the windows and front door open, the turntable in the salon spinning *The Essential Tom T. Hall* and "The Year That Clayton Delaney Died" as she worked and dabbed off the blood with a cold, wet towel. He figured it would stop bleeding, but halfway home from Tupelo, holding an old rag against his head, he knew he'd need some stitches.

"Doesn't have to be pretty," Quinn said. "My hair will cover it."

"As short as you keep your hair?" Maggie said. "I don't want anyone saying that Maggie Colson did a half-ass job sewing up her husband's head. Now sit still and let me finish it up."

"Reggie got slashed with a knife over at the Club Disco this summer and said Raven sewed him up so nice and neat you couldn't even see the scar."

"You want me to stick you with this needle?"

"No, ma'am."

"Then sit still and be quiet."

It was that in-between time in late August, right after sundown but before night when everything was lit up in a fine, hazy gold. The soft light fell over the cow pasture and the meandering creek, now completely dry. The cows had wandered out from under the oaks and pecans, getting some relief from the heat, swatting their tails at flies. The air smelled of dried manure and brittle brown weeds, a trumpet vine with bright orange flowers growing wild on the cattle guard.

"Damn," Maggie said. "You might need some staples on this one. Just what exactly did they hit you with?"

"A metal pipe."

"How many of them?"

"Three," Quinn said. "There was a fourth guy. But he didn't do much but talk."

"That's the one pulled a gun?"

"Yep."

"What would you have done if Lillie hadn't shown up?"

"Curtis Creekmore wouldn't have shot me," Quinn said. "He's a crook. Not a killer."

"You seem pretty confident about that."

"Yes, ma'am," Quinn said.

Quinn reached for his coffee mug filled with Jack Daniel's and took a long pull. The best thing about not being on the job was being able to drink when he felt like it. Nobody felt comfortable having a sheriff with whiskey on his breath. But a sheriff on temporary leave was something completely different.

He set down the mug as Maggie held his head tight in her hands, surveying the work. "I'd say that's a fine and professional job," she said, removing her latex gloves. "I take both cash and credit."

Quinn reached for her hand and pulled her onto his lap. Her pregnant body weighed heavy on his legs but felt solid and strong, her hair worn loose and long down her back. He leaned in and kissed her neck, hands against her tight belly. She had on her scrub pants and a man's tank top, the material nearly busting at the seams.

"Don't you think it's time to get off your feet?"

"Another week."

"You don't have to look out for anyone but Brandon and this baby," Quinn said. "Tibbehah County can take care of their own for a while."

"Might say the same for you," Maggie said. "No need

for you to do what you've been doing. Although you seem to want to keep that to yourself."

"Just poking around," Quinn said. "A little recon helps with the boredom."

"What if I told you I'd like you to quit for a while?" Maggie asked. "Until the baby comes and then for a while after that."

"Can't do that."

"And I can't take off time at the hospital until I'm ready."

"Yes, ma'am."

Quinn kissed her again on the neck and moved his hand down her inner thigh. She didn't speak as he inched his hand upward, moving his lips down her neck, goose bumps raising on her skin. "You know that makes me crazy."

"Yep."

"Then how come you're doing it?"

"I like you when you're crazy," Quinn said.

"We have to meet your momma in an hour for dinner."

"I know."

"My head hurts, my feet are swollen, and I have to pee every ten minutes," she said. "Does that sound sexy to you?"

"Talk a little slower," Quinn said. "I like the sound of that husky voice."

"Damn, you are hard up, Quinn Colson," Maggie said, pushing up off his legs to stand and bending down to kiss him on his hurt head.

"Worth a shot."

"Well, it does lower blood pressure and helps you sleep."

"Yes, ma'am."

"And even boosts your immune system."

"See," Quinn said. "I'm just trying to do what's best for the health of my family."

Without another word, Maggie headed back into the house, screen door thwacking closed behind her. Quinn stood up, hearing her feet on the steps leading up to their bedroom. He reached down and drained the rest of the whiskey as the cell phone began to buzz in his pocket. It was his momma, probably wanting to remind him again about meeting at the El Dorado for supper.

He didn't have to take it, but if he didn't, she'd just keep on calling and calling until he answered. He picked it up on the fourth buzz.

"El Dorado in an hour," Quinn said. "I haven't forgotten, Momma."

"Did you pick up Jason from school today?"

"No, ma'am."

"Well, he wasn't at football practice," Jean said. "Coach said he never showed up after school. You think your sister would've let me know if he was sick. I've been calling her for the last half hour and can't get her to pick up. I'm worried sick, Quinn. And I'm too damn old for that mess."

13

The van had stopped a few times that night, at gas stations along the interstate that circled Memphis, where Angel led the girls back and forth from the bathrooms. He had a gun now and seemed real proud to show it off on his belt, continuing to give Jason mean stares and shoving him a few times. Jason didn't fight back, waiting for the right moment, waiting for a time when he could grab Ana Gabriel and they could run off. When they'd stopped earlier, he'd seen a Memphis police car and tried to get their attention, but the patrol car had hit the flashing lights and drove off into the darkness. Angel slapped him in his head and told him if he tried that again, he'd shoot him in the leg. Angel was just a damn kid, but talked to him like he meant it. Jason knew he would shoot him.

It was dawn now, a light gray and blue, as cars and trucks zoomed down the nearby highway. Both the driver and Angel were out of the van, and through the front windshield, Jason saw them talking to a tall black man with long braids down his back. It was early and already warm, but the man was dressed in a full-length coat, like dusters in old Westerns.

"What are they talking about?" Ana Gabriel said.

"I think they are trying to make a deal."

"A deal for what?"

"A deal for all of y'all," Jason said. "That son of a bitch Angel never planned on taking y'all to see your families. He saw y'all as a business opportunity."

"I'm so stupid," she said. "He gave his word. He seemed so honest, saying he was worried about me and my family."

"Because he's a damn liar," Jason said. "Tell me it doesn't make sense. Why are we in Memphis? What else would they be doing? You saw that kid point that pistol at me. I say we make a run for it right now. We got a better chance causing a commotion out here than letting them drive us around to God knows where."

"What about the others?"

Jason looked around the van, the girls sleeping on their backpacks, one of them, Marisol Gonzalez, on her knees praying. The first time they stopped, sometime around midnight, Angel and the driver had taken all their cell phones and put them in a sack. They'd promised to give them all back when they got to the prison, but now they knew that was nothing but a bunch of bullshit. They were just going around and around Memphis until those boys could figure out how to make a few bucks. Damn, he wondered what his momma must be thinking right about now. His grandmother, Uncle Quinn, and Aunt Maggie.

Jason knew he'd made a mess of things, but now it was up to him to make it right. He reached into his waistband and pulled out the Buck knife that Uncle Quinn had given him.

"Wait," Ana Gabriel said. "Wait. What are you doing?"

"I'm gonna get y'all out of here and that metal-mouthed bastard better not try and stop me."

Quinn hadn't slept all night. He stayed up with Caddy and his mother at Jean's house, drinking coffee and smoking cigars, and calling up every kid that Jason knew. They talked to his teachers and his coaches, Quinn and Boom taking to the back roads and the places Jason would most likely hide if there was some kind of trouble. Tree stands and fishing holes, old dry creeks and abandoned houses deep in the piney woods. He and Boom parking the truck on gravel roads and hiking into the woods, flashlights scattering up and around the trees, calling Jason's name into the dark.

"He wouldn't run away," Caddy said. "He had no reason. There wasn't any trouble. He just started football season. You know how much he loves it. It's all he's been talking about since camp at Ole Miss."

Quinn and his sister stood across from each other in the house where they both grew up. Quinn held a cigar in his hand, letting it burn while he listened to what Caddy had to say. Behind the ranch house was a gentle, sloping hill where Quinn used to play war and Caddy kept a small kitchen under their play fort.

"What about folks at The River?" Quinn asked.

"Are you asking me about the sketchy folks, perverts, convicts, and all that I sometimes help?"

"Didn't say that, Caddy," Quinn said. "I'm just trying to help the best way I know how."

"Doesn't make any sense," she said. "Does it? God. It's so warm out here and I can't quit shaking."

"He have a girlfriend?" Quinn asked.

"He's just twelve," Caddy said.

"Almost thirteen," Quinn said. "Who's he friendly with?"

"There's this little girl staying out at The River," Caddy said. "Her name is Ana Gabriel. I tried checking with her before I left but her little brother said she was sound asleep. I figured I'd head back and try again. I don't think she knows anything. Jason didn't know her that well."

"Mommas are always the last to know."

"Not this momma."

"Go on and wake her up," Quinn said. "I'll track down Brock Tanner and get him to send word to the folks on patrol."

"Brock Tanner?" Caddy asked. "You really want to do that?"

"No time for pride and bullshit," Quinn said. "I already reached out to Reggie and sheriffs in surrounding counties. You said he finished up school but no one saw him leaving?"

"Never showed up for practice," Caddy said, starting to cry again. "Does that sound like Jason?"

"Whatever happened, he must've had a good reason," Quinn said, reaching his arm around his sister and pulling her tight. "We'll find him. I promise. Everything is going to be just fine."

Donnie Varner had made a black skillet filled with two fried eggs, some Jimmy Dean sausage links, and Wonder Bread grilled in butter when five trucks rolled on up into the Magnolia Drive-In. He stood there in his tighty-whities, mud boots up to his knees, and terry cloth robe open, staring into the headlights blazing into the dawn.

A truck door opened and a fat little fella wandered out. Donnie wasn't able to make out his face.

"Picture show is closed," Donnie said, raising his voice to the trucks. "Hadn't had movies out here since John Wayne kicked the bucket. Try that new Malco over in Tupelo."

The man kept on walking, dust and grit all kicked up by the mud tires, the man emerging close to where Donnie stood on his wooden steps. The little fella was dressed for combat, black tactical pants and black shirt, a pistol worn in a side holster. It was one of the boys he'd met over at Zeke's Value City, one of those Watchmen folks.

Donnie held the skillet in his right hand and closed his robe with his left. Man had to have a little dignity.

"You're a tough man to find, Donnie Varner."

"Hell no, I ain't," Donnie said. "In case you hadn't seen a damn map, Tibbehah County is nothing but a little postage stamp of property."

"You never called us back."

"Still working out a few details," Donnie said.

Other truck doors began to open and more of those wannabe-military fruitcakes crawled out in their combat gear and black hats. Some of them had guns. Most of them wore beards, headlights still shining bright too damn early in the morning.

"Sorry but I don't have but a few more sausages in the fridge," said Donnie. "I ain't exactly equipped for no pancake supper."

The man walked up close to the wooden steps. A half-dozen or so of those other boys joined them. With all the scraggly beards and dark shades, they looked like the goddamn Oak Ridge Boys were back on tour.

"We gave you a list."

"And a fine list it was," Donnie said. "But gathering all that weaponry ain't exactly like stopping by the Piggly Wiggly and filling up your cart with Ding Dongs and Fruity Pebbles. You boys got to understand this stuff takes time. It's about making contacts, gaining trust, and some hard-nosed negotiation. Y'all got to trust me and give me some space."

"We think you're pulling our goddamn peckers," one of the men said. The boy was a spitting image for William Lee Golden with the long gray hair and beard that drooped down over his chest, or that old sallow-faced fucker on *Duck Dynasty*. That show sure had been a big hit at the correctional institution. Boys laughed and laughed at that old hambone country wisdom he dispensed.

"We heard some federal folks made their way down here," the short turd said. "You know anything about that?"

"No, sir," Donnie said. "I most certainly do not. And I resent the holy fuck out of the implication. Do you have any idea what it's like to spend the last decade in lockup being told when to eat, sleep, and shit? I'm no friend to the federal people. I can promise you that. Those people, and one redheaded woman in particular, cornholed my ass long and good. I hadn't been able to sit down for years."

The men, standing in a semicircle, exchanged glances with each other. The Oak Ridge Boy nodding over at the little fat fucker who Donnie figured was the leader of this Mickey Mouse Club. The man looked up at Donnie, who just wanted to sit down and have breakfast before his eggs cooled off.

"Yeah?"

One of the fellas, dressed head to toe for combat operations, dropped a rucksack on the bottom step.

"What the fuck's that?" Donnie asked.

"Down payment."

"Hold the phone for a second," Donnie said. "Let me get back to you on a few things. I mean that was one hell of grocery list y'all gave me. It's gonna take time."

"You've got one week," the little man said.

"Yep," ole Oak Ridge Boy said. "Or we'll hang your ass high on that movie screen out there. We're not an organization who puts up with bullshit and insubordination."

Donnie picked up a sausage link from the skillet and took a bite. He looked down at the little crew all waiting for Donnie to make good on the promise. He just stood there and stared, the edges of his bathrobe opening and closing in the hot summer wind. At a time like this, he sure was glad he slept in his underwear.

"I promise y'all I'll do my damn best," Donnie said, holding up his free hand and offering them a salute. "Cub Scout's honor."

Jason yanked back the van door but heard a chain clanging outside. They'd locked them all in. But as he moved into the driver's seat, tugging at the door handle, it budged open and he whispered to Ana Gabriel and all the girls for them to get the hell out of there. He hit the pavement, reaching up for Ana Gabriel's backpack, motioning for the others, not even turning to see who was following. Jason had the Buck knife in his belt loop now, carrying it like ole Jim Bowie from the books, and scooted fast through the air pumps and car wash and on behind a Pirtle's Chicken, looking across the big road to an abandoned car dealership. *Mt. Moriah.* Jason figured if they could lose Angel and his buddy, they could maybe stop a car or find another gas station where they could call the police.

Jason and Ana Gabriel hid behind a dumpster outside Pirtle's, catching their breath, and listening for anyone following. There was some yelling in Spanish and the screeching of a car back behind the gas station. They were still too damn close, but here in Memphis, right out by the interstate, there wasn't a tree or a blade of grass to hide behind. They'd need to cross the big road and get on behind that car dealership to get free. He swallowed, motioned to Ana Gabriel, and they both sprinted across the road, waving their arms for someone to stop and help. But no one did. They kept on running toward an abandoned building, racing through busted glass and NO TRESPASSING signs.

"We have to help," Ana Gabriel said, panting and out of breath.

"We will," Jason said.

"The girls will be punished."

"Come on," Jason said. "We'll find them some help."

He ran up behind the car dealership, looking for a place to hide, the asphalt spreading out in the morning light, busted up with weeds poking through the cracks.

"Where's your backpack?" she asked.

"Wasn't time to fool with it," he said.

"So stupid," she said. "Angel promised he'd look out for us. He said he'd make sure we got to our parents. He said his father was taken, too. But that was probably a lie."

"Probably," Jason said. "No time to think on it. Let's keep moving. Always keep moving."

"Your uncle taught you that?"

Jason Colson nodded, pushing in a beat-up metal door, the doorknob long gone, wandering into a wide-open space that had been the showroom at one time, with buckled linoleum floors and ceiling tiles hanging loose or laying broken on the floor. Pipes and wires dangled down, desks and chairs overturned. A yellowed poster for HONDA SALES DAYS 2010 spiraled down to the floor. Half the plate-glass windows were busted, and the air was already hot inside the building. Jason looked out onto the big empty lot, hearing tires squealing and then that goddamn white van came roaring toward them, busting through a chain draped across the entrance and coming to a rest by the showroom. Jason and Ana Gabriel ran far into the back rooms, through puddles and darkness and into the old maintenance building. They stayed there, huddled behind a pile of old tires, and waited.

A few minutes later, after what seemed forever holding his breath, Jason watched as Angel and the tall black man in the duster and the long cornrows strolled inside the showroom. He seemed as cool and collected as if he was about to put a down payment on a new ride.

"The girl is yours," Angel said. "I'll take care of that little boy free of charge."

It wasn't even eight a.m., but Tanner was where dispatch told Quinn he'd be, seated in a spinning barber chair in front of a woman with a big bouffant giving him a trim over his ginormous ears. The woman's name was Faye Randolph, and before she started cutting hair she'd been in the business of breeding Chihuahuas with squirrel dogs. She called them Taco Terriers. But all that had stopped when one of her dogs nipped her next-door neighbor and Quinn had to come out personally to take the report.

"Miss Faye," Quinn said.

"Sheriff," she said.

Quinn stood in the middle of the barbershop, looking over at Brock Tanner, who didn't acknowledge he'd walked in the door.

"Brock," Quinn said.

The man just gave a lazy, uninterested look up at Quinn. The whole idea of him sitting there at Quinn's barbershop, dressed in a uniform with Tibbehah County patches, wasn't exactly pleasing. But Quinn knew he had Brock Tanner's damn number, knowing exactly who he was, why he was put there, and what he intended to do on the job in north Mississippi. Unfortunately, right now he needed the SOB's help.

Quinn's friend Don, who owned and ran the place now, was seated in a far barber's chair, reading a copy of the *Daily Journal* and looking up every few seconds at a TV on top of the Coke machine. The news channel was running a promo for a new show where a woman with bleached blonde hair and lots of gold jewelry talked about the continuing persecution of people of faith. The commercial let the viewers know that they provided Biblical answers for those under attack in today's America.

"We need more people like Miss Ainsley," Faye said. "Y'all know we are all being persecuted for our faith. Just for being white people."

"Is that a fact?" Quinn said. "Has that happened to you? Or you just hearing it?"

"It's all over the news," Miss Faye said. "Haven't you heard? We got to protect our rights or this country's going to hell in a handbasket."

Brock grinned and cut his eyes over at Quinn and then up at the television, the news proclaiming it was CELEBRATE AMERICA MONTH. A flag unfurling and fireworks popping from the screen.

"Can I help you with something?" Brock Tanner said.

"My nephew Jason is missing."

"Yeah, I heard," Brock Tanner said. "Wish there was more I could do. Got some boys on patrol on the lookout for him wandering the back roads. I'll let you know if they spot him."

"I was hoping for a little more than that," Quinn said. "His mother asked y'all to put out an Amber Alert and I hear that hasn't happened yet."

"You got any proof he was abducted?"

"He didn't run away," Quinn said. "He's been missing since after school. He's not the kind of kid to wander off and not tell us."

"But you don't have any proof?" Tanner said, Miss Faye working the scissors across his forehead, his nose long and upturned like an old wooden puppet. "No witnesses? No information? Nope. I can't put out an alert half-cocked. Did he have a fight with his momma or something? That sister of yours can be a real pistol."

Quinn didn't answer. He looked up to the television now with two grown men screaming at each other about how Congress was taking a wrecking ball to the Constitution and how soon gun owners would be targeted. The station went to a commercial break and a woman came on the screen talking about her husband's erectile dysfunction. Quinn walked over to the television and turned it off. He couldn't hear himself think straight through all the damn noise.

"Call me up if you hear something different," Tanner said, closing his eyes as Faye worked. "I got to follow the law. You recall that."

"I don't think you're hearing me, Brock," Quinn said. "I'm asking as a personal favor."

Don looked up from his paper, folding it back, sensing something tense between the two men. He turned to Quinn. "Give you a trim, Sheriff?"

Tanner's eyes opened up, not liking the sound of Don addressing Quinn as sheriff. He opened his eyes briefly and then closed them, looking like a man trying to relax and shut out the intrusions.

"Not today, Don," Quinn said. "Appreciate it."

Faye shaved Tanner's neck, washing the razor off every few swipes. Quinn stood there watching her work until Tanner opened one eye and then snapped it shut. "Didn't get the family connection when I got the picture last night," Tanner said. "That boy sure doesn't look like he'd be your people."

Quinn stepped up to where Faye worked the blade against Brock Tanner's neck. The woman stopping for a moment when she saw what was in Quinn's eyes and put away the blade. Quinn hovered over Tanner, noting the small grin on the man's little mouth, almost like a bass.

"Things always tend to shake out in this county," Quinn said. "You'll find that out soon enough."

"Oh, Lord," Tanner said with his eyes closed. "I know you're not making a threat."

"Count on it," Quinn said.

Quinn winked at Don and nodded to Miss Faye and headed out the glass door, the bell tinkling overhead. Boom sat in the passenger seat of the bright blue Ford Highboy. He had his good arm folded over his big chest, head down where he'd been catching a few moments of sleep. They'd been up all night.

"What he say?"

"He's not gonna help."

"Didn't figure he would."

"What now?"

"Circle back to Caddy," Boom said. "Maybe she's heard something by now."

Quinn cranked the ignition, knocked the truck in reverse, and headed out of the lot. The morning coming up bright blue and spreading across the bottomland of Tibbehah County.

14

"Ana Gabriel's gone and her little brother won't talk," Caddy said. "I know he's scared as hell, but so am I, Hector. I need you to talk to him, make him feel comfortable, let me know what he knows. I'm so damn worried for those kids. Please help me. Please."

She stood with Hector Herrera outside the Huddle House along Highway 45. He'd agreed to meet her there after driving back from an early morning meeting in Tupelo, trying to gather a coalition of priests and pastors to sign a petition for humane treatment for those in federal custody. From behind him, Caddy could see the monstrous Tibbehah Cross, a so-called civic project from last year that would've fed and clothed countless families. Instead, it had become a local joke, the target of a laser light show from Vienna's Place. SIN TODAY, REPENT TOMORROW, the cross would read at sundown.

"I know of six other girls who are gone," Hector said. "Where is the boy?"

"He's here," Caddy said. "In my truck. Will you speak with Sancho?"

Hector smiled at her, placing a hand on her shoulder. "Of course," he said.

Caddy walked back to her old GMC and opened the creaky passenger door. Little Sancho sat sunken down in the front seat playing with the knobs on the radio, cutting between country music and talk radio. Sort of listening in a mindless way—Kane Brown's "Lost in the Middle of Nowhere" and a sound bite of Governor Vardaman talking about Mississippi being on the cutting edge of technology and education. Caddy wasn't sure the boy was even paying attention to the songs or what was being said as three eighteen-wheelers rolled past, back to back to back. The trucks flew south along the highway, passing by the Jericho exit and the Huddle House, the Golden Cherry Motel, and the Rebel Truck Stop that offered "the best chicken fried steak in the South."

Hector's head was clean shaven that day, gleaming like a cue ball, his mustache and goatee an inky black. He wore a LOS TIGRES DEL NORTE T-shirt and khaki pants cut off ragged into shorts with a pair of blue Crocs. His gold cross was huge and heroic hanging from his neck, the chain thick enough to lock up a gate. *"Sancho, es bueno verte esta hermosa mañana,"* Hector said, smiling. *"¿Ya comiste? ¿Estás bien? Escuché que no hablarás con la señora Caddy."*

Sancho shrugged. He kept on spinning the dial on the old radio.

"Esto es muy serio," Hector said. *"Por favor. Debes escucharme, mi amigo."*

When Sancho didn't answer, Señor Hector reached over him and shut off the radio. The man leaned into the open window and rubbed his face with his hands. He looked to be composing himself. More than once this morning, Caddy had wanted to shake the kid until the fillings came loose from his teeth. But you couldn't and she didn't, instead asking plain pleading questions and getting nothing in return. His sister was missing, disappeared, and her son with him. Her only son, her sweet boy Jason, gone off to God knows where.

"No lo sé," Sancho said, shaking his head. *"No lo sé."*

"Por favor. Por favor, Sancho," Hector said. *"Te necesitamos. Tu hermana corre mucho peligro."*

Caddy closed her eyes, praying the Lord would give her strength. She wasn't exactly sure everything Hector was asking but she could tell it wasn't helping. She leaned in the window opposite from Hector and looked across at the boy. Sancho wouldn't give her his eyes, head dropped, black hair scattering in the wind off the highway. He spoke in a low muttering voice, barely understandable with all the noise from the highway.

"Sancho," Caddy said. "Your sister may be in some real danger. Where are they? Where did they go?"

Sancho inhaled a big breath and shook his head. *"Yo prometí. Le prometí a mi hermana que no lo diría."*

Caddy rested her chin on her forearms. "Is she with my son? Is she with Jason Colson?"

Sancho turned his head and looked Caddy right in her eye. The boy started to cry and gave a small nod.

"*¿Y estaban con las otras chicas?*" Hector asked.

"Yes," Sancho said, staring down at his fat little hands, nails bitten down to the quick. "They left after school with the others. Ana Gabriel said they were going to find our mother, who is in jail for nothing. You understand? You must understand, Señor Hector."

"And Jason went with her?" Caddy asked.

Sancho didn't speak. And then turned to look at Hector Herrera. Herrera nodded to the little boy. The boy's chin began to quiver a bit as he wiped the tears from his eyes. "Yes," Sancho said. "Jason Colson is with her. She says he wanted to protect her. Why? What is the matter? Did something bad happen? Something very awful? Are they all dead?"

"No," Hector said. "But we can't find them. Who drove them? Who took them away?"

Sancho swallowed and began to cry, heaving into his hands. Caddy opened up the truck door and crawled inside, the bench seat covered in an old blanket, pulling the chubby little boy close to her. He shook and cried for a while and then finally looked up and wiped his big brown eyes. "You know this boy? The one they call Angel?"

Caddy shook her head, her eyes also filling with tears, and then over to Hector; Herrera had backed away from the truck, turned to stare down at the highway, up and down, north and south, and then back to Caddy. "I know this boy," Hector said. "He is not one of us. His mother worked at the plant. This boy Angel would leave and come home when he needed money. They lived at that place people call the Skid Bucket. There was talk of drugs and threats to another family. I'm afraid he is a very bad kid. *Este chico es malvado.*"

"Where can we find him?"

"I don't know," he said. "Perhaps someone at the trailer park knew him?"

Sancho swallowed and looked to both of them. He shook his head in full agreement. "This boy, Angel," Sancho said. "He is a very big asshole."

Jason knew damn well they were screwed. There were two, possibly three, dudes coming into the old car dealership, kicking over desks, looking in hidey holes and mildewed offices and poking around until they would find him and Ana Gabriel. From what he heard, the tall black dude with the braids went by the name of T-Rex. Angel seemed to be real familiar with the man, saying, "T-Rex coming for you" and "Watch out, kids, T-Rex ready to eat." Angel was a stupid kid and stupid was worse than mean and evil, or maybe it was the glue that tied those things together. At one point, for no reason whatsoever, Angel fired off a shot from his pistol. "Give it up, *chico*. You don't have nowhere to go."

Jason and Ana Gabriel stayed crouched together behind the piles of worn-out tires, not far from a busted window where you could see the interstate and a long stretch of high grass and trees, a meandering creek separating them. Jason nodded to Ana Gabriel, and she saw it, too. Both of them waited for Angel and T-Rex to head back into the showroom, knocking over chairs and toppling partitions to offices, making a whole lot of racket as they worked.

Jason figured Angel thought his bullshit was scary.

"Where did you meet that kid?" Jason said, whispering.

"Church," Ana Gabriel said. "He came to the Catholic church over in Pontotoc."

"Pontotoc?" Jason said. "Yeah. That sounds about right. Those folks ain't right in the head."

Jason reached for his Buck knife and nodded to Ana Gabriel. The girl ran toward the window, jagged pieces of glass sticking out like blades on the lower parts of the frame. Jason knocked the glass shards out with the blade of his knife, but the pieces didn't fall quietly. He followed Ana Gabriel through the opening, careful not to cut himself. The girl sprinted toward the tree line, through the eroded dirt and weeds covered in sacks from Pirtle's Chicken, crushed cans and bottles, rubbers, old lost shoes, and discarded car parts. The girl was fast, already deep into the little brittle trees and briars, the interstate close almost enough to touch, cars zooming along in the first light.

He was almost there when he heard the gunshot. *Twice.* And then a third time. Angel's dumb ass yelling behind them. Jason kept on running, diving into the tree line and searching for Ana Gabriel through the kudzu, weeds, and brush. If they could get down to the creek and up that hill on the other side, they could find the road and try and flag down a car. Or at least follow the road until someone stopped for them.

At first, he couldn't find Ana Gabriel.

She was already down at the edge of the shallow creek, backpack on her shoulder and following the crooked, twisting water. The backpack was bright purple and a hell of a target as she crossed. Jason tried to recall all the things Uncle Quinn had told him about making yourself invisible, finding concealment when you can, cover when it was available. There was little concealment and no damn cover. It was just him and the girl trying to make it through that little slice of nature between the car dealership and the road. It seemed like one of the few spots in Memphis someone just forgot to pave over. A strange little patch of woods in the middle of all that concrete.

He knew they'd have to cross that little creek but he couldn't see a good place to pass without being followed. Not far beyond where they stood, he saw where the Mt. Moriah bridge spanned over the creek and the interstate, a big, empty, shadowed spot below. On the other side of the creek were big rocks and sandy shoals where they could climb out and away from these bastards trying to catch them. Jason now thinking of the other girls, wondering how many of them broke loose and got free.

Jason prayed they were all all right.

When he turned back to the hill, he spotted T-Rex coming out from the scraggly trees. The black duster swirled behind him as he rushed forward and raised a big black pistol in their direction.

"You know, you don't need that shit," Boom said.

"That's what Maggie tells me," Quinn said.

"Your wife is, you do realize, a fucking nurse."

"You once thanked me for not judging you," Quinn said, shaking two pills into his hand. "Appreciate you returning the favor."

Quinn had parked outside the old Calvary United Methodist Church, right next to the cemetery where both his sets of grandparents and his Uncle Hamp and Aunt Halley were buried. It was a small, simple white-frame structure with a slanting silver roof, reminding him a lot of his farmhouse. He'd been attending church there most of his life; his mother, too. He and Maggie married there. Quinn's parents were supposed to get married there before they hightailed it to Vegas. Quinn wondered where in the universe his father, the original Jason Colson, landed after once again leaving Jericho in shame.

"You think you can't face another day without them," Boom said. "But you sure as shit can. Pills, booze. Man, it's like falling into a feather bed. Nothing matters. Nothing hurts. You just kind of live in that in-between world. Everything fuzzy at the edges like an ole-time photograph. Don't you want to be sharp, clearheaded, and see the world? It's about gratitude. About appreciating what God laid at your feet."

"Damn, you sound like Caddy."

"Where she at anyway?" Boom said.

"She texted me she'd call when she can," Quinn said. "Said she's meeting up with Hector Herrera. She believes he might can help her with that kid, Sancho. Boy won't say shit to Caddy, pretends he only knows Spanish."

"He's scared."

"Damn straight."

"Caddy sure Jason's with that girl?"

"Yep," Quinn said, reaching down for his metal thermos. He poured himself a tall cup of coffee and then offered some to Boom.

"I'm good."

"It's coffee," Quinn said, grinning. "Just coffee."

Boom didn't say anything, leaned all the way back in the passenger seat. He cut his eyes over at Quinn and then stared down the long gentle slope of the cemetery, the morning sun coating half of it in bright white light. His people were buried far on the opposite side of town behind a clapboard church in Sugar Ditch where his dad served as a deacon.

"Want to smell it?" Quinn said.

Boom turned to Quinn and yanked the thermos from his hand. He sniffed at the coffee and then handed it back. He didn't say a word.

"Just trying to get through the day," Quinn said. "Get things done. Move ahead without falling. I'm not hurting anyone. I'm not doing anything wrong. This is a doctor's prescription. I was shot. Remember that? Four times in the back."

"Your momma says what Elvis took came from a doctor, too."

"I'm not Elvis."

"You know when we were kids, after your daddy left, I had this feeling that Elvis was your real daddy," Boom said, staring straight ahead. "Your momma had just showed us that movie where Elvis is that half-breed. What's his name?"

"Charro."

"Yeah, Charro," Boom said. "One of those movies

where he don't sing and don't dance. Just shoots guns and looks mean, trying to be Marlon Brando or maybe Clint Eastwood with that skinny cigar. I left y'all's house, your momma going on and on about what a good man Elvis had been, and thought to myself, yeah, that woman, Miss Jean Colson, done messed around with the King of Rock and Roll."

"And then you did the math."

"Yeah," Boom said. "I did. Kind of disappointed me, you being born three years after Elvis died. I figured we might at least be able to get a free tour at Graceland, maybe take out one of his cool-ass dune buggies or one of those pimp-tastic Stutz."

"It's a damn fact," Quinn said, taking a sip of coffee. "I am Jason Colson's boy."

"Oh, I know," Boom said. "I know you. You always been crazy as fuck."

Quinn winked at him, already feeling the pain go away in his shoulders and lower back. He took a deep breath and looked back down at his cell, waiting to hear from Caddy. He snipped the end of a fresh cigar, a new Liga Privada from the humidor Maggie had tried to hide from him, and lit it up with his old busted Zippo. A gift from a Ranger who'd served in Vietnam before Quinn had left for his first deployment a million years back.

"I'll get straight when this is done," Quinn said. "When we get Jason back and all this shit is over."

"You think it'll ever be over, man?" Boom said. "Shit. You know this is Tibbehah County. Been cursed since your people fucked over the Choctaws."

Quinn was about to answer when his cell phone

buzzed. He looked down and saw the message from Caddy. *Can y'all find that crazy old man Manuel? Looking for a kid named Angel in Skid Bucket.*

From up the hill, T-Rex fired once. And then again.

Jason figured the son of a bitch was trying to scare them, not make too much trouble for himself with two dead kids up by the interstate. He told Ana Gabriel to drop that damn backpack and make a run for under that bridge. Jason knew if they could get under the bridge, over that creek, and to the road, they'd be safe. No one could mess with them up there. They'd wave down a car or a truck, and get someone to slow down and help. You'd have to be a real heartless bastard not to help out a couple kids hitching on the roadside. Maybe they'd get spotted by the police or highway patrol. Up on 240 at least they'd get a fighting chance.

Under the bridge, it was dark, quiet, and cool. The creek ran slow and sluggish over stones and little sandbars situated between them and the other side. Jason knew ole T-Rex and Angel would be on them in a minute if they didn't cross. Jason jumped from stone to stone, off a little sandbar littered with busted bottles and plastic bags, Ana Gabriel following him fast, hopping onto another stone, trying to make it across. Above them, Jason could hear the zooming cars on Mt. Moriah Road. Jason had been to enough Vacation Bible School to not like being in the land of Moriah where old man Abraham was about to sacrifice Isaac. Hell, the man had been a hundred years old but was going to do as God had told him.

Putting a blade to his own boy's neck, saved in the nick of time by an angel of God and a stray sheep.

"You're dead," Angel said, yelling.

Ana Gabriel turned, falling from a rock and into the shallow water. Her face gone white as she pulled herself up onto a sandbar and held her ankle.

"Come on," Jason said.

"I can't."

"They're going to flat-out kill us," he said. "I said leave that backpack. Come on. We got to go."

Ana Gabriel dropped the backpack and moved from one rock to the next, gritting her teeth in pain as Angel and T-Rex were on them now, in the darkness and up under the bridge. They yelled and taunted them, Jason pulling Ana Gabriel along the sandy shoal and up into a thicket of trees and kudzu. Uncle Quinn told him to find concealment when he could, make yourself small and quiet, and always be on alert. Something he preached called "situational awareness." They stopped for a moment and Jason looked down at the girl's ankle, all swollen up and thick-looking.

Jason didn't speak, only pointed up the hill where they could hear the cars passing. They moved through the scraggly trees and all that trash thrown out of windows and up into the little patch of woods. The kudzu was wild and thick, clinging to the eroded hillside and up into the tree branches, blinding and choking them, catching Jason's legs as he headed farther up the hill. The heat had come on strong and he and Ana Gabriel were sweating. Jason tried not to look back, only move forward. There was no slowing down now.

He could see the road, a highway breaking off from the interstate, a good place to rejoin the world and be seen. They had to be seen if they wanted to make it out. Jason figured they'd take Ana Gabriel but leave him shot up in the ditch, bled out and lost among the broken bottles, scattered hamburger wrappers, and assorted trash. Keep moving. Don't look back. Keep moving ahead. *Rangers Lead the Way*. They'd never give up, keep moving, keep on the march. His mission was to bring the girl home safe. He wouldn't be Isaac or that sheep his daddy ended up killing. No sacrifices today. No sacrifices today.

Jason reached up to a root, offering a hand to Ana Gabriel. The girl was crying in so much pain, hobbling up that eroded hill. As he looked up, he stared right into the ugly face of the black man with long braided hair.

"Goddamn, kid," T-Rex said. "You sure fucked up."

Jason pulled the Buck knife and stuck ole T-Rex hard in his foot. The man howled as he flew backward, holding his foot, Buck knife down deep into the bone. He fell onto his back, pulling the knife out and tossing it in the woods, coming for Jason now, limping with that big pistol in his hand. Angel and the dude driving the van had Ana Gabriel, pulling her toward the roadside, where the van door lay wide open. She screamed as Angel yelled for T-Rex to jump in with them.

T-Rex limped forward, dragging his foot, and lifted the gun and fired. Jason turned and tumbled down the hill, rolling and rolling in all the grit and trash, lying down deep in a thick tangle of kudzu. Stealth was key when trying to meet up with friendly forces. Keep the mission moving. Be invisible. Be silent.

He heard the gun fire again and more yelling.

And then up on the roadside, the van door slammed and the engine whined, tires spinning in gravel.

Jason stayed in the kudzu trying to catch his breath as the morning light shone through the leaves in broken shafts. Under the blanket of kudzu leaves, he saw broken bottles and a crushed Coors can. He worked to steady his breath and his heart, lay still and quiet. They could still be out there. T-Rex. Angel. Any of those bastards.

And now they got what they wanted. They had Ana Gabriel.

Jason felt like a damn rock was in his throat. He started to cry, crawling loose from the tangle of all that kudzu, and headed up the hill. Along the roadside, the van was gone. Only a pair of thick ruts remained, cars and trucks zooming past, going about their daily business. No one noticed what was going on. No one even seemed to give a damn.

Jason looked along the shoulder of the highway and finally saw the glint of the Buck knife in the sun. He walked over and picked it up by the bone handle. Wiping the blood on his jeans, he slid it back in his sheath, following the roadside to the next exit.

She was gone. Ana Gabriel was gone.

The old man's name was Manuel and he lived at the far edge of Skid Bucket, a collection of three trailer parks north of the Square and east of the Big Black River. Manuel had built a shack fashioned of bricks, concrete blocks, discarded windows, and a roof slapped together from tar paper and old shingles. Everything came from materials he'd scavenged around Tibbehah County. He was old, wrinkled, and toothless, dressed in a white T-shirt that ran down to his knees and thread-worn blue jeans. No shoes. Quinn had seen him many times walking drunk along the roadside. Sometimes he worked as a brick mason or on a paint crew. But mainly the old man sat among his chickens and drank tequila.

When Quinn and Boom drove up, the old man sat by an empty fire pit, tossing stale bread to a giant black rooster.

"This one is very mean," Manuel said. "Make no sudden movements. Show no aggression. This chicken is better than a pit bull. He will growl. Have you ever known a rooster to growl at you like a wild animal?"

"Good to see you, Manuel," Quinn said, offering his hand. "You know my friend, Boom."

The man seemed leery of Boom's prosthetic hand, the sight of it seeming to make him uneasy. He instead raised the tip of his Pepe Lopez tequila in Boom's direction.

"Señor Manuel," Quinn said. "We're looking for a boy called Angel. Used to live up in these trailers with his mother. Do you know who I am talking about? Skinny with a shaved head. He is about sixteen, seventeen years old."

"No, no," Manuel said. "I don't know this boy. Come. Sit down with Manuel. It's early. But not too early for a drink. Come. I have clean cups in my house. Or you can drink from the bottle. I don't mind. I have no germs. Pepe Lopez kills all diseases. He is so very good to your system."

Quinn shook his head. He took a seat in a folding chair by the empty fire pit. The black rooster approaching him, raising its feathers, scratching at the dirt.

"This chicken would walk a hundred miles to fight," Manuel said. "Five hundred if a hen was involved. He has the heart of a champion. The mind of a warrior. Is the sun always so bright? It is hard to see you both. You look as if you have a glowing halo around your heads."

"This boy Angel runs with a man who has a white van," Boom said. "They took some girls from the trailers around here. They promised to take them over to Louisiana to see their folks. The people caught up at the raid out at the chicken plant."

"Yes, yes," Manuel said. "So very unfortunate. Those people were stupid. They thought they could come here, be given decent jobs and live. You don't live in this place. You can exist. Sure. You can make enough change perhaps to get by. But living isn't something you can afford. Are you sure you don't want a sip? It would make a man very happy if you joined me."

Boom shook his head, looking over at Quinn. "I know ole Pepe Lopez," Boom said. "Me and him ain't friends. Last time I shot some tequila, I ended up clearing out a juke joint down in Sugar Ditch."

"I thought you were drinking moonshine," Quinn said.

"All of it," Boom said. "I was drinking all that shit."

"You know my sister," Quinn said. "Caddy Colson."

The old man shrugged. The skin on his neck as tanned and thick as old shoe leather. His eyes black, hard, and bloodshot.

"She has short hair," Quinn said. "Almost as short as mine."

"Sorry, my friend," Manuel said. "I don't know her."

"Yeah, you do, Manuel," Boom said. "She came out here looking for the father of Ana Maria Mata. She and a black girl named Tamika Odum had disappeared. You told her what had happened to Ana Maria's father, run out of town by a couple peckerheads. Remember? Caddy used to bring you food and blankets, too. She looked out for you."

Manuel thought on it, nodding a bit, and then drinking. He nodded some more and drank some more. The tequila seeming to infuse the neurons in his brain with energy. He drank as if the clear white liquid was nothing more than water.

"Perhaps?" Manuel said, wiping his mouth with the back of his hand. "Whatever came of Ana Maria Mata and her father?"

Boom shook his head. "Don't know, man," he said. "We never found those girls."

"You never find them?" Manuel said.

Boom shrugged. He tossed a stray stone into the empty fire pit, sending the rooster in a rage, flaring its wings and rushing toward Boom. Manuel picked up a handful of dirt and sand and tossed it at the old black bird, sending it sprinting away making cackling sounds, almost like it was laughing.

The men didn't speak for a while. Quinn and Boom knew that if the old man was going to talk, they couldn't push it or shake it out of him. They just sat there watching as he drank more and more, the bottle glinting in the early afternoon light. Quinn tried to be patient and controlled, worried sick about Jason and where he might be. Manuel picked up a long, blackened stick and poked in the pit as if there was a fire and it wasn't ninety-eight degrees.

"So those girls are gone?" Manuel said. "They never come back to Jericho?"

"Nope," Boom said.

Manuel nodded. "I don't know this boy Angel," he said. "But there is a man here. A young man who drives a van like you say. Tattoos of *Mara Salvatrucha* on his neck. His name is Ramos and he comes and goes. Comes and goes."

"He lives here?" Quinn asked.

"Sometimes here," Manuel said. "Sometimes in Memphis. He's gone for long weeks in Texas or perhaps to the far reaches of space. We do not know."

"What does he do?" Boom asked.

"He brings young women here to work at that place by the highway," Manuel said. "Only the prettiest and freshest of the young women. Like young flowers, fragrant and new. You know which one? The place where the naked women go up and down on a brass pole. They say it has cold women and hot beer."

"I think it's the other way around," Quinn said.

"Perhaps," Manuel said. "I can't remember things. My head hurts so much in the early morning. That woman by the highway pays for flesh by the pound. The young women find work there. The old women must go to kill and clean the chickens. What else is there for them to do?"

"What else do you know about Ramos?" Quinn said.

"I know he is a criminal," Manuel said. "He wears the MS-13 tattoo on the back of his neck. He is no good. Not a man of value or worth. I worry for these children. Why did you bring so much worry and concern to Manuel this fine morning?"

15

D amn," Donnie said. "What the hell is this place?"

"Amazing Pizza Factory," Akeem Triplett said, as if Donnie had gone soft in the head. "Or couldn't you read the big-ass sign outside?"

"I got your message and saw the damn sign," Donnie said. "But why'd you want to meet here? Ain't exactly a quiet and peaceful place to plan out a robbery."

"Nope," Akeem said, looking over at Rerun, the fat man waiting for his double dip scoops of chocolate ice cream. "But sure is a good place with a lot of noise and energy and shit in case someone wants to listen in on what we got to say. You want some ice cream? I got some vouchers. Strawberry, vanilla, goddamn butter pecan?"

"This your place?"

"This is Mr. Sledge's place," Akeem said, looking down and absently scrolling through his cell. "He bought into the franchise last year."

"Thought he was into funeral homes."

"Mr. Sledge is into everything," Akeem said, grinning. "He's one diverse motherfucker."

The Amazing Pizza Factory was wedged into a storefront down in South Memphis between an empty Toys "R" Us and a Planet Fitness. The wide-open space, once a cavernous old Kmart, was choked with a mini roller coaster, bumper cars, electric go-kart track, and a fifties-style diner and ice cream shop. The ice cream shop was located right by the big chocolate fountain and pizza buffet. But whatever factory made the fucking pizzas looked like it had been in Taiwan and shipped them frozen. The pies sat thin and dry under heat lamps, kids skittering up to the buffet to pile it on their trays along with unlimited soda refills.

"I prefer the catfish buffet at Pap's," Donnie said. "How much y'all pulling in?"

"More than the titty bar we got up on Summer Avenue," Akeem said. "Mr. Sledge thinking about shutting down that place, opening up another Amazing Pizza Factory. What do you think?"

"I think that would make a bunch of grown-ass men cry."

Rerun's fat ass joined them, licking his double scoop chocolate as they walked, following behind, Akeem stopping off every few minutes to check out the different video games. He found one he liked, *The Terminator*, and slid in his game card and picked up a laser gun. According to the screen, more than three million lives had been lost in the damn Robot Apocalypse of 1997. The terminators coming out of all the rubble and busted-ass buildings, Akeem Triplett now being humanity's only hope.

"Shit's coming down in a week," Akeem said, firing off that laser at those wild red-eyed robots. "You ready? You got the truck? You got an exit plan? You got the damn balls to pull this shit off?"

"Don't you worry none about my balls," Donnie said, turning his head. Rerun walked right up on their ass, finishing off that big top scoop, tonguing the whole melting mess like a cow on a salt lick. "My balls are solid brass. How about you, Akeem?"

"Me?" Akeem said. "Shit, man. I ain't going with y'all. You crazy? I got too much to lose. This you, Rerun, and Tyrell's show. I'm just orchestrating the deal."

"Son of a damn bitch," Donnie said. "That wasn't the agreement."

"OK," Akeem said. "That's cool. I'll hand it over to my nephew. He ain't but eighteen but could pull this shit off when he was twelve. Drive in, load up, drive out. You got that? I mean, shit, country boy. This ain't fucking *Mission: Impossible*. You ain't gonna have to rappel your redneck ass on fishing wire, poison folks with blow darts, or commit yourself to a HALO parachute drop. This thing is easy and cool. We got IDs. We got uniforms. We got clearance. *Drive in. Drive out.* No different than ordering up a buttermilk biscuit at Mickey D's. And then you make that sale you promised. You get straight on the money with me and all will be fine."

"Then why not do it yourself?" he said. "If you don't need my country ass."

Akeem Triplett missed the shot and got rushed by a

mess of futuristic robots. *Dead. Game Over.* Akeem slid the electronic ray gun back into the holster and turned around. "Man, you made me fuck up. We lost the goddamn apocalypse and those mechanical motherfuckers gonna fuck us in the ass for a thousand years."

"I said, 'If it's so damn easy, why not do it yourself?'"

"'Cause Mr. Sledge been told me you were the man to see in north Mississippi," he said, pointing a long finger at Donnie's chest. "That you got them connections to make a sale mean and quick for cold hard cash and we all go home happy. High score. Top player. Best of the goddamn best."

"Sure," Donnie said. "OK. You got that right."

"OK, then?" Akeem said, backing off the arcade game, sliding his hands into the pockets of his white silk workout jacket. "Follow me. We need to get your ass straight."

Donnie followed Triplett through all the fat ladies and kids, mouths covered in pizza sauce and chocolate. One black woman had hair the color of dandelions, weaved and braided down her back nearly to the damn floor, and carried a matching purse. There was so much damn yelling and screaming, bing-bonging, electric-zapping, mush-mouthed, grabby-handed fun that Donnie felt like he needed some fresh air and was damn glad when he and Akeem and Rerun headed out the front door.

He followed them into the half-filled parking lot, sun up high and hot over Memphis. Akeem going straight for his electric green Impala, twenty-inch chrome rims, hitting a button on his key chain and opening up his trunk.

"Come on, man," Donnie said. "Not here. Not damn now. What the hell?"

"This is my town, Mr. Varner," Akeem Triplett said. "I am the king of the Southern jungle and know when and where my watering hole is safe. We safe here. Go ahead and get your shit. Just make sure you get that truck."

"I'll get the truck," Donnie said, mumbling. "Shit. Already got the damn truck."

Inside the trunk, Donnie spotted a neatly folded and shrink-wrapped brown UPS uniform, complete with a box of black shoes and a lanyard with an ID badge.

"How about we do this later?"

"Ain't no time like the goddamn present," Akeem said.

Donnie started to turn and walk away, not liking any of this shit, when an MPD patrol car hit the blue lights and sped right toward where he stood with Akeem and Rerun. A voice from a speaker told the men to raise their hands high and step away from the trunk.

Donnie stepped back and did as he was told.

Damn. They were fucked five ways from Sunday.

Caddy tried calling Donnie almost a dozen times but he wouldn't answer, already thinking that maybe Quinn had been right not to trust him. Back in high school Donnie had always been getting girls in trouble, sneaking them out at night and once getting his back window shot out by Skylar Bright's daddy. He raced trucks and sold a little weed. But she'd always felt Donnie had a good heart. Maybe he was always trying to take a short-cut to being a big deal, but when it mattered he'd been someone she could rely on. But here it was, near lunch-time, and all she got from Donnie Varner was a voicemail greeting.

"What is it?" Hector asked, nodding to her phone.

"Nothing," she said. "Just trying to reach a friend."

Hector pulled into the Fiesta Mercado, just north of the Square on Main Street, in front of what had been the Blue Label Grocery, an old cinder-block building painted white with a rusty tin roof. They walked inside the store, which was hot and smelling of tortillas and spices, a portly gray-headed woman named Rosa Jurado working the cash register. Hector introduced them in English and Caddy did her dead-level best to smile.

Mercado was the place, Hector explained, addressing both Caddy and Rosa, that you came for telephone call-ing cards, to wire money back to Mexico, or buy good Mexican laundry detergent or spices they don't carry at the Piggly Wiggly. Dried chilies and herbs. Caddy smiled and looked attentive as her hands shook loose and useless at her sides. Her entire body felt quivery and her stomach queasy.

"No more," Rosa said. "You the first I see today."

Hector said he was sorry.

"I have no customers," she said. "Those who weren't arrested have left town. Or are afraid to be seen in public. I have to pay electricity. I have to pay rent. What's to do? This town is dead."

Rosa Jurado was a plump woman with a pleasant face and dark, intelligent eyes. She had on a plain white peasant blouse, the same as she sold on a rack behind the counter. The store was crowded with soccer jerseys, straw hats, rows and rows of dried beans, spices, and a big cooler of Mexican soft drinks that glowed a Day-Glo green and red.

"Do you know a young man named Ramos?" Hector asked.

"I know many men named Ramos."

"This man drives a white van," Hector said.

"No, no." Rosa shrugged and shook her head.

"He has a tattoo on the back of his neck for MS-13," Caddy said, stepping up beside Hector and sharing the information that Quinn had passed along from the old man. Quinn telling her that he'd do all he could to track him down.

Rosa Jurado stopped smiling. She looked to Caddy and then back to Hector Herrera. She just shook her head.

"Rosa," Hector said. *"Por favor."*

"My son," Caddy said. "He and a boy named Angel took my son."

"Took your son where?" she asked. "In that van?"

"They took him," Caddy said. "Stole him."

"I no longer allow that man or his people to come inside," Rosa said. "He like to scare people. He lets people borrow money from him and then he doubles what they owe. If they don't pay, they get hurt. No. If I am here, he looks at me and runs out the door. He knows not to do his business at the Fiesta Mercado. I wish I seen him. But I have not seen that boy for a long while."

"Do you have children?" Caddy asked.

Rosa didn't answer, pulling on a pair of reading glasses, and shuffling through a handful of envelopes. Her chin had dissolved into her thick neck as she read, eyes away from Caddy and Hector. She checked through a half-dozen envelopes and then set them on the counter, eyes peering over the half-glasses.

"They also took at least six others," Caddy said. "Young girls. Latinas. The oldest was maybe fifteen. They were told they were going to visit their mothers who'd been arrested by ICE. But I don't think that happened. I think they stole these kids. It's happened before. Two years ago, two girls disappeared and were never found."

"I will ask," Rosa Jurado said. "OK? But I want no trouble with that man. Or his people up in Memphis. They know who is illegal. They know these people have nowhere to turn or no one to trust. They will take your money. They will take your children. These are men without heart or honor. They are at his mercy."

"I'm scared as hell, Rosa," Caddy said, reaching across the counter and touching the woman's forearm. "I threw up three times this morning. Please help me."

"I pray for you, Caddy Colson," she said. "For you, your son, and those girls. I pray they are found."

Quinn and Boom pulled up in front of Vienna's Place not long before noon, four hours or so before she'd be opening for happy hour and two-for-one lap dances, according to the sign outside. But Fannie Hathcock's Lexus was parked nearby, along with a few other cars, and Quinn figured she'd be inside, up in her roost, high lights on as her minions detoxed and swabbed down the vinyl furniture and brass poles. The big metal door wasn't even locked as they headed on into the club, not seeing Fannie but instead spotting Nat Wilkins behind the bar, looking up at them both as she unloaded a box of whiskey bottles. "We're closed," she said. "Didn't y'all see the sign?"

"We saw the sign," Boom said. "Came for some personal business with Fannie."

"Personal business," Nat said, acting like she'd never seen either of them in her whole life. Or that she and Boom had grown friendly and intimate two years back when he found out he was trucking drugs for the Syndicate and tried to help Nat bring them down. "What do you want?"

"That's between us and Fannie," Boom said. "Reason it's called personal."

Nat gave the slightest of grins, wearing a small and tight pink Vienna's Place T-shirt with a retro pinup girl in a bikini. Quinn couldn't imagine how a federal agent felt pulling that shirt on every day and having to head on down to Tibbehah County to pour drinks and make small talk with lonely truckers and skeevy businessmen passing through. Nat had her afro full out today, big and wild, looking like a kick-ass black woman from a 1970s B-movie, Nat Wilkins in *Undercover Mama*. Quinn didn't look at her again, passing by the bar and heading up the spiral staircase in the faint red glow of the overhead lights.

"Hold up," Nat said, calling out. "Fannie ain't in yet."

Quinn bounded up the steps anyway and quickly found Fannie seated behind the kidney-shaped glass desk, speaking with two young women in short shorts and tank tops. One of them had on a pair of baby blue flip-flops clasped with a plastic daisy. They looked like they were in a hard, come-to-Jesus meeting with the youth pastor.

"Didn't you hear?" Fannie said. "I'm not in yet."

"I heard."

"But you bust in anyway?" Fannie asked. "Ladies. Give me a second. I think the sheriff here has some personal business with Miss Fannie. Go on and get your pay out from Nat. But if either one of you don't show up tonight, don't you ever darken my fucking door again. I may be charitable but I'm not damn stupid."

"Yes, Miss Fannie," both of the girls said in unison.

Quinn wandered in as they brushed past, both short and blonde, spray-tanned, and smelling like strawberry perfume. One of the girls grinned up at Quinn as if he might sometime soon be a potential customer.

"Aren't you gonna remove your cap?" Fannie said. "I heard that about you. *Quinn Colson sure is a Southern gentleman, won't ever catch him indoors with a hat on his head.* Whether it's down at the Fillin' Station diner or at Sunday service."

"I need a favor, Fannie."

Fannie's face split in a big wide smile, eyes lighting up, shoulders rounded and squeezing her large breasts together, a ruby pendant rocking between them. She leaned into the desk and bit the corner of her lip. "Goody goody," she said. "I've wondered how long that might take."

* * *

"You from around here?" Nat Wilkins asked Boom.

Boom leaned his back against the bar, elbows on the cool marble, looking in the opposite direction toward the empty DJ stand. Two Hispanic women were cleaning chairs and sofas near the main stage, one running a vacuum, the other wiping down the seats with disinfectant spray. Boom figured Vienna's must smell like a damn zoo by the end of the night.

"All my life."

"What do you do?" she asked.

"Drive trucks when I can," Boom said, afraid to turn back to Nat. Afraid like hell someone would see the familiarity that would pass between them. "Fix shit."

"What kind of shit do you fix?" Nat asked.

"All kind of shit," he said. "Mainly engines on trucks. County vehicles and the like. I like to tinker. Play around with things."

"Mmm-hmm," Nat said. "Is that right?"

Boom couldn't see her, but more felt her working behind him. He'd missed Nat like hell. They'd gone through so much together, working to bring down Wes Taggart and J. B. Hood, both of them now dead and long gone.

"Dr Pepper?" Nat asked.

Boom turned around and leaned his left hand on the bar, his prosthetic draped against his leg. He nodded and Nat poured from a spray nozzle, eyes locked and intense. Boom tried to read what she was telling him, looking more bored than scared, setting down a napkin and the drink. "That'll be ten dollars," she said.

"You got to be kidding."

"We don't offer discounts to veterans," she said. "Sorry."

"How'd you know I was a veteran?"

"Lucky guess," she said. "Unless you lost that arm jerking your monkey."

Boom couldn't stop himself from grinning, reaching into his pants and setting down a twenty on the bar. He picked up the cold Dr Pepper and took a sip, eyes wandering up to the catwalk and the office of Fannie Hathcock. He could see two shadows behind the plate glass and he wondered how far Quinn was getting.

He'd told Quinn coming here was a big mistake. A terrible idea. And now standing here, not two feet from Nat Wilkins, he was scared their presence would bring some heat and attention she didn't need.

There weren't a lot of women like Nat Wilkins. Sometimes he missed her so bad it hurt.

She set down his change and turned her back to him.

"Come on, now," Donnie said, hands raised in the center of the parking lot. Heat radiating up off the busted asphalt in South Memphis. "Nothing's going on here. Just hanging out. Ain't no law about hanging with your pals and eating some pizzas. Did you know they have a whole damn roller coaster there? A roller coaster. Inside."

The cop was black, a little younger than Donnie, and a few inches shorter. He was clean-shaven and wearing mirrored sunglasses, muscled and compact, with a small round belly. Man didn't look like he saw any humor at all in the situation.

"Y'all got something good in that trunk?" the cop asked.

"No, sir," Donnie said. "Not really. Just some left-overs from my little girl's birthday party. She ate so much of that chocolate pizza it about made her puke."

"Where she at?" the cop said.

"Oh," Donnie said. "She's inside with her momma. Me and her are divorced, but we try and make a good thing from a bad situation. Long, sad story. Enough for a half-dozen country songs. Appreciate you stopping by. We sure do feel safer with you boys in blue patrolling the streets."

"You mind if I take a look?" the cop asked.

Donnie exchanged glances with Akeem and Rerun. The cocky smiles both dropped as the cop headed toward them, his patrol car still running in the heat of the day. Donnie having half a mind to jump inside the vehicle and head on back to Tibbehah County. He sure as hell didn't need to be caught right here with his pants down and pecker out in front of the Amazing Pizza Factory.

"You boys work with UPS?" the cop said, pulling out the uniform, giving it a once-over and then tossing it back inside the trunk. "Because if you don't, I may need to check up on things. You know you can't have someone roll on up to that facility and fill their damn truck with whatever shit's in the warehouse. Happened last year. Hold on, now. Let me call this in."

The cop stepped away. Donnie looked to Akeem, who had his hands in his pockets. The son of a bitch shrugged. Shrugged! Like it wasn't any big deal some Memphis cop was riding their ass and might fuck the whole damn show.

"Come on now, Officer," Donnie said. He raised his hands. "Maybe we can all come to some kind of agreement. I bet my friend here can get you vouchers for your whole damn family. You have kids? Hell, bring your whole family. Aunties, grandmommas, all them. They can eat pizzas till they damn well bust."

"Like your little girl?" that smart-ass cop said. "The one inside with your baby momma?"

"Just like her," Donnie said. "Her name is Tammy. Little Tammy Jo. She's only six, but holy hell, how that little girl can put that pizza away."

"Hands on the vehicle."

"Shit."

"I said, hands on the vehicle."

Donnie closed his eyes and shook his head. All of this. From FCI Beaumont back to Tibbehah County and now arrested in a pizza palace parking lot. "Son of a damn bitch."

As he let out all his breath and finally laid his hands flat on Akeem Triplett's electric green ride, all of them started laughing. At first it was Rerun's fat ass, then Akeem, and then the fucking cop. The fucking cop laughing harder than anyone, doubling over and cackling, having to run back to his car, bent over and doing a little circle, until coming back and slapping hands with the other two men.

Donnie Varner now felt like the kid at the back of the short bus, taking his hands off that hot car and turning to the three of them.

"Tyrell?" Donnie asked.

The cop winked at him and offered his hand. "I can get y'all in," he said. "But getting out's gonna be y'all's own damn business."

"Ramos?" Fannie said. "Never heard of him."

"He drives for you sometimes," Quinn said. "He trucks over the talent from Houston. You may not know his name. Drives an older white van, sometimes hauls girls from Skid Bucket up to Memphis."

"Skid Bucket?" Fannie said, laughing, tapping her long red nails on her cell phone screen. "Is that somewhere near Dogpatch? Place where Li'l Abner and Daisy Mae knock boots?"

"Ramos and his partner, a kid named Angel, picked up a bunch of kids from behind Tibbehah High yesterday," Quinn said. "One of the kids was my nephew Jason. I'm asking you to tell me how to find him. I don't want any trouble or need to know how you're connected. I just need you to tell me how I can get to him."

"Ramos?"

Quinn nodded.

"I don't know anyone named Ramos," she said. "I don't hire too much Taco Talent at Vienna's Place besides the ladies who clean my toilets. I prefer good old American USDA prime cuts. White or black or brown doesn't much matter to me. Titties are titties. Big, saggy, or itty-bitty. Do you have any idea how many girls around here can't wait to turn eighteen and hop on my brass pole? I don't have to recruit my goddamn talent from Texas or down in

Mexico or anywhere else. No, sir. Miss Fannie does it on the level and legal and if you know anyone says different, bring them straight to me."

"How's Dana Ray doing?" Quinn asked. His mouth felt dry, his right hand opening and closing at his side.

"I fired that little piece of country trash," Fannie said. "Wasn't nothing but trouble to me. She and that short little peckerhead Bradley Wayne. Did you know he went back to Parchman this summer? Got caught over in Grenada robbing a gas station Subway. How goddamn stupid was that? You really think a Subway keeps a few hundred in the till?"

Quinn didn't answer. Both he and Fannie knew why he'd asked about the woman who called Quinn out to an ambush. Fannie only tilted her head, turning back and forth in her swivel chair, closing one eye. Flirting and fucking with him at the same damn time. He didn't have the patience for either.

"Just need some direction," Quinn said. "This is family."

"Kinda funny you coming to me for help," she said. "After all I heard you been saying about me in town. Tramp, criminal, and even an attempted killer. You told plenty of folks I was the one who set you up out on Perfect Circle Road."

Quinn didn't answer. He crossed his arms over his chest. He took a deep breath and waited. For Jason, he could take about anything from that woman. Quinn nodded, controlling his breathing, trying to stay still and direct.

"Don't blame me for all your problems, Quinn Colson," Fannie said. "Between us, I'd start checking the want ads in the *Tibbehah Monitor*. You might could find a little part-time work to pay for that growing family of yours."

"Ramos," Quinn said. "White van."

Fannie ran her tongue over her teeth, nostrils flaring. "Never heard of him, doll," she said. "Sorry you had to sully your reputation by walking through my fucking doors."

Quinn turned to leave. "Don't say I never gave you a chance."

"For what?" Fannie said, laughing. "Fucking myself? No thanks. Good luck finding that kid. Wish I could help."

Quinn walked out from Fannie's glass office and down the spiral staircase to the main floor. Boom pushed himself off the bar and headed toward him, Nat Wilkins nowhere to be seen. They walked out of Vienna's together from the dark haze of reddish light into the blinding sun of the parking lot.

Quinn got in the truck. Boom saddled up in the passenger seat.

"She didn't say shit," Boom said.

"Nope."

"Didn't figure she would."

"I had to try."

Boom nodded and Quinn started the truck, heading on back toward Jericho. Quinn tried Caddy but didn't get an answer. He waited a few minutes and tried again. Nothing.

He and Boom hit the Square, circling the gazebo and veterans' memorial shaded by the old oaks. They passed the old movie theater, Western wear shop, and fluff and fold laundry. Quinn took another turn around the Square, contemplating heading back to the house until they got some news.

The cell buzzed and Quinn picked it up.

"He called," Caddy said, out of breath. "Jason called. He's free and safe. God, Quinn. These people wanted to sell those girls and tried to kill my son."

16

It was twilight when Donnie drove up to Miss Jean's house, sliding out of his daddy's gold GTO and marching up the driveway. Boom stopped him right there and then, the Colson family not needing Donnie Varner's particular brand of crazy tonight. They'd been through too much all night and most of the day until Caddy got that call from Jason. The kid had broken free of those boys he was with and found a ride down to Byhalia, where he called his momma to come and get him.

"Byhalia?" Donnie said. "What the hell's Jason doing up in Byhalia?"

"Obviously you ain't been tuning in, man," Boom said. "Jason ran off with some Mexican kids yesterday after school. He was looking out for his little girlfriend and thought they were all headed to Louisiana where her momma was being held."

"Damn," Donnie said. "I sure wish Caddy had called me."

"She did," Boom said. " 'Bout fifteen times."

"That girl's momma one of those chicken gutters?"

"Yep," Boom said, smoothing down his long black beard while eyeing Donnie to gauge the man's sincerity. "Jason's got too much of his momma in him. Trying to help folks out even when he know it's gonna come back on his young ass."

"Where's Caddy?"

"Where you think?" Boom said. "Rode up to Byhalia with Quinn. I'm sitting here with Miss Jean until they get back. You know what Miss Jean does to Caddy when she gets nervous. Figured it best that she waited here."

"Miss Jean making some margaritas?"

"It's five o'clock somewhere, ain't it?"

"I sure could use one of them right about now."

"How about you head on down to the Southern Star then," Boom said. "Happy hour starting right about now."

Donnie nodded, looking over Boom's shoulder at the front door and then back at his daddy's GTO. Donnie had been riding around in Luther Varner's prize machine like he owned it now. That was the thing about Donnie Varner, he never wanted to work a day in his life. Always acting like the world owed him an ass-pocket full of favors.

"I tried calling her back," Donnie said. "Must have left her a half-dozen different messages."

"She said she couldn't find you," Boom said. "Where you been, man?"

"Up in Memphis."

"Memphis?" Boom said. "What's up in Memphis?"

"Doing a little business."

Boom nodded, still stroking down his beard. Donnie grinned back at him, hands on his waist, wearing an old yellow T-shirt that read DISCO SUCKS. Donnie thinking shit like that was funny as hell.

"I'll tell her you stopped by," Boom said, crossing his arms over his chest.

"So it's like that?"

"Just don't think now is a good time for you to be messing with Caddy's mind."

"Damn, I'm sorry, Boom," Donnie said. "Thought Quinn was Caddy's brother. Not you."

"All the same," Boom said. "Doubt Quinn would feel any different."

Donnie shook his head and rubbed at the back of his neck. His hair shaggy and blond, a dark five o'clock shadow on his face. He turned to Boom, a look of hurt in his eyes. Boom wasn't buying it. Donnie had been pulling that hurt-my-feelings shit since they were twelve. Like that one time Donnie took Boom's dirt bike to go mud riding and then acted all sad when he was caught, talking about how his daddy couldn't afford such an extravagance. Country-ass twelve-year-old Donnie dragged out the word *extravagance* like he'd been itching to use it after hearing it on his momma's soap operas.

"I did my time," Donnie said.

"Didn't say you didn't."

"Don't see the problem, then," Donnie said. "Sorry I'm late to the fucking party. But I didn't get Caddy's message till I was leaving Memphis. Holy hell, man. I can't be on call twenty-four/seven. I got business like anyone else."

"But you can be on call for Fannie Hathcock?" Boom said. "Trading favors and wares out back of the Rebel."

"Who told you that?"

"Ain't nobody told me," Boom said. "I saw it myself."

Donnie nodded. Damn, Boom loved Donnie like a damn brother but he was getting too old for his shit. And he sure as hell didn't want Caddy mixed up with a man like that. Not after all that girl had been through in her life. Her home torn apart in that big tornado that hit Jericho. Watching Jamey Dixon die right in front of her. And then Bentley Vandeven's trifling, privileged ass.

"Don't play with Caddy's mind," Boom said. "This is goddamn Tibbehah. I know what kind of business you got. I heard you been at Vienna's Place enough times to get your punch card filled for a free lap dance."

"Man can't look at titties?" Donnie said. "Maybe drink a cold beer or two? Since when did you get so damn judgy, Boom Kimbrough? I'm trying to make a fresh start. I got all kinds of pressures and obligations riding my ass. You got no idea. Since when are you too damn big to trust a friend? Maybe recognize I got the situation by the gonads and I'm working things out just dandy and fine."

"Always had a way with words, Donnie."

"Can't deny that."

"It's only the deeds that I ain't got time for," Boom said. "How about you come and call on Caddy and the Colsons when you work all that shit out. Until then, you're gonna have to go through me."

"Shit," Donnie said. "Do you even hear yourself?"

Boom nodded back to the gold GTO parked on the street. "See you around, Donnie Varner."

Quinn drove Caddy north, a little more than an hour away to Byhalia and a little restaurant off 78 called the Whistle Stop. The waitresses had been looking out for Jason since he arrived, one of them letting him use her cell and another offering him anything he wanted on the menu. Apparently he'd already downed a large cheeseburger and French fries before they'd gotten there.

It had been a big, emotional hug fest with Caddy when they walked in the door. Caddy cried and held him tight, trying to get the gathering of three other women to take her money for taking care of Jason. They all refused and showed them to a little table away from most of the other customers. Quinn grabbed some coffee, checking back and forth on his cell with Lillie Virgil, Lillie already making some connections with some cops in Memphis to be on the lookout for a van like Ramos used. Although they were all sure he'd dumped it by now.

"You sure you were up by Mt. Moriah?" Quinn asked.

"Yes, sir," Jason said, now eating a slice of chocolate pie the waitresses brought him without asking. "That's where we got loose and broke into that old car dealership."

"You did good," Quinn said.

"I stabbed that bastard right in the damn foot."

"Jason," Caddy said.

"I think he's earned a little cussing," Quinn said.

Caddy nodded, inhaling deeply, eyes closed and hands clasped in front of her. Quinn smiled over at Jason, the little boy still wearing the Buck knife he'd given him on the side of his belt. People in Byhalia, or Tibbehah, wouldn't give him a second glance for carrying that knife.

"You have to find her," Jason said. "I think they caught some of the other girls, too. Me and Ana Gabriel were just running so fast we didn't even look back. I did like you said, looked for cover and tried to make myself invisible. You always told me I had a better chance of living outside a vehicle and I got gone just as quick as I could."

"You did good."

"Lord God," Caddy said. "Please don't ever do that again, Jason. We were so scared and sick with worry. You could've been killed."

"I didn't know."

"But you know what you did is wrong," Caddy said. "You lied to me and took off without my permission. If Ana Gabriel had to go find her mother, you know I would've helped. I would've helped right away. It hurts me that you didn't even ask."

"It all happened real quick, Momma," Jason said. "I'm sorry. I'm so sorry."

Quinn turned his head from the table, steam rising from his cup, as he spotted a black Dodge Charger zoom in and wheel hard into the lot. Lillie Virgil crawled out, dressed in a fitted white top, blue jeans, and boots. She had her Marshal's badge hanging around her neck and

Sig on her hip. As she walked toward the front door, she took off her sunglasses and headed on inside.

"Damn, kid," Lillie said, standing over their table. "I heard you stabbed a pimp."

"Yes, ma'am."

"Don't think they make a merit badge for that," Lillie said. "But they should."

Lillie sat down and reached out for Caddy's hand, squeezing it and smiling at her. Lillie shook her head and pointed her index finger right at Quinn.

"You coming with me back to Memphis?" Lillie asked.

"Planned on it."

"Good," Lillie said. "Time to hunt down these rotten motherfuckers. Anyone takes my godson and I'll bag 'em and tag 'em before they know what's coming."

Jason looked up, straight-faced, and gave a big nod.

They locked Ana Gabriel and two other girls in a windowless brick building along with the white van. One of the other girls, Marisol Gonzalez, kicked and screamed at the metal door long after Ana Gabriel and the other girl, Alida, had quit trying. The side door of the van was wide open, the two of them resting on the pillows and blankets the other girls had left. Marisol finally quit the banging and fell to a heap on the concrete floor, sobbing.

"What happened to the others?" Alida asked.

"They got away," Ana Gabriel said. "Jason got away, too. He will find help. And they will come for us."

"He is your boyfriend?"

"He is a friend who is also a boy," Ana Gabriel said. "But yes. He is."

"When you both ran, I became frozen," Alida said. "I was paralyzed. I couldn't move or scream. When I finally was able to control myself, Ramos was on me. He's the one who did this to me."

She pulled back the long hair from her face, a dark purple welt against her temple. "He said if I screamed or moved again, he would shoot me. Why are they doing this? What are they going to do with us?"

"Jason said they were going to sell us," said Ana Gabriel. "He said the tall black man with the braids was going to take us somewhere. To make us all whores in cheap motels and the back of trucks."

The girl, a few years older than Ana Gabriel, looked as if she might get sick. She got onto her knees and then crawled out of the van, walking to a far corner of the big concrete room. Her shoes echoed on the floor against Marisol Gonzalez's endless crying.

Jason would get back to his mother and Señor Herrera and both of them would find out what this boy Angel had done. How could she have been so stupid to trust a boy she barely knew and who so many had warned her about? They called him a drug dealer, a thief, but he spoke to her with such kindness. Saying his mother had been taken, too, and if they didn't help their families they would be sent back to Mexico. How could she not help? How could she not act? She imagined her mother alone and in a place very similar to where she was now. Locked away and caged like an animal. Hungry, cold, and ashamed. Why was there so much shame in something you didn't do?

"I'm very hungry," Alida said. "When will they come back?"

"I hope never."

"And then we will die here or be sold to the man with the long braids?" she said. "So they could turn us all into whores?"

"This place is impossible to escape," Ana Gabriel said. "It's hard for me to walk with this ankle and I believe I might have broken my hand pounding on that door. We can yell and we can scream. But they've taken us somewhere far away with no one around. All we can do is wait."

"And trust your friend will find his way home."

"He will," Ana Gabriel said. "He has a very strong home and a very strong family. Would you like to pray? Perhaps that would make us feel better."

"We are not alone," Alida said, taking Ana Gabriel's hand. "We must never believe that."

17

By daybreak in Memphis, Lillie and Quinn had a pretty damn good handle on what was going on. They'd nailed down Ramos as being Ricardo Ramos, a known MS-13 shitbird who operated out of Houston and Memphis and Atlanta. His little brother, Angel, was lesser known since he was a juvie but he'd still had time to rack up a nice little record since moving to Mississippi two years ago. He'd been in Pontotoc and Lafayette County, going to school for a few months in Southaven. Mainly the Ramos Brothers ran drugs and girls. The older brother was a known associate of a fella called El Jaguar, who ranked high on the U.S. Marshals' Most Wanted. Lillie didn't have to do much to move finding the Ramos Brothers to a top priority.

Quinn and Lillie had spent most of the night running up to North Memphis and over to Summer Avenue to check in with some informants. Quinn was impressed, but not surprised, that Lillie had the town wired.

"Selling out your own people is the lowest of the fucking low."

"We should know," Quinn said. "A Tibbehah County specialty."

"You hear why the Ramos Brothers ended up in Tibbehah?"

"Why do you think?" Quinn said.

"I can't stand that damn bitch," Lillie said, popping a stick of gum in her mouth. "I'll shoot off fireworks on the Jericho Square when they flush her big-titted ass down the commode."

"Ramos Brothers," Quinn said. "Sounds like a car dealership."

They were on Lamar, headed south from South Parkway, hitting that big epic lonely stretch of broke-ass motels, shuttered fast-food franchises, a couple all-night gas stations, and a big intermodal facility with thousands of Conex containers coming and going on semis and trains. Lillie turned into a dimly lit motel, the sign outside offering Elvis Week Specials, Memphis's finest barbecue, and *de*-luxe rooms with hot tubs.

"Who's your guy?"

"My guy is a gal," Lillie said, double-parking in a slot behind the pool. The water glowing a bright shimmering green in the early morning light.

"Working girl."

"Mm-hm," Lillie said. "Hardest working girl in town. She's the CI from my partner, Charlie Hodge."

"You know Elvis's right-hand man was named Charlie Hodge?" Quinn said.

"You're starting to sound like your momma, Quinn Colson," Lillie said, chewing her gum, tapping out a message on her cell. "Elvis on the brain. You can stuff all the romance down on South Lamar into a fucking thimble. Worst place for a working girl. Sadists, pedophiles, and killers prowling this road. Working girl prays like hell she'll just make it through the goddamn night."

"Looks like some of the working girls are dudes," Quinn said, nodding up to a broad-shouldered woman with a square jaw and an ill-fitting blonde wig.

"Oh, yes," Lillie said. "When I was a rookie, patrolling down here, we busted this big old corn-fed country boy from Red Banks. He'd come on up to the city to unwind and find a little loving, swearing to us we'd just rolled up on a little fun between him and his date. When we got them out of his truck, my captain yanked down his date's skirt to prove that hooker was really a man. That old country boy fainted out cold. Took us twenty minutes to revive his sorry ass."

Quinn laughed and reached for a Styrofoam cup of coffee. The light was coming up a dull, hazy gray over the old motel and down Lamar Avenue, the potholed road that led south out of Memphis and on to Tupelo, eventually back to Tibbehah County. He promised Jason he'd bring Ana Gabriel back and he wouldn't leave until they found her.

"How's Rose?" Quinn said.

"Wondering why her mother works so damn much," Lillie said. "I promised her I'd take her to the zoo this weekend and maybe over to the Pink Palace. They're showing a movie about dinosaurs on that IMAX screen. She's obsessed with dinosaurs these days. I've had to watch fucking *Jurassic Park* so many times, I hear that theme song in my head. I'm thinking I'm no different than those crazy folks trying to corral those animals, get them back in their cages, and out of harm's way. I swear to you, Quinn, some of these people we have roaming free out here need an electric anal probe to get them to pay attention and get their mind right."

"You don't mean that," Quinn said.

"Hell I don't," Lillie said. "You know anyone in law enforcement who thinks they're communing with God's great and wonderful master plan? We're just running a zoo that most civilians don't even know they're sharing with the animals."

Quinn noticed a slim, brown-headed girl coming down the steps of the motel. She had her hands in the pockets of a gray hoodie, her hair greasy and slicked back, eyes darting around the parking lot. She didn't look like she'd quite reached eighteen.

"That her?"

"Don't know," Lillie said. "Never met her."

She flashed her lights, reminding Quinn of times long ago when he and Lillie met up with girls working for Johnny Stagg at the Rebel. Those days almost seemed quaint and innocent compared to what they had now. At least with Johnny Stagg, you knew where you stood.

Lillie let down her driver's-side window. "Brandy?"

The young girl nodded and leaned down toward the window.

"Mr. Charlie said you had cash."

"Yes, ma'am," Lillie said. "Heard you know a little about where those Ramos boys keep house up here?"

The girl had big brown doe eyes, her face scrubbed of makeup but still looking dirty. The girl reminded him of Caddy when she first went off the rails, dead to the damn world and without any fear. Feeling no pain and not giving a damn about herself or her brother when he was sent over to the other side of the world to make America a safer place.

"One of their buddies sliced up a friend of mine."

"Sorry to hear it," Lillie said, reaching into her shirt pocket for a wad of cash. "You got a fucking address, Brandy?"

Fannie was waiting for Brock Tanner as soon as he walked out of room twenty-three of the Golden Cherry Motel. He wasn't dressed in the sheriff's uniform he'd stolen from Quinn Colson, instead looking like a goddamn insurance salesman in a red polo shirt and pleated khaki pants. Leaving the room with two of her top girls with a little wave and a joke, closing the door with a soft click as if not to disturb anyone. Tanner about jumped out of his pants when he spotted Fannie sitting on the hood of her white Lexus, smoking down the back half of a cigarillo, looking at him up and down, taking in his whole sorry ass.

"They're good, aren't they?" she asked. "Belinda and Destiny could make a dead man raise up his head."

Tanner didn't answer, a pair of sad brown loafers in his left hand, red polo untucked and wrinkled. His black hair unplastered and sticking up wild over those damn ears that reminded her of two wide-open car doors.

"You sure aren't shy about calling on room service," Fannie said. "First it was a black one. And then it was a black one and a white one. And then you wanted three girls jumping on beds and fighting it out with pillows. Do you have any fucking idea how long it took to clean up all those feathers?"

"Something you need, Miss Hathcock?" Tanner said.

"'Miss Hathcock'?" Fannie said, placing a hand to her chest, her breasts pointed and proud at the world in a scoop-necked green silk top. "I've never asked you for much, Brock Tanner, besides staying the hell out of my goddamn way. And in return, I've kept you and your savage thieves neck-deep in old whiskey and young poontang."

"Not here," he said, pulling the keys from his pocket and walking over to a new black Jeep parked by the empty swimming pool. "Not like this."

"Good a time as any," Fannie said, spewing smoke out of the corner of her mouth. "How about you come on in my office and we'll talk it out."

Tanner laughed and shook his head. "Me seen across the street with you?" he asked. "Have you lost your damn mind?"

Fannie slid off the hood of her Lexus and pressed unlock on her car doors. She pointed to the passenger side before she crawled behind the wheel and pulled on a pair of Chanel sunglasses, taking the hard, blinding light out of her eyes.

Tanner stood there for a moment, Fannie having half a mind to crank the car and run his ass over. Instead, she clicked her long red nails on the wheel and then lifted up her left hand and crooked her index finger.

Brock Tanner did as he was told, crawling inside to all that fine wood and rich leather. The inside of the vehicle smelled like goddamn money, all the wealth and finery and fucking power that Fannie Hathcock deserved.

"Which one did you like best?" Fannie said.

"Oh, I don't know," Tanner said, face coloring, eyes glancing back in the rearview. "Does it matter? Didn't mean anything. Not to me. Just a little fun is all."

"That's funny," Fannie said. "Destiny told me that you promised you were going to leave your wife as she walked your bony white ass around on the carpet in a choker and dog leash. Don't you dare tell me that you were lying to one of my fine ladies. It just might break her heart."

Tanner swallowed, his neck as long and skinny as Ichabod Crane's, arms ropy and pale as he turned back to look at Fannie. The man was trying, but failing a great deal, to gain some kind of foothold in their conversation. "What do you want?"

"Don't you worry, Brock," Fannie said. "I'm not in the shakedown racket. We didn't record any of your bowwow fun at the Golden Cherry. That would be unethical as hell. Since I'm the queen of Mississippi hospitality, how would that look to my customers? They'd ruin my fine ass on Yelp."

Tanner waited. His black eyes narrow pinpoints, looking uncomfortable in all that smoke. Fannie finally leaned forward and crushed out the cigarillo.

"What?" Tanner said. "Get to the goddamn point."

"Our friends down in Jackson have a problem," Fannie said. "They've asked me to be in touch, as going through the governor would be unseemly as hell. Vardaman has fish to fry and fuck. Same as you."

"I know what you want," Tanner said. "It's been discussed. You don't need worry your pretty red head about any of it."

"I don't give a shit about it one way or the other, but the governor asked for it special," Fannie said, sliding down the windows, letting the last traces of smoke whirl and spread out into the hot morning. "And this is my fucking show and my fucking county. Got that straight? 'Cause I sure would hate to end these little slumber parties of yours. Pigtails, pom-poms, and pussy ain't free for the taking, Sheriff."

"Won't be long," he said. "OK? We're working on it."

"That goddamn wannabe Cesar Chavez in Crocs is making it hell for some folks in Jackson," Fannie said. "Make sure that stops now. Until then, you're cut off from the Golden Cherry, from my girls, and from any dog walking. Understand?"

Tanner didn't answer, reaching for the door. His face and jug ears lit up in a bright red.

"I said, do you understand Miss Fannie?"

Tanner swallowed again, opening the door. "Yes, ma'am."

"You mind hanging back while the Feds take care of the Ramos Brothers?" Lillie asked. "Or will your masculine pride be too injured?"

"You and Charlie Hodge?" Quinn said. "Sorry. It still makes me think of Elvis. He brought Elvis bottles of Mountain Valley water and silk scarves."

"Me, Charlie Hodge, and your pal Holliday," Lillie said. "Since we can't work with the local assholes down in Tibbehah, the report had to originate with the Feds. Holliday, God bless his weird tattooed ass, made quick work of the warrants. The Ramos Brothers might actually help us grab El Jaguar by the nutsack."

"My momma says you cuss too much."

"And Miss Jean thought Priscilla was a virgin until her wedding night."

"Swears on it," Quinn said.

He and Lillie had been on the warehouse for the last two hours, twice spotting Angel Ramos coming and going in a Toyota Tundra, navy blue, busted up and dusty. The first time he'd come back with sacks from McDonald's. But he was gone again, leaving the warehouse back lot empty and wide open. Lillie figured it was best to come in with extra firepower just in case. "I don't want to skip into some Cartel fuckfest with my thumb jacked up my ass," she'd said.

The warehouse was about as unremarkable as it gets, blond brick, two loading bays shut off with an accordion gate. Two metal entry doors out front and a single door in the rear. Two security cameras by the front doors. At some point, the old building had several big arched windows, but they had been walled off in the same blond brick, creating a bunker effect to the whole place. Lillie said it was registered to a place called Mid-South Enterprises, LLC. But a little further digging showed the company and all its properties and assets had been in Chapter 7 for years, the property up for sale for almost as long.

"I liked that girl," Quinn said. "Brandy."

"Yeah," Lillie said. "She was a real fucking hero for two hundred bucks."

"Led us to the Ramos Brothers."

"I saw you got that Beretta on your hip."

"Wouldn't feel right if it weren't," Quinn said. "Same as putting on pants."

"You drop one of these turds and you might have to hire me back," Lillie said. "Feds are a little nitpicky about shit like that."

"I'll hang back," Quinn said. "Finish this fine Pirtle's chicken biscuit and cold coffee."

"Thatta boy," Lillie said. "Knew you had it in you."

Forty minutes later, coming up on 0800, they moved two blocks away into a cleared lot and parked beside a black SUV as a silver sedan quickly pulled up beside Lillie's Charger. A medium-sized man with gray hair and a thick gray beard got out of the sedan. Jon Holliday followed from the black SUV.

"Back door swings out and has a keypad lock," the gray-headed man said. "No cameras. We bust in and move in fast. You said you think it's only the two of them?"

"May only be one of them," Lillie said. "Or none of 'em."

"How many girls?"

"My nephew said there were about ten of them in the van," Quinn said. "Don't know how many got free yesterday."

The gray-headed man nodded and looked to Quinn. Lillie introduced him as her partner, Charlie Hodge. Quinn decided it would be an inopportune moment to ask him about having a famous namesake.

"I knew your daddy," Charlie Hodge said. "Long, long time back."

"How's that?" Quinn asked.

"Conversation for another time," Hodge said. "You wouldn't believe it if I told you."

"Lillie won't let you come along and play?" Holliday said.

"Says it may complicate matters."

"Not for me," Holliday said. "Officially you're still the sheriff of Tibbehah County. We're just acting on a tip you provided."

"Appreciate that."

Holliday nodded and winked back, the four of them crossing a barren South Memphis street on over to the warehouse, finding a narrow path lined with rusting chain-link fence overgrown with weeds and trumpet vines. The trumpet vines pretty in the early morning heat, growing hearty and free from the cracked asphalt.

Charlie Hodge had brought a nifty little entry tool and a sledgehammer and carried them both as they found an open space in the fence and crossed to a back door. As they got close to the door, he handed the sledge to Quinn and slid the entry tool against the lock.

"Figure you've busted in a few doors, Ranger."

"Just a few."

"Yeah, right," Hodge said. Lillie had told him that Hodge had been a Marine back in the seventies. He didn't look a hell of a lot older than Quinn's father.

Quinn hammered the tool, Hodge trying to rip the door open. Quinn hammered it again, the tool sinking hard in the metal, getting a solid hold of the door. Two more strikes and they were in, moving into darkness, Lillie turning on a flashlight over her Sig, moving and communicating through the open space, Holliday identifying them as federal officers.

They crossed through one door, and then another, and into an empty warehouse with skylights. They found an abandoned office area toward the front door and two blue doors padlocked from the outside. Charlie Hodge lifted the tool and broke through the chains, moving fast and hard into a cavernous brick warehouse with a lone white van inside.

A black man with long, woven hair came toward them, hobbling on a bandaged foot. As he reached for a pistol in his sweatpants, Quinn swung the sledgehammer into his ribs, dropping him fast and hard.

Somewhere on the far side of the warehouse, they heard a toilet flush.

Another man, shirtless and wiping his hands on a towel, came from the bathroom and looked up in surprise. Lillie, Holliday, and Hodge all had their guns trained on him. He dropped the towel and raised his arms. His flat, skinny chest was decorated with black tattoos, the image of a horned devil on his belly, MS-13 inked on his left arm. It was Ricardo Ramos.

"Where's your brother?" Lillie said.

He didn't answer. Lillie walked up hard on him and took his legs out with her shotgun, sending him onto his back. *"Pájaro de mierda,"* she said. Quinn wasn't sure if *shitbird* was an insult in Spanish, but it sounded like it should be.

Quinn and Holliday walked over to the white van, hearing nothing but the moans of the pimp who had tried to shoot Jason. Holliday slid back the van door and they saw three young girls shaking and huddled together, backs pushed against the front seats.

Quinn recognized one of the girls from the picture on Jason's phone.

"Ana Gabriel?"

The girl's eyes were huge. She was trembling but slowly nodded.

"I'm Quinn Colson," he said. "Jason's uncle."

The chicken plant—HILL COUNTRY POULTRY INC.—had opened back up three days previous, but Hector Herrera had not returned until this morning. He parked his truck near the security gate, the main building surrounded by chain-link fence topped with concertina wire, and smoked several cigarettes while scanning the property for familiar faces. The company had given statements about firing plant managers and said they'd never condoned hiring illegal immigrants. It was just talk, lies that no sensible person believed but that the community accepted.

Hector had worked in plants like this for more than

twenty years in Texas and Louisiana, but he'd never been in a state more corrupt than Mississippi. His people, the hundreds of workers who made so much money for the plant owners but earned little in return, had been taken and carted off like animals. Few in the community seemed to realize, or care, they were even gone.

He lit another cigarette and leaned against the tailgate of his truck, feeling blessed that his friend Caddy's prayers had been answered. He knew her son had been returned and prayed that the other children were safe, too. The arrests at the chicken plant had caused disruptions in families and chaos in their little community, exposing the weak to thieves and criminals.

The morning had grown hot and sweat dripped in his eyes as he held up a camera with a long lens and took photos of several men and two women who worked as managers. The thieves in Jackson had done nothing to change the business, only harass and expel those who dared raise their voices. He wiped the sweat with his forearm and snapped off several more pictures of a grouping of foremen by the intake dock, where the chicken trucks had already started to arrive. White feathers stirred in the gravel lot.

When the arrests first took place, he'd heard from Tibbehah's citizens that what happened to the people at the plant had been wrong. So many of those arrested had been in the county for years and years, making this place their home. They shopped on the town square, attended many churches, and had their children enrolled in school. Despite what anyone argued, they were here and living the American dream.

Hector scanned the loading dock through his camera lens, looking for more details. He didn't hear the heavy-set man with wild white hair and gold glasses when he first approached Hector. The man wore a blue security guard uniform and held a walkie-talkie. "You can't park here."

"It's a public street," Hector said. "I can do as I please."

"Well," the man said. "Don't be taking pictures of the plant. You can't be going and photographing a private business. Do it again and I'll call the sheriff on you."

"Please," Hector said. "Please do. My attorney loves when I get harassed."

"You that fella Herrera?" the man said. "Ain't you? Haven't you caused enough damn trouble? You're the reason they was forced to round up them illegals. If you'd just kept your damn mouth shut, it'd be business as usual."

"For men and women to work for next to nothing?" Hector said. "In dangerous and filthy conditions? Let me ask you something, sir. Would you eat a chicken that was slaughtered here?"

The man looked as if he might be choking on a jagged stone and then averted his eyes, heading back down the driveway to the little guard shack. Herrera stayed at the tailgate, taking more photos until the buses began to arrive. At first, he thought perhaps this was another raid, rounding up all new employees who'd just started work-ing at the plant. But these buses were different, old, painted a flat white, and marked on the side NORTHWEST MS CORRECTIONAL.

Hector watched as the four buses parked side by side and men in orange uniforms were marched out onto the loading dock, prodded along by guards holding shotguns.

The sons of bitches hadn't hired local citizens at all. They were trucking in private prison labor.

Hector took photos until two more men approached the guard shack. The man in the gold glasses pointed up the hill to Hector's truck. Hector dropped the camera in the passenger seat and crawled behind the wheel. He'd gotten what he came for.

He had so many to call. So many to inform of the situation. Attorneys, journalists, families of those taken. These men who owned the plant had no honor or shame.

Hector drove out of the Johnny T. Stagg Industrial Park and headed back toward the town square. As he sped past that long vacant stretch of road back to town, he began to scroll through the names of television stations in Tupelo and Memphis on his phone. They had covered the raids and later reported without questioning the official lies that the plant would reopen for local citizens in need of work.

He was about two miles from town, passing a stretch of grazing cattle and a few sweet potato fields, when he saw the blue lights flashing behind him. At first, he thought the patrol car was trying to pass, speeding up closer and closer in his rearview mirror. But then the sheriff's office cruiser just stayed there, closing in within an inch or two of his rear bumper, hanging there, until Hector slowed and moved toward the side of the back road.

The patrol car followed. And as he jammed the truck into park, another deputy's car approached from the north, moving close to the front of his truck and boxing him in. The windows were down and the road silent. The blue lights flickering and flashing as two deputies, one from each car, got out and approached him.

Hector placed his hands on the wheel and waited.

"Please step out of the vehicle," said one of the deputies.

"Sir," the other one said. "Hands up, move slow and easy."

"Can you at least tell me what I have done?" Hector said. "I have done nothing. You have no right."

The men didn't answer. Both had their right hands resting on the butts of their pistols, watching from behind dark sunglasses.

"I wasn't speeding," Hector said. "Wait. Do you wish to see my license? I have insurance as well. Please. Tell me what you want."

"Get out or I'll drag your sorry Mex ass out," one officer said.

"Excuse me?"

The officer reached for the truck door and wrenched it open, yanking Hector from his seat, ripping his T-shirt at the neck and pulling him tumbling to the ground. His Crocs fell off his feet as he fell onto his side and looked up into the men's grinning faces.

"He has a gun," one of the men shouted. "Look. Look. He has a gun!"

18

Donnie had to hand it to ole Fannie Hathcock. As far as titty bars went, Vienna's was a first-rate, top-shelf joint. It may have seemed like nothing but an old metal barn out back of a truck stop, but step inside and your ass was down a magical rabbit hole. The pulsing music, the soft red glowing light, the comfy leather furniture and long onyx bar was something out of a cellblock wet dream. She poured drinks straight and uncut and offered up a stable of women that looked as if they'd stepped right out of the pages of a vintage *Playboy* magazine. Donnie should know. Despite Luther's recent return to the cross, his daddy had every issue from 1962 onward wrapped in plastic and organized by date in his work shed. *Damn,* Donnie thought, holding a cold beer as he watched two women going at it in a brass birdcage. *Not a bad place to pass a few hours.*

"Miss Fannie wants to see you," said a gorgeous black

woman with a big, bouncy afro. She had high cheek-bones, large green eyes, and the longest legs he'd ever seen. Whoever she was, she looked too damn good to be working it down in Tibbehah County. "Up the spiral staircase and to the left. Can't miss her."

"Hard to miss Fannie," Donnie said. "Say, what's going on tonight? Y'all offering free draft beer and chicken wings?"

"Oil wrestling," the woman said. "Or as you country boys call it, rasslin'."

"Y'all sure do draw in the true sports fans," Donnie said.

"That big table behind you flew in from Shreveport. Rotary Club special," she said. "Got bets laid down and everything."

Donnie turned back and watched a crew of gray-heads in cowboy hats with half-nekkid women sitting on their laps. The men had dollar bills fanned out in their hands like a deck of playing cards, the women taking turns trying on their hats.

"Those old coots should be ashamed of themselves," Donnie said.

"Hmm," the woman said. "You really think so? Step inside Vienna's and you leave any shame at the door."

Donnie looked the woman up and down and took in a deep breath, shaking his head. "You seem too damn smart for this side hustle," he said. "What's a quality woman like you doing in a place like this?"

"Upstairs to the left, Mr. Varner," the woman said, winking. "Fannie doesn't like it when you're late."

Donnie nodded and stood up, his legs aching and feeling a bit wobbly. He'd been sitting in front of that main stage for the last two hours, showing up early after Boom turned him away from Miss Jean's house, deciding to have a few cold ones till he met up with Fannie Hathcock. It still chapped his damn ass how Boom had treated him. If he only knew the shit he'd been through since getting back to Jericho.

As he moved on past the old coots in the cowboy hats, Donnie pulled a shot of tequila from an old man's shaking hand. The old fella didn't seem to mind, as his bald head was buried between the biggest set of titties Donnie had ever seen in his life.

Donnie tossed back the tequila and set the glass on a table before taking the spiral staircase, round and round through that weird red light, up to Fannie's office.

Fannie Hathcock wasn't at her desk but instead at a little grouping of purple velvet chairs and a sofa. A big man Donnie hadn't seen before, a muscle-bound Indian with long black hair pulled into a ponytail, was sitting with her. His black eyes turned to Donnie as he entered, looking cool as an ice cream social in a black suit and skinny black tie, Fannie Hathcock laughing at something he said while holding a tall glass of champagne.

"Sorry to interrupt," Donnie said.

"No interruption," she said. "This is Sam. Sam, this is Mr. Varner."

That big Indian nodded in his direction. Big silver rings on his fingers and a belt buckle inlaid with turquoise. *Sam.* Hell of a name for an Indian.

"Smells good in here," Donnie said, taking a seat with them, a round glass table between them. "What is that, patchouli?"

"Pussy and cash money," Fannie said, opening up a silver case and extracting a skinny brown cigar. "Best scent in the world. Midnight Man said you wanted to talk some business. What's on your mind, doll?"

"You sure get right to the matter," Donnie said, crossing his legs and pulling a pack of American Spirits from his shirt pocket. "Well, I just met up with some fellas out of Memphis who say they represent the interests of Marquis Sledge. Y'all might have heard of Mr. Sledge. He runs a string of funeral homes and jerk shacks down in South Memphis. Ring any bells?"

"Maybe," Fannie said, tilting her chin and blowing smoke up the ceiling fan. Sam the Indian didn't answer, still and silent as if made of ancient cypress.

"Well," Donnie said. "I'd like to know if I can throw in with them."

"You want me to vouch for the character of a bunch of thieves?"

"That's about the tall and short of it," Donnie said, blowing out a big cloud of smoke. "I just wanted to know if Marquis Sledge and his people can be trusted. See, I'm taking one hell of a risk as I've only recently been released from incarceration and have little or no interest in returning to watch my cellmate read poetry on the commode. Man preferred the works of Lord Byron to Emily Dickinson. Or so I was told. I kind of like being here, among civilized people drinking good liquor and watching nekkid women wrestling in hot oil."

"Oil wrestling is only once a month," Fannie said. "Always on the last Saturday."

"Y'all know these folks?" Donnie said. "Or should I be watching my damn back so as not to get cornholed?"

Fannie wet her lips, cutting her eyes over at Sam the Indian, and then back to Donnie. The woman had on some kind of fancy-ass, short silver dress, the hem riding up high on her shapely pale legs. "Sam?" she said. "You mind leaving me and Mr. Varner for a moment? We need to have a heart-to-heart."

Sam didn't say a word, only stood, looking even taller and meaner at full height, walking from the room and out the door without a glance back. Guess everything couldn't be said straight and true out in the open. Donnie took his warm seat and leaned back in the comfortable leather, hearing the pulsing music from down on the floor, the DJ promising that the oil wrestling match would start shortly. "Pour Some Sugar on Me" playing loud and proud.

"And just what does that fella do for you?"

"He's on loan," Fannie said, taking a long drag on her cigar, sharp green eyes taking him all in, mouth popping into a big O as she exhaled a smoke ring. "Makes sure everyone plays fair up in north Mississippi."

Miss Fannie kicked off her fancy high heels and stretched her million-dollar legs up on the glass table. Her toes so perfect and manicured, little nails painted a lovely shade of red. "Yeah, I sent Sledge your way," Fannie said. "You said you need guns. Right? Isn't Sledge gonna get you guns?"

"Enlighten me," Donnie said. "Just how do you profit

off this here deal? A woman like you doesn't set something in motion unless there's something in it for her."

Fannie nodded and wiggled her cute little toes, tilting her head at Donnie as if seeing him for the first time. "Mr. Varner," she said. "Would you mind standing up, removing that T-shirt, turning your pockets inside out, and dropping those blue jeans for a moment?"

"Come on now, Miss Fannie," Donnie said, winking. "Got to talk a little dirty to me first."

Fannie smiled and shrugged, reaching down for what Donnie first assumed was her lighter, but instead pulled out a fucking framing hammer. "You get naked right here and right now or I'll be knocking your goddamn nuts from here to Natchez."

"Yes, ma'am," Donnie said, taking off his shirt and unbuckling his pants. "Yes, ma'am. All you had to do was ask. Damn if you didn't make it crawl up a little."

Quinn was back at the farm making supper for Brandon, Maggie again working late at the hospital. He had three nice size pork chops, butchered local in Tibbehah County, frying them up with butter and Tony Chachere's in a black skillet. Some fresh turnip greens and field peas simmered on the back burners. Brandon sat up high on the kitchen table as Quinn worked, thinking how funny it was that Quinn slipped an apron over his pressed khaki shirt. Even funnier, as it had been Miss Jean's and said I LIKE PIG BUTTS AND I CANNOT LIE.

"Why do we have homework every day?" Brandon

said. "Even the weekend. I hate homework. That's for old kids."

"I thought you'd finished up."

"No, sir," Brandon said, shaking his head. "I have to read some book called *Brave Harriet*. It's about the first woman to cross the English Channel in an airplane. That was more than a hundred years ago. Who cares?"

"Sounds like a tough woman to make that crossing," Quinn said.

"I don't know," Brandon said. "Haven't finished it yet. But I figure she makes it across. I guess it'd be a sad story if she crashed in the water. No one likes reading bad endings."

Quinn forked a pork chop out of the skillet and onto an old green Fiesta plate, adding a lot of field peas but only a small portion of turnip greens. Brandon hated turnips of any kind but tolerated the greens if they weren't cooked too long.

"Can you believe people had just started flying a hundred years ago?"

"This house didn't have electricity or indoor plumbing sixty years ago," Quinn said. "You'd have to read by kerosene lantern. Folks went to bed early and got up early."

"That would stink."

"I think I'd like it," Quinn said. "No telephones, either. You raised, shot, or grew what you ate. No television."

"What?"

"Yep," Quinn said. "My uncle didn't put up a television antenna out here until the nineteen seventies and that was only to watch *Gunsmoke* and *Mayberry R.F.D.* My Aunt Halley also loved watching the morning show out of Tupelo. They had a country band that would kick off the day fronted by Buddy and Kay Bain."

"You stay out here a lot?" Brandon asked, picking up the pork chop and turning it over in his hands. When he decided it was cool enough, he nibbled a bit off.

"My daddy wasn't around," Quinn said. "And my mom worked liked your mom. Aunt Halley and my Uncle Hamp looked out for me."

Brandon ate some more and Quinn fixed his own plate and sat down across from his son. Brandon had a wide, pleasant face with lots of freckles across his nose and cheeks and wild, straw-colored hair, looking like Huck Finn from an old paperback. Quinn had gotten back from Memphis just in time to pick him up, about two hours after the Ramos Brothers were transported to 201 Poplar in Lillie's Charger. The man Jason said went by T-Rex was taken for medical treatment on his sliced-open foot, a concussion, and several broken ribs.

Real shame, Quinn thought as he sipped reheated coffee from an old chipped Fillin' Station mug.

"When are you and Momma gonna decide on a name?"

"It's a long list," Quinn said.

"How about Halley?"

"That's on the list."

"Or Harriet?" Brandon said. "You know she's gonna be brave."

"Sure," Quinn said. "Why not?"

The front and back doors were open, letting in a soft, warm breeze from the front pastures. The radio above the refrigerator playing Mississippi Public Broadcasting, a show based out of Oxford called *Highway 61*. This night's show dedicated to the old-time songs of the late, great Jimmie Rodgers, the yodeling brakeman.

Quinn still had on his khaki shirt and Levi's, his boots left by the front door. He hadn't slept in forty-eight hours but figured he'd catch a little rest once Maggie got home. Jason was safe and so was Ana Gabriel. Caddy said Jason had cried when they brought the girl back to The River, hugging her tight and apologizing for letting those men take her away.

"Momma says she always knew I'd be Brandon," Brandon said. "On account of her friend who got killed. I guess you know all about that."

"Yes, sir," Quinn said. "I do."

Quinn had gotten up to get some more coffee when he heard a car pull up outside. He walked to the wide front porch, meeting Reggie Caruthers as he climbed up the steps. Reggie had his hat off and had a pained look on his face. Quinn's stomach sank.

"Hector Herrera has been shot," Reggie said, shaking his head. "He was stopped by Tanner and his chief deputy. They claim they pulled him over for speeding and he got out of the car raising a pistol."

"That doesn't sound right."

"Nope," Reggie said. "Just left the hospital. Herrera's dead, Quinn. Those boys wanted him shut up for good."

*   *   *

Caddy often thought of Mingo and prayed that perhaps he was still out there and alive. She recalled his quiet ways, long black hair, and gentle smile, knowing he shouldn't work for a woman like Fannie Hathcock but not knowing much else. He was just a kid when he disappeared, not long after he tried to help Caddy and Boom find two lost girls, Tamika Odum and Ana Maria Mata. He was who'd first told her and Lillie Virgil about the underage girls, many who didn't speak English, trucked through Fannie's compound out at the old airfield. Lillie and Quinn were about to shut everything down when Mingo just up and disappeared. That had been what? Two, three years ago? There was little doubt who'd been responsible.

Caddy steered her old GMC out the front cattle gate of The River, wiping the tears from her cheeks, white-knuckled on the wheel toward town. She couldn't sit back anymore and wait for Brock Tanner or the county supervisors to do any damn thing. The past couple years, she had pushed down what likely happened to Mingo and those girls. Swallowed it as something she couldn't change—not yet—and moved on.

But now that evil woman could've killed her son. Her *son*. It was too damn much.

She drove on up to the Square and then east along the highway, passing Sonic and Piggly Wiggly, aiming her truck right at the colorful lights of the Rebel Truck Stop. The old truck sprayed gravel into the Vienna's Place parking lot, where the pink and blue neon blazed in the late August twilight.

She was dressed in ragged jeans and Jamey Dixon's old flannel shirt over a tank top. Jamey had been on her mind constantly after he appeared to her these last two nights, once in her bedroom and another time at The River's barn after she and Jason got back from Byhalia. Jamey's spirit had tried to make her feel calm when she called Vienna's a den of iniquity, a black hole that swallowed children and lost souls. Jamey only repeated the words she'd known he'd say: *Do not be overcome by evil, but overcome evil with good.* Caddy was sure she'd seen him, damn well knew it, with his long brown hair and beard, smoking a cigarette. His entire body seemed to be made of fading gold light and smoke. He'd been there. Right?

"That place needs to be burned to the ground."

Hatred stirs up strife, but love covers all offenses.

"Not this time," Caddy said to the figure in the spinning dust and fading sunlight slowly receding from her view. "No, sir. That bitch almost got my son killed."

Caddy jumped out of the truck and slammed the door closed, marching toward the front doors of Vienna's. A busty woman with pink hair worked the entrance in a short black robe. "You here for the oil wrestling?" the woman said. "It's amateur night. We pay out five hunnard to the winner."

"I'm here to see Fannie Hathcock."

"Is that a fact?" the young woman asked, hand on hip, showing off her goodies under the robe. "You're looking a little old to be working that pole. Maybe ask Fannie about a gig as bartender."

Caddy didn't answer as she shoved past her into the

hazy blue and red light and looked up to the glowing white box of the woman's office in the rafters. The main room was jam-packed, two topless women coated in oil flipping each other around in a kiddie pool. Everyone was on their feet watching the action as Caddy's boots banged up the spiral steps.

"Are you satisfied?" Donnie said, grinning, tucking his key chain and his wallet back in his blue jeans. His red Take Off Grill T-shirt tossed over his pointy-toed cowboy boots on the floor. "Or do you need me to bend over while you pull on a pair of rubber gloves?"

"I'm satisfied," Fannie said, pouring herself some champagne out of a fancy bucket. "You can never be too careful. I know Sledge. And I know all about that man who came to see you, Akeem Triplett. I don't care how many touchdowns he made at State, don't you ever mention my name to any of those folks."

"Not one damn word," Donnie said. "Glad to hear you're making a little off this deal, Miss Fannie."

"Baby," Fannie said, taking a sip from a tall crystal glass. "I profit from every damn thing in Mississippi. Do we have a buyer? Or not?"

"Oh, yes, ma'am."

"And who's that?"

"Some good ole boys meanin' a lot of harm," Donnie said. "You know those weirdos who marched in Oxford last summer to save the Confederate monuments?"

"The Watchmen," Fannie said.

"I don't care to get too damn political," Donnie said.

"If they think a truckload of AR-15s is gonna help the South rise again, good on them. I just want to get my cut."

"You sure you're OK with that?" she asked. "I heard you and Sheriff Colson used to be friends."

"Long time back," Donnie said. "When we were kids. But had a bit of a falling-out after he arrested me and then testified against me in federal court."

"Y'all don't talk?" Fannie asked.

"Once," Donnie said. "On the town square. Why?"

"I just don't want you to get cold feet on the deal."

Donnie grinned and rubbed the stubble on his jaw. "No, ma'am," he said. "Not at all. Fuckin' over Quinn Colson will just make the deal that much sweeter."

Fannie took another sip of champagne and nodded Donnie over to a little rolling cart filled with about every damn kind of liquor known to man. He poured himself a little shot of Patrón Silver and was about to propose a toast to Fannie when he turned to see Caddy Colson marching straight into the office. She was out of breath and sweating, wearing a dirty tank top and an old flannel shirt. She pointed her finger right at Fannie and opened her mouth, but then looked over to Donnie standing there shirtless and shook her head like he was the sorriest bastard she'd ever laid eyes on.

Fannie reached down and grabbed Donnie's T-shirt and boots, tossing both to him. For the first time in a long while, Donnie couldn't think of a thing to say.

"You know what kind of woman you're screwing?" Caddy asked him. "Fannie's chewed up and used this county since you left. Young girls are nothing but products to her, whether they're homegrown or brought in from over the border. Remember Tamika Odum, Fannie? Ana Maria Mata?"

Fannie shrugged. "Got a lot of talent down on that stage," she said. "Can't blame me for not recalling real names."

"They never worked here," Caddy said. "But you sold them through a pipeline up to Memphis. Same thing happened to my son two days ago. You were working with the Ramos Brothers and they stole my son, nearly got him killed. They were shooting at him. He's *twelve*. This cesspool you've cooked up down here is what did it. If not for you, none of this stuff would happen in Tibbehah County."

"Sure," Fannie said. "It was all moonlight and goddamn magnolias when Johnny Stagg ran the Rebel. Isn't that who recruited you into the life?"

Donnie took a deep breath and turned his head. Son of a damn bitch. He knew what was coming but sure didn't want to see it. Caddy walked on up to Fannie, seated in her high-backed purple velvet chair, and slapped the champagne glass from her hand. It busted apart on the wall, dripping down to the carpet.

"My son almost died because of you," she said.

"Caddy," Donnie said, slipping into his boots. "Come on."

Caddy turned her finger to Donnie and told him to shut his filthy mouth. That was when that big ole boy called Midnight Man came huffing and puffing up the stairs along with that mean-ass Indian. Caddy Colson was a damn hellcat, but he needed to get her out fast without something bad happening. He reached out and touched her arm, but she shook him off hard. Fannie lifted her eyes to the two men standing right behind Caddy Colson's shoulder. She leaned back in the chair and crossed her legs, cocking her head and staring right at Caddy. She smirked. "So fucking what?"

"Is your soul that damn black?" Caddy said. "Is that what you told yourself when you had Mingo killed?"

Fannie's grin melted off her face, her skin seeming to drain of all color. Fannie leaned forward and started to stand.

"Mingo was a decent person," Caddy said. "Not that you'd understand, but he got right with God before you had him killed. He couldn't live with himself anymore, seeing what you did with those girls you trucked up through here, packing them in like a bunch of cattle, eyes looking out in the darkness. Needing some help. He stepped up. He did the right thing, and you couldn't stand that he crossed you."

"That's a damn lie," Fannie said. "I would've never harmed that boy."

"You killed him," Caddy said. "You made those girls disappear and now you nearly killed my son. Good luck, Donnie. Just watch your back while y'all lay side by side in her satin sheets. I heard she's a talent with a framing hammer."

"Liar," Fannie said, getting on her feet. Her face had turned a bright red.

Caddy walked up on her and slapped the damn taste out of that woman's mouth. Half of Fannie's face turned a bright red, a little blood trickling off her lip.

Donnie reached around Caddy's waist, Caddy kicking and screaming as he picked her up and pulled her from Fannie's office. Caddy was slight but fighting like hell as he dragged her down that twisty staircase, not giving up until they got to the ground floor. She pulled loose from his grasp and headed straight out the door. Donnie ran after her, calling out to her in the parking lot.

"You're gonna get yourself killed," Donnie said. "That wasn't nothing. Come on now. You don't get it. You don't see what's going on."

"Letting you in was a mistake," Caddy said. "You're as dirty as all of 'em. Don't you ever come around me or my family again, Donnie Varner."

"Just a damn second," Donnie said. "Let me talk."

"Why don't you buckle your pants first," Caddy said, stomping to her busted-ass GMC truck and jumping behind the wheel. She screeched off, blowing up a mess of gravel and dirt, headlights waving wild and crazy through the Rebel Truck Stop until she hit the road back toward town.

Donnie took a deep breath, reached down and buckled his damn pants before pulling on his T-shirt.

That federal agent Jon Holliday never promised this shit was easy. But damn if Donnie thought he wouldn't have been better off still at FCI Beaumont. Putting your ass on the line and getting your heart shattered wasn't no damn picnic.

"I left Brandon with my mom," Quinn said. "What the hell happened?"

Maggie sat beside him in Boom's old truck. He'd picked her up near the emergency entrance of the hospital and circled to the far corner of the parking lot so they could talk in private. She'd changed back into her street clothes, a maternity top that was stretched nearly to its limits. Quinn wishing like hell she'd take a few days off, slow down until the baby came.

"It had been called in as a gunshot victim," Maggie said. "The doctors were prepped. But he was dead when he got here. He'd been shot a bunch of times, the front of his shirt and his face a bloody mess. I didn't even make the connection until an hour ago. We were told not to say anything by the sheriff's office since they were trying to notify his family back in Texas."

"They say anything else?"

"To me?" Maggie said. "No. But they definitely tried to keep his identity quiet. They didn't want a bunch of media attention. It wasn't but thirty minutes later, the state people showed up and took the body."

"Was Ophelia Bundren here?"

"Nope."

"They can't release the body to the state unless Ophelia signs off on it."

"They did," Maggie said, face half hidden in the shadow of the truck cab. "The body's gone."

"I met Herrera a couple times," Quinn said. "He was stand-up."

"Poor Caddy," Maggie said, playing with the bracelets on her wrist. "She's already been through enough."

For the first time in weeks, rain started to fall, pinging the windshield and across the dusty hood of the Ford

Highboy. It rained quiet and soft for a few moments and then began to fall in great, thick sheets across the parking lot, slanting into the lamps along the edge of the hospital.

"What is it that you wanted to tell me?" Quinn asked. "That you couldn't say on the phone?"

"I heard they're saying it was some shoot-out," Maggie said. "That's the word around town."

"Yep."

"Only thing I know is that man was killed at close range," Maggie said. "I don't need any medical examiner to tell me that. Someone put a gun right between that man's eyes and blew the top of his head clean off."

19

Don't you want to touch it?" old Zeke Coldfield said to Donnie Varner, licking his cracked, dry lips and holding the antique sword up to the dim light inside Zeke's Value City. It was early morning with just a few overhead lamps on, the only illumination coming from the old wood display cases glowing in the dark. Coldfield sat at the head of a long dinner table situated up on a display platform, wearing a worn-out kepi cap and a moth-eaten cape over a pinstripe suit. "It's a piece of living history. Taken from the hand of Nathan Bedford Forrest's brother as he lay dying, not five miles from where we stand."

"No shit," Donnie said, pulling the cigarette out of his mouth. "Ain't that something."

"That's what spurred Forrest to run those goddamn Yankees out of Tibbehah County," Coldfield said. "He held his brother in his lap, saying 'Poor Jeffrey,' and then mounted his horse Roderick, the way Forrest always did, standing tall in the saddle, saber raised as he busted right through a line of Union soldiers that was trying to link up with that rotten bastard Sherman."

Donnie took the sword, spewing smoke from the side of his mouth, finding it surprisingly heavy, blade dull and tarnished. Damn if it wasn't much nicer than those samurai swords they sold to the truckers out at the Rebel.

"This one was made by Mansfield & Lamb up in Rhode Island," Zeke said, his cataract-blue eyes shiny with excitement. "My granddaddy bought it off a nigger man up in Memphis whose daddy had stolen it from the Forrest family. He was using it to cut the heads off chickens out back of a fillin' station. Can you imagine the disgrace of such a prestigious piece of our heritage? Exactly what we were all fighting for. If we'd had more men like the Forrest boys we'd have won that war."

"Me and some of my buddies used to go hunt for Minié balls down in the creeks in Sugar Ditch," Donnie said. "Found me a bayonet once. Guess there'd been a lot of action down that way."

"They were trying to protect that breadbasket of the Confederacy," Coldfield said, taking the sword back from Donnie's hand and sliding it into its leather scabbard. "Sherman wanted everything south of Jericho plundered and burned. The wheat, the corn, and cotton. They say when our boys were tearing into those Yankees, there was smoke and fires as far as the eye could see. Ole Forrest and his boys greeted by hoots and hollers of folks on the town square as he sought out that coward Sooy Smith for the Second Battle of Jericho."

"Second battle?" Donnie asked. "Just when was the first?"

"Biblical times," Coldfield said. "Our boys were as mighty as the Israelites that day, blowing their trumpets, attacking that weakling and coward Sooy Smith. *Hee-hee-hee*. Must've been a sight to see him and thousands of them troops turn tail and run up the road to Pontotoc."

"All this stuff must be worth plenty," Donnie said, looking about the cavernous darkness, the display cases glowing a hot white light. "Ever think about selling out and maybe taking a cruise down to Mexico or down to the Bahamas? Some of them Princess cruises have discos and waterslides, too."

"Why on earth would I do that, son?" Coldfield asked. "Third-world countries are filled with crime and vermin. I seen it all on *Fox & Friends*. And that was plenty for me."

Donnie nodded, watching the old man at the head of the table unwrapping a Nutty Buddy. He shoved the whole damn thing in his mouth, mawing it up with his dentures clicking and slipping. He wasn't sure why the old man was wearing the musty, tattered Confederate garb and didn't ask, Coldfield meeting him at the front door with that shit on as if it was normal and expected.

"Well, you boys are in luck," Donnie said. "Looks like I'll take delivery over the weekend and we can go ahead and seal this here deal by the start of the week. How's that sound?"

"Good, good," Coldfield said, licking his fingers clean. "You're a fine man, Mr. Varner. Ever think of maybe joining our ranks? We sure could use someone of your military experience for the upcoming battles."

"Come again?"

"The upcoming battles," Coldfield said. "Damn Yankees want nothing more than to come back down here and finish us all off. Take our statues and our heritage. Forrest headed them off then, and later when he organized the Klan. Now it's up to the descendants of those brave souls to stand our ground. We don't need none of what they're selling. Jigaboo music, diet lemonade, and Hollywood homos. Just the other day I seen two men kissing each other in the Walmart parking lot like they was Ozzie and Harriet. That's the last time I'll go to that place and get me my treats. You don't see none of that mess at the Piggly Wiggly."

"No, sir," Donnie said. "The Pig offers a more wholesome clientele."

"If any of those sonsabitches try and take that statue off the town square, I'd chain my old bones to that ole soldier standing guard over our values," he said. "Yes, sir. Ain't no way Zeke Coldfield would lose his history without putting up a good fight."

"Glad I could be of service, sir."

"This is a grand time to be alive," Coldfield said. "I never thought we'd see the likes and fiber of a man like J. K. Vardaman again. His ancestor was a great man, a grand figure with a vision of the past and the future. I swear to the Lord, our current governor is the spitting image. That's the man we voted for and that's the man who's gonna see us through."

"You Watchmen are a damn supportive crew."

"Why wouldn't we be?" Zeke Coldfield said, standing up and hobbling off the steps from the display. He hit a few more hidden switches on the walls and walked on through the tiny spotlights. "Governor Vardaman is a founding member of our society. He's one of us. Hell, he's gosh-dang family."

"Just exactly how many of y'all are there?" Donnie asked.

"Son, if I told you, you wouldn't believe it," he said. "You couldn't throw an old shoe at the statehouse without hitting one of our brothers in arms right in the damn head."

"Did Herrera call you or tell you anything?" Quinn asked.

"Nothing," Caddy said. "The last time we spoke he said he was working with the law school at Ole Miss, hoping to get those folks out of jail. Maybe help get them some work visas."

Quinn looked at his sister, standing there on the farmhouse porch, the rain not letting up since the other night, drenching the pasture and pouring off the tin roof. Caddy leaned on the porch railing while Quinn stood in the doorway.

"These people are so reckless and arrogant," she said. "They can do whatever they want to anyone. It doesn't matter. No one cares."

Quinn nodded. He hadn't told his sister everything about the shooting. The details about Herrera's body had been between him and Maggie and now him and

Jon Holliday. Quinn took a puff of his Liga Privada and let out a big cloud of smoke.

"We care," Quinn said.

"That chicken plant is back open," Caddy said. "It's been working behind locked gates for a week now. I don't know who they've hired or where they're coming from. Do you know anyone who's gotten a job there?"

"Caddy."

"You want me to slow down?" she said. "Leave it alone?"

Quinn shook his head. He watched Caddy drop her head into her hands and start to cry. He moved from the doorway to a porch swing and took a seat. The rain blew across the front yard and over the dirt bike Brandon had left in the front yard. Hondo wandered out the front door from the kitchen where he'd been sleeping and looked at the rain, bending down deep into his front paws and lifting his butt up to stretch.

"I'm sorry," Quinn said.

"Hector was a very good man," she said. "Maybe one of the best."

"Momma told me about those dreams you've been having."

"They're not dreams, Quinn."

Quinn nodded, cigar smoldering in his hands. He was barefoot, cowboy boots muddy and placed by the front door. Hondo looked up and dropped his head on Quinn's knee. Quinn scratched the dog's old gray head, Hondo making pleasant grunting sounds. Rain dripped down off the sharp edge of the metal roof and patted onto the thirsty flower beds. The pink four-o'clocks had been nearly dead.

"I didn't tell you this," Caddy said. "But the other night, right after I got Jason home, I drove out to Fannie Hathcock's place. I couldn't stand it, Quinn. I had to face her or I felt like my insides would explode."

"That was a bad idea, Caddy," Quinn said. "You should've called me."

"Wouldn't have mattered," Caddy said, wiping her face. "Even Jamey couldn't talk me out of it. He tried his best to get me thinking right with Scripture."

Quinn didn't say anything, watching his sister speak, hoping that she knew this was all crazy talk. But she didn't let on, going on and on about her conversation with a dead man inside that old barn at The River. She never even stopped for a moment to put stock in what she was saying.

"I slapped her," Caddy said. "All that big talk I make about loving your neighbor and turning the other cheek got thrown out the window like trash onto the highway. I didn't give a damn. I wanted to hurt her. I slapped that damn bitch so hard I made her mouth bleed."

"She's a dangerous woman," Quinn said. "Maybe even worse than you think."

"I hope it hurt," Caddy said. "I hope it hurt like hell. For Jason. For Ana Gabriel and those girls. For Mingo and Ana Maria and Tamika. And now for Hector Herrera. God, Quinn. All of this for what? All of those lives for some greedy and godless men in Jackson to gorge on the north Mississippi trough. It's got to end. Right? When will it end?"

"Soon," Quinn said, standing and placing a hand on Caddy's shoulder. "I promise."

She wiped her eyes again with the back of her hand and stared out into the pasture, the air thick with the smell of mud and manure. A mess of cattle huddled together in the center of the field, their legs and hooves coated in mud and shit, shifting and swaying, looking for some kind of solid ground. Hondo barked at them from high on the porch and then ran faster than he had in a long while to gather a few strays from the herd.

"That old dog's still got it," Caddy said, wiping her nose.

"Damn straight."

"Sam, why won't you drink with me?" Chief Robbie said. "Just one drink. A toast to our future, or a toast to look back on the past. We have come so far. Look out there, look at all those people giving us their money. Do you remember the government trailers? The worn-out secondhand clothes the white people handed down to us when we were kids? Now we control two hotels, the casino. I've even been taking lessons to fly my own helicopter. That way I can get down to the Coast, when Takali is built, and back within less than an hour. Think of it."

"I don't want to drink," Sam said, standing with the Chief in his office, the great gold mirrored plate-glass window looking out onto the casino floor. "And you should know better. When did you start again? The drunken Indian is a cliché from the Westerns. I've been that man. I lost my family because of it. You know what became of Norma. And later of Mingo. If I had been a father, I'd have come back for him."

"Please, Sam," Chief Robbie said. "Leave it alone. Leave Fannie Hathcock and Mississippi. Go to your lovely condo in Tulsa and be with that young woman you told me about. The one with the beautiful face, the golden hair, and the wide hips. Spend the money you've made, live the life you have earned. You built this place the same as me. If not for a few pieces of bad fortune, you're the one who'd have been chief."

"I've made many mistakes, Robbie," Sam said. "And you know them all. I could never have been chief. I'm a killer. I was trained to kill at Parris Island. I killed as a Marine and I've been doing it since I got back to the Rez. That's who I am."

"Promise me you won't kill Fannie Hathcock," Chief Robbie said, reaching for a fancy crystal decanter on his desk and pouring out some whiskey. "When you called, I was worried you were about to make a bad mistake for the entire tribe. Why? Because some crazy white woman threatened Fannie and said she'd killed Mingo? It sounds like this woman is unstable. Why risk the peace and all our business dealings for the unhinged ramblings of a woman you don't know?"

"She's the sister of the sheriff I shot."

"Even worse," Chief Robbie said, taking a sip and then sitting behind his huge wooden desk with the eagle-claw feet, turning back and forth in his leather seat. "Leave now. You can have my big Mercedes. You can drive all night and be in Tulsa by morning. OK? You will feel much better then. You can come back when we've settled all this mess."

"I can't ever come back," Sam said. "You've told that to me many times. There is a U.S. Marshal after me. They have photos and information. They know who I am and what I've done."

"It can be corrected," Chief Robbie said. "In time. Trust me."

Sam shook his head, watching Chief Robbie drain the glass of fine whiskey. The Chief poured himself another half glass of the brown water. Sam noticed how soft his old friend had gotten around the jawline and thick in his smiling cheeks. The Chief had sworn off alcohol many years ago, getting healthy and fit, and Sam never thought he'd ever see his friend touch the stuff again.

"This woman will hang herself," Chief Robbie said. "She's made too many enemies. So many people want her dead, she won't make it another year. And then, well . . . We will be there to take over."

"Do you recall that time in New Orleans?" Sam asked. "When you found me living under I-10 like a wild animal? I had gone on a drunk for two, three weeks. You wrestled me to the ground and chained me in the back of your truck. The whole way back to the Rez, singing old hymns in Choctaw, playing Metallica as loud as you could. Why did you do that? Why did you come for me?"

"You'd lost your wife," Chief Robbie said. "The government had taken away your children. You had lost your way."

"I'm not lost anymore," Sam said. "I know what to do."

"I would offer you money or position, but none of that means anything to you, Sam Frye."

"Stop me from leaving," Sam Frye said, turning toward the door, exposing his broad back to his old friend. "I have a long walk through the casino and out to my car. You're chief. You can do as you please."

"I can't," Chief Robbie said, tossing back the second glass. "But I will be there to clean up whatever follows."

Jason and Ana Gabriel took a walk from the little shotgun cabin she shared with her brother Sancho. The sun had finally gone down and the rain had stopped, leaving the grassy fields and the small rutted paths choked with steam and humidity. They found an old fallen tree to sit on and watch the lightning bugs come alive in the nighttime heat, thousands of them flickering their yellow tails on and off like tiny flashbulbs.

"We should do something to honor Señor Herrera," she said. "He should be remembered and respected for all he tried to do for us. While we were gone, he found my father in Atlanta. He's coming for us, Jason. I didn't know how to find him and Señor Herrera told him about my mother and that we were left alone."

"You're leaving?"

"For now," she said. "What else can we do? They say they're sending our mother back to Mexico. How will we find her? I've never even been to Mexico."

"Are your mother and father together?"

"No," she said. "Not for a long while. He has a new wife and new children. But my mother said he was a good man, always sending money to help us. But I don't know what will happen. Me and Sancho living with his new family in Atlanta. What if they hate us?"

"When is he coming?"

Ana Gabriel reached out and snatched a lightning bug out of the dusky air. She turned to Jason, gave a soft smile, and then opened her hand. The lightning bug's tail glowing weak and slow in an old rhythmic pulse. They both watched the bug as it flickered its wings again and flew out into the night.

"I don't know," Ana Gabriel said. "He left a phone number here at El Rio. Your mother had me call and leave a message. I haven't heard back. But I will. He's not the type of man to ignore family."

"You can stay here," Jason said. "My momma said you and Sancho can stay here as long as you like."

She reached out and grabbed Jason's hand, squeezing his fingers. "We're not safe here," she said. "I worry for Sancho. Everything that's happened. I know this is your home, but this is an evil place, filled with evil and dangerous people."

"Only home I've ever known," he said. "I guess you get used to it."

"The things I've heard about your uncle, the sheriff, and his friend, the big black man."

"Boom," Jason said.

"Why do they stay?" she said. "Why do all of you stay? You can start a new life anywhere. My father came from Juárez, not from El Paso. He told me that he left to be something better and bigger for his family. He works so hard, Jason. Not only does he send money to us, but to his mother as well. And his mother takes care of his younger sisters and cousins. How is that a bad thing?"

"It's not a bad thing," Jason said. "Who would say that?"

"The people here," she said. "I hear what they whisper behind our backs, the names they call us. They say we steal food and jobs from people who want to work. They say we are dirty and have no value."

"Not me," Jason said, squeezing her hand back. "You're the prettiest and smartest girl I've ever met in my life, Ana Gabriel. If I hear someone saying something about you and Sancho, I'd punch them right in the throat."

"Your mother wouldn't like that," she said. "Would she? She says to forgive others as Christ Himself forgave, seventy times seven."

"My mother thinks on things different," Jason said, smiling over at Ana Gabriel. "She always has. She feeds other folks before she can eat. She brings clothes to people out in the county while she's got holes in her own blue jeans and holes in her shoes. That's just the way she is."

Ana Gabriel nodded, looking down at their hands clasped together, their skin a similar brown. "And this makes her happy?"

Jason didn't answer. He looked out into the field, thousands of those bugs lifting off into the night, searching for their mates. He remembered seeing maybe twice as many back in June, those bugs having one last big party before fall set in down south. The air was so thick and wet outside, it was tough to breathe.

"I don't know if my momma is ever really happy," Jason said. "She seems only content when life is real hard."

"Why is that?" Ana Gabriel said. "Why would anyone want that for themselves?"

"I don't know," Jason said. "She always says she'll get her reward in heaven."

"But not here?" Ana Gabriel said. "Not in the comfort of a better place, away from all this death and violence?"

"I don't know," Jason said. "I always figured what she was doing was right for everybody."

Ana Gabriel put her head on his shoulder. "Everyone but herself," she said. "I feel very sad for your mother."

20

Donnie couldn't go home. The thought of staring at the walls of that old trailer or that big blank movie screen made him physically ill. He didn't want to see his daddy at the Quick Mart, watching him chain-smoke Pall Malls and lecture about Jesus. And he sure couldn't see Quinn and Boom now that both of the best friends he'd ever known thought he was as crooked as a wild duck's pecker. Instead, he headed on into the Dixie gas station and bought a case of warm Coors, set it into a Styrofoam cooler along with a bag of ice, and placed the cooler in the seat beside him, the beer riding shotgun, icing itself colder and colder each country mile. He finished beer after beer, crawling up on those old gravel roads as twilight turned to night, breaking into a straightaway on the old Jericho Road, passing that dark place where he'd heard Diane Tull and her friend were attacked back in '77, three years before he was born. So many damn sad sights on the grand tour.

But he had Waylon in his daddy's tape deck, a nice little buzz working as he wandered the back roads of Tibbehah. "The Chokin' Kind." "Anita, You're Dreaming." "Just to Satisfy You." *Someone's gonna get hurt before you're through. Someone's gonna pay for the things you do.*

"Damn," Donnie said. "Goddamn." He tossed another empty can of Coors into the back of the GTO, speakers thumping and jumping, windows open, warm humid air blowing through the car, lightning bugs in the wild brown field clicking on and off, humping the hell out of each other out in those weeds.

Everything he'd ever tried to do was for a good purpose. But somehow, someway, he always ended up cornholing himself. He thought when he was over in Trashcanistan that nobody would really miss a few dozen of those rifles and that maybe he could put them to good use back home. Everybody else was getting a check from Uncle Sam back then, why not him? In the end, he got those damn guns into the hands of good folks who needed them. Luz and her people were taking on the fucking Cartel, back in Cherán, the Cartel owning the damn town, the federales strip-clearing every tree in what had been a crazy, wonderful forest. But that had cost him. Doing the right thing, fighting the bad guys, landed his ass in prison.

And when that federal agent showed up at FCI Beaumont last Thanksgiving, Donnie was just trying to get through his day, thinking about that turkey and dressing the trusties were fixing up for him and his buddies Luis

and Salvador. Salvador even sneaking a bottle of Casami-
gos tequila into the prison along with his regular supply
of cell phones.

Help out his friend Quinn Colson? You bet your ass.
But nobody would think Donnie Varner was a fucking
good guy even if he wore a Nudie Suit the color of vanilla
ice cream and a white hat taller than Tom Mix's.

Donnie headed down that curvy stretch of the old
Jericho Road toward town, the bright lights of the Jericho Square beckoning. Maybe hit the pool hall or the
Southern Star, but goddamn if that golden GTO didn't
have a mind of her own, its nose pointing south at the
Fillin' Station, Donnie heading down into Sugar Ditch
and knowing full well that he was headed to The River
to see Caddy. He'd missed her so much, knowing wherever he went and whoever he'd been with, he'd always
wanted Caddy Colson. Caddy was home. He could wander around and around this earth and never find a
woman as quality as Caddy. And right now, he didn't
give a good goddamn what anyone thought or what he
wasn't supposed to say. Caddy needed to know just what
the hell Donnie Varner was all about.

He slowed down as he approached that big hand-
painted sign, the ribbon of cracked asphalt working its
way past the cotton and cornfields and then into the low-
lands of Sugar Ditch. He turned at the cattle gate, open
big and wide, and slid on down the muddy road, back
tires slipping and sliding as he headed to the barn. Take
it to the barn. Take it on home. He could see the light on
in Caddy's office, a beaten white single-wide cast off and
unwanted, that old GMC truck, two-tone brown and

white, parked crooked out front. Donnie knocked the car into park and crawled out of the GTO, taking a final sip of the can of Coors as he wandered down the path, children playing and singing songs in the barn as he headed up the beaten wooden steps and pounded on the door.

Nothing. And so he pounded more. Caddy finally opened the door and looked Donnie up and down and shook her head. "Why don't you just quit?"

"Not in my nature."

"Fannie Hathcock?" she said. "Good God."

Donnie put a hand on Caddy's slim sun-brown arm and said, "Baby, don't you believe half of what you're seeing."

"Good night."

"Come on, now."

Caddy shook off his arm and turned back to the trailer.

"I love you."

"Bullshit."

"I said, I love you," he said. "Damn it, Caddy. You know. Hell, we've always known."

She turned to him, hands on her hips, jaw clenched. She was mad as hell but she looked like the most beautiful thing he'd ever seen.

"You don't know a damn thing about love," Caddy said. "You lay with filth and evil. I can smell it on you now."

"No, ma'am," he said. "That's just a little Rocky Mountain spring water."

Donnie shook his head, feeling something that sure felt like tears sliding down his cheeks. He turned toward the music coming out of the barn, some kind of service in Spanish. He knew the hymn, the music familiar but the words coming out foreign. He leaned in to kiss Caddy but she turned her head away from him.

He leaned in and whispered into her ear. "I'm working for the goddamn FBI," he said. "That's how I got out early. I'm working to bring all these bastards down. Same as Quinn and same as Lillie Virgil. I'm one of the goddamn good guys."

Caddy backed up as if seeing Donnie for the first time, a kind, passive light coming across her face. Donnie loosened up, thinking he was about to get one hell of an apology. But instead took Caddy's small tight fist right in his face.

It knocked him back on the heels of his pointy-toed boots. She sure popped his ass good.

"Go," she said, pointing back to Luther's prized vehicle. "Get off my property. I'm too damn old and too damn smart to be told such ridiculous lies."

"It's late, Skinner," Quinn said. "What do you want?"

"Plenty," Skinner said. "How about you take a seat, Sheriff."

"I'm fine with standing."

Both of the men stood in the dimly lit First Baptist Church late that night, not three days after Quinn had picked up Jason in Byhalia. Quinn was tired, already headed to bed when his cell phone rang. He got up, dressed, and took two pills to ease his back on the ride to town. Seems like he couldn't get on his boots without a little help, and he hated it.

"How's your wife doing?" Skinner said. "Heard she's about due. That's a wonderful thing, becoming a parent. Changes everything. Now I know you two have a young son, but having one of your own, one that looks just like you. Well, that's the Lord's work."

Quinn didn't say anything. Even with the two pills, his lower back ached like hell. He took a seat in the second church pew from the altar. Skinner, Stetson in hand, collapsed his lumbering body in the pew ahead of him, staring up at the cross, no doubt for effect. He then lapsed into a coughing fit, Quinn waiting for the old man to finish and get on with it.

"I've made a lot of mistakes," Skinner said.

If ever an understatement had been made.

"Done things I'm ashamed of."

No doubt.

"Everything I've done is to help the folks of this county."

A lie.

"But sometimes I made a buck or two on the side."

Truth.

"You don't talk much, Sheriff," Skinner said, eyes sliding down to his own lap. "Kind of remind me of ole Gary Cooper in that way. Never forget seeing that picture he was in with Grace Kelly, wandering down that barren street alone. Everyone'd turn tail and run, afraid of Frank Miller and his gang."

"My family's asleep," Quinn said. "And tomorrow, I got work to do."

"If you don't mind me asking," Skinner said, "just what kind of work are you doing with the governor setting up his own men up here? You know he doesn't just aim to sideline you for a few months. He's got plans for that Brock Tanner to run this county for a long, long time. Tanner himself says he has plans on running in the next election."

Quinn looked up at the big stained-glass window behind the pulpit. An empty wooden cross topped with a crown of thorns and wrapped in a purple sash, a beam of golden light shooting down from heaven. He waited for Ole Man Skinner to tell him that his family had bought and paid for that window, bought special from an artist up in Illinois when they rebuilt the church. Everyone in Jericho had heard the story more than once.

"As a leader in the community," Skinner said, starting to cough a bit again, "I had to make a few compromises. Work with folks of low integrity for the bigger picture of this county. Those millions of dollars from Jackson don't flow up to Tibbehah easy. No, sir. Sometimes you got to turn that river, make money and business come our way. I have broken bread with godless men and women. I have looked the other way while evil was being done. And I do believe I have been in the presence of the living, breathing devil."

Skinner turned his pale blue eyes to Quinn, his jowls loose and sagging.

"I'm the sheriff," Quinn said. "Not a preacher."

"I'm et up with cancer, Sheriff," Skinner said. "Only the Lord knows how much time I got left. But in that time, I'm gosh-dang sick and tired of bending to the wills and ways of evil. I don't like that Brock Tanner and he doesn't like me. I'm sick to my stomach at the filth and immorality that's come here. And believe it or not, I feel compassion for the Mexicans who lived here in good faith, only to get rounded up like cattle and shuttled over to Louisiana, leaving the little children behind. Folks owned that company knew right what they were doing."

Skinner began to cough some more. Quinn sat up straighter in his seat, studying the old man's face as he hacked into his fist.

"Sorry to hear you're ill."

"Ha," Skinner said. "Appreciate you saying it. But I know how you feel about me, and can't say I blame you. I tried to run roughshod over your mission back here at home. I know now you studied on things seriously, a true military man looking at the best course of action."

Quinn nodded. The church had that pent-up library smell of old hymnals and Lysol, the faint trace of ladies' perfume from the Sunday service.

"And as a military man, I'd like to offer you a little intel, son," Skinner said. "Yes, sir. I may not have much time, but by God, I'm gonna do my best."

Quinn waited, the air-conditioning blasting through the sanctuary, nearly freezing where the two men sat. Quiet and cool, the air humming through the ductwork overhead, rattling the wilting flowers on the altar.

"Fannie Hathcock's got a big party coming to town," Skinner said. "Folks from Jackson flying up to enjoy the hospitality at that big new place on Choctaw Lake. I can imagine what kind of barnyard acts will be offered, along with a river of whiskey flowing from the devil's own hand."

"What's that to me, Skinner?"

"The governor will be the honored guest," Skinner said, his pale blue eyes flat and impassive. "Figured someone might want to catch that SOB with his pants down around his ankles."

Fannie was alone.

She'd driven out into the county to the series of Quonset huts by the old airfield, most of them stuffed to the rafters with stolen televisions, jewelry, truck parts, and tires. But one of the huts, the second from the far end, is where she made nearly all of her money. That's where she'd set up the servers for the online sex trade, working cribs in the back rooms of Vienna's, several units at the Golden Cherry, and hundreds of remote locations from Memphis to Los Angeles. Any girl who wanted to be part of Fannie's team just had to sign up, turn on her laptop or cell phone camera, and welcome in the prying eyes of the big wild world of perverts. Fannie could've never imagined working without even having to leave her apartment. But she had housewives, college students, broke-ass immigrants, and a few has-been names in the porn business. *Ashlyn Fox. Silvia Steele*. These women put in maybe one or two hours of work and sometimes pulled in a few thousand a day. One of her VIP stars might make ten, fifteen grand for a private show. Damn, the perversion of men was an unlimited commodity.

Fannie sat there in the control room, servers softly humming in the dark, the dozens and dozens of screens on the wall flashing images from bedrooms and bathrooms all over the country. She had eighteen domain names under her control, eight shake joints, and two historic bars in the French Quarter. Fannie sat there in a cheap spinning chair and pulled a half-empty bottle of gin from her purse.

She poured out a good swig into a red Solo cup and looked up and around at all those girls, all those pretty faces and a few ugly ones. Black, white, brown, yellow. Skinny and fat, blonde, brunette, redhead, doing things on camera that Fannie used to do as a teenager out back of cut-rate motels in Gulfport and Biloxi for less than fifty bucks. She'd wander home, dirty and degraded with skinned-up knees. Sore, with a busted lip and a bruised coot, having to go back and do it again. And again. As she tilted the gin up to her lips, she realized she didn't have any more of a feeling for these girls than folks she'd see on a television sitcom or the silver screen. They'd chosen their dirty, crooked path and Fannie had helped them make some money from the privacy of their own homes.

She lifted her eyes to the security monitor, seeing Midnight Man standing outside her waxed white Lexus, leaning his fat black ass against the passenger door. He was locked and loaded with a big-ass pistol on his hip, worried that some kind of bad end would come to his meal ticket. But she'd assured him everything was gonna be just fine. Miss Fannie had come a little undone earlier, getting too sloppy and drunk, firing one of her girls who'd fallen off the big brass pole, the one that stretched up to the catwalk, and busted her collarbone.

She was fine. Miss Fannie was fine. There was no goddamn way Sam Frye paid any mind to Caddy Colson. Sam knew that girl was flat-out crazy, coming to her saying those things about Mingo. Who on earth would ever believe that Fannie Hathcock would've stood by and watched a boy, one she valued and treated like her own son, get killed? Fannie seeing him now with those two faceless, shadowed men, up on the levee getting his brains blown out. A backhoe sputtering to life before he'd even dropped down to the mud. *No way.* No way Fannie would stand by and order that done. No way a professional man like Sam Frye would see that happening, see her driving him up to that levee, to those shadow men, lying to his face that everything was fine, they were fine. After all, it was that tub of whale shit Buster White who made it happen. He killed Mingo. Right? He killed the kid and told Fannie to ask no questions.

Her hands, manicured red nails, and lovely body wrapped in lace from La Perla up in New York City were clean and spotless and blameless. But goddamn, why did her hands shake so on that red Solo cup filled with straight gin? Why did her stomach feel hollow, sloshing with a belly full of alcohol, Fannie not having eaten in two days? Why the fuck did she let Midnight Man come home with her and sleep out on her couch? And why did she feel like a big hand had reached into her chest and was crushing her heart? Fannie reached up, touching the ruby locket around her neck, a gift, an heirloom from her lovely, sainted grandmother, who'd run the most successful cathouse in Alcorn County for nearly three decades.

Fannie looked up at all those screens, all those faces, all those naked bodies, closed eyes and mouths gagging on one more digital dollar. Fannie felt like she was coming loose from her skin, standing up, knocking the chair over and heading to a trash bucket.

She got down on her knees and started throwing up. Choking and coughing, she got to her feet, pushed open the metal door out to the gravel lot. Midnight Man backed off her car and walked over to the driver's side.

"You OK, Miss Fannie?" He put his big paw on her little shoulder.

Fannie stared into his big, broad dark face and nodded.

"Maybe I should drive," Midnight Man said. His voice nothing but a croaked whisper. "Until you feeling better."

"Heard that Fannie is hosting a pool party for some good ole boys flying in from the capital," Jon Holliday said, meeting Nat in the woods and out of the moonlight, high up on that fire road. The Big Woods and the Tibbehah hills stretched out far, inky and deep. No "hi" or "hello," just Holliday starting to talk. "And that maybe Vardaman himself may show up."

"You think he's that damn stupid?" Nat asked.

"You bet," Holliday said. "I think it has something to do with that poultry plant. They're trying to limit fallout from bringing in prison labor. One of his buddies is in deep shit for making that call. Immigrant labor in jail. For-profit prisons trucked in to do the dirty work. Lot of local folks down here aren't pleased. Won't take much to connect all this back to Vardaman and his good ole boys.

At least Johnny Stagg had the damn sense to keep his business under the table and pretty much off the books."

"Vardaman's too damn egotistical to care," Nat said. "Who's gonna call him on it?"

"In this state?" Holliday said, pulling at his graying beard.

He was a good-looking man, about her height, which was a little under six feet. He had a shaved head and a brushy beard and a damn road map of tattoos that she could see on both arms. She knew he'd been Special Forces in the Army, longtime veteran of the FBI, did a couple years' undercover work here in Tibbehah County and was largely credited with bringing down Johnny Stagg alongside Quinn Colson.

"We've entered a golden age of stupidity and corruption," Nat said. "If I were Vardaman, I'd stay way the hell away from Fannie Hathcock. What's he need that woman for? He got his money. He got elected. You think he'd be done with all those country-ass crooks."

"You've heard the same as me."

"That he's got special needs?" Nat said, smiling. "Oh, yeah. I've tried to talk to Fannie about that, making sly little jokes here and there. But if she knows that man's into something kinky, she's not saying. She's open as hell about the drugs. Talks about the trucks coming and going as if she's the goddamn manager of the Walmart. Pills, weed. All the same. But on the kinky shit she plays it real close. What'd you hear?"

"I know," Holliday said. "But can you believe I'm embarrassed to say?"

"Because I'm a woman?"

"Because you're a person," Holliday said. "Vardaman isn't far removed from stepping out of the barnyard."

"Holy damn hell."

"Yes, ma'am," Holliday said. "Can you get close to where those boys will meet?"

"I can try," Nat said, shifting from one leg to another, not finding it easy to work all night in platform heels, and walking out some dark, country road to meet Holliday made it even worse. "Fannie has a poker room in the back of that lodge. She doesn't allow anyone in there besides Midnight Man and herself. If those good ole boys want private company, that's done in their rooms or out at the pool. But she keeps that poker room sacred."

"Can you get in beforehand?"

"Maybe."

Holliday reached into his shirt pocket and pulled out a black box no larger than an ice cube. He tossed it to Nat and she caught it in midair. She'd used similar ones in a ton of criminal cases up in Memphis, some phones in pens and others in smoke detectors or clocks. There were smaller units but few with better audio and video. She wasn't sure what she could get, but she'd damn well try.

"You said Fannie has been off her game," Holliday said. "Maybe this is an ideal time."

"Caddy Colson, the sheriff's sister, busted in her office the other night," Nat said. "Raising holy hell. Blaming Fannie for something that happened to her kid. I heard she slapped her right across the face."

"Her son got mixed up with a girl marked by some human traffickers," Holliday said. "The boy broke free but Colson and Lillie Virgil had to track down the girl. They arrested two brothers who were running kids."

"Damn," Nat said. "You talking about the Ramos Brothers?"

"Yep," Holliday said. "And I think they're gonna co-operate once all this comes together."

Nat played with the black cube in her left hand, whirling it end over end in her fingers. When this was all over, she was going to take a long hot shower, change out of these trashy hoochie-mama clothes and tall-ass heels. She hoped to hell she'd never have to come back to Tibbehah County again.

"What are you thinking, Nat?"

"Wondering how men who got that much money smell that damn cheap."

"Is it getting to you?" Holliday said.

"If we bust that woman on her worst damn day, when supplies are low?" Nat said. "Shit. We'll still be legends. Nobody seen this much drugs moving north since the goddamn eighties and Barry Seal's crazy ass."

"Southern arrogance."

Nat nodded. "At its goddamn finest."

Caddy had agreed to see Donnie once Jason was asleep, and at midnight, his phone buzzed. Donnie dozed on his daddy's couch and jostled awake to his "Gimme Three Steps" ringtone. Old Luther snored to the back half of *The Sons of Katie Elder*. Donnie did his best not to wake him, the old man cradling a worn-out leather Bible in his lap. He grabbed his car keys and slipped out the side door, taking Caddy's call as he cranked the gold GTO and pulled out.

"I knew you'd come to your senses."

"Donnie."

"Don't say nothing," he said. "Not on the phone. Don't trust these damn phones. Can you slip out to my place?"

"Slip out?" Caddy said. "I'm a grown-ass woman."

"I got a bottle of tequila and more of that Acapulco Gold."

"I don't drink. How many times do I need to tell you?"

"I'll leave the front gate and door unlocked."

"It's the middle of the night," she said. "We're sleeping over at Momma's."

"Then you have no excuse," he said. "Come on."

"You really think that's wise?" Caddy said. "Considering what we discussed."

"For you, Caddy Colson?" he said. "I'm willing to take my chances."

Donnie was standing at the sink in his Airstream about thirty minutes later when he heard the old truck rumble up. He peeked out the curtains and then quick-footed his way over to the couch. He lay down like he was chilling out and watching TV, some movie on called *Moonrunners* about a couple bootleggers over in Georgia when the revenuers still gave a shit. Damn, those were the days. His granddaddy and Quinn's granddaddy raising fucking hell on the back roads of north Mississippi.

The screen door opened and Caddy walked into his

trailer. She wouldn't look at him as she moved toward him, staring at the floor and away from his gaze. The trailer was tiny inside, not a lot of personal space, and Donnie hung back just in case she decided to deck him again.

"Can I get you something to drink?" Donnie said. "If you don't want that tequila, I got some cold beer and Kool-Aid. Sorry, that's about it."

She shook her head, looking so damn pretty in faded Levi's and a little white peasant top with embroidered roses like Mexican women wore. Her hair seemed even shorter than last time he'd seen her, buzzed up on the neck and the sides. Shoulders and face sunburned, those cute little freckles spread across her nose and cheeks.

He stood up, wanting to kiss her hard on the mouth. Caddy shook her head and told him to sit.

"All right then."

"I don't want you to come out to The River anymore."

"Listen now."

"Enough," Caddy said. "OK. Enough with the bullshit. I shouldn't have hit you. But damn, Donnie. Screwing Fannie Hathcock? Why the hell would you do that? It's so damn two-faced, you coming out to The River and helping me with the families and then heading out to the titty bar at night, getting a private dance from that crazy woman up in her chicken roost."

"It's not what it seems."

"Oh, right," Caddy said. "You're some kind of damn Secret Squirrel special agent, working for the govern-

ment while tooling around in your daddy's gold GTO
and listening to CCR. Come on. You can lie to me. But
just don't treat me like I'm stupid."

"I swear, Caddy," he said. "I swear it's the truth. Why
else do you think they let me out of jail? For all the shit
I pulled, I should be in jail for the rest of my life. No. I
was brought back here to get in with the folks that got
your brother shot up. I'm working something right now
that will be the end of it. Something good. But I need
you to trust me. At least for now that I'm doing the right
thing."

"Who let you out?"

"I shouldn't be telling you none of this."

"And I shouldn't be so damn stupid to come over here
and listen to more of your horseshit."

Donnie nodded, understanding.

The trailer was a tidy little space not much more than
his recliner and TV, a kitchen and a bed against the far
opposite end. Besides some vinyl and a record player, he
only had the slot for poor old Chi Chi, a shellacked ar-
madillo, laying on his back and holding a bottle of Lone
Star.

The jalousie windows were open, and in the silence
between them they could hear the sounds of the cicadas
out in the fields beyond the old movie screen. He smiled
at Caddy, knowing he could trust her with anything.
"Quinn ever talk of a federal agent by the name of Holliday?" Donnie asked.

Caddy's eyes widened and she tilted her head.

"He came out to Beaumont not long after Quinn got
shot," Donnie said. "He told me what happened and

who was responsible. I've been working with him and some other folks since I got back. We're gonna tear down that mean-ass woman's playhouse. I promise. I'm all in. But I don't want to lose you while I'm doing it."

"Don't you lie to me," Caddy said. "OK? Please don't lie to me."

"I may be full of shit," Donnie said. "But I'd never break your heart, Caddy. I've loved you since we were kids."

"Yeah?"

"I've fucked up plenty and I'm doing my damn best to set it all straight," he said. "Just stick with me, OK? It's all gonna work out. We can't tell Quinn or anyone else what I'm doing. But I swear to you we're gonna get the folks who tried to kill your brother."

"You better," Caddy said, wiping her face with her hand.

"And when this is over, I'm going to work for the rest of my life to make you happy," Donnie said, reaching around her waist and pulling her close. "How does that sound?"

He felt Caddy's body stiffen when he said it and he cradled the back of her head in his hands.

Donnie remembered all that long gorgeous hair she used to have, running down her back and tied up in long braids. What happened to that girl? Where the hell had she gone?

"I'm here, Caddy," Donnie said. "I'm not going nowhere."

21

Four days later, midnight and raining like hell, Donnie was headed back to Memphis, stopping off at the Flying J truck stop in Olive Branch. He sat in the empty section of the Subway shop eating a meatball sub after filling up a Peterbilt he'd gotten on loan from Fannie Hathcock. The sub wasn't too bad, a nice little snack before rolling out, loading up, and driving back through the night. Nobody expected much trouble. Nobody ever did. Hell, he never thought he'd have been caught in the crosshairs of the damn ATF just trying to help some good folks from south of the border. But there you go. A good deed that sure as shit wasn't left unpunished but came back and cornholed him high, hard, and good.

The plan was to pass through the security with a wink and a wave and join up with Rerun's fat ass on loading dock 23. The truck had been painted the perfect brown with UPS decals on each door. Any problems at the gate, or out along Winchester Road, and Tyrell and a few of his buddies would arrange a police escort to the state line. *What could go wrong?* Donnie started to laugh at the thought, taking another big bite. At least he wasn't hanging out in Beaumont watching a fuzzy television playing the damn Home Shopping Network or reruns of *Judge Judy*. Some of them boys so damn hard up, they started wondering what was under that old woman's robe.

Donnie dropped a little marinara sauce on his T-shirt, staring at the rain sweep across the parking lot and the diesel pumps. Lonely hours up here in north Mississippi. He looked across the way at a tired old woman with her hair in a net mopping the floor. A young black woman at the cash register nodding off as she watched something on her phone. Canned laughter and some sitcom banter. Rain tapped, tapped, tapped against the glass as he looked down at the time on his cell, knowing it wouldn't be much longer.

The airport and warehouse was a straight thirty-minute shot on up Highway 78. He would drive through the gate at a little after one, during the security shift change.

"Sure is a real frog strangler out there," the old woman said.

"Yes, ma'am," Donnie said, looking up from his sad little table. Two salt shakers and a big cup filled with Mountain Dew.

"Sure did need it," the old woman said. "This drought dried up my tomato plants and killed off my flower beds. All this rain almost seems like an insult."

"God's middle finger."

"What's that?"

"I said yes, ma'am."

"Where you headed, good-looking?" the old woman asked.

"Tucumcari," Donnie said. He'd never been there himself but liked the way it sounded. He heard it once or twice in some Western Luther had been watching. For some reason Eli Wallach coming to mind.

Donnie stood up and dumped off the wrappers and leftover chips from his tray. The woman stopped mopping and then leaned on her mop for a moment, looking for all the world like Carol Burnett on her variety show.

"Married?" she asked.

"No, ma'am," Donnie said.

"Shoot," she said. "Don't believe that. A handsome fella like you?"

"Well, I may have found the right one."

"I like the sound of that," she said. "She sure must be something special."

"She is," Donnie said. "One of a kind. Known her pretty much my whole life."

"What are you waiting on, son?"

"Things been a little complicated these days," Donnie said. "Hoping it will slow down real soon."

"Never does," she said. "Never a good time for doing nothing. Better get to it while the gettin's good."

"Don't I know it."

"And if it don't work out, my name is Lynette," she said, leaning hard on that mop handle. "If you call, ask for me special."

Donnie walked over to her, bent down and kissed her on her cheek, and headed out into the rain. He was completely soaked by the time he got up in the rig and started the engine, the whole cab shaking and shuddering to life.

Sam Frye followed Fannie from the strip club parking lot and onto the town square where it spiraled off onto Jericho Road. He thought she was headed back to her condo outside Memphis, but now she was driving out to the big sprawling cabin on the lake where she'd killed Buster White with that hammer.

Sam was cool and well rested. He switched cars and headed out of the Rez that night, taking his time, knowing Fannie Hathcock's routine down cold and how long it would take her to shut down. She never trusted anyone with the countdown or the cleanup. Fannie Hathcock was tight-minded about the cash, making sure every one of her girls tipped out every dime before they left the club.

As soon as he knew where she was going, he dropped back, careful not to scare her on that back-county highway out to the lake. He could take his time, driving and enjoying the night. The rain already passed through, leaving the twisting asphalt covered in a misty fog rising up off the pastures and farmland. Hand-painted signs advertised rattlesnake watermelon, okra, sweet potatoes, and jams and jellies. You could buy rabbits and chickens or worship at homemade church houses in busted trailers off the main road. Sam followed the road till the signs changed to ones for boat landings and bait stores, a restaurant called the Captain's Table that advertised with a small billboard promising fresh fried catfish and Gulf seafood. He slowed, taking an unmarked road away from the restaurant and out to where the asphalt turned to gravel, driving for at least four miles until he saw the glowing green light atop a pillar of rocks. His headlights hit a brass marker that read PRIVATE ENTRANCE. NO TRESPASSING.

Sam drove on farther and parked behind an abandoned trailer, the rain coming back again and patting against the windshield. The big cabin wasn't far down that road, only about a quarter mile. Sam knew it was best that he walked in, did a little recon, and then waited for the proper time to kill that woman.

He felt shame for not realizing she was the one to blame all along. Of course it was that redheaded bitch. Buster White had no more interest and business in north Mississippi than Chief Robbie did. This was a private territory with a nice tribute being paid down to the coast. But Buster White had no reason to want his son dead. The only one that Mingo could've hurt by talking would've been Fannie, with her nasty business trucking those girls in from Texas. Something Chief Robbie had warned her about time and again. Every time she tried to bring him some underage Mexican girls who didn't speak English, he would turn her away. The Chief didn't mind the skin trade, but he drew the line at slaves and children. If a grown woman chose to sell herself, that was her business, the Chief would say.

At one a.m., Sam got out of the car, popping the collar on his rain slicker, leaving his go-to Ruger .357 Redhawk and taking a cheap .45 someone had pawned back at the Rez. He placed it in the pocket of his long black coat as he walked in the rain, following the straight gravel road to the big wooden cabin, glowing yellow and warm from behind the glass. Sam felt comfortable in the rain, knowing it lessened any chance of being watched or having to deal with security guards walking the property.

Sam realized he might have to kill the big black man, too. He liked Midnight Man. He had a bit of humor to him, joking with him when Fannie had been slapped, giving Sam a sly grin as Fannie ran to the bathroom to clean the lipstick smear from her face and blood from her lip. But he'd chosen his path. And Fannie hers. And now Sam Frye would put a bullet into her pretty head and then drive all night for Oklahoma City.

Sam stood away from the cabin under a stretch of tall pine trees. He watched the empty glowing house, Fannie's white Lexus parked outside.

He figured she'd come to stay the night or was attending to details of Vardaman's visit. Sam watched from the shadows, seeing her disappear from the huge room she used to entertain. He saw a light on the second floor click on. Sam walked toward the cabin, boots crunching on the wet gravel, smelling the fetid muddy scent of the lake.

He found a large oak with long fat branches where he could take shelter and keep watch. There was no sign of Midnight Man or any of her people. He figured Fannie had grown complacent and sloppy, not realizing that Sam could not stand for what she'd done.

He pulled the cheap gun from out of his coat, screwed in the suppressor, and held it loose at his side. On the second floor, Fannie looked out the window and began to disrobe.

Untying a black dress from the side and pulling it open, she stood tall in a red bra and panties, looking out onto the empty black lake. Her breasts were two of the largest he'd ever seen in his life, her hip bones carved and prominent from the thin strap of the panties. She began to twist the piles of hair off her shapely shoulders and into a bun on top of her head.

The woman's skin was like porcelain, her hair such a rich Technicolor red and limbs so long and willowy that the breath left his chest. How could a woman who looked like that be so entirely evil? Why would she do the things she'd done?

Nobody stopped Donnie as he rolled through the gates at UPS, past the guard shack and down the service road toward the big warehouse facing the airport. A cargo plane sat on an empty runway behind a long chain-link fence, red light flashing on its wings and tail. Donnie moved on past dozens of trucks that looked just like the one he drove, letting down the window on the semi and craning his neck to see where he was headed. He found himself driving around the entire compound until he doubled back toward the main entrance and spotted the loading bay. He slowed the rig, hit reverse, and backed in smooth and easy to number 23. When he stopped and hit the hissing parking brakes, he saw Rerun standing on the dock wearing a Carhartt winter mask up on his head, the rest of his fat white body exposed in the hot lights.

He held up the flat of his hand as if telling Donnie to stop, like he'd been the one guiding the truck into the bay and not Donnie's expert driving.

Donnie reached for the UPS hat down between the seats, mashed it down on his head, and hopped from the Peterbilt. When he walked up to the platform, Rerun had already opened up the trailer, smiling bigger than shit. "More space than we'll need."

"No shit," Donnie said. "Don't you remember the conversation? I said it was better to be too long than too short and you thought that was real funny. Laughed like hell for five minutes."

"Already knocked out those cameras," Rerun said, not remembering a damn word. "Pinged 'em with my little twenty-two."

Rerun gave a grunting little laugh as Donnie headed back into the loading bay where a black fella he'd never seen before sat high in a forklift. The kid, a damn teenager, sitting up and scrolling through his cell.

"Who the hell's this?"

"Deshaun."

"And who the fuck is Deshaun?" Donnie said, turning to Deshaun. "No disrespect, man. Just don't like new people being sprung on me."

"He's cool," Rerun said, sporting a big diamond earring in his left ear. White man trying his dead-level best to be cool. "Deshaun is Akeem's second cousin."

"Well, that makes me feel a fuck ton better," Donnie said. "Can you drive that forklift, kid, or you just resting your ass?"

"If you'll get out of the way, man, he'll load us up and

we can get gone," Rerun said, wandering over to a stack of boxes on several wooden pallets. "Or do you want to sit around and jaw about it all night?"

"You," Donnie said, pointing to Rerun. "Shut the fuck up. And you," he said, now pointing to Deshaun, "start that fucker up and let's load up. Let's git 'r done and git gone, gentlemen."

A logo for RED RIVER ARMS had been stamped on the flat, long cardboard boxes. Donnie slashed through the plastic security band of one and opened up the lid to find a fresh, clean, and well-oiled AR-15. The side of the box marked LAW ENFORCEMENT ONLY.

"Honey, hush," Donnie said.

"Already checked the boxes," Rerun said.

"Well, I ain't," Donnie said. "How many?"

"As good as promised," Rerun said. "Four hundred and forty-two."

Deshaun started up the forklift, the engine puttering away, as he backed up and turned toward Donnie and Rerun, scooting right by them and sliding the rails up under a pallet stacked high with dozens of boxes loaded with the guns. Damn, if the kid wasn't good.

Donnie stood back, hat down in his eyes, and noticed three big-ass trucks pass the loading docks and snake on back to Winchester Road.

He lit a cigarette and watched the convoy driving in the rain. All he had to do was start her up, pull out, and he was as good as gone.

"Too easy?" Donnie said to Rerun.

"Ain't no such thing," Rerun said.

* * *

Sam found the side door to the kitchen and walked inside, his rubber-soled boots soundless as he moved on through the darkness and into the great room, wood-paneled and wide open, to where he'd watched Fannie kill Buster White. The room, big enough for a game of stickball, different now, with more fine carpets on the polished wood floors and leather furniture, six large televisions on the walls and a mirrored bookshelf stocked with dozens of bottles of whiskey. The woman had turned the cabin into a playhouse for rich men with big appetites and money to burn.

He kept searching for Fannie's men but saw no one. He heard nothing but knew she was somewhere upstairs, perhaps in the shower or already in bed. Sam mounted the stairs, thumbing off the safety and listening. The walls of the staircase had been decorated with paintings of fancy hunting dogs and old advertisements of white men duck hunting. After he was done, he'd toss the gun deep into the lake.

Everything was so quiet and still. He couldn't have asked for a better night to find Fannie. He only had one question for her: *Where is Mingo's body? What have you done with my son?* If he felt she answered straight and true, he would kill her with little pain. If not? Well, he had until daybreak.

He moved up to the second floor and searched the rooms against the far wall, where he'd seen her standing in those red panties contemplating the lake. In the second room, he found Fannie's black wrap dress on the bed and a pair of tall velvet heels close by. Her purse was open and a bottle of gin sat on the nightstand with a glass of ice.

He checked the bathroom. He checked the hallway. All done easy and slow and with stealth. He waited each breath for the woman to come at him with a hammer or a gun. He wasn't so arrogant or stupid to think she couldn't have spotted him on the drive out from Jericho. All through the second floor, he could smell her expensive perfume and the faint tinge of cigar smoke. She had been right there. Right there.

The .45 felt old and clunky in his hand as he took the steps back down to the great room, finding Fannie Hathcock sitting on a long, padded sofa, looking like a velvet painting that might hang over the bar in an Old West saloon. A black kimono lined with bright flowers hung loose and open over her large breasts, red hair twisted up on her head.

She tilted her head as he came into the room.

"Peekaboo," she said.

"How'd you know?"

"I've been waiting for you every night since that country trash marched into my office and slapped my face."

"So is it true?" Sam said. "Was it you who killed my son?"

"Take a seat, doll," she said. "How about a little heart-to-fucking-heart."

Donnie knew better. Once you got cocky and lazy, that's when it was Cornhole City, USA.

They'd just loaded the last pallet into the trailer when he saw the flashing blue lights through the windshield of the truck. An MPD patrol car sped in and parked crossways in front of his Peterbilt, and a second later Tyrell stepped out into the rain and walked toward the loading dock. He had on a cop hat and a long plastic slicker.

"How y'all doing tonight?" he said.

"Loaded up and ready to roll," Donnie said. "You mind moving your vehicle, son? I got me a long ways to go and a short time to get there."

Tyrell didn't say anything, walking up the steps onto the loading dock, exchanging a quick glance with Deshaun and then looking back over to Rerun. Rerun narrowed his eyes, looking uncomfortable as hell with the whole situation. What the fuck was Tyrell trying to pull at this late hour?

"You boys mind standing against that wall?"

"Yeah, I would," Donnie said. "I ain't got time for games, man. Now if you would just back that car out of my damn way, let's all get gone. Maybe you can escort me the fuck out of here like we had planned."

"Like we had planned?" Tyrell said, turning down his mouth. "I don't know you. How about you show me your driver's license and registration? Security guard said you didn't stop at the checkpoint. You know you got to stop and show them ID, man. Don't you know that? Do you even work here?"

"For fuck's sake, Tyrell," Donnie said. "I ain't got time for no bullshit."

Donnie had barely had time to say the "shit" after the "bull" when goddamn Tyrell pulled out his sidearm and aimed it right at his ass. There was a *blam-blam-blam* and the echo of a small gun somewhere inside the loading dock. Tyrell, the fucking Memphis cop, was down and bleeding. When Donnie turned, he saw Deshaun's ass hanging off the side of the forklift, a gun clattering to the concrete.

Rerun smiled up at him from where he stood, real proud he'd shot both those fellas, a pistol hanging loose in his chubby little hand. Donnie's ears rang with the sound of the gunshots as he smiled back, not sure what the hell was going on.

Rerun wavered on his feet and then fell to his damn knees, clutching at his stomach.

Donnie hadn't even had time to reach for the .38 at the small of his back. Now he was standing in a heavily guarded facility with a truckload of weapons, a dead kid, a dead Memphis cop, and a big fella bleeding out on the dock.

"What the hell, man?" Donnie said. "What was that?"

"Wasn't Akeem," Rerun said. "Tyrell threw in with Deshaun and fucked us. Wanted it all to himself. Goddamn. Son of a bitch, man. I'm shot right in the fucking gut."

Donnie didn't know what time it was. But he sure knew it was time to bust out that gate and head on back to Tibbehah County.

"Can you walk?" Donnie said.

Rerun nodded, but it sure was a chore getting that big ole boy to his feet.

"C'mon."

* * *

"Did you want an apology?" Fannie asked. "Do you want me to get down on my hands and knees and grovel for my life?"

Sam Frye didn't answer. Little beads of water dropped off his black slicker and onto the hardwood floor. He fingered at the old .45 with the long suppressor in his hand.

"Good," she said. "Because I'm not going to do any of that shit. I'm going to sit here in my comfortable silk robe, have a smoke and a drink to unwind from a hell of a goddamn day, and tell you what happened to your son. I do believe when it's all over, you'll understand just what I did and why I did it. You're a professional, Sam. You know the ways of the fucking world."

"Tell me," Sam said. His mouth felt dry. It had been a long time, many years, since he'd felt so nervous. His hand shaking around that cheap pistol.

"Mingo was my friend," Fannie said, clicking on her golden lighter and firing up that tiny cigarillo. "You know he worked for me down on the Rez with the big chief. And then came up here for a few years. Best damn employee I ever had. I swear to that. I loved that boy as if he was my own."

"You've said that," Sam said. "Only he wasn't your own. And you had him killed. Or did it yourself."

"Just wait, Sam," she said. "Please. I'm getting to all that. Let me just say, that boy really opened up to me. Told me all kinds of things about you and your ex-wife. What was her name? Norma. Yes, Norma. Y'all sure did love to party. Wow. Sounds like that bitch put your lovesick ass through the wringer. All those goddamn men. The shame. The drugs. What a fucking mess in high heels."

Sam steadied his hand. He raised the weapon. It would be so easy. Just a flick of his index finger and Fannie Hathcock would quit talking and cease to be.

But he couldn't. Not now.

He just had to know about his beautiful little boy.

Donnie didn't slow down as he hit the security gate, inches from the bumper of another semi he followed out onto Winchester, the road to the airport empty and lonely at one-thirty a.m. Donnie drove easy and cool, passing by the apartment buildings and strip malls, going right by the Take Off Grill, where he'd first met Akeem and Rerun and took first damn place in the Hot Wing Challenge. They were slow rolling solid and easy past Dixie Belles strip club, all lit up in pink neon, with a sign outside reading: GIRLS WITHOUT UNDERWEAR DON'T GET THEIR PANTIES IN A BUNCH.

"How you doing there, partner?" Donnie asked.

Rerun grunted something, leaned against the passenger door and window looking pale and bled out, eyes glassy enough they refracted the neon of the strip club.

"Think you can hold on till Tibbehah?"

Rerun didn't answer.

In truth, they didn't have a damn choice. He couldn't exactly roll up to Baptist Memorial in that big rig and drop off a gunshot victim without drawing a little attention to himself. No, ole Rerun would just have to hold on until they crossed the state line and he could dogleg it somewhere around Red Banks. Maybe then he might be able to stop off and check out what exactly Rerun was dealing with. But right fucking now, the best he could offer was the jacket from the UPS uniform pressed against his big belly, praying like hell that his guts didn't come tumbling out.

"How about some music?" Donnie said. "You like some music, big man?"

Rerun grunted. Donnie reached up to the stereo above the windshield and flitted about the channels, searching for some decent music as they headed south along Highway 78 and down toward the state line. This was a solid area to pass through, hundreds of eighteen-wheelers coming and going out the intermodal facility and the Love's truck stop. He finally found a classic rock station, 98.1, playing ole Joe Walsh. "Life's Been Good." *Hell yeah.* That would get 'em through the night.

Donnie thumped at the big wheel, downshifting as they hit the line, rolling into Mississippi. A shit ton of guns in his trailer and a nearly dead fat man riding shotgun.

"Don't know why people always shit on the Eagles," Donnie said. "It always impressed the hell out of me how Don Henley could play the fucking drums while singing. I love 'The Long Run' so damn much. I don't give two shits what anyone else said. I'd fight any bastard who says that's not a fine song. What do you think, Rerun? You old enough to listen to the damn Eagles?"

Rerun didn't answer. His head lolling on his shoulder, tongue hanging loose.

"Almost there, buddy," Donnie said, shifting down, looking to the next exit. "Don't let your big ass be dying on me."

"Now do you understand?"

Sam didn't answer, seated across from Fannie Hathcock in the cavernous room, dead animals everywhere, watching them with glass eyes. The chilled air in the room smelled of cigar smoke and women's perfume. Not of the expensive stuff Fannie wore, but cheap body lotion, cherry and strawberry stuff sold by the gallon. There were tiny bits of glitter all over the leather couch where she sat from strippers wriggling in the seats. Looking closer, pinpricks of cigarette burns in the full-grain leather.

"I don't want trouble," Fannie said. "I can help you bring Mingo home."

"How?"

"I can take you to where he was buried."

"You know?"

"I was there, Sam," Fannie said, leaning forward and touching his knee. "I cried like a baby for days. Buster White killed him. Why won't you listen to me? Why would you take the word of some country trash off the street? She blames me for everything. Anything bad goes on in Tibbehah County it's Miss Fannie's fault. But you? You are in the goddamn life. You know when you are outmaneuvered and outgunned. There was nothing I could do but watch. God. Just to think about it. Why do you think killing Buster White gave me so much goddamn pleasure? Every whack of the hammer brought tears to my eyes thinking about that boy. He was so good, Sam. He was a good man. A loyal, hard worker and a friend to me."

Sam didn't speak. His heart raced and mouth felt dry as he watched the woman take a swig of some gin. Her voice had a slight tremor, hands shaking on the glass.

"Search me," she said. "I don't have a gun. I don't even have my hammer, baby. I just wanted it to be you and me. I wanted you to sit down, take a load off, and listen to why I couldn't tell you. I just couldn't tell you, Sam. I'm so sorry. I'm so fucking sorry."

Sam wasn't sure what to say. Mingo and his daughter had been his biggest embarrassment. He was a failure. A missing father. A loser who never offered guidance or love. He only saw the boy maybe four or five times after Norma died. He let others care for him, left him to be raised on the Rez by aunts, uncles, useless cousins while Sam was out doing for Sam Frye. He let out a long breath and stood, gun loose in his hand.

He had failed his son completely. The woman leaned back, cigarillo pointed upward in her mouth, opening her knees as she reclined.

"He had your eyes," Fannie said, speaking to the ceiling. "You know that. So kind and dark. Handsome. So very handsome."

The woman started to cry and Sam walked away from her as she leaned up and took another drink from the crystal glass. The ice clinking loud behind him as he headed out the big twin doors of the porch, propped open and letting in the hot, humid air off the dark and endless lake. Choctaw Lake, named for his people but built long after they'd been run from Mississippi or had to hide out like animals in the wilds of the hills. *Choctaw Lake.* Sam stepped outside to have a cigarette, listening to the sounds of the woods, the crickets and frogs deep-throated and loud, the ticking of water off the leaves.

The lake seemed to go forever, a fog lifting off the surface and twisting into the mist.

He slipped the gun back into his pocket, unsure what he needed to do. Was the woman now offering herself to him? She knew he'd been watching. She had wanted him to come to her.

Sam Frye knew as soon as he heard them. The security lights of the grand house on the lake clicked on and flooded out onto the rich green lawn. Four men with rifles stepped out toward the porch, all of them wearing sheriff's office uniforms and pointing guns straight at him.

Sam Frye didn't speak. What can a man say in his last moments? He flicked the half-spent cigarette out into the wetness, looking the jug-eared man with the tin star on his chest straight in the eye.

The rain tilted sideways across the green lawn and lake as they started to fire.

22

Quinn found Bentley Vandeven at his family spread, a sprawling three-thousand-acre compound called Cedar Grove down in Pocahontas, Mississippi. He hadn't been there in years, not since tracking down his father there years ago, living in a rusted-out trailer and tending to the horses and stables for the Vandeven family. Jason Colson was supposed to be elsewhere, Los Angeles, Austin, maybe even up in Wyoming. Some rumors even had him playing a stunt double in a new Indiana Jones movie. But nope, Quinn's father had been hiding out not more than two hours from Tibbehah County, teaching Bentley to ride and shoot skeet and, if the rumors were true, spending even more time with Bentley's mother, a well-known socialite named Mary-Margaret who'd been Miss Ole Miss in the eighties and later a runner-up Miss USA.

Bentley rode up to the stables in a golf cart, dressed for the hunt in khaki pants, a pressed blue shirt with a shooter patch on his right shoulder, and rose-tinted sunglasses. "Damn good to see you, Quinn," he said, stepping out of the cart. "Wish you'd called first. Been out with a few guests hunting quail."

"Y'all stocking or transplanting?"

"Stocking," Bentley said. "Too many coyotes around here to transplant."

"Most folks think the bush hog killed the quail in the South," Quinn said. "Destroyed their habitat."

"Or armadillos eating their eggs or pesticides," Bentley said. "We stock pheasants, too. You should come down sometime. It's a hell of a good time. Love for you to be my guest."

"I don't hunt for sport," Quinn said.

"Those birds get a fair shake," Bentley said, standing next to a tall fence painted black and a small corral where Quinn's dad used to train Tennessee Walkers. His face appeared thinner than Quinn recalled, almost sallow, and he looked as if he'd lost twenty or thirty pounds. "We let 'em out that morning and they get plenty of time to scatter. It's mainly about watching those bird dogs work. They just love it. Have you seen our English setters? They come from a line in Oxford that goes back sixty years."

Quinn shook his head, watching a blue roan stallion and a coal black mare galloping around the paddock. The riders were young women, looked to be about college age, dressed in tank tops and short shorts with tall riding boots. Both of them waved to Bentley as they practiced with the horses.

"Friends of my sisters," Bentley said. "Silly girls. They're just visiting."

"Y'all do have plenty of space."

The stable had dozens of private rooms on the second floor, the entire structure built of river stone, cypress beams, and copper fixtures. Jason Colson had given him a tour when Quinn had come to confront him. His father seemed proud of the work he was doing for the Vande-vens, not ashamed in the least of hiding out from his own family.

"Something on your mind?" Bentley asked.

Quinn leaned his elbows on the black rail fence, watching the women sit high in the saddle, the Walkers cantering in a fine, smooth gait around the paddock. He recalled his dad saying something about Tennessee Walk-ers riding so smooth, you could hold a cup of tea in your hand without spilling a drop.

"Haven't seen you around lately," Quinn said.

"Things with Caddy didn't really work out," he said. "I think everyone saw that crashing and burning from the start."

"Because you were using her to keep tabs on me."

"I think it was more about the age difference," Bent-ley said. "Your sister is six years older. If Caddy was a man and I was a woman, nobody would say a thing. My mother is twenty years younger than my dad."

"Yep," Quinn said. "That must be it."

Caddy had once told Quinn that Mary-Margaret Vandeven had moved on from the aging stuntman to the owner of a BMW dealership and now an Argentinian horse trainer half her age.

"The only reason I'm back here now is because Daddy decided to open up Cedar Grove," Bentley said. "I run the hunts and my sister Anna runs the wedding parties. We built a beautiful little chapel by the lake. You can stay out here with your whole family, have the entire grounds to yourself for a weekend. It's not what I want, but it allowed us to keep the land. It's not all roses and sunshine down here, Quinn. We have troubles, too."

Quinn looked at Bentley, not really being able to see his eyes behind the rose-tinted glasses. For a young man in his early thirties, he was looking haggard. He needed a haircut and a shave pretty badly. The shirt was tailored and probably expensive but hung off his skinny frame like it was on a scarecrow.

"Caddy said you were leaving Jackson."

"I hate my daddy about as much as you hate yours," he said. "I guess I'm just biding my damn time before he keels over."

"Hard to hate someone that you barely know and seldom see."

"Haven't heard from Jason lately?" Bentley asked, taking off the sunglasses and placing them in the pocket of the hunting shirt with the shooter patch, two pockets, and all types of bells and whistles.

"Haven't heard from him for three years," Quinn said.

"Me, either," Bentley said. "I think your daddy is ashamed of what happened with that big land deal in Jericho. Maybe blames some of that on me, since it was my father who was supposed to back him. I'm real sorry about how that worked out."

"My father has a hard time seeing things through,"

Quinn said. "His most death-defying stunt has always been confrontation."

"Most folks think my father is one hard-nosed, tough-as-nails businessman," Bentley said. "But he inherited most of what he's got and my mother runs this family and all of Cedar Grove. That man is only held together by Glenfiddich and duct tape."

Bentley let out a long breath and joined Quinn, leaning against the top rail. Quinn faced the corral while Bentley leaned his back against the fence. The sun was high and very hot, the pasture and paddock still moist and muddy from the rains.

"Don't suppose you drove all this way for us to talk about daddy issues?" he said.

"Nope."

"You know we own a piece of those chicken plants," he said. "And you came to find out what I know about that man who got shot, the one who was suing us for workplace conditions."

"Hector Herrera," Quinn said. "But you knew his name. You warned Caddy not to get too close to him. That it wasn't safe."

"With these people?" Bentley said. "I'd call that an educated goddamn guess."

"You've heard something."

"My father and his people didn't care for Herrera," Bentley said. "He was suing them for ten million dollars. What the hell do you think?"

"I think you know more than how to open the cages of a bunch of birds and teach some rich folks where to aim," Quinn said. "A lot more, I'd say. Who's trucking in those prisoners from those private jails?"

"Shit, Quinn," Bentley said. "Why do you think I'm here driving folks from New York around in golf carts? Once my father got involved with the Watchmen, I was out. I wanted nothing to do with him or any of these people. All of this has gone too damn far. Vardaman. He lives off the hate he knew was festering under the surface with those people. He did his dead-level best to cultivate and grow them to make him stronger. Make them feel better about their own pathetic lives. That's not the Mississippi I know."

"Your daddy didn't get rich by playing by the rules," Quinn said. "And y'all didn't earn this big stable and all these grounds by the sweat of your brow."

As the women circled back by the fence, Bentley turned to the paddock and forced a smile and waved. He spoke between clenched teeth. "I know what I am," he said. "And who we are. Sometimes I wish I could scrub all the bullshit right off me."

"Always time to stand up."

"For what?"

"Help me find out what the hell's going on in my county."

Bentley started to laugh, cackling so much it sounded like he might choke. Bentley turned from the fence and spit, eyeing Quinn with a reddened face.

"You want me to turn on my own father?"

Quinn turned his head to Bentley. He adjusted the brim of his cap, looking him straight in the eye, and nodded.

"And possibly land his ass in prison?" he asked. "Lose everything my family has left?"

Quinn didn't answer.

"Damn you, Quinn Colson," Bentley said. "That's a hell of a thing to ask a man. You might could turn on Jason. But damn. I can't do that. That's too damn much."

Quinn watched one of the women, one hand on the reins with a light touch as she moved the horse into a steady gallop, going round and round. The horse fighting her at the bit, tossing its head back and forth but finally taking the direction, the hooves clomping in a steady, elegant rhythm.

"My daddy's coming later tonight," Bentley said. "When he hits that fourth scotch, there's not a man alive who can shut his damn mouth."

Quinn turned to him and offered his hand. "You know where to find me."

Bentley waited for a second and then shook it.

It was almost as if nothing had happened at all. The rain had gone away and the sun had come out and Caddy and Jason were making their weekend rounds to the food banks, grocery stores, and churches in Tibbehah. She had the windows down on the old truck, thank God running again after she replaced a bad battery that morning, and now they were headed south from the Yellow Leaf community, richer by a few hundred cans of food and some cooking oil. Mac Davis's "I Believe in Music" coming from an old cassette she found at her momma's house, Jean telling her that Mac had not only written songs for Elvis but had hosted some of the best Christmas specials ever made. Jean made the seventies seem like some weird, mystical time, like a Redneck Camelot.

"When do you think Coach will let me back on the team?" Jason asked.

"That's between you and Coach."

"But what I did should count for something."

"Running away?" Caddy asked.

"No, that other thing."

"Depends on how impressed your coach is with you stabbing a pimp in the leg."

"Wasn't his leg, Momma," Jason said. "I stabbed that son of a bitch right in the foot."

"Jason?" Caddy said. "How about you tone down the cussing. Just for a few days. You can talk like that in front of your Uncle Quinn and Boom. But I'm your mother. OK? Not your fishing buddy."

Jason nodded, Caddy taking those gentle curves down toward Jericho, Mac Davis now singing his own rendition of "A Little Less Conversation," a funky, down-home version of the song Elvis made famous. It was slow and cool, good driving music, Caddy thought, heading into the sun and reaching for her cheap white sunglasses on the cracked dash.

They passed over the Big Black River bridge, a slash of heavy-duty concrete built beside the old train trestle. Caddy could never pass over the water and see that boat landing without thinking about poor Milly Jones, doused with gasoline and set afire for trying to tell the truth, a trucker finding her walking from her car in flames.

Caddy glanced over at Jason and patted his knee,

thanking the Lord that he'd escaped and made it back home safe. She'd always hoped and prayed that the darkness would never touch her son's life. Caddy had more than her fair share of darkness, living in sin and desperation until she crawled out from her hole into the sunshine. She felt she'd left those people behind, the ones that clawed at you and tried to hold you down. Jason looked over at her and smiled, brown-skinned and blue-eyed, looking more and more like her father every day and a little like some man she couldn't even recall.

"Slow down, Momma."

"What's that?"

"Slow down," he said.

Caddy looked into her rearview, noticing a Tibbehah County Sheriff's patrol car coming up behind her. In the past, she'd never given them a second glance. Being the sheriff's sister definitely had its advantages. Not to mention, the sheriff's office didn't mess much with speeding tickets and traffic violations. But after what happened to Hector Herrera, just the thought of a cruiser tailing her made her blood run cold. She turned down that fun, funky music and placed both hands on the wheel. She made sure her seat belt was buckled and told Jason to do the same, even though he always wore his seat belt.

"What is it?"

"Nothing," she said. "Just in case."

"Just in case what?"

She saw the patrol car speed up close to her bumper, Caddy looking back and praying it was someone she knew. But it wasn't. It was a white man wearing dark sunglasses, and soon he hit the flashing blue lights, riding her tail until she slowed and rolled over onto the shoulder. They weren't two miles from the Jericho city limits.

Caddy looked over to Jason and tried to compose herself. She reached into her purse for license and registration, Quinn always telling her to have it ready, just to put the deputy at ease.

"You know why I stopped you?" the deputy said.

"I sure don't," Caddy said, trying to be polite, although she knew what was coming.

"You were driving twenty miles over the speed limit."

"In this old truck?" she said. "That's not possible."

The man didn't answer. He had narrow, sleepy eyes and a pockmarked, bloated face. Something about his hair made her think of a child's, cut off with scissors in a straight line across his forehead. His eyes red, unfocused, and bleary, breath that smelled like liquor and onions.

He walked behind her truck and wrote down her tag. "License."

She handed over her driver's license, noticing the name tag on his uniform said M. DANBURY.

"You kin to the old sheriff?"

"The sheriff is my brother."

"And who's this colored kid?"

"Excuse me," she said. "What the hell did you just say?"

Two motorcycles came off the Big Black Bridge and sped past them, going twice the speed Caddy had been going. M. Danbury didn't even look at them as they passed, their exhausts blasting loud down the hills and into the straightaway.

He looked over the license and then tucked it into his

shirt pocket. He turned his head to spit and then looked right back to Caddy, staring hard at her and then to Jason. Her heart was beating so damn fast, hands tight on the wheel while her left leg started jumping up and down.

The deputy turned and headed to the patrol car, hefting his thick body behind the wheel.

"What's going on?" Jason asked, whispering.

"I don't know."

"Were you speeding?"

"No."

"Then what does he want?"

Caddy couldn't lie. Had always promised to always be straight and truthful with Jason. "He's trying to make trouble."

Neither of them spoke until Danbury got out of the patrol car and shuffled back to Caddy's open window. Caddy looked in her rearview mirror, hoping like hell that someone she knew would pass by. Maybe someone who'd stop off and notice her, realize what this man was trying to do to her and Jason. Her son had already been through enough.

"Your tag is expired."

"Is it?"

"Expired two months back," Danbury said, his mouth working into a tight little grin. "And this insurance card is from two years ago. What do you think we should do about that?"

Caddy didn't answer. She was so damn mad, she was shaking. That was the worst of it. The humiliation of letting this man try to scare and intimidate her. But she'd had enough. She knew full well Jesus was riding shotgun and would look out for her and Jason and there was nothing this man could do to them.

"I guess you were one of the men who shot and killed Hector Herrera."

Danbury grinned some more. He turned his head. He spit.

"Y'all are killers," she said. "The real criminals."

"I'd be careful with that attitude," he said. "You might be figuring that the little camera on my dash is on and you can smart-talk me all you want. But you'd be wrong, Miss Colson. That camera's dead-ass broke. And what happens out here is between us."

"And my child," she said. "You want to do this in front of a child?"

"Honestly, I don't give a fuck about you or your colored boy," he said. "How about you agree to shut your damn mouth and I'll give you your license back."

Caddy was about to answer when she spotted a second patrol car roll up behind Danbury's. When the door opened, Reggie Caruthers jumped out and marched up to where Danbury stood. He didn't say a thing, just hung there on Danbury's shoulder, staring him down. The fat man's face was red and sweating as he reached into his pocket and tossed her license to the ground.

Danbury swore a few times before pushing past Reggie, knocking shoulder to shoulder, and jumped into his patrol car. He burned some rubber on the pavement and sped on past them on the way back to Jericho.

"Y'all all right?" Reggie said. "Jesus. Heard him call in your license on the radio."

"God, Reggie," Caddy said. "Who the hell are these people?"

Boom got a strawberry ice cream cone at Lipscomb's Drugstore and walked across the street to the Square to see what the hell was going on. A crowd had gathered by the gazebo and veterans' memorial with a couple TV news trucks parked downtown. Cameras had been set up and aimed at the gazebo steps where Brock Tanner appeared to be holding a news conference. He was dressed in the khaki uniform Quinn always wore, minus the Wranglers and the cowboy boots, black hair slicked down against his skull and jug ears jutting out like handles on a sugar bowl.

Boom stepped in the crowd and stood by Betty Jo Mize, who was scribbling notes onto a steno pad for the *Tibbehah County Monitor*. She didn't even seem to notice Boom while she worked, writing fast on the page with eyes up on Brock Tanner speaking at a makeshift lectern.

"At approximately one a.m. this morning, the Tibbehah County Sheriff's Office answered a trespass call on a private property near Choctaw Lake. There we came into contact with Samuel Teschu Frye, who was wanted on numerous felonies by the sheriff's office, the FBI, and U.S. Marshals Service. When members of the sheriff's office rapid response team cornered Mr. Frye, he began to fire on myself and three of my deputies. Through quick action and quick thinking, we were able to neutralize Frye. He was pronounced dead on the scene by EMTs. This man was considered armed and dangerous, the main suspect in a raid that happened at our sheriff's office almost a year ago. He was believed to be the suspect who gained entry to our county jail by unknown means and killed a prisoner. That prisoner had known ties to a criminal syndicate on the Gulf Coast and this incident was considered a contract killing."

Boom could see that Tanner loved to talk, continuing on about his daring raid and all the brave deputies in his employ had done. He thanked his military training and the Maker above.

"We believe Mr. Frye was also involved in a shoot-out with my predecessor last October when the sheriff was nearly killed," Tanner said. "A task force was set up a short time later by Governor J. K. Vardaman to get to the root of how Frye was allowed entry to the jail and how a dispute between him and the then-Sheriff Colson erupted. The findings of that inquiry should be made public in the coming weeks."

Betty Jo Mize elbowed Boom hard in his ribs. When he looked down at the little gray-headed woman, she shook her head. She looked disgusted at the whole sorry carnival that had set up on her beloved Jericho Square.

As soon as she could, the woman wove her way through the crowd and TV reporters to the front of the gazebo and Tanner's lectern. "Last week your deputies were also involved in a deadly shooting with a man named Hector Herrera," Mize said. "Since that time, y'all haven't answered a single question about how or why it happened."

Tanner looked annoyed, not used to getting straight talk or basic questions. But Mize stood her ground, while the other, much younger reporters kept quiet and waited for a reply. The old woman's gray hair stiff and teased, a pencil slipped behind her right ear.

"I told you several times that shooting is an ongoing investigation," Tanner said. "Since you've been around since the Civil War, Miss Mize, I figure you'd understand how law enforcement works."

Tanner gave a little grin, happy with himself, shuffling the papers in front of him. Boom wanted to walk up to that boy and grab him by the throat with his hook, toss his ass far and wide from the memorial and town square.

"I've covered a lot of fine law officers in this county and some sorry ones, too," Miss Mize said, raising her voice enough that people in the crowd took note. "Want to guess what category you fall in?"

Tanner's face colored and his nose flared. He shook his head and made a twirling motion around his ears, letting everyone know he believed Miss Mize had gone senile. Boom had known Betty Jo Mize since she used to cover his little league football games. She'd once written a sympathetic editorial about his father when he joined in with some other black cotton farmers to get fair prices at the local gin.

"Hector Herrera had been fighting to get those poultry plant workers freed," Betty Jo Mize said. "He'd also filed a ten-million-dollar lawsuit on their behalf. Are you telling us that he just happened to jump out of his vehicle and start firing on y'all one day? What kind of stupid do you think we are, boy?"

Tanner shook his head, announcing there would be no more questions. He left the lectern, walked from the

Square, and met up with his right-hand man Mitchell Danbury, who'd just parked his cruiser. Danbury stood by the open door of his patrol car and leaned into Tanner's ear to whisper something.

"Goddamn, this sure stinks," Miss Mize said. "Where's Quinn?"

"You know, I was just about to call him," Boom said.

"Tell him to call me, too," Miss Mize said. "That jug-eared son of a bitch just accused him of being in bed with organized crime. Sure would like to know what Quinn has to say about that."

"Oh, you know Quinn," Boom said. "Few words. Lots of action."

"Tell him to hurry," Miss Mize said. "Like ole Porter Wagoner sang, I've enjoyed as much of this as I can stand."

"Yes, ma'am."

Flowers.

Nat Wilkins watched as Fannie brought in more fucking flowers, huge arrangements of white roses, birds of paradise, and orchids, to her intimate and personal dinner party. Of course, those men from Jackson wouldn't notice. The only thing they cared about was young cooze wiggling in their laps and old scotch being poured into their crystal glasses.

Nat had worked most of the day stocking the bar with bootleg booze from Fannie's trucker contacts. So many whiskeys and bourbons that weren't allowed to be sold within the state of Mississippi now being set high on the mirrored shelving of the bar. She made sure they had some tequila, vodka, and good gin, too. But mainly this was about the whiskey, cigars, and women for Vardaman's inner circle. The centerpiece being that damn swimming pool made of river rocks out back where Fannie would bring in a dirty dozen in the tiniest of swimsuits and probably nothing at all, making sure those young girls told those old fat men, bald and graying with hairs coming out their ears, just how attractive they were.

"Don't forget the soda pop," Fannie said, sneaking up behind Nat.

"Yes, ma'am."

"Some of these old boys would fuck a light socket but won't touch a sip of liquor," she said. "Better make sure you can pour a tall Coca-Cola on ice."

"Yes, ma'am," Nat said. "You think we're good on that Pappy Van Winkle? Only have four bottles. I know that's all these folks gonna ask for. *Pour me a big ole bourbon and Coke with the best damn whiskey y'all got.* Damn heathens."

"I'd take exception to it if I didn't know it's nothing but Jim Fucking Beam in those bottles," Fannie said. "They won't know the damn difference."

Nat nodded, watching Fannie fiddle with the towering flower arrangements along the center of the long cypress table. From the place settings, it looked as if Fannie was expecting ten to twelve men, with Vardaman at one end of the table and Fannie at the other.

It was damn hot inside that lake house with the French doors propped open for the deliverymen to come and go. Nat had already started to sweat in her black tank top, her hair worn in long braids down her back.

"What happened to the afro?" Fannie asked.

"Decided to switch it up a little."

"Can you change it back?" Fannie asked. "Already had two good ole boys wanted to know about that fine girl with that big bouncy afro. I'll pay whatever you need to get it back styled high and right. We want everything to look and feel perfect for this little dinner party."

"You mind me asking what this is all about?"

Fannie winked at Nat. "Half business," Fannie said. "Half hail to the goddamn chief. Make sure all that beer gets iced down, too. We want those bottles cold as can be when those first planes touch down."

Nat nodded, watching Fannie walk out of the back doors and speak to the foreman of the crew setting out leather recliners and rocking chairs and staking tiki torches at the edge of the pool. Another twenty minutes passed before she saw Fannie heading out a side door, saying she'd be back later.

Fannie acted like she was more secure and in charge with Sam Frye dead. But Nat knew what this was really about was making those good ole boys fat and happy and on her damn side just in case Chief Robbie wanted to make trouble. Those boys loved their gambling, but there wasn't a man alive who couldn't be caught in a trap made of whiskey and cooze.

Nat wandered through the great room and back to the opening by the staircase, pushing in through the heavy oak doors decorated with stained-glass peacocks that led into the poker room. The green felt of the tables now covered over with black leather, surrounded by a dozen or so heavy leather chairs with brass nailhead trim. Ashtrays set about the side tables and along the bookshelf. Yeah, this is where the cigars would be lit, the whiskey would flow, and the men would get down to business.

Nat searched the bookshelves loaded with bottles of Pappy, Blanton's, Glenfiddich, and Johnnie Walker Blue. She was looking for the right place to slide in that little black cube Holliday had passed her. A good spot to take it all in but also in a spot where it wouldn't be seen or moved. In the middle of all the glass decanters and old leather-bound books, some decorator had propped up a framed photo of an old Civil War general, bearded and grim-faced, eyes black and dead, something like a phantom as he stared out at Nat. Put a red baseball hat and some blue coveralls on his grizzled ass and that son of a bitch would look right at home changing her damn oil.

She scooted the gilded frame over and found the perfect nook for the cube. Yep, this would do damn nicely. Only the smallest sliver of space between the books and the antique portrait.

Nat turned the unit on, slid it into position, and headed out of the poker room back into the lake house, where no one had noticed a damn thing.

23

Donnie never left the big Quonset hut out on Fannie's airstrip after he rolled through the gates in the UPS truck at dawn. Midnight Man and some rough old dude named Carl had met him, Carl being one of the Byrds, a family of thieves who'd gotten busted running chop shops back in the eighties. Carl hadn't said much, just grunted and took the keys of the Peterbilt and drove off into one of the other cavernous warehouses, most definitely to cut that semi into a million different pieces. Donnie had helped unload the trailer, Midnight Man working a forklift maybe even better than the late, great Deshaun, setting the boxes from Red River Arms into a separate trailer that he'd take to where Ole Man Coldfield and his boys in gray wanted to meet. Finally, Donnie had found a shower and a cot in the back of one of Fannie's warehouses to get some sleep.

Damn, what a shitshow.

Rerun died not long after they crossed the state line and Donnie dumped his body behind a burned-out barbecue joint somewhere around Guntown. If he'd had time, Donnie would've given him a proper burial. But all he could do was place Rerun's Carhartt cold-weather mask down over his face and say the quickest prayer he could: "Sure do appreciate you killing those motherfuckers before they killed me. I didn't know much about you other than you was kinda fat and liked hot wings. A white man who wasn't a bigot and associated with black folks. *The Lord is close to the brokenhearted and saves those crushed in spirit.* Sorry, dude, that's all I got. And I got to go. *Amen.*"

Donnie had been awake for a day and a half when he finally laid on that cot in the warehouse and closed his eyes. He didn't wake up until Akeem Triplett himself shook him by the shoulder. Akeem looking down at him, cool and reserved in that white satin suit, black shades, and little toothpick tucked at the corner of his mouth.

"It's about game time, Donnie Varner," Triplett said. "You ready?"

"Yeah, man," Donnie said, pushing himself up off the cot and looking down at his cell phone. "You coming with me or what?"

"I don't think they'd dig someone like me at that Cracker Barrel convention," Triplett said. "No, sir. You unload those guns, get that money, and meet me back here. We'll take care of the split then. Cool?"

"Cool."

"Sorry with all that shit back in Memphis with Tyrell," Triplett said. "Motherfucker got greedy and tried to slice your ass out of the deal."

"Hadn't been for Rerun my ass would be dead."

"Deshaun," Triplett said. "Damn. That's my heart, man. I loved that boy. Can't believe he'd stab me in the back and throw in with fucking Tyrell. I shoulda known better. Talked about it with Mr. Sledge. Mr. Sledge offered his apologies for the lack of hospitality in South Memphis. When we split that money up, you'll get part of Rerun's cut, too. Cool?"

"Cool," Donnie said again.

The warehouse was cavernous, the guts of the building filled with floor-to-ceiling heavy-duty metal shelving like they had at a Costco. Crates and boxes filled with appliances, car parts, commercial grade tools, and electronics. Earlier Donnie had marveled at all the shit that runs through Tibbehah County, so many damn tractor-trailers hijacked and sold through Fannie's little operation here. He had to admit he was impressed.

"You nervous?" Triplett said.

Donnie shook his head, stood up and reached for the fresh T-shirt he'd found in the warehouse. The brown UPS uniform he'd been wearing was covered in Rerun's blood. This shirt was white and advertised Pap's Place. WHERE CATFISH IS KING AND JESUS IS LORD.

"I used to get real nervous before kickoff," Triplett said. "I'd be keyed up as hell before that whistle blew and I saw that ball flying high in the air. Soon as it hit my hands, all that shit was gone, adrenaline pumping, running full the fuck out with all those boys trying to take my damn head off. Wasn't the action making me nervous. It was not being able to do something about it. Once it was game time? Shit, man. It was on."

"I don't trust these folks," Donnie said. "Real squirrely group of white boys."

"That's why we've arranged for this shit to go down in a controlled environment," he said. "I don't give a shit what that crazy old man say. You tell him to meet you out back of the Rebel Truck Stop. They got this truck wash for big rigs that you can just roll in and out of. Make this thing as easy as going through the drive-thru at Mickey D's. You hear what I'm saying?"

"I don't know if the Watchmen will go for that," Donnie said. "I kind of get the feeling they want me to deliver to the furniture store."

"Damn Zeke's Value City."

"Yep."

"Fuck that shit," Triplett said. "They ain't getting no home field advantage. We do this in Fannie Hathcock's world, those motherfuckers ain't gonna know what to expect. But they know what happens if they try to grab those guns and not pay. Shit, man."

"But you'll be close by."

"You know it." Triplett took out the toothpick and winked at Donnie. "Tonight, they got half-price beer, chicken wings, and UFC fights on the big screen over at Vienna's Place. Yeah, me and my boys will be real close by in case some shit goes down. But let's hope it all goes smooth, you know. No bullshit. No lies. You get that goddamn money and meet us back here. I'm told we can even order in a little talent to keep us busy while we count cash. I heard that Miss Fannie has a few cases of some damn Dom Pérignon somewhere back here."

"I'd settle for a cold six of Coors Light."

"Let me ask you a question," Triplett said. "You ever tried to hit that?"

"Hit what?"

"Oh, hell," he said. "You know. Miss Fannie."

"No way."

"Smart man," Triplett said. "I'd be half afraid that woman's pussy got some sharp teeth down there. Rip my pecker clean off."

"I don't know about all that," Donnie said. "That woman's got more twists and turns on her than Six Flags Over Georgia. Figured she might be one hell of a time."

"I heard this story, don't know if it's true or not, that Fannie Hathcock done fucked a man to death."

"Yeah?"

"Yeah," Triplett said. "I don't care how good she looks. You better keep your ass away from that. I'm just saying."

Donnie nodded. Akeem Triplett offered his fist and Donnie bumped it back.

"Like Coach used to tell us," Triplett said. "You either demand some respect or expect defeat. Which way's it going to go?"

"It's cool," Donnie said. "I'm ready."

"You ready to hit it like a black man?"

"Come on now," Donnie said. "Shit."

"Say it," Triplett said. "I want to hear you say it loud and proud."

"I'm ready."

"To what?"

"Hit it like a black man."

"I said loud and proud."

Donnie yelled, the words echoing through the expanse of the big tin warehouse. Triplett grinned big as Donnie's cell phone began to chirp, one of the numbers the Watchmen boys were using this week.

He looked to Akeem, nodded, and accepted the call.

"Bentley Vandeven," Boom said, sitting behind the wheel of his big jacked-up Chevy, Quinn riding shotgun. "That's the whitest damn name I ever heard in my life. Never did like that dude. Big teeth and big hair. Had him a real frat boy attitude."

"He came through," Quinn said. "Stood up. Said it took his daddy four scotches before he started to talk about the Watchmen. Bentley said his old man was finished with all those people, called them white trash out of the hills. He said whatever support they gave in the last election was over. The good ole boys doing all they can to keep them far away from Vardaman."

"They don't think goddamn J. K. Vardaman is white trash come to town?" Boom said. "Shit. That motherfucker smells like chicken shit and kerosene, same as Johnny Stagg."

"Johnny Stagg, J. K. Vardaman, the Watchmen—all of them come from the same place," Quinn said. "Me and you been fighting them ever since we came home."

"Been here long before me and you were born," Boom said. "And they gonna be around long after we die."

"That's a hard take," Quinn said.

"Do I lie?"

Quinn and Boom had parked on the far side of the

Confederate cemetery under the rusted West Jericho Water Association tower. Bentley's daddy said that the Watchmen were back doing business in Tibbehah County, just to thumb their nose at Vardaman, working a big gun deal through some old man that collected Civil War memorabilia and ran some kind of two-bit museum. Quinn knew straight off they were talking about Zeke Coldfield, a crazy old coot often called the town's unofficial historian and keeper of the flame, with his furniture store next to a Confederate graveyard. More than five hundred soldiers were buried there, a few fine old homes in and around Jericho serving as hospitals for those wounded at Corinth and Brice's Cross Roads and the Second Battle of Jericho. It was a barren, stark place. The rows of headstones in the flat field a solemn reminder of what had happened in America not that long ago.

"What do they aim to do with all these guns?" Boom said.

"Doubt they even know," Quinn said. "This whole thing started as some kind of fanboy movement for Vardaman. But now it's out of hand."

"Out of hand," Boom said. "Shit. That's all you got to say about it?"

"Vardaman doesn't need them anymore."

"Now that the killer from the Rez is dead, they're the only ones left who set you up."

"Nope."

"You talking Fannie?"

Quinn nodded.

"Y'all ain't ever gonna catch that mean-ass bitch," Boom said. "No way. Y'all might take down these crazy folks and maybe Vardaman, but we'd still be stuck with Fannie Hathcock. Might as well get a historic marker for Vienna's Place, the jewel of U.S. Highway 45."

"We got Stagg."

"Stagg fucked his own damn self," Boom said. "Doing business with morons like ole Larry Cobb. That man ever gets out of prison, I promise you he won't make the same mistake twice. Unlike a dumb son of a bitch we both know."

"Donnie?" Quinn said. "Thought had crossed my mind."

"A big gun deal in north Mississippi? Donnie Varner's crazy ass gotta be involved," Boom said. "What are the chances?"

"Maybe we go and talk to Donnie."

"Man wouldn't say shit if his mouth was full of it," Boom said. "I love Donnie. You love Donnie. But hell, man. You can't trust his ass. Never could."

"If this damn deal is as big as they say, someone's been tipped off."

"Who you thinking?"

"Big money, stolen goods."

"You talking Curtis Creekmore?"

"He lied to me and Lillie before," Quinn said. "He owes us something."

"Who would've thought Bentley Vandeven would actually come through?" Boom said. "Rich white boy trying to make good in this world."

"If the damn rednecks ever realized how much the rich despised them."

"Better catch up," Boom said. "My folks figured that shit out a long time back."

* * *

Two hours later, Curtis Creekmore walked out of the Waffle House picking his teeth and patting his belly after polishing off a T-bone steak, two eggs sunny-side up, and a side order of hash browns scattered, smothered, and covered. Yes, sir, it was gonna be a hell of a fine day in Tupelo. He had a shipment of Stihl chain saws and weed eaters coming in from Birmingham, some Milwaukee tool sets in from Columbus, and some jumbo Bluetooth speakers from Mobile that would be just right for a pleasure boat on the Tombigbee.

"Hello, shithead," Lillie Virgil said.

"Damn, woman," Creekmore said, jumping back three steps. "You're gonna give me a goddamn heart attack sneaking up like that."

"And the world would be a brighter place," she said.

"I've gone straight, Miss Virgil," Creekmore said, swiveling the toothpick in his mouth. "Yes, ma'am. Got right with the Lord. Found me some of that old-time religion. Like ole Peter said to Jesus, *I don't have silver or gold but what I have I'll give to you.*"

"Damn, Curtis," Lillie said, leaning against her Charger. "Could you be any more full of shit?"

Creekmore couldn't help it, starting to snicker himself. Lillie Virgil knew what side she was on and he knew what side he was on. It was like two players from opposing football teams meeting outside the arena. *Yes, sir.* He figured that he and that woman Marshal had some mutual respect going on.

"You're pretty goddamn stupid, Curtis, if you think

you can hand off some bullshit to me without retribution," Lillie said. "What did I say?"

"You said you'd let me go if I told you where to find that big Indian," he said. "And I told you. Isn't that how y'all blasted his ole nuts across Choctaw Lake? Oh, I see. You come out here to give me some kind of citizen reward. No, ma'am. I'm fine. I don't need no recognition. Just glad to assist."

"You lied to me and Quinn Colson," Lillie said. "Sam Frye wasn't hanging out at Fannie's lake house. He was headed out to kill that woman."

"Hell, I don't know all the particulars," he said. "I gave you what I got. That's the best I can do."

"I need more," Lillie said, stepping up. She patted his cheek like he was nothing but a boy. "Or you're coming with me to Memphis."

"For what?"

Lillie reached into her pocket and began to read out a list of charges that went clean back to 1993 and things he'd been accused of that he'd long since forgotten about. He figured some of those charges had gone off the books with time being what it was, statute of limitations and all. But Lillie Virgil was here for her goddamn pound of flesh right out of his narrow country ass.

"Someone is running guns in Tibbehah County."

"Ha," Creekmore said. "Someone's always running guns in Tibbehah County. Every man, woman, child, and critter is armed in that place. I heard the goddamn possums carry derringers."

"Someone is running guns today or tomorrow," Lillie said. "They were stolen from a UPS facility in Memphis.

You might have seen it on the fucking news given that you own a million TVs."

"No, ma'am," he said. "Don't know nothing about that."

Creekmore grinned, knowing damn well Donnie Varner was back in business, whether he boosted them guns or not, and had turned them back around to sell them to old Zeke Coldfield and his band of Confederate soldiers or whatever the hell they were. Creekmore kept grinning, working some gristle out of his back teeth with the toothpick. Maybe if he acted cool and stupid, she'd get back in that Dodge and leave him alone.

"Turn around," Lillie said. "Hands behind your back."

"Really?" he said. "Right in front of a fucking family-friendly place like the Waffle House?"

"Where and when?"

"Oh, shit."

"Where and when?"

Creekmore stood back from his truck, letting out a long breath and weighing his options. Staring back at that big tall woman in the mirrored shades, he knew he didn't have too damn many. Not unless he wanted to be trucked up to Memphis tonight and deal with a whole list of charges going back to when he'd been running electronics for old Johnny Stagg and his two-bit Dixie Mafia.

"OK," Creekmore said. "OK. Can you at least give me a damn second, woman? Let me make a couple phone calls."

"Don't screw me, Curtis," Lillie said. "I promise you, you sure aren't my type."

24

Donnie and Midnight Man had unpackaged all the guns and reloaded them into a Little Debbie delivery truck. Little Debbie under that wide-brimmed straw hat painted on the sides, grinning to the goddamn world that she had AMERICA'S NUMBER ONE SNACK CAKE. Donnie had chosen the truck special out of several in Fannie's warehouse, pretty sure that old Mr. Coldfield would nearly shit his pants thinking about Swiss Rolls, chocolate cupcakes, and AR-15s to kick off the Third Battle of Jericho. *Yes, sir, that would be too good to resist,* Donnie thought, punching up Jon Holliday's cell on his ride into Jericho.

"You good?" Holliday asked.

"Ain't there a French singer with your name?" Donnie asked.

"That's Johnny Hallyday," Holliday said. "He had a big hit called '*Requiem pour un fou.*'"

"What the fuck does that mean?"

"Requiem for a fool."

"You shitting me, man?" Donnie said. "That should be my damn theme song as I roll up into the Rebel Truck wash in a Little Debbie's snack truck loaded down with four hundred and forty fucking AR-15s."

"Hope it goes better than last night."

"Three men dead, one of them a damn Memphis cop," Donnie said. "Yeah, tonight should be a real cakewalk. Unless one of those Watchmen gets paranoid. All I need is an army full of nutcases with automatic weapons on my ass. What I want is a goddamn vacation."

"Soon."

"Shit," Donnie said. "You're always saying things like soon. And not much longer. I mean, shit. How long am I indebted to you boys?"

Donnie took the turns from up in the Tibbehah hills, down Highway 9 and toward the bright lights of Jericho, glowing over the wilderness miles away. Both hands on the wheel, looking back in his side mirrors to make sure he hadn't been followed.

"Keep at it, Donnie," Holliday said. "You may not see us. But I promise we're with you every step."

"Side by side with those gun-toting monkeys from the Watchmen Society?" Donnie asked. "I believe if any of those boys got a taste for real war, not just playing pecker-pull GI Joe in the booger woods, they'd shit their damn britches."

"You know it," Holliday said.

"And when will y'all bust 'em?" Donnie said. "Or is this fact-finding mission gonna last from now until judgment day?"

"Soon as the money exchanges hands," Holliday said.

"Just make sure to activate that device I gave you. Step up close on those boys and when you're ready, say the magic word."

"Come on, man," Donnie said. "Can't we come up with something better? You and me both know that sounds damn corny as hell. You really want me to say *tasty*? Besides, I don't know how the hell I'm gonna say that when I get the cash. I mean you try and say fucking tasty in a sentence."

"That's the word," Holliday said. "And I'm sure you'll think of something, given the vehicle you'll be driving."

"You Feds are about as funny as a bad case of the hemorrhoids."

"Hang in there," Holliday said. "We appreciate all you've done."

"We gonna get these folks?"

"You know it," Holliday said. "Everything is contained and controlled."

Donnie smiled, turning into a straightaway, passing the old Dixie gas station as he plucked an American Spirit into the corner of his mouth. "Last time someone told me that, damn hadjis opened up a little box that sent my ass flying far and wide. Didn't wake up until a month later."

"Don't worry," Holliday said. "Just do your part and I promise to get you out safe."

"I knew it," Boom said. "I damn well knew it. Donnie just can't help himself. Here he gets a gift from God, an early damn release, and what does he do? Goes right on back to selling guns as if those last eight years didn't mean a damn thing. If he's lucky enough to get out of this alive, he ain't never gonna get out of prison. Just what do you think that'll do to Luther?"

"You think we can reason with him?" Quinn said.

"Hell no."

They were headed back out from the Magnolia Drive-In after finding the gold GTO gone and Donnie nowhere to be found. Boom drove fast back toward the Square, the mufflers on his big V-8 growling.

"You think maybe we can hit him up and get rid of those guns before he shits the bed?"

"Worth a shot," Boom said.

"Lillie said it's definitely tonight," Quinn said. "Out back of the Rebel. If we can't find him before then, we got to be there."

"To stop the Watchmen?"

"To catch Fannie," Quinn said. "And maybe stop Donnie from getting killed."

"What about your buddy, the Fed," Boom said. "Holliday."

"Already left him four messages," Quinn said. "This can't wait."

"Me and you might get arrested by Brock Tanner and that shitbird monkey with the schoolboy haircut," Boom said. "Want to remind me why we're doing this?"

"Because Donnie's our friend."

"Oh, yeah," Boom said. "I almost forgot."

It was nearly dark when Donnie drove the Little Debbie truck back behind the Rebel Truck Stop and idled by the

bay door to the big corrugated tin building. Donnie
flicked the high beams, the bay door started to rise, and
he headed on into the washing bay. The Watchmen, bless
their hearts, were already there and waiting, dressed
head to foot in the latest stylish military uniforms. Sort
of like men without a country, the only patch on their
arms that of the stars and bars of the Confederacy. There
were eight of them, plus old Zeke Coldfield. Mr. Coldfield looked the same as he did in his local commercials
in that funeral-black suit and powder blue tie, golden
glasses with thick lenses. Donnie swore the old man
licked his damn lips when he saw Little Debbie's picture
smiling down at his ancient ass.

Donnie killed the engine and hopped down out of the
truck.

"You mind if we check on the inventory, son?" Coldfield said.

Donnie shook his head and four of the Watchmen
opened up the truck and trotted on inside as the older
fella with both eyeglasses and a black patch, ole One-
Eyed Willie himself, came up to where Donnie stood
with Zeke Coldfield. The *Duck Dynasty* fucker with the
long gray beard joined them and looked Donnie over as
if inspecting a dog turd.

"The general told me you'd come through," *Duck Dynasty* said. "At first I didn't believe him."

The general? Holy Fucking Christ. These ole boys
were crazier than a truckload of shithouse rats.

"Don't mean to be greedy or impolite," Donnie said.
"But y'all got the money?"

One-Eyed Willie nodded and lifted his chin over to

his *Duck Dynasty* commander pulling at his beard, the buttons damn well about to pop off his uniform. Who knew? Maybe this fucker was the goddamn admiral of their fleet of bass boats or maybe the damn captain of their Southern-made zeppelins. Donnie looked the SOB right in the eye and saluted. Shit, he just couldn't help himself.

Mr. Coldfield reached into his suit pants pocket and pulled out some keys on a jingly ring. He tossed it to Donnie and Donnie caught it in his right hand. "That little round one opens the trunk."

Donnie swallowed. He wasn't too excited about opening up a car trunk with some heavily armed nutcases at his back.

"How about *you* open it?" Donnie said.

"You don't trust us?" Coldfield said. The old man looking genuinely sad and disappointed, like a grandpa who's just been told no one gave a shit for his corny jokes no more. "Take the car and the cash. Just like ole Bob Barker might say on *The Price Is Right*. Son, you just won yourself a 1991 Buick Park Avenue and a half million dollars."

"What about a trip to Acapulco?" Donnie said, walking over to that old car and popping the trunk. He counted out the money the best he could, given the time constraints, the pressure, and the fact that he couldn't keep the money anyway. "And a couple of them models in bikinis with big ole knockers."

Coldfield looked as if he wasn't listening, staring over Donnie's shoulder. Donnie turned to see the Watchmen coming out of the back of the Little Debbie truck, all holding brand-new AR-15s and looking happier than some broke-ass kids at Toys for Tots. They passed around the guns, each of them working the rifles, aiming and dry firing.

"Pleasure doing business with you, son," Coldfield said. "Please give your daddy my best. A true American hero."

Donnie waited for the bullets to start flying or someone trying to snatch up his ass and stick him in the trunk. But no one did. Those boys too damn happy with their surprises in that Little Debbie truck to even notice he was leaving. Donnie got behind the wheel of the Buick, cranked her up, and waited for the big bay door to open and let him free and loose into the night.

He was about to mention those wonderful tasty treats old Mr. Coldfield enjoyed when Donnie noticed the big yellow truck, jacked up on massive tires, idling right in front of the bay doors.

Quinn and Boom got out, both of them carrying shotguns.

"Hey, boys," Donnie said. "Funny running into you here. I was just washing down my delivery truck. Did I tell you my daddy got me a job delivering Little Debbies? I'm peddling them snack cakes all over north Mississippi. I'm gonna be a hero to every little fat kid with a sweet tooth."

Quinn nodded at Boom and they walked into the truck wash. Quinn carried his Remington 12-gauge and Boom carried a cut-down J. C. Higgins he could balance in his good hand. Donnie stood back from the grouping of men in black tac gear, no mistaking the damn Watchmen, along with old Mr. Zeke Coldfield himself. Coldfield looked like a circuit preacher who'd been discovered in the back room of a Memphis cathouse. His pale blue eyes wide and barren, jaw hanging open as Quinn and Boom corralled the boys like Hondo working a herd of cattle.

"Don't see why this is any of your concern, Quinn Colson," Coldfield said. "I thought you was on an extended vacation."

Quinn didn't answer. He and Boom moved clockwise around the gathering. Boom had his gun raised in his good hand and Quinn had his 12-gauge against his shoulder. Four of those boys had pulled AR rifles up to their shoulders, barrels trained on him and Boom. But Quinn almost wanted to walk over and pat those old boys on the back. All four of their guns were missing their magazines. They were aiming empty guns at him and Boom.

Boom noticed it, too, smiling slightly as he walked slow in a ring.

One of the men, who Quinn recognized from his online posts as Silas Pierce, a self-proclaimed general of the crew, wore glasses with one lens blacked out, an Australian slouch hat, and a big revolver. This guy was dead serious, staring Quinn down with that one beady and mean eye, gun stretched out in his hand, level and ready to fire.

"I know who you are," the man said. "My boys should've finished you off out on Perfect Circle Road."

Quinn stood maybe eight feet from the man and could cut the son of a bitch in half with the twitch of a finger.

"You come in here with a shotgun and a one-armed nigger," the man said. "My boys'll turn y'all into hamburger and wash you down these here drainpipes."

"Them magazines sold separately?" Boom said, nodding.

The one-eyed man swallowed, stepping back, his eye wandering around and noticing the gravity of the situation. In all the years Quinn had been sheriff, the one thing he realized was that stupidity had no bounds. The one-eyed man wandered up to Quinn. He kept his gun aimed at him.

"You boys are gonna step back and let us take that snack cake truck outta the wash."

"And let y'all take all the guns?"

"Guns?" Pierce said. "Ain't no guns. Just a truck filled with ole Ho Hos and good old sticky buns. Me and the boys get real hungry out on the range, training and prepping. You better be doing some of that, too, Sheriff."

"Come on, Quinn," Donnie said, palms outstretched, stepping back toward the entrance. It was a step-by-step, slow retreat, but Quinn noticed it. "Just let me work this little deal and we can catch up later. Man's got to work."

"Damn, Donnie," Quinn said. "Working with these turds is beneath even you."

"That hurts, Quinn," Donnie said.

"Hold on, hold on, hold on," Zeke Coldfield said, hobbling on up to where Quinn worked the room with his Remington pump. The old man addressing Quinn as if he'd just stopped him after church to see how his momma and them were doing. "Perhaps we might come to some kind of financial arrangement. I'm a wealthy man and would be glad to fill your coffers a bit. I know times are tough since you got laid off. You just don't understand the gravity of the current situation we have in Mississippi. This is our last stand. This is no different than the selfless act of Nathan Bedford Forrest back in the winter of '64 when he lost his own brother, committing his mortal remains into these wild hills."

"Step back, Mr. Coldfield," Quinn said.

One of the Watchmen, an older guy with a long gray beard, had lowered his empty AR and started to reach for the gun on his hip. Boom flipped the shotgun around and rammed the stock right into the man's nose, sending him down on the wet concrete floor, blood sputtering into his hands.

"And can y'all please lower your damn weapons," Quinn said. "Having empty guns drawn on me is an insult to my intelligence."

"We can work this out, son," Coldfield said. "Me and your granddaddy were good friends. That ole boy made the finest moonshine in eight counties and damn, how your daddy and his crazy brothers could drive."

Quinn turned the gun on one-eyed Silas Pierce, leader of the shitbirds, and told him to lower his weapon or he'd splatter his brains across Little Debbie's pretty little face.

Pierce didn't move.

"I got it," Donnie said. "I got it. Y'all stand down. I fuckin' got it."

"Back up, Donnie."

Quinn had been so intent on saving Donnie and corralling old Mr. Coldfield and the Watchmen that he hadn't noticed Donnie walking up on him from the side. He had an AR-15 of his own now, this one with a full clip inserted, and pointed the gun at Quinn, walking forward.

"Y'all go ahead and git," Donnie said, nodding to the Watchmen. "And I'll hold these boys right here. Sorry for the inconvenience. Enjoy them snack cakes. They're just tasty as hell."

Donnie shouted the last sentence. The room was silent. Donnie looked right at Quinn and winked. Quinn looked at him sideways, trying to figure out just what in the hell he was up to.

"*Tasty* stuff," Donnie said. "Yes, sir. Tasty stuff."

Quinn held the shotgun on Pierce. Mr. Coldfield mumbled something and walked toward the delivery truck. But all the other men looked to Pierce for direction, stopped cold and holding those empty guns.

"Drop the damn gun," Quinn said to Pierce. "Get facedown."

"Like hell," Pierce said, raising his revolver.

Quinn shot Pierce in the chest, sending him hard and quick down on his back. The Watchmen all scattering, searching for cover behind a big trailer with JESUS SAVES painted on the side. A few of them hopped up into the delivery truck and another boy tried to run past Boom toward the open bay door but Boom tripped his ass, sending him skidding headfirst across the soapy wet floor.

The rear door rolled open and from the front and

back of the truck wash, men and women wearing vests that read both FBI and ATF rushed into the building. They got everybody down on the floor in seconds. It took longer for old Mr. Coldfield, who needed assistance to get down on his arthritic knees and place his hands behind his neck.

Jon Holliday walked up to Quinn, who was down on the floor with his hands behind his neck. Holliday reached out a hand and helped Quinn to his feet, nodding down to the dead man on the floor, slouch hat in a pool of blood.

"Might've called me first."

"I did," Quinn said. "Four times with four messages."

"That who I think it is?"

"Yep," Quinn said. "Silas Pierce. First time I'd seen him outside his YouTube videos."

Quinn watched as a woman in an ATF vest and a blue ball cap helped up Donnie and cuffed him behind his back. As she walked him out toward the big bay doors, Donnie gave Quinn a weak smile.

Quinn looked away, unable to look Donnie in the eye. So disappointed that his good friend would work with the men who'd tried to kill him.

"That one is on me," Quinn said. "I should've warned y'all Donnie was back. And probably up to no good."

Holliday nodded, placing a hand on his back. "Let's get you out of here before Brock Tanner shows up," he said. "Me and you got a lot to discuss."

25

Fannie sped toward Choctaw Lake, stopping and slamming her Lexus into park. Two Tibbehah County patrol cars were parked up under a single lamp shining outside the barren Captain's Table Restaurant, the kind of place that served greasy fried fish with a gallon of tartar sauce on the side. The place hadn't been open in years, but the air still smelled of catfish and hushpuppies as Fannie got out, tossing her cigarillo down into the gravel lot full of dirt and weeds.

She walked up toward the shadow of the building where Brock Tanner stood with that dumbass Mitchell Danbury, both of them having the good goddamn sense to keep their mouths closed and let Momma talk.

"What in the fuck is going on out at the Rebel?" she said, speaking direct to Tanner, Danbury not worth her attention.

"Feds busted some of those Watchmen folks," Tanner

said. "They were buying guns off some local boy named Donnie Varner. You know him?"

"Why didn't we know the Feds were down here?" Fannie said. "I mean Christ Almighty, what good are you if you don't know the Feds are working in Tibbehah County? You got to be some kind of stupid not to notice."

"We hadn't been informed," Danbury said, his wide, pockmarked face shiny with sweat, his little bangs combed straight down over his forehead.

"I'm not talking to you," Fannie said. "I'm talking to the fucking sheriff here who's supposed to be watching my ass while I run my damn business. Are you listening to what I'm saying? What in the hell is the FBI doing operating right out my own back door? I heard somebody was killed."

"One of the Watchmen," Tanner said, tightening up his cheek, a little tic in his left eye. "Man named Silas Pierce. He was the leader of the whole crew. Figured you must've done some business with those boys at one time or another."

"Holy hell," Fannie said. "What flaming pile of shit have y'all left on my back door?"

Tanner kind of kicked at the ground with his boots, lifting his eyes up at Danbury, who pursed his tiny mouth and narrowed his eyes. He looked away, out into the lake. Over the water, Fannie could see the lights of her lake house, the dinner party of Vardaman's good ole boys in full swing by now. She'd have to be the one to drive up with the good news. *Sorry to interrupt your crooked little pecker pulls, Governor, but the goddamn Feds are in Tibbehah County and may be watching every single move you make. Don't worry, the cooze and the booze is on the house. Just relax and drink.* Shit. They were screwed.

Danbury caught Tanner's eye again and slowly shook his head.

"Y'all working out some goddamn Morse code?" she said. "What? What is it? I swear to God, if you boys are holding back, I'll reach out and snatch up your nuts in Miss Fannie's hand and squeeze those things until y'all beg for mercy."

"Quinn Colson was there," Tanner said.

"What do you mean Quinn Colson was there?" she said. "Colson was where? At the fucking Rebel?"

"He and that big nigger he hangs out with," Danbury said. "They bust in shooting up the truck wash and I heard one of them is who killed General Pierce."

"How about you wash the redneck out of your fucking mouth?" Fannie said. "You must be tied in with those Watchmen boys, Danbury. Got yourself a ticking pocket watch tattooed on your ass? Yeah, they've done favors for me before, but I'll never work with them again. Too unreliable. Too damn crazy."

Mitchell Danbury didn't answer, dumb black eyes dead on Fannie's, then turned and reached for a tin of Skoal up in his shirt pocket. He thumped at the can and took a little pinch with his thumb and his forefinger, just like the old commercial used to say.

"How many Feds?" she asked.

"Six," Tanner said. "Maybe eight."

"What else they have going on?"

"I think that's it," Tanner said. "The guns Varner was selling were stolen from that big UPS facility up in Memphis. They were onto him and also looking for some black dude named Akeem Triplett, the one and the same Akeem Triplett that used to play at State. Hell of a damn football player before he shattered his ankle."

Fannie heard Triplett had gotten away, shagging ass from Vienna's Place just about the time the Feds busted into the truck wash. She'd tried calling him and Marquis Sledge up in Memphis but hadn't heard a word back. Whatever was going on, they'd blame Fannie for the deal turning to shit.

"Are they gone?"

Tanner nodded. The little tin light over the entrance to the Captain's Table shuddered in the warm wind off the lake, making small squeaking sounds. From where they stood, Fannie could barely make out the sound of music from over at her compound. She wished to God she was there already, pounding a double Dirty Shirley and locking herself in with the governor, making damn sure he continued to insulate and support her good works up in Tibbehah County.

"Is that a party going on?" Danbury asked.

"Not for you, fucknuts," Fannie said. "Y'all need to get out and do some goddamn work. Did you do what I asked you on that woman Caddy Colson?"

Danbury shrugged. "Pulled her and her kid over. I think I scared her pretty damn good."

"That's it?" Fannie said. "I was promised that you both knew how to take care of business. I asked you to handle someone for me and you write them a goddamn ticket? That had to put the real fear of God into Caddy Colson. A fifty-dollar fine."

Fannie thought she could just make out the song playing way out on the lake at her party house. Sounded to her an awful lot like "Everybody Loves Somebody." The notes caught her off guard, nearly leaving her to stumble in her Jimmy Choos. She walked ahead of Tanner and Danbury, moving out through the weedy gravel and toward the dock, straining to listen and knowing she was right. *Ray.* Damn, it was his favorite song. She touched the ruby pendant on her neck and closed her eyes. She breathed for a moment, trying to regain her composure, but still tasted the blood in her mouth after Caddy slapped her hard on her face. Just what would Ray have said about that? Any small transgression, however slight, wasn't to be accepted. Ever.

She opened her eyes and walked back to where her two lawmen for hire languished by their patrol cars, waiting for their orders.

"I want that bitch gone," she said. "Tonight. I don't care how you have to do it."

"Shouldn't we wait?" Tanner said. "Until the dust settles in town?"

"You said the Feds got their prize and are gone," she said. "Right?"

Tanner nodded.

"I don't care what you have to do or how you do it," Fannie said. "But I'm sick of that whole damn Colson clan. Burn that bitch out."

"I know I shouldn't be saying this," Governor J. K. Vardaman said. "Not in this era where every red-blooded man might find himself in front of the firing squad. But ma'am, you sure got a fine body on you. All those bumps and curves. Just sitting here, watching you bend over to fill the water glasses, I'll be damned if I forgot what I came here to talk about."

Nat smiled, wanting to take that serving tray and whack that son of a bitch upside his head. But instead she just thanked him for the compliment and asked if she might get him another scotch. "What was it again, Johnnie Walker or Glenfiddich?"

"I think I'll have some of that Macallan Rare Cask I saw up there," the governor said, smacking his lips, slumped down in a spinning leather chair and eyeing Nat up and down. The man looking a little different than on TV, no suit and tie, just some khaki pants, zipped at half-mast, a blue plaid shirt, and a big-ass jangly gold watch on his wrist. His silver hair had been combed back up off his long, tanned face, hound dog eyes not moving off her breasts.

They were alone in the poker room, Vardaman getting led straight back for his private cocktail while some of the other men mingled under twinkling strands of white lights by the lake. The men had gone straight for the buffet table, scooping nachos in crab dip and shoving chicken wings into their chubby cheeks, pulling the bones out clean. Midnight Man was playing Sinatra and the rest of the old Rat Pack, those boys from Jackson really happy to meet up at Miss Fannie's little dinner party. Later on, there would be charbroiled steaks and cold raw oysters from down around Apalachicola.

"Later on, me and you should have a drink," Governor Vardaman said. "Upstairs."

"Sorry to disappoint you, sir," Nat said. "But I'm not on the menu. I'm just a bartender."

"Damn shame," he said. "Always had me a sweet tooth for black women. Just what are you? Is your momma or daddy white?"

Nat felt the silver tray in her hands, thinking about how she could hold it tight and swing, using it as a sharp-edged weapon aimed right for his Adam's apple as he took a swig of that scotch.

"Oh, they were just people," she said, not being able to resist. "Same as me."

"But you're mixed, aren't you?" he said. "I know some folks have trouble with that, but mixed folks have the damn prettiest babies. You may not know your history, but quadroon and octoroon women were prized down in New Orleans. Y'all have the most lovely skin, like cream in coffee. Yes, ma'am. You are one fine-looking woman and I'm not afraid to say it out loud."

Nat wished she could've told the dumbass crook she'd been a history major at the University of Memphis and studied slave narratives from the antebellum and postwar Deep South. *Yeah, motherfucker, I know all about how white men "valued" mixed women two hundred years ago. I sure as hell don't need a history lesson from the dumb hick who ran on the platform of turning back the clock for Mississippi.*

When Nat turned to set out two more water glasses, she felt the man's small hand run up her bare thigh and almost make it up into her shorts. She knocked the governor's hand away with a smile and a laugh. "Oh, Governor," she said between gritted teeth. "You're such a rascal."

"Darling, you got no idea," he said. "What's your name, baby?"

"Nat," she said, winking at him.

"Nat," he said. "I like that. Simple and cute as a button."

"Good," she said. "You'll be hearing that name again real soon."

"Oh, yeah?" he asked, sleepy-eyed. "Counting on it, sweetheart."

The governor smiled, his leathery sunburned skin bright red against his silver hair and tuft of fur from his open shirt collar. He lifted the scotch again as a few more men, guffawing and back-slapping, entered the room. They had heavy country accents, so garbled and thick it sounded like they had marbles in their mouths. Most of them wore red and blue polo shirts, big expanding bellies hanging over their khaki pants, two with brown leather belts adorned with the logo for Ole Miss. She noticed that one of the men, paunchy and leathery with what looked like a brown squirrel on top of his head, wore a white polo with CEDAR GROVE STABLES embroidered on the chest.

That man going on and on about how glad he was they'd sent all them chicken chokers back to Mexico. As they gathered, she refilled their water glasses and took drink orders.

Vardaman got to his feet and stared down at the leather-topped card table. "How about you leave us for a few minutes, baby," he said. "We got some man talk to do."

Nat smiled. "Y'all just let me know if you need anything," she said. "Anything at all."

Nat Wilkins left the poker room and closed the stained-glass door with a tight little click, the guttural voices muffled from behind her.

Ana Gabriel hadn't left The River since getting back from Memphis. There had been a tearful homecoming with her friends, talk of returning to school, and then an unexpected phone call from her mother. She wasn't sure how it happened, only that Miss Caddy had handed her a phone and told her who was calling. There was so much to say, so much to tell, Ana Gabriel leaving out most of what had happened with the Ramos Brothers, only saying there had been a little trouble but all was fine now. Her mother cried. She cried so much and begged Ana Gabriel to take Sancho and go with her father to Atlanta.

"I can't leave you," Ana Gabriel had said.

"It's finished," her mother said. "They are sending us back. There is nothing to be done."

Ana Gabriel hadn't slept much since then, talking twice to her father, finally agreeing that yes, she and Sancho would come next week. She hadn't told Jason they were leaving so soon. How could she? That boy had risked his life for her. How do you throw away such a gift?

That night she'd gone back to the small cabin, turning off the light where Sancho had fallen asleep reading *Charlotte's Web*. She kissed her brother on the head and changed into a secondhand nightgown Miss Caddy had given her. The nightgown had belonged to someone long ago, white cotton worn thin, comfortable and light as she slid into bed and turned her head to the window, looking out onto the wide-open space behind the barn and the houses where the dry creek had just started to flow.

Tomorrow, she would tell Jason. She and Sancho would return to the old trailer and start to pack whatever they could bring. They would start again. The thought didn't scare Ana Gabriel; her entire life had been about packing up and moving on. That's why she seldom made friends, never liked people to get in close. They were just people she'd never see again on the road to somewhere else.

As she turned her head to the cool pillow, delighted to see the last flickering of the lightning bugs, she smelled the smoke.

Ana Gabriel moved from the bed to the front windows of the cabin and stared into the darkness. She couldn't see much, but the smell was so strong. She opened the front door and walked out onto the gravel path that connected all the cabins at The River. She could hear a crackling, creaking sound. The smoke was coming from the great old barn where they held church.

She crept down the small hill, the nightgown feeling like gossamer against her small body, finding refuge behind Miss Caddy's old truck and hearing the sound of men laughing. As she looked around the grille, she saw a heavy man with a pockmarked face and angular haircut lift a bottle to his lips and then toss it into the barn. He and another man, one she couldn't see but only hear, were laughing, stumbling back to a truck parked down the main road to The River.

The fire was going strong now, flames erupting from the center of the barn over the church pews and bales of hay where they sat during service. Smoke poured from the big open mouth of the church, the two windows of the loft lit up in fire like glowing eyes.

The breath left Ana Gabriel as she sprinted back to the cabins, the nightgown tight and restrictive on her legs as she knocked on doors and screamed for help. Sancho ran out and found her, clutching her elbow and tugging her back from the barn.

The entire structure crackled and burned. Even from where she stood, she could feel the heat radiate off her face and smell her long black hair start to wilt and smolder.

"Why won't they leave us alone?" Sancho said, crying.

"Because they are afraid," Ana Gabriel said, wrapping her arms tight over her chest. "They are all cowards."

The men had left a damn mess.

Nat set about picking up paper plates of chicken bones, dry cheese, and cracker crumbs. Cheese dip that had fallen onto the floor and empty crystal glasses wet with melted ice left on the porch railing. The welcome buffet looked as if it had been attacked by a pack of wild dogs. Not much left, and what was left was filthy and nasty, men leaving half-eaten crackers in the dips, bits of cigar ashes on the cheese tray. Whoever believed in the myth of Southern gentlemen needed to meet these old boys.

She wiped her face with a paper towel, drinking water from a red Solo cup Fannie had given her.

"Apologies," a weathered old voice said behind her as Nat dumped ashes and empty plates into a trash bag. She turned to see a lumbering bald-headed man standing there. He had on a sky blue golf shirt with a small embroidered gold cross on the chest and stiff pleated khakis, a white cowboy hat clutched in his hand.

"Just part of my J-O-B," Nat said, smiling. She took another sip of the ice water and surveyed all the mess that was still left to clean.

"I'm ashamed how those men were acting," he said. "The things they said to you and those other young ladies that welcomed them here. They had no right."

"I think we both know some of those fine young ladies were part of the buffet line."

The man nodded, his pale, almost translucent eyes looking sad. He just stood there on the big deck overlooking Choctaw Lake, almost as if he was waiting for the right words to say.

"Can I help you with something?"

"No, ma'am," he said. "I believe I'm on my way out."

"Oh," Nat said, looking into the windows to the great room. "Y'all's meeting over?"

"No, ma'am," he said. "Just beginning. But I decided I'd rather not be a part of it. I'm too old and too worn out to listen to such filth."

Nat looked the man in the eye and nodded, going back to what she was doing, straightening up and resetting the buffet line for when they headed back outside. The next course would be big silver trays of oysters on ice and shrimp po' boy sandwiches cut into little wedges. She figured if they couldn't beat and bust these old boys' asses, maybe they could just feed them on a chow line until their hearts stopped.

"You remind me of my granddaughter," he said. "If those men spoke to her the way they spoke to the rest of you women, I think they'd have to call in the National Guard."

Nat smiled, tilting her head. "What's your name, sir?"

"Clarence," he said.

"Nice to meet you, Clarence," Nat said, offering her long, lean hand, jangling silver bracelets on her wrist. "I'm Nat. You seem like a good man."

"Well," he said. "Not for a good long while."

He placed the cowboy hat on his head and delicately reached for the porch railing, looking out onto the still, black lake. "My daddy helped build that lake back in nineteen thirty-three," he said. "There is a whole little town under there called Easonville, covered up when they put up the dam and blocked in the river. I don't have any recollection of it, but it had always haunted me. A whole town, little grocery store, and an old filling station down there in all that blackness."

"Are you OK, sir?"

"Just a stupid old man," he said. He looked to lose his footing for a second as he reached out to grab the railing, hat falling down to the porch, knees looking weak.

Nat brought him over a metal chair and the man sat down as she reached for his cowboy hat and placed it in his lap. He used the brim to fan his face. "Looks like I forgot to take my pills," he said. "Would you mind getting me a glass of water, too, Miss Nat?"

"Yes, sir."

"Sure is nice meeting you," he said. "You truly are a ray of sunshine."

Caddy was headed out to The River late that night with Jean, wanting to check on a few things for tomorrow's Sunday service. She knew that tomorrow they'd double capacity with the band Southern Flair, a gospel bluegrass group that she loved, coming to town. This would be the last big fund-raiser before the Christmas season, not only for those immigrant families left in trouble but also for her entire ministry. She was running almost eight thousand dollars behind now, but raising three would maybe allow them to keep their doors open for a few more weeks. It was a tight spot but not an unfamiliar one.

"I think your brother and Boom are way too hard on Donnie," Jean said. "Always have been."

"Donnie deserved some of it."

"But not all," she said. "He was such a cute little rascal. I remember y'all riding those dirt bikes all over town like a bunch of heathens. And when y'all were obsessed that there was real buried treasure out on the old railroad line. You spent that whole summer riding up and down those old tracks, carrying shovels and picks. Set you were going to find it."

"That was pretty dumb," she said. "We nearly got ourselves killed."

"Donnie's handsome, too," Jean said. "Nice eyes and smile."

"OK, Momma," Caddy said. "I get the point."

"Just wanting you to be happy is all," she said. "Every

mother wants that for her children. I prayed and prayed for Quinn. And then he found Maggie. She just appeared in town like I had hoped."

"Sure," Caddy said. "That was a real Hallmark special, calling the sheriff's office on her criminal ex. That man blowing Quinn's truck into a million pieces."

"Worked out fine," she said. "Just want you to find someone. I want you to be happy."

"I am happy," Caddy said, headed on a straight shot south to The River, noticing a strange yellow glow in the distance. "Why is everyone accusing me of not being happy?"

"Look at your hands on the wheel, baby," Jean said. "You've worn your nails down to the quick, hands blistered and cracked. Life doesn't have to be like that."

"I don't have to be with someone to be happy," she said. "Isn't that why you kicked Daddy loose? You weren't happy with him. Y'all were never happy together."

Jean didn't answer, and for nearly a quarter mile, Caddy thought she'd overstepped. Her mother was pretty sensitive on all matters of the original Jason Colson. Caddy turned to see if she'd made her cry but only saw Jean staring straight ahead, a worried look on her face. "Baby," she said. "I think something's a matter."

"That's nothing," she said. "Just some farmer with a burn pile."

"No," Jean said. "I don't believe so. Look again."

Caddy couldn't see more than a few feet ahead of her in her headlights, the big glowing yellow light expanding as they got closer. Now she smelled the smoke and saw the glow was at The River, or pretty damn close to it. She mashed the accelerator and rushed toward the cutoff road.

"I'm sure it's fine," Jean said. "Maybe a little bonfire."

"On a ninety-degree night?" Caddy said.

"Maybe you better call the fire department," Jean said. "Oh, Lord. Do you see that?"

Caddy turned hard off the main road and down past the open cattle gate. The fire department was already there, Caddy driving closer and seeing the arcs of water shooting into the barn and dousing the tin roofs of the cabins. Everything was on fire, lit up like a bright sun in the dark night.

Caddy parked on the gravel road, feeling like someone had punched her square in the gut, and got out of the truck with the engine still running.

She could hear her mother yelling at her to get back, but she didn't listen, just drawn to that heat and flame, knowing everything she'd worked to build was gone.

Skinner heard the commotion going on in the kitchen but didn't pay it much mind. He'd taken his pills, cleared the cobwebs from his head, and felt good enough to stand up and drive home. Reaching for the porch rail and pulling himself to his feet, he heard that redheaded devil Fannie Hathcock herself say, "You didn't need to be in there. That room is off-limits. Looked to the governor like you were eavesdropping, Nat. Why would you do that? Why did you even feel the need to be here tonight? I got Feds crawling all over my ass like fire ants and you better pray to the good Lord above that you sure as hell aren't part of that."

"Hold on, Miss Fannie," the nice girl named Nat said. "I feel like I'm gonna be sick."

"Are you listening to a damn word I've said?" Fannie said. "You've scared the ever-living shit out of the governor. Son of a damn bitch."

"Can you give me a second?" Nat said. "I can't breathe."

Skinner turned his head as the back door opened and he saw Nat stumble outside, Fannie Hathcock following, shoving Nat's shoulders. Fannie plugged a skinny cigar in the corner of her mouth like a gosh-darn man and fired it up. Skinner didn't know what had happened, but Fannie looked mad as hell. Skinner placed his Stetson on his bald head and nodded to the two women. "Evening."

"Let me get my purse," Fannie said, ignoring him. "I'll take you back to Vienna's. You've done enough for one night."

"Are you OK?" Skinner asked.

"She's fine," Fannie said, returning back into the kitchen, screen door thwacking closed behind her. "Please get out of the damn way."

Nat didn't look fine, giving him a weak smile, her eyes big and glassy. The young lady walked on up to him, reached around his neck, and hugged him like a grandchild might, saying loud, "Sure was nice meeting you, sir. Hope you had a good time."

"Appreciate the dinner," Skinner said. "Hope you get to feeling better."

With her mouth not an inch from his ear, Nat whispered, "I'm a federal agent. Make sure this gets to Quinn Colson."

"Ma'am?" Skinner said, stepping back. His face coloring from the young woman getting so close and intimate, the words she said at first an afterthought and then sharpening. *Just what in the gosh-dang world was happening?*

"Come on down to Vienna's anytime," Nat said, holding on to the railing for support, looking into the black night and swallowing hard as Fannie came out from the big stone house.

"Come on," Fannie said, grabbing Nat's upper arm and tugging at her. "I'll drop you in town. What's the matter, Skinner? You waiting for this girl to pass out and get you a little prime-time poon?"

The vulgar words sounded vile and sharp in Skinner's ears as he watched them disappear down a softly lit path lined with gardenias. He craned his head to see Hathcock's fancy white car start up and then drive off into the black night. Just what in the Sam Hill was going on?

Skinner reached into his pocket for his keys, but instead he found a strange black cube.

He studied the little cube for a moment in the light of the porch, smiled, and then tucked it away. Gosh darn. *Quinn Colson.* The Lord sure did work in strange and mysterious ways.

26

The next day, after bouncing from Jericho to Oxford and then over to Tupelo, Quinn stepped out from meetings with Holliday's task force to finish the rest of his cold coffee and burn a fresh Liga Privada. He'd gotten two hours' sleep at the Garden Inn by the BancorpSouth Arena where all the Feds had gathered to plan the nighttime raid. If Holliday hadn't secured those no-knock warrants from Judge Percy in Oxford, he would've headed straight home. Jean had called and told him what had happened out at The River. There wasn't much he could do now but keep focused on the mission.

Holliday said they would hit Fannie's lake house, the Rebel, Vienna's Place, and the sheriff's office at sundown. None of the folks from the DEA had heard from Nat Wilkins since last night.

"Who would've thought that bald-headed fuck would come through?" Lillie asked.

"I think Skinner has been studying on his legacy for the last few months."

"You think?" Lillie said. "What's in it for him? Always something for Skinner at the trough."

"Redemption," Quinn said.

"Nope," Lillie said. "Old man is a fuckwad, but he isn't an idiot. He smells which way the wind is blowing. He's trying to save his ass."

"Little more to that story."

"Maybe you can tell me sometime when I give a shit."

Quinn nodded, turning his head to blow the smoke away from Lillie. He'd gotten a call from Skinner in the middle of the night, wanting them to meet up by the Tibbehah Cross. The old man hemming and hawing about finally seeing the light and being washed in the blood of the lamb before handing over that lovely little black device. After Skinner had left, he'd jacked it into his laptop and watched it for two hours in his truck before he saw the scene Nat wanted him to have. The honorable J. K. Vardaman, sitting at the head of a big round poker table, talking about the ordered killing of Hector Herrera. Quinn had to play it three times before he was sure he heard it right. But there it was live and in glorious living full-color video.

The Feds already had plenty. But Holliday called this the cherry on top.

The late August afternoon was pushing nearly ninety-nine degrees outside the Hilton. Next door, the Ban-corpSouth Arena was hosting a Monster Truck Jam over the weekend. They'd been listening to the big engines growl all morning while breaking into four-member teams for Operation Deliverance. Quinn would roll with Holliday and a team of federal agents to the sheriff's office. Lillie would ride with her partner Charlie Hodge and two folks from the DEA having the honor and pleasure to capture Fannie Hathcock and gather all the evidence they needed from her office at Vienna's and the Rebel.

Lillie had said she wouldn't have it any other way, smiling through the entire meeting in the Hilton banquet room. Holliday tossed her the file on Hathcock that Nat had put together.

"Nat's been silent for a reason," Lillie said. "Fannie must suspect something. Remember what she said about Sam Frye recognizing her?"

"Skinner said Nat looked sick," Quinn said. "The last he saw her, Fannie was taking Nat back to Vienna's."

"Nat wouldn't have gone with that woman at gunpoint," Lillie said. "She would've run."

"Skinner said she looked like she was about to throw up," he said. "That she couldn't stand up straight."

Lillie nodded. Quinn not liking the vacant look on Lillie's face.

Quinn turned as the loudest, most unholy racket sounded from within a tractor trailer and Grave Digger XX headed out nose first, the driver gunning its engines and shaking the other vehicles in the lot. After a few moments, another big truck started to rumble, the noise killing all conversation. He and Lillie watched as Megalodon, the big truck shaped like a massive shark, rolled out of another trailer and wheeled right behind Grave Digger, rolling slow and loud in a mini parade into the open mouth of the arena.

"Goddamn rednecks will pay to see anything," Lillie said.

"I took Jason and Brandon last year."

"Just to prove my goddamn point," Lillie said.

"I'm sure Nat's OK," Quinn said. "She may have hopped off the grid if Fannie was asking too many questions."

"She better be," Lillie said, reaching for Quinn's cigar and taking a puff. "I've been waiting for this moment since that bitch and her circus rolled into town. I don't really give a good goddamn how Fannie leaves."

"You don't mean that," Quinn said, taking back his cigar.

Lillie just stared right at him, not wavering, the smoke floating off into the parking lot and scattering into the hot wind. "Damn shame to hear what those people did to Caddy."

"I wish I'd been out there," Quinn said.

"Can't look out for everyone, everywhere, Ranger," Lillie said. "Did Caddy really step up to Fannie and slap her across her face?"

Quinn nodded.

"I sure do admire the hell out of your sister."

"And now she's left without a church or a mission," Quinn said. "How do you think that'll go?"

"You mean will she go off the rails?" Lillie said. "Like last time? Nah, not this Caddy. Not Caddy now. That woman has been forged in damn steel. She'll rebuild or finally get smart and get the fuck out of Tibbehah."

"Like you."

"Yep," Lillie said. "I'm the only one from that damn county who has any sense. Look at Donnie Varner. Do you really think it was worth an early release to nearly go and get himself killed? He should've told Holliday no thanks and kept on trucking until he could walk out a free man and keep on heading west."

"Took out the Watchmen for me."

"Those old boys would've hung themselves one way or another," Lillie said. "Not exactly a brain trust with their people down in Jackson."

Quinn held his cigar in his right hand and flicked the long ash away with his left middle finger. He took a draw and let it out, feeling that familiar buzz of caffeine and nicotine in his system, already doing his best to get down to two pills a day, cutting it down in half. Not all the way like he'd promised Maggie. But he'd learned long ago, way back when he was nineteen at Fort Benning, you did everything you could to complete the mission. He'd keep running on empty until Tibbehah was cleaned out.

"What about that jug-eared monkey wearing your uniform?" Lillie asked.

"Holliday and I get to pick him up," Quinn said. "Along with a few of his deputies."

"After he's busted, you think he'll still sign his fucking book for me?" Lillie said. "*Honor and Duty.*"

"Sure," Quinn said. "Being arrested will only up his book sales. You know how he'll spin it."

"Persecuted for his politics and faith?"

"Yep."

"Mind if I walk over to where Grave Digger laid down those tracks and puke?"

"Be my guest."

Lillie tugged on her gold sunglasses and smiled at Quinn, dimples formed deep in her cheeks. "This is gonna be one hell of a time, Ranger," Lillie said. "Just like the old days."

"Love you, Lil."

"Damn straight," Lillie said. "You and Maggie ever figure out what you're gonna name that kid? Lillie Virgil Colson sounds awfully nice."

It was early afternoon when Fannie pulled around back of Vienna's Place in a borrowed blue Chevy Impala. Heat radiated off the asphalt as she got out. Being forced to drive a domestic car with no air-conditioning from Memphis had made her sweat through her black tank top, hair lifeless and damp across her face. Vardaman's people had tipped her only two hours before that the raids were coming either tonight or at first light tomorrow. Whenever it went down, Fannie wanted to make sure her ass was long gone.

She should've known a woman with Nat's looks and brains coming hat in hand to work at an interstate titty bar was a Fed. Fannie should've seen it all straight off, but had wanted someone smart and competent under her. So many idiots had come and gone over the years that she was willing to believe it. Of course a woman like

Nat would want to work under Fannie Goddamn Hathcock. It was gonna be just like *The Devil Wears Prada*, but instead of *Vogue* magazine, Nat was there to learn from the high priestess of steaks and titties.

Fannie unlocked the back door and headed into the club, the house lights off, a red glow coming off the bar and down in the VIP rooms. Every time she walked away and came back in, the damn smell nearly knocked her out. It wasn't a bad smell, it was a like a massive Jolly Rancher fart of sugars and cherries and personal lube and whiskey. She'd worked in titty bars all the way from Mobile to Biloxi to New Orleans and that smell was the same. No amount of bleach could get rid of it.

She mounted the steps, walking round and round up onto the catwalk. She unlocked her office and turned on the lights, getting down on her knees to punch up the combo on her safe. She'd grab the laptop and the extra phones and all the standby cash and credit cards she kept. This was the shit she'd been prepping for since she opened up Vienna's. But truth be known, she was kind of sad to see it all go. The entire bar built as a monument to the only person in her family that she gave a shit about, the straight-talking, lovely, and accomplished Vienna. Her mother had been a drunk. Her father had been a creep, turning her out to old men before she had her first period. That old woman knew what she'd gone through, lived and breathed in that old trailer on the Coast, and let her know there was a better world out there, filled with silk dresses and steak dinners. She let it be known that Fannie's mother had been a disappointment, letting men eat her up and destroy her. Vienna understood her granddaughter was smart and capable, made of stronger stuff, sitting there in that wheelchair and grasping her hand. "You got a little something extra, don't you?"

Fannie loaded a big leather travel bag with the money and yanked the laptop off her desk, cord and all, scattering a pile of little pink vouchers for two-for-one lap dances and free buffet dinners Saturday night at the Rebel. The Rebel an afterthought to Vienna's, a joint that only a peckerhead like Johnny Stagg could've loved. Leaving that place every day made you smell like smoked hickory and burned meat.

This was going to work. Everything would be fine. If the Feds came for her, they wouldn't find shit. And nobody, absolutely nobody, would ever hear from Nat. Fannie had made sure of it.

Fannie reached for her bag, weighing a goddamn ton, and placed the laptop under her arm. After she headed back downstairs and moved toward the front door, she caught a quick glimpse of herself in the mirrored walls. Gucci sweatpants, black tank, and a goddamn trucker's cap from the Rebel on her head. Damn if she didn't look like country trash come to town.

If she could just make it to her car and back out to the warehouse and her airfield, she'd be sipping Sazeracs at the Roosevelt in New Orleans by midnight. She'd leave J. K. Vardaman to mop up this Mississippi shitshow and make things right.

Until then, Miss Fannie was shutting down for a short while.

So long, big-ass chicken fried steak. So long, ponytailed truckers with halitosis. So long to ice-cold cocktails on that vintage bar and the whir of the money counter. Damn, it's been a grand old time.

Fannie Hathcock took one last look around at the little islands with the brass poles and the catwalk in the rafters where she could view all the house action and then turned off the lights.

Quinn and Holliday hit the sheriff's office right at 20:00, getting intel that both Brock Tanner and three of his deputies were still inside. They'd rush the dispatch and the deputy meeting room while a team of four would secure the jail guards and the exits in case any of the men made a run for it.

They found Mitchell Danbury first. The chief deputy was seated at the SO conference table parceling out a bucket of chicken and cold biscuits from KFC to other men who'd been special hires by Brock Tanner. Tanner and Danbury had been buddies in the Army, Tanner bringing him up to Tibbehah after Danbury got fired in Louisiana.

Danbury didn't show much. He set down the box of chicken and raised his hands, his right still holding a drumstick, as he muttered, "Goddamn son of a bitch."

The front of his Tibbehah County uniform was dirty and stained with grease, his pockmarked face downturned and dark. Holliday ordered Danbury and the other deputies to lie down on their stomachs and he and Quinn worked to disarm them and zip-tie their hands behind their backs.

"You want to tell me what the fuck's going on?" Danbury said, face flush to the linoleum floor.

"You boys are being charged with accessory to murder," Holliday said.

"Murder?" Danbury said. "Whose fucking murder?"

"Hector Herrera," Holliday said.

"You Fed boys are goddamn crazy," Danbury said. "Been that way since Hoover tried on his first set of pantyhose."

Holliday placed a foot on Danbury's shoulder blades and told him to shut his mouth.

Quinn headed out back into the hall, passing the empty, unmanned dispatch station as he walked back to his old office, the door slightly ajar. He could just make out the profile of Brock Tanner rushing away from his desk and buckling on his gun belt. Just as he hit the doorway, Quinn elbowed him hard in the throat, sending Tanner reeling backward, holding his neck.

Tanner reached for his gun and Quinn knocked his hand away. He head-butted Tanner, knocking him down on his ass. Quinn lifted the Remington pump onto his shoulder.

"We knew y'all were coming," Tanner said, wiping the blood from his nose.

"Glad to see you prepared."

Quinn reached down and pulled the Glock from Tanner's holster, tucking it inside his belt.

"This is a joke," Tanner said. "Your ass will be in prison and those Feds will be out of their goddamn jobs."

"Is that a fact?"

Holliday and another agent from the Memphis office

walked into the room. Holliday reached onto the desk and tossed a box of Kleenex to Tanner. "Got a little something on your face."

"This is nothing but a damn witch hunt," he said. "A big ole nothing burger of lies."

"Talk to your boss, Vardaman," Holliday said. "He's the one who sold your ass out."

"Bullshit."

"I'd tell you more," Holliday said. "But I'd hate to spoil the surprise. Y'all will hear it all at your first appearance."

"Hear it all?" Tanner said. "What the hell are you boys talking about?"

Tanner pushed himself up by his elbows, ripping Kleenex from his box and mopping at his face. Tanner's face, which always looked perpetually dirty from a five o'clock shadow, was a mess of blood flowing from his nose and smeared across his jaw.

Quinn looked around the office, the walls bare and blank, his framed American flag off the wall and hidden in a dusty corner, a side window open with a box fan whirring away the August heat. The desk was a mess of files and papers, Styrofoam cups and empty cartons of half-eaten food.

Holliday reached down and ripped the silver star from Tanner's sunken chest. He tossed it over and Quinn snatched it in midair.

The weight of it felt right in the palm of his left hand. Quinn nodded.

"Sheriff," Holliday said. "Please secure these prisoners for transport back to Oxford."

* * *

At that same moment, Lillie and her partner Charlie Hodge burst into Vienna's Place carrying guns and wearing their black U.S. Marshals vests. Lillie yelling up at the DJ playing a goddamn Post Malone song to please shut the fuck up.

"I hate Post Malone," Lillie said.

Charlie Hodge, slim and gray-haired, looked over at her and shrugged.

"You don't have a fucking clue what I'm talking about."

"Can't say I do, Lil," he said. "Last time I was in a joint like this they were playing Boots Randolph."

The big room had gone wonderfully silent, the women onstage just standing there dazed, not sure whether to drop down and gather up all those crinkled dollar bills or put their hands up. Lillie reminded them to stand still as two teams from the DEA gathered up all the patrons, twenty or so fine gentlemen, to line up against the far wall.

One of the agents, a black man with a bleached blond afro named Horatio Jones, was talking to the bartender and pointing up to the darkened crow's nest. The woman shook her head.

"Where is she?" Lillie said.

"Says Fannie hasn't been in all night," Jones said.

"Check it out," Lillie said. "Look behind the bar and under the sofas in that VIP jerk parlor back there, too. She's around. No way that woman crawls out of Tibbehah County."

Lillie took the spiral staircase up to the catwalk, holding her flashlight under the chrome Sig Sauer she had in her right hand. She walked slowly into Fannie's office, checking over the big glass desk, coffee table, and bright purple chairs. In one corner of the room, a big, old-fashioned safe sat open and empty.

Someone hit the overhead lights and she turned to see Charlie Hodge leaning in the doorway. "Just how did she know we were coming?" he said. "Girls working to code, too. Topless with those little G-strings on. Everyone nice and cooperative as a church social."

"Where's Midnight Man?"

"They got him over at the Rebel," Charlie said. "Want to head on over?"

Midnight Man was working the giant brick barbecue pit inside the restaurant. He had on sloppy big black pants, an XXXL white T, and an apron coated in blackened streaks and red sauce. His face was sweating, eyes bloodshot from the smoke, and looked to be genuinely surprised some federal agents had come to ask him a few questions.

"Where the fuck is Fannie?" Lillie said.

"Don't know," he said in a croaked, soft whisper. "Y'all try the bar?"

"Yeah, we tried the fucking bar, Midnight Man," Lillie said, leaning against a stainless steel table with pork half-pulled in aluminum containers.

"Don't know what to tell you, Deputy Virgil."

Lillie held out the badge that hung from around her neck, clearly stating she was a U.S. Marshal. Damn.

Lillie shook her head, reached out for a slab of pork

and tasted it. Lots of bad things you could say about Midnight Man, mainly the company he kept, but no one would ever complain about his barbecue. Half the town had mourned when he'd stopped working the pit regular to work security for the titty bar.

"We're looking for Fannie and a woman named Nat who worked over at Vienna's," Lillie said. "You know Nat?"

"Yes, ma'am."

"You know where Fannie took her?"

He slowly turned his big head, left and right. He stood silent as the meat sizzled on the grill, spitting and popping, smoke getting sucked up into the vent.

"You remember when we busted Johnny Stagg's ass?" Lillie asked.

"Yes, ma'am."

"And do you recall how your ass didn't get thrown in jail with him?"

Midnight Man stared, his giant eyes watering as he lifted up his apron to wipe them dry.

"You're a smart man," she said. "The more you help, the less time you'll get."

Midnight Man didn't react. He just stared, flat-footed and dead-eyed in the restaurant at the Rebel. "Where you think?" he said in a croak. "Y'all do realize that woman has her own goddamn airplane."

"Is that where she has Nat?"

Midnight Man didn't answer.

"Come on now, Midnight Man," Lillie said. "Ain't no good barbecue in prison."

"Why you asking me a question that you already know the answer?"

"She's dead," Lillie said, a damn rock in her throat. "Right?"

Midnight Man just stared back at her, his eyes flat and lifeless. "Miss Hathcock the meanest got-damn woman I ever met in my life."

27

Fannie was a half mile from the old airfield when she spotted the flashing lights and the roadblock. Cresting the hill and taking that curve at seventy, it was too late to U-turn and head back to town. She slowed, catching herself in a line with five other cars and trucks, waiting her time, trying to keep calm as she felt like her heart was about to jump out of her chest. She pulled the trucker cap down in her eyes and knotted her hair into a ponytail. Moving up inch by inch, a few more car lengths until some asshole from the highway patrol shined a goddamn flashlight in her face.

"Oh, Lord," Fannie said. "What's going on?"

"License, please." The trooper was big and white with a square jaw and a head like a cinder block.

Fannie reached into her Birkin bag and gave him the ID from one of her dancers, a nice-looking young woman from Baton Rouge named Debbi Dupont who danced under the name Aquamarine. She had red hair and gorgeous green eyes and the biggest set of natural tits Fannie had seen since she herself had turned eighteen.

"Where you headed, Miss Dupont?"

Fannie tapped at the wheel of the Chevy, staring out behind the MHP cars, the burning flares and the shadowed purple hills in the distance. A damn half mile away.

"Church," she said.

The patrolman eyed her, looking her up and down, the black bra up under her tank top on regal display. She glanced down at her large freckled titties and then lifted her eyes up at the patrolman. She softened her smile and gave a dumb little shrug.

He stared at her a long moment, licking his lower lip, and then handed back her driver's license. "Y'all have church this late at night?"

"We have church every night, baby," Fannie said.

"Y'all must be some real holy rollers."

Fannie turned her head and under her breath said, "Bet your fucking ass."

The patrolman's jaw hung open for a moment and then he motioned his flashlight to the highway back behind her. "Road's closed, ma'am," he said. "You're gonna have to double back and find another route to that prayer meeting."

By the time Quinn and Holliday made it out to the airfield, the Feds and their SWAT team had cleared all the buildings and arrested fifteen of Fannie's most trusted employees, including Carl Byrd, who looked to have returned to fine form, chopping up eighteen-wheelers and reselling the parts. The Feds had gathered Fannie's people into one of the old Quonset huts to interview them before sending them to the jail for processing.

Quinn wore his Tibbehah County Sheriff's cap, the silver star pinned to his plain khaki shirt. He had his Beretta clipped to his belt, Remington pump in his right hand.

"No Fannie," Holliday said, walking back from where he'd been speaking to an older black woman in an FBI vest. "No Nat."

"Could she have already flown out?" Quinn asked.

"Nope," Holliday said. "We've been watching this field since sunup. Nothing has come in or out."

"Someone tipped her."

"Lots of folks loyal to Vardaman in Oxford," Holliday said. "They knew something was up as soon as we brought in the Watchmen."

"Lillie said one of Fannie's people said Nat's dead."

"Midnight Man?"

Quinn nodded.

"He would know," Holliday said. "Right there walking behind Johnny Stagg and Fannie. That ole boy is a survivor. Right now, he's got nothing to lose."

Quinn didn't say anything, and Holliday got quiet. Holliday had put Nat on point and dead center of the action, the same spot he'd been in years before when he became Johnny Stagg's right-hand man to bring him down. Nat was a tough woman who'd personally busted apart the whole Pritchard Brothers dope empire, but the big prize was always the Syndicate. She put herself up front to take on Fannie. The thought of what happened to her made Quinn feel uneasy, wishing he'd been doing something besides just recon with Boom up in the hills. *Boom*. Damn. He'd have to tell him.

"If we can't find her," Holliday said, "maybe I'll leave you alone with Brock Tanner at the jail."

Quinn thought about it. The woods around the airfield dark and endless, no moon out tonight. "Then I'd be just like him," Quinn said. "That's something I'd like to avoid."

"I hear you," Holliday said. "And with those ears, Tanner probably heard you, too."

"Honor and duty," Quinn said.

"Those without it are always the loudest."

Quinn nodded, walking out to the edge of the gravel road, staring at the runway, which was freshly paved, small lights blinking red and blue. He recalled being out here several years ago, trying to catch an escaped convict named Esau Davis. Davis came after Caddy's boyfriend Jamey Dixon on account of some stolen loot Dixon had used to start his church, The River, now burned up and gone. He could still see Dixon's head exploding in a pink mist and hear his sister's screams. Quinn wished they would bulldoze this whole damn place, let it return to nature.

As Quinn and Holliday headed back up to the Quonset huts, one of the agents called them over to the hut farthest from the road. Quinn had already been in and out of three of them, marveling on how Fannie had expanded her operation over the last few years. The warehouses were lined floor to ceiling with stolen electronics and truck parts, commercial grade tools, and even workout equipment. One of the huts contained countless classic cars and trucks, a collection that might've rivaled the old Tupelo Auto Museum.

Quinn followed Holliday and the agent inside the hut and saw two semis, four dually trucks, three Dodges and a Ford, and a dirty, but new, white Lexus. Holliday, careful not to touch the car, leaned through an open window and looked inside.

The floor was oil-stained and dirty, one of the semi's engines out on a massive workbench in several pieces. Holliday looked over to Quinn and pointed inside the Lexus. Quinn saw what Holliday had found. The gray leather backseats were coated in blood, the headrest a damn mess.

Holliday borrowed Quinn's flashlight and shone it into the open window. Caught in the sticky mess on the leather, looked to be human skin and a clump of black curly hair.

Quinn felt all the air leave his body.

He walked out of the Quonset hut to catch a breath. The air was humid and thick, frogs making a racket down in a nearby creek. He stayed there for a long moment looking out at the blue blinking lights on the airfield. What had that woman done?

As he gritted his teeth and turned back to the gathering of Feds, his cell vibrated in his pocket. Message from Maggie. *She's coming early. Headed to Tupelo with your momma.*

Lillie was with Reggie Caruthers now, just like the old days when they were both working for Quinn at the sheriff's office. Reggie had met her out at Fannie's new lake house, a big, sprawling compound of river rock and cypress, an outdoor fireplace large enough to park a Buick. Reggie had gone ahead inside with two folks from the DEA as Lillie finished a phone conversation with Charlie Hodge, who'd met Quinn and Holliday at the airfield.

Nothing. Nada. That woman had pulled an Elvis Presley and left the fucking building. They had roadblocks on every major highway in and out of town, the Rebel and Vienna's Place shut down, and now it looked like not hide nor red hair of that bitch could be found out on Choctaw Lake. Lillie had to admire the damn balls on Fannie, opening up her own high-end pussy palace for the sleaziest and neediest turds in the South. A private club for old men hopped up on Viagra and bourbon, horny enough to hump the shit out of the old Confederate statue at Ole Miss.

"Hadn't been inside before," Reggie said, walking up, shotgun thrown over his shoulder. "Nice place. Wonder what all that cost her? The land, shipping in all that stone from up North? Shame it's all going to be owned by the government now."

"Yeah," Lillie said. "I just might start to cry. What a fucking loss for the entire community."

"You think she's long gone?"

"Yep."

Reggie nodded. He was still in good shape, short and compact and strong. He looked sharp in his fitted tan uniform and silver star on his chest. She'd trained him from the start, after Quinn had been beaten by an insurance salesman in an election a few years back. She'd taught Reggie the difference in law enforcement and the Army, just as she'd done for Quinn Colson ten years ago.

"But if she was still around," Lillie said. "And spooked."

"I heard Fannie might've had a few safe houses in the county," Reggie said. "Don't know where. Place I saw her car parked most was over at the Golden Cherry. I told Brock Tanner about her webcam girls over there but he never paid me no mind."

"Feds had surveillance on the motel all day," Lillie said. "They said it was nothing but truckers and travelers. Cool AC and color TVs with cable. Fannie even had the pool filled in just in time for summer."

"I don't know about all that," Reggie said. "But that place would've been the second spot I would've hit. Right across the street from the Rebel and Vienna's. Maybe they're right. No way she'd go back there."

"Oh, yeah?" Lillie nodded over to her Charger. "How about we take a little ride, Reggie? Just to satisfy our damn curiosity."

"What do they know?" Fannie asked Nat.

Nat's face was a bloody mess, one eye closed and lip busted. She could taste the blood in her mouth, metallic and hot, as she turned her head and spit on the motel carpet. The blinds were drawn, slats of light from outside the U-shaped motel shining onto the bedspread and a little grouping of a table and chairs by the window. Over a big queen bed was a full bronze starburst, a relic from the fifties that had survived all these years in this shithole.

"I'm not tired," Fannie said. "And I don't have anywhere to go."

"They're coming for you," Nat said. "Won't be long now."

"Shit," Fannie said, grinning. "You really think so?"

When Nat came to that morning, Fannie had pulled on a pair of weighted leather gloves, bragging to Nat how the knuckles had been filled with twelve ounces of steel shot. She said they'd been a gift from some steroid freak cop who used to visit Vienna's on a regular basis. And man, they sure did pack a wallop. Fannie's slim hand in that weighted goatskin felt like a big old rock being tossed right in her face with each punch.

"They want just me?" Fannie said. "Or Vardaman, too?"

Nat shook her head, feeling the warm blood and spit run down her chin. The front of her white T-shirt covered in blood as she mouthed the words "all of it," knowing it didn't make much of a difference now. They were on her, fire ants crawling over Fannie Hathcock's world.

"I fucked up trying to kill the sheriff," Fannie said. "I'm a big girl. I admit that whole thing had a touch of arrogance about it."

Nat leveled her good eye right on Fannie and said, "And Hector Herrera."

Fannie stepped back, ripped the Velcro from her wrist. "That little Mexican man in the Crocs?" she said. "You've got to be fucking kidding me. Just what did you hear Vardaman say?"

"I didn't just hear it, bitch," Nat said. "I got y'all on damn video."

Fannie turned her back and then came back at Nat hard, knocking her jaw nearly sideways. Nat shook her head as her mouth filled with more blood and loose teeth.

She turned her head, spit, and smiled. "That all you got, woman?"

Holliday drove Quinn at ninety miles an hour over to the hospital in Tupelo. Quinn was out of the car before it even stopped, opening the door and running into the reception desk. His mother, Jean, and Maggie's friend Raven were standing there waiting, Jean pointing her finger right at Quinn and saying, "There's the father. That's him." She said it like she was accusing him of shoplifting at the Piggly Wiggly.

"Her water broke two hours ago," Raven said. "Your sister is with Brandon. She didn't want to worry you."

"I'm not worried," Quinn said. "Do I look worried?"

"You've been through this before?" Raven asked, leaving Jean and walking Quinn back through security. Raven, a nurse who was also Maggie's doula, was dressed in hospital scrubs and handed Quinn an ID badge. "Right?"

"Not with one of my own," Quinn said. "Helped a young girl out a long time ago in a camp out in the woods. We had a doctor with us but had some complications getting to a hospital."

"No complications here," Raven said. "Come on in."

Maggie sat on the edge of a bed, head down, eyes closed, swaying slightly from side to side. A nurse gripped her hand and rubbed her back through the thin, papery hospital gown. The nurse waved Quinn over and gave

Maggie's hand to him. He squeezed it and Maggie finally looked up, surprised to see him. Her eyes were slightly unfocused from pain, but she smiled.

"We haven't called the doctor in here yet," Maggie said. "The contractions are too far apart. How in the world did you get here so fast?"

"A federal agent who puts Richard Petty to shame," Quinn said.

"She's coming, Quinn," Maggie said. "She's ready. She just wanted to come on out a little early."

"I'm here," Quinn said. "Everything is going to be fine. Just relax and breathe."

"Really?" Maggie said, eyes closing lightly. "Relax? Do you really think I can relax?"

Quinn reached up and brushed the bangs off her forehead. He leaned down and kissed her on her freckled cheek.

"Everything's OK back home?" Maggie asked. "Brandon's OK? Our farm is OK? Right. Everything is right where we left it? They burned Caddy's barn. They tried to kill her, Quinn."

"Don't worry," Quinn said. "All that's over. We've got everything in hand."

"If you lie to me," Lillie Virgil said to the front desk clerk at the Golden Cherry, "I swear to God, you'll be bunking with the biggest, nastiest gangbanger in Parchman, buddy. No swimming pools or movie stars down in the Delta. Just long nights, a lot of pain, and that damn freight train hammering on home to Memphis."

"She's here," the little man said. "Room twenty-three."

He was old, skinny, slack-jawed, and gray, wearing a Hawaiian shirt two sizes too big open at the collar with tan Sansabelt slacks and flip-flops. Living his best goddamn life out on Highway 45.

"Don't you dare touch that dial and warn her ass," Lillie said, reaching for the key. "Or my offer still stands. I know motherfuckers in that joint who'd fuck a rhino cross-eyed."

She looked over at Reggie. Reggie shaking his head but grinning, too, well aware of Lillie's light touch, friendly approach when getting close to a suspect. They walked out into the hot night, and Lillie popped the trunk of her silver Charger, pulling out her favorite shotgun. A sweet Mossberg 590 Shockwave, heavy-duty and quick-loading. Lillie grabbed a handful of shells, thumbed in a few, and packed the others into her U.S. Marshal's vest.

From where she stood, Lillie spotted a dozen or so sheriff's cruisers from surrounding counties and several news trucks in front of the Rebel. The entrance onto Highway 45 still blocked off by the highway patrol, blue lights flashing in the dark.

"Shouldn't we wait?" Reggie asked.

"For what?" Lillie said. "A goddamn invitation? Come on, let's go snatch up that bitch."

Fannie reached down and touched Nat's bloody face, gripping her chin and moving her head from side to side. She may have actually done it. The woman was breathing, but just barely, and not saying a goddamn word. Little bloody bubbles formed at the corner of her mouth.

Fannie walked over to the queen bed, where she'd spread out another change of clothes: a Lilly Pulitzer beach dress, strappy leather sandals, and a big wide straw hat. She'd already packed her trunk with everything she'd pulled out from Vienna's Place and would get on the road just as soon as those state troopers opened up Highway 45 south. She'd head on down to Mobile and then west to New Orleans. She had lots of friends and lots of business in New Orleans. That would be a fine place to regroup and see exactly what happened to Vardaman. She only half-believed the shit Nat had told her while doped up. She had to be lying when she said Vardaman had admitted he wanted Herrera dead. Fannie had been damn careful never to talk about that side of business. She didn't say anything to Vardaman. Did she?

She walked past Nat, duct-taped to the plastic chair, and into the narrow little bathroom. She checked her new hair, dyed jet black against her pale skin with no eye makeup or lipstick. Just plain ol' Jane trucking on down to the beaches. Nobody would ever imagine she was still in town. The hounds howling all about the woods while the fox patiently waited.

Fannie held on to the sink and closed her eyes. Just one more thing to do.

Fannie reached into her purse and found a lovely silk hankie. Turning back to Nat in the dim light of the motel room, Fannie held the hankie and the flat of her hand to the woman's mouth while pinching her nose shut. Nat shot awake for a moment, pulling at the tape on her wrists and ankles and screaming into Miss Fannie's hand. But Fannie had it. "Shh, baby," Fannie said. "Just hush."

It was then the motel room door splintered off the fucking hinges and in walked a big-ass woman with broad shoulders holding a shotgun.

Damn if it wasn't Lillie Virgil.

"I can't do it," Maggie said, screaming through gritted teeth. "Holy hell, y'all. Jesus. I have to stop. I just have to stop."

"Can't stop," Quinn said. "She's ready. She can't wait any longer."

Maggie was surrounded by Raven and a trio of nurses, the doctor down between her legs, ignoring her and telling her to keep on pushing. She had Quinn's hand, gripping it tight, breathing in and out, trying to be cool and relaxed like the books she'd been reading and all those natural childbirth classes she'd taken before Brandon had been born. But the pain was crushing her whole body. She knew there was no way her body could get through it without ripping apart. She'd have to split apart to get the baby out. The panic started rising and she grabbed Quinn's hand, looking down between her raised knees at the doctor, the doctor again telling her to push.

"I'm doing this natural," Maggie said.

"I know."

"That means I'm in an awful lot of pain."

"Of course."

"Goddamn it, Quinn Colson," Maggie said. "Are you hearing what I'm saying?"

Maggie screamed. Raven had told her to scream low down in her belly, not high, because high screams make you panic and hyperventilate. Maggie screamed so low she growled. The doctor looked up from down below and shook her head. Raven told Quinn they needed Maggie on her feet and they needed his help.

"You can't shake that baby out?" he said.

The doctor pulled down her mask. "Yes, sir," she said. "We sure can. Come on. Grab her up under her arms."

Quinn and Raven helped Maggie slide off the table, feeling as if she'd entered another damn time zone with the pain, her head lolling around, her whole body untethered. Maggie had never even considered taking an epidural, saying she hadn't with Brandon and that it hadn't been that bad. Quinn may have been shot in the back, stabbed, dragged behind a moving truck. But he never in his life had gone through something like this. If he told her to Ranger Up, she felt she just might smack him.

Raven put Maggie's arms around Quinn's neck and showed him how to hold her, Maggie's legs hanging loose, barely touching the floor, almost feeling like she was floating.

"Push," Quinn said.

"Goddamn you, Quinn Colson."

"Push," Quinn said.

"You did this," Maggie said. "You put this in me. I can't do it. I can't push."

But she did. She pushed, her arms dangling from

Quinn's neck at first but then planting her feet in the floor and pulling downward with all the force she could. She could feel her baby's head finally inch past her pubic bone.

Quinn and a nurse, a heavyset woman in scrubs with pink flowers, helped Maggie get back on the birthing bed, the doctor down below calling for her to push some more. *Push. Push. Push.* Damn, she was pushing, feeling like she just might split in two.

"I see her," the doctor said, as calm and easy as could be. "Your baby is coming, Mrs. Colson. I see her little head. You're almost there."

Lillie didn't say a word moving into the motel room, dim from the artificial light outside the plate-glass window, slats of white across the bedspread and over a slumped figure in the far corner.

The woman standing in front of her was Fannie Hathcock but sure didn't look like Fannie. She had black hair and a plain, simple face, wearing a black tank top and tacky-ass sweatpants. She stared at Lillie as Lillie moved forward, the Mossberg up on her shoulder.

"And here we are," Fannie said.

Lillie cut her eyes briefly over at the slumped figure, not seeing more but knowing it was Nat. Lillie looked back up at Fannie, who was smiling, confident and cool with a shotgun in her face, a deputy in the doorway, and state troopers blocking every exit out of town.

Lillie was careful to listen, to watch, to make sure no one else was in the room with them. She moved around Fannie and nodded over to Reggie to check the bathroom. He walked in and out fast, heading back to his place in the doorway. All was clear.

"Don't suppose y'all would be interested in a few million bucks in the back of my car?"

"What did you do to her?"

"Y'all help yourself and let me be on my way," she said. "Easy transaction."

"What did you do to her?"

"Y'all think you were so fucking smart," Fannie said. "Busting up in here, crashing my party, and shitting my damn bed. How about we talk in a few months. Once Governor Vardaman gets hold of your ass, you'll be writing tickets on the Jericho Square, doll."

"Hands up," Lillie said. "Against the wall."

Lillie couldn't help but look down at Nat's slumped head, bloody and bruised, one eye snapped shut, blood all down the front of her T-shirt. When she glanced back to Fannie, Fannie hadn't moved, the woman peering over at something on the nightstand.

In the dim light, Lillie couldn't tell what it was. To her, from where she stood, it might've been a gun.

"Can y'all at least let me snag a smoke," Fannie said. "It's been one hell of a long goddamn day."

"Nope," Lillie said. "Hands up against the fucking wall."

"What are you gonna do, Lillie Virgil?" Fannie said, dead-eyed and staring. "Shoot me? Oh, hell."

Fannie turned and walked over to the nightstand, Lillie trailing her with the barrel of the shotgun as Fannie Hathcock blocked whatever she was reaching for with her back, leaving Lillie to yell at Fannie to drop it and turn around. Fannie spun around quick and hard, that silver object caught up in her hand just as Lillie squeezed the damn trigger and knocked that bitch back hard against the far wall, toppling the lamp off the nightstand and sending her sliding down the wall, blood across her chest and on the bed, on the carpet, and goddamn near everywhere.

"Shit," Lillie said, lowering the shotgun, smelling the smoke and seeing the mess.

Reggie not paying any of it any mind, only running to Nat and checking on her. He put his face up close to hers and then reached for his radio. "We need an ambulance right now."

"She's breathing?" Lillie said, feeling the tears run down her cheeks.

Reggie nodded, taking a folding knife from his uniform and cutting Nat loose from the chair. Lillie took a few steps forward, the fallen lamp casting a strange light up across the bloody wall and the toppled body of Fannie Hathcock. Queen of Mississippi.

Fannie's mouth hung open, eyes glassy, and fingers topped with long red nails splayed open. A few inches away was a small silver case, tiny little cigars scattered across the motel room floor. Lillie could just barely make out the etched inscription. FROM RAY WITH LOVE.

"I warned you, woman," Lillie said. "I've always warned you. But you wouldn't have it any other way."

28

"Did you tell him that you loved him?" Sancho asked. "Perhaps kissed him on the mouth and promised yourself to him? I understand that in Mississippi you could marry at sixteen. That isn't long, Ana Gabriel. So very exciting."

"Where do you learn this stuff?" Ana Gabriel said. "Why do you talk this way? You're too young to understand any of this."

Sancho shrugged. "I am truly wise beyond my years."

She and Sancho again found themselves in Atlanta, living with their father, going to a new school and trying to figure out what was next. Which road do they take? Which way is home? Would they go back to Mexico? Or stay here with these Southern people and lose their culture and their language, melt into that long drive of strip malls and fast food. Never escaping. Every big city looking the same, so forever and anonymous that it felt to Ana Gabriel as if it all might swallow her whole.

"Or did you take off your necklace and press it into his hand?" he asked. "The good one from our grandmother. The crucifix made of gold. That would mean something. That would show that you loved Jason Colson forever."

"You're such a silly boy," Ana Gabriel said. "I text him. We have talked on the phone. OK? Is that what you want to hear?"

Sancho nodded, sipping on a Coca-Cola in the back booth of a Mexican buffet out on Buford Highway. El Toro. The bull. Their father had taken a job as a cook and their new stepmother was a waitress, the winter setting in, the night coming on faster. It was only five but already dark outside the restaurant. Their stepmother working to fill up the big buffet with meat, cheeses, tortillas, green Jell-O, and fried fish heads. There was a taco station and a dessert bar, but despite the big feast, it was empty.

It was early, she and Sancho sitting in that last booth working on their homework, waiting for the time when they would close and they would all go home to the apartment they shared with their stepbrothers and stepsisters. They would watch soccer or bull riding and then fall asleep to the sound of cars zooming along the busy roads. Sometimes Ana Gabriel missed the quiet of the Frog Pond Trailer Park, the woods and creeks they had to cross on their way to school.

"Will we go back to Mississippi?" Sancho asked. "One day if our mother is free?"

Ana Gabriel looked up from her math book, placing

her pencil's rubber eraser to her mouth, thinking on it. "I don't know."

"I miss her," Sancho said.

"I miss her very much," Ana Gabriel said. "With all my heart."

"Perhaps it was all a dream that we will wake from," Sancho said. "Or maybe it really was the Rapture and we are living in what some people call heaven. Or that in-between place people go."

"Purgatory," Ana Gabriel said.

"Yes," Sancho said, looking out behind the buffet and over the mass of empty tables and chairs. The neon sign blazing OPEN in the big plate-glass window. "Yes. There."

"Would you like to call her tonight?" Ana Gabriel said. "Mother gets very lonely where she's been taken. Waiting. So much waiting."

"Will it be much longer?" Sancho said. "They can't keep her locked away forever. Can they?"

"I don't know," she said. "I only know that one day, we will all be together. That I can promise."

"I'm really sorry, Quinn," Donnie said. "I didn't mean to mind fuck you like that. With all you had on your plate, getting kicked out of your office, Feds crawling all over the county, and your wife being pregnant. How is that little girl, by the way? Caddy told me she's about the cutest baby she's ever seen in her life."

"All babies are cute," Quinn said. "But yeah. She's something special."

"Y'all are calling her Halley," Donnie said. "After your aunt?"

"That's right."

"Pretty name," Donnie said. "I like those old-fashioned names. I've had it with those Brittanys, Madisons, and Tiffanys. Or whatever they're called these days. If I ever have a child of my own, I'd name her after my momma. *Delores*. I know that's not the coolest or loveliest name that you've ever heard. But that would mean something. That'd mean something to me."

"You talk to Caddy about that?" Quinn asked. "I don't know if she's up for more kids."

"Oh, I'm just talking," Donnie said. "You know how much I like to talk."

Quinn nodded, taking a sip of coffee. He and Donnie sat around the fire pit in the open field behind the farmhouse. Tomorrow, Donnie would be leaving town, and Caddy and Jason were going with him. All of them moving on to Austin, where Donnie swore he had an Army buddy who had hooked him up with a great job driving a beer truck. Caddy said she'd find something to do, there was always work for people willing to work hard. She was more worried about moving Jason in the middle of the school year, picking up and going to a new state, a new city after all he'd known was Tibbehah County.

"Heard you turned down Luther's offer on the GTO."

"I know," Donnie said. "Can you believe my incredible integrity? He handed over the keys and shook my hand. This, of course, coming after he learned I wasn't a Grade A fuckup and had actually been working for Uncle

Sam. He was right proud of it. Said he always knew that someday I'd do the right thing."

"How's it feel?" Quinn said.

"Doing the right thing?" Donnie said, thinking on it in the glow of the fire. It had been two months now since the raid at the Rebel and the night Fannie Hathcock had been killed. "I guess it feels good. Got my ass out of prison and nailed those damn bastards who got you shot up. I'm only sorry you didn't bag that big Indian yourself. There ain't a shred of honor shooting a man in the back."

"He was just an instrument of Fannie's," Quinn said. "Following orders."

"A soldier," Donnie said. "That's just fucking ironic as hell. How's Lillie doing with all this mess? Heard she's on leave from the Marshals. Any chance you'll bring her on back to Tibbehah?"

"Can you see Lillie moving back to Tibbehah County from Memphis?"

"She did it before."

"And swears she'll never do it again."

Quinn took a big sip of some Four Roses Single Barrel in the coffee mug. He placed his cowboy boots up closer to the ring of stones, warming his feet. That moment might've been 1955 or 1885. He thought about all the folks who'd built a fire in the back pasture over the years, coming and going, fading with time. Choctaws, Confederate soldiers. His grandparents, Uncle Hamp, and Aunt Halley all watching them from the darkened corners of the woods. Sometimes he swore he could feel them walking in that old house, moving about as Quinn rocked with Halley in his lap.

"I promise I won't fuck up again," Donnie said. "I love your sister. I'll do my dead level best to take care of her."

"Driving a beer truck?"

"Hell yes," Donnie said. "Driving a beer truck. Did I tell you it was Coors? Maybe sometime, someday, I'll just take the whole load and head eastbound and down to Tibbehah County. How would that sound, Quinn Colson?"

Quinn poked at the fire with a long stick and looked across at Donnie. "How about you hold off on that, bud. Least for a while."

They had moved before, once even losing everything in a tornado. But this was altogether something different, Jason decided. Now they'd be leaving Jericho, maybe for good this time, and he'd be leaving everything he'd ever known. His momma tried to remind him of all those horrible apartments in Memphis, but that was so long ago that he couldn't even quite place it. And then there had been some time at Uncle Quinn's farm and at Grandma Jean's. His mother said to remember that nothing was permanent, the only home you really had was with family.

"I think that's true," Brandon said after Jason told him what he'd been thinking. "With my old daddy, my mom said we weren't living unless we were living out of boxes. You'll get used to it."

The two boys sat out on the curb of the little bungalow on Stovall Street, not two blocks from the Square. Mr. Donnie and Uncle Quinn working to load up a U-Haul truck while his momma and Grandma Jean packed up more and more boxes.

"Texas ain't Mississippi," Jason said.

"Maybe that's a good thing," Brandon said. "Momma said y'all will have better schools and better roads. I also heard everybody wears cowboy hats. Is that true?"

"I don't know," Jason said. "But Mr. Donnie swears he's gonna buy me and him one, both. I swear to you that man is crazy."

"I'm going to miss y'all," Brandon said. "Are you sad?"

"Naw," Jason said, picking up a stick and raking it in the little gutter. "Best I've seen Momma in a long while. She was laughing and smiling with Mr. Donnie, cutting up this morning about what they were going to do with his old trailer."

"What are they gonna do with it?"

"Leave it with y'all," Jason said. "Maybe you can use it as some kind of fort. You know we'll be back for Christmas. Probably the summers. Maybe y'all can visit Texas, too."

Brandon nodded. He was a cool little kid, had almost been like Jason's little brother for these last two years. Uncle Quinn taking them both hunting and fishing, showing them those old Westerns on TV, telling them the legends of Jimmy Stewart, Randolph Scott, and Gary Cooper. Jason had taught Brandon to hunt for arrowheads and even whistle. Now that kid whistled like a damn bird.

"Dad says this has something to do with finding y'all's grandfather," Brandon said. "Is that true?"

"Don't know about that," Jason said. "But wouldn't surprise me. Grandma Jean said he was over in Texas somewhere, playing hotshot stuntman."

"What's he like?"

"Grandpa?"

"Yeah," Brandon said.

"My grandfather is a damn nut," Jason said. "He's nearly seventy years old and still would climb the tallest tree in Tibbehah County just for the hell of it."

Brandon stood up and brushed the dirt off his jeans. Jason followed, watching Uncle Quinn and Donnie load in a big mattress. Jason turned to Brandon and reached behind his back. "Figure you might could use this," Jason said.

"Your Buck knife?"

"I got two."

"Holy shit," Brandon said.

"Yep," Jason said. "You'll be using it a lot come hunting season. And you can wear it right on your belt. Just like Daniel Boone."

Brandon took it in both hands and thanked Jason. Jason looked at his little cousin and placed a hand on his shoulder. "And if things go south, you can always stab a fella right where it hurts."

"What in the world do you think those boys are talking about?" Maggie asked.

"What do all boys talk about?" Caddy said. "Trucks, hunting, and girls."

"Brandon still hasn't discovered girls."

"That's when it all changes," Caddy said. "Jason is still mooning over Ana Gabriel and she's been gone two months. I don't think it's gonna end anytime soon."

Halley started to cry from the little baby bucket she'd brought her in. Maggie lifted her up and cuddled her in her arms. The kitchen so empty that their words echoed off the wall and floor. The little girl was tiny and light, eyes bright and inquisitive, looking around a world that she couldn't quite focus on yet.

"Now girls," Caddy said. "That's gonna be two times worse."

"You really think so?" Maggie said.

"What do you think?"

Maggie passed Halley over to Caddy and the baby stopped crying. Caddy was so good with kids, humming softly and rocking her back and forth.

"Promise me you'll look out for Momma," Caddy said. "She can be a piece of work."

"I will."

"And don't forget Hondo with all this going on," Caddy said. "I sure love that dog."

"Me, too."

"I would say Quinn," Caddy said. "But that's the most self-sufficient bastard I've ever known. He could live off beef jerky and whiskey for years."

"We have a full house," Maggie said. "It feels good."

Caddy reached out her index finger to Halley and

Halley grasped it in her little hands. "I don't know what she'll be," Caddy said. "But you can bet Halley Colson is gonna be a pistol. It's in her DNA."

Ole Man Skinner died two weeks before Christmas. Quinn rode with Boom to the church service and later the burial. It had been a cold day, drizzling rain, and the reading had been short and sweet, sending on his small group of family and friends over to Pap's for a catfish buffet with a gospel group from New Albany taking on some of Skinner's favorite hymns. According to the program they'd kick things off with "Rock of Ages" and follow up with "In the Sweet By-and-By."

"Never saw us being at that man's burial," Boom said.

"Never saw him coming around."

"But he did," Boom said. "Hadn't been for him, Vardaman's ass wouldn't be headed to federal prison and Nat Wilkins would be dead."

"Before he died, he told me that compromises and excuses would erode your soul."

"True," Boom said. "But he sure did tote that water for Vardaman for a while. Can't believe that man was so almighty stupid to admit he ordered Herrera getting killed."

"These days?" Quinn said. "Arrogance and stupidity walk hand in hand."

"Take a left here," Boom said.

"Pap's is straight ahead."

"I know where Pap's is at," Boom said. "You don't need to tell me where to get catfish."

Quinn turned onto a freshly graveled road down toward the County Barn, where Boom had worked for a number of years and where he'd just started back on the job. Everything from dump trucks to backhoes to patrol cars got repaired or fueled up. Quinn had no idea why Boom wanted to head back here tonight.

They got out of Quinn's vehicle, an old Cherokee that had been put in service when he'd first become sheriff ten years ago. He followed Boom out in the rain while Boom opened up the bay doors and walked into the garage.

"How you doing with those pills?" Boom said.

"After I saw what Maggie did," Quinn said, "on her own? I flushed them down the toilet."

"All you can do," Boom said. "Pain won't stop. But you get used to that shit in time."

Boom hit the overhead lights to spotlight a green Super Duty F-250 truck with a fat light bar on top of the cab and the silver star of the Tibbehah County SO on the doors. The truck had been given a tall lift, custom rims, a winch, and big-ass mud tires and looked ready for the apocalypse.

"This what Skinner had me working on," Boom said. "When he first got me hired back on."

"For who?" Quinn said. "Brock Tanner?"

"Skinner knew you'd be back," Boom said. "Said get that boy ready for whatever's next. I don't know what he was thinking, but he must've been expecting a real shit-storm headed our way."

"I can't take it."

"Skinner knew you'd say that, too," Boom said. "Truck is used. Two years old and all the customizations came out of his own pocket. Called it a gift."

Boom pressed a button on the key fob and the truck rumbled to life, blue lights flashing on the cab and scattering around the garage.

"What do you think, man?" Boom said. "The new Big Green Machine? Or what?"

Quinn nodded, lifting a cigar from his jacket pocket and firing it up. He nodded some more, the smoke twirling up into the lamps. "You did all this?"

"Everything is custom," Boom said. "From nose to damn tail. But you ain't seen the best part yet."

Boom opened up a rear door where Quinn could hook up prisoners to a D-ring.

Behind the driver's side, Boom had strapped in and fitted a baby seat to the rear bench.

"That baby can't be riding in that old beater," Boom said. "You know I'm right."

On Christmas Eve, the Rebel Truck Stop was doing a fine business from both the locals and the folks headed up and down Highway 45 for the holidays. For several months, Vienna's had been shuttered and locked up and the only sign that shone along the highway was a billboard offering the finest chicken fried steak in the Mid-South, not to mention that Kids Eat Free!

The waitresses had decked out the diner side of the truck stop with silver garland and blinking colored lights. A hand-painted sign showed Christ being born in the manger under the Star of Bethlehem, the words PEACE, JOY, & LOVE. JESUS GIVES US ALL written below. The waitresses twirled about in their blue and white uniforms delivering super-sized dinner platters and refilling coffee mugs while Brenda Lee sang "Rockin' Around the Christmas Tree."

There was no snow and ice that night, north Mississippi a rainy and dark fifty-two degrees, with more rain expected for Christmas Day. Everyone was so caught up in their conversations and holiday plans that no one seemed to notice the skinny, gray-headed man wander in from the diesel pumps. If it weren't for the double-breasted blue suit and blue paisley tie, the man might've walked right out of a Walker Evans photo. He had the ruddy complexion of a dirt farmer and the pompadoured hair of a 1950s rockabilly star.

As the man headed on into the Rebel, he seemed to know his way around, waiting until a young woman finished busing a booth in a far back corner. The woman looking up at him as he patiently waited, asking if he had more folks joining him.

"Just me," the man said.

"This is the family table," she said.

"Well, ma'am," the man said. "I am family."

The woman gave a confused look and left with the dirty dishes, the man sitting down at the table and taking in the entire room while popping a peppermint into his mouth and crunching on it with his back molars.

After a few minutes, Midnight Man appeared from the kitchen, holding a coffeepot and a clean mug. He set down the mug and filled it to the rim. Steam rose from the top.

"Wrapped up testimony yesterday," the man said, not even glancing up. "Boy, they sure got Vardaman's ass good. Watched him on TV say he ordered that killin'. Live and in Technicolor. Looked better than damn *Gone with the Wind* on the big screen."

"Good to have you back, boss," Midnight Man said. "Can I get you something else?"

Johnny Stagg added two big tablespoons to his coffee and stirred, thinking on it. "You know, I sure have been craving some of our fine chicken fried steak. And maybe a slice of that hot pecan pie with a big old scoop of vanilla on top. Yes, sir. That'll do the trick."

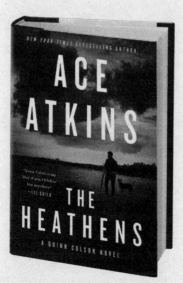

Tanya Jane Byrd, known to her friends as TJ, never gave a damn about being famous. But here she was, four days on the run from Tibbehah County, Mississippi, with that girl Chastity passing along the burner phone to show they now had more than a hundred thousand followers on Instagram. They only had six posts, the newest one from just two hours ago after TJ cut her hair boy short, dyed it black as a raven's wing, and made her ultimatum to that cowardly son of a bitch Chester Pratt. She called him out for not only her mother's murder but the money she and her little brother John Wesley were owed.

On the forty-five-second clip shot outside the Tri-State Motel in Texarkana, she held up her fist on the diving board to an empty pool and said, "Fair is fair," remembering the line from one of her mother's old VHS tapes in the trailer.

"What do you think?" Chastity asked.

"I think I better drop that phone into the nearest creek."

TJ saying *crik* as she had her whole life, never caring about talking proper or right. To hell with how other people said it. At seventeen years old, TJ had no intention of being no different than she'd always been. Famous leader of the Byrd Gang or not. Five feet tall, skin as white as a china plate, and eyes that folks said reminded them of a Siberian husky.

"When we gonna eat?" John Wesley asked. Her nine-year-old brother lying on the other twin bed, kicking his legs back and forth while watching a show about street racers in Memphis. The host some middle-aged douchebag in sunglasses and a tight tank top to show off his big belly and sleeve tattoos.

"We eat when it's safe to go out," TJ said. "Damn, John Wesley. You just downed a pack of them little Krispy Kreme donuts. I swear to Christ, your stomach is gonna get us all kilt."

In the motel room, it was just her, John Wesley, and Chastity. Holly Harkins, TJ's best friend since kindergarten, had decided enough was enough and left them on the side of the road, saying she planned to walk all the way home. Now it was night, they were flat-ass broke, and TJ's boyfriend Ladarius had headed out to steal them another car. They stole the one they had now from a marina parking lot back in Hot Springs after escaping the cops and riding in a boat across Lake Hamilton. TJ was worried as hell about Ladarius after the news of their escape from the law had been broadcast damn near everywhere. *Grisly discovery. Teenage lovers on the run.*

It had been more than a week since her mother had gone missing and five days since they'd found her body stuffed in that oil barrel over in Parsham County. The law didn't take long before looking right at TJ, accusing her and Ladarius of things that weren't true, had never been true, trying to make it seem like some kind of race thing, even though her mother had never been too interested in TJ's personal business. Why they decided to up and blame her, she had no idea, but wasn't about to stick around and find out. Her whole life had been a struggle, trying to break free of folks trying to put her down or use her up. TJ Byrd wasn't standing for that shit anymore.

"Hope Ladarius steals a fast one," John Wesley said.

"Hope he steals a nice one," Chastity said. "Maybe a Lexus. Or a Mercedes like mine."

"Just what are you getting out of all this?" TJ asked.

"Don't you know, TJ?" Chastity asked. "Justice. I want justice for all y'all."

TJ looked over to Chastity, with her ringlets of blonde hair and wide-set blue eyes and that hooked nose that kept her just on the wrong side of being pretty. The makeup and clothes perfect, down to her three-hundred-dollar frayed jeans and little frilly white top. The only frayed jeans that TJ had came from her pants getting worn slap out. All this damn talk about being a social media influencer and reaching the world with a message of truth was giving her a headache. The only reason they let Chastity come along with them was on account of her threatening to call the police back at that mansion on the lake. Of course, the girl did have a point, since the house belonged to her rich daddy, and TJ, Ladarius, Holly, and

John Wesley had busted in and made themselves at home. Two days at the big house and an endless buffet of stolen steak dinners, smoked almonds, cocktail olives, and mini cans of Coca-Cola had allowed them to rest, catch their damn breath, hole up, and think on where they'd be headed next. *California? Texas? Florida?* Spin the damn bottle, boys.

"I know you're innocent," Chastity said.

"Good," TJ said. "So do I."

"Only your people back home don't want you to be."

"What do you know about back home?"

Chastity gave a reckless little look while she played with the tips of her hair and shrugged her shoulders, a mess of freckles across her chest and a half dozen thin gold chains around her neck. One with a diamond-crusted compass on it saying, DADDY'S LITTLE GIRL IS NEVER LOST.

"You think Holly will go to the police?" Chastity asked.

"Nope."

"How can you be so sure?"

"Because she's Holly Goddamn Harkins," TJ said. "My best friend since we was five, before you showed up and damn well elbowed her to the side."

"I think she got pissed we pretended I'd been kidnapped."

"No shit, Chastity," TJ said. "Why else do you think she gave me the middle finger?"

Chastity didn't say anything but gave a small grin as TJ pushed herself up off the bed and walked over to the curtains. She looked out onto the empty pool and the abandoned storefronts across the road, not a mile over the

Texas border from Arkansas, the first time TJ had been in either state. Furthest she'd ever been out of Tibbehah County was a visit up to Memphis to the zoo or Incredible Pizza on John Wesley's birthday. He ate a million pepperoni slices and stuck his whole hand right into that chocolate fountain. He puked all the way back home.

TJ let the curtain drop and headed back into the bathroom, closed the door, and turned on the rusty faucet. She had on a flannel shirt over a red tank top from Walmart and a pair of green camo pants. Her daddy's old .38 was stuck into her waistband with plenty of bullets jangling down in her side pockets. Splashing cool water up into her face, she barely recognized the girl she saw. Her skin pale white, newly black hair up off her head. It had been Chastity's idea to do it. She said it made her look just like some French woman who got burned at the stake.

When she walked back into the room, Chastity had taken her place on the bed, head up on the pillow and scrolling through a new phone they'd bought at Walmart right after leaving Memphis.

"I don't think you should be doing that," TJ said.

"Why?" she said. "It's not registered to you. There's no way to track us. Wow. You should see these hits. We added five hundred more likes in five minutes. I've never seen anything like it."

TJ nodded, her mouth feeling dry and her stomach empty. She nodded to Chastity.

"And what are they saying?" TJ said. "All these people?"

"Lot of boys want to see you naked," she said. "But mostly folks calling you a hero."

"A hero?" TJ said. "For what?"

"For snatching me up to your cause," she said. "For sticking it to that greasy Chester Pratt."

"What the hell do you know about Chester Pratt?"

"Only what you told me," she said. "And that was plenty."

"And you're sure they can't track us?"

"No way." Chasity said, not looking up from the phone. "We're all being too careful."

Deputy U.S. Marshal Lillie Virgil hung up the phone, turned to her partner Charlie Hodge, and said, "They're in Texarkana," she said. "The McCade kid just got caught trying to steal another car."

"Why couldn't these little bastards steal a car back in Memphis down on EP Boulevard?" Hodge said. "I haven't been home in two days. I need a shower and some decent food."

"Kid's in bad shape," Lillie said. "Some dogs got to him."

"Dogs?" Hodge said. "Holy Christ."

For the last twenty-four hours, they'd been working out of the Marshals office in downtown Hot Springs, an ancient government building up the hill from Bathhouse Row and across from the abandoned veteran's hospital. The big brick fortress with dark windows reminded Lillie of an old-time asylum.

"That'll teach him to throw in with TJ Byrd," Lillie said. "Ladarius should consider himself lucky."

Lillie stood up, reached for Hodge's black slicker, and tossed it to him.

Lillie was nearly six feet tall, with broad shoulders and a walk that some whispered looked a little like John Wayne's. She'd been in law enforcement for nearly twenty years, working in Memphis, down in Tibbehah County, and now with the Marshals. She was stronger than most men, a better shot than all, and suffered few fools. Lillie reached for her Sig Sauer and Winchester 12-gauge while she waited for Hodge to follow.

"I haven't seen Rose all week," Lillie said. "That doesn't exactly make me mother of the year now, does it?"

"Who's driving?" Hodge said.

"Now you're just trying to be cute," she said. "With you behind the wheel, we'd be lucky to hit the state line by sunup."

Charlie Hodge was in his last years as a Marshal, nearly twenty years Lillie's senior. A wiry fellow with flinty blue eyes, gray hair, and a thin gray beard, he'd been both a Marine and an undercover agent in Mississippi, working for years against the Dixie mafia. They'd spent the day going over the mansion where those kids had hid out for two days on Lake Hamilton and later checking out the marina where they'd parked their boat and stolen a brand-new Kia Sorento.

"What about Quinn?" Hodge said, slipping into his jacket. "You gonna call him?"

"Rather not," Lillie said, already headed to the staircase. "I didn't leave things on the best terms."

"And that Sheriff Lovemaiden in Parsham County?" Hodge said, walking in tandem with Lillie down the steps to the street.

"You trust that bastard?" Lillie asked.

"Nope."

"Me neither," Lillie said. "He and Chester Pratt have gotten to be thick as thieves and neither one of them have got the sense God gave a squirrel to keep their fucking mouths shut. Gina Byrd was a good friend before she got on drugs and flushed her life down the toilet. Her people had quit on her. But I won't."

Lillie unlocked her Dodge Charger—a special model called the Hellcat confiscated from a drug dealer in Orange Mound—crawled behind the wheel, and pressed the starter. She revved the engine, making it growl and purr as Hodge got in. "Damn, Lil," he said. "Can I at least buckle my belt?"

"Hold onto your nuts and call the locals," she said. "We're southbound and down. These goddamn kids aren't getting away twice."

Sheriff Quinn Colson drove up to Olive Branch, Mississippi, to meet Holly Harkins at a Huddle House off Highway 78. He'd been up for most of the past few days, sleeping little since the body of Gina Byrd had been discovered over in Parsham County. As a retired U.S. Army Ranger and sheriff for nearly a decade, he was used to operating on little to no sleep. In fact, he prided himself on being able keep moving while living off good cigars and black coffee.

"I'm glad you called," Quinn said.

"You ain't gonna arrest me or nothing?"

"There are warrants," Quinn said. "For you, TJ Byrd, and Ladarius McCade."

"They didn't kill Miss Byrd," Holly said. "You got to believe me, Sheriff. I always liked you. You were always real sharp and stand-up when you came to high school to talk to us about the dangers of drugs and staying away from Fannie Hathcock's place out on the highway. Hadn't been for you, I might've ended up working the pole like my cousin."

"That warms my heart, Holly."

Quinn was a trim, muscular man, now nearly forty, with a face full of sharp angles and dark hair cut high and tight like a man still in the service. That night, and as always, he had on a crisp khaki shirt with a silver star, starched and creased dark jeans, and a shined pair of Lucchese boots. Some folks said he reminded them a little of a young James Garner. He liked that, as he'd admired the man who'd marched with Dr. King and played both Major William Darby and the lead in *Support Your Local Sheriff!*

"I can't go to jail," she said. "I didn't do nothing. I was just trying to help TJ. If we hadn't gotten out of town, she would've ended up in a trash barrel just like her momma."

Quinn knew the investigation wasn't his yet, still officially belonging to Sheriff Bruce Lovemaiden, but there was little doubt that whatever happened to Gina occurred in Tibbehah County. The Byrd family, like the Colsons, had been in Tibbehah since well before the Civil War. Gina Byrd's grandfather was an associate of Quinn's grandfather, running moonshine and evading Treasury agents back in the day. She'd been classmates with Quinn and would've graduated with him had she not shacked up with Jerry Jeff Valentine, a man ten years her senior, a part-time house painter and full-time accomplice of the biggest fence in north Mississippi.

"How about you start from the beginning?" Quinn said.

Holly looked behind the counter, all the eggs and bacon and hash browns sizzling on the grill. The air was thick with grease and burnt coffee.

"When's the last time you ate?" Quinn asked.

"That trucker I hitched a ride with gave me some beef jerky."

Quinn handed her a laminated menu slick with oily fingerprints.

"Anything I want?" Holly asked.

Quinn nodded. Holly Harkins sure was a goofy-looking kid, with her mousy brown hair and sad brown eyes. She was tall and gangly with a freckled pug nose, sitting there bland and awkward in a sequined T-shirt of Minnie Mouse reading from the Holy Bible.

"What they're saying about TJ and Ladarius are a bunch of lies," Holly said. "I saw the news. They're trying to turn this damn family tragedy into some kind of redneck Romeo and Juliet. Miss Byrd didn't care at all who TJ was seeing. She was always too damn stoned or drunk most of the time. Like a damn zombie. She didn't know when TJ was coming and going from the trailer. You know the Byrds. You know their ways."

"Unfortunately."

"TJ's not all bad," Holly said. "She does what she does to take care of John Wesley. If she and him didn't steal shit, they wouldn't have anything to eat. TJ's been keeping the lights on in that house since she was thirteen."

"Her little brother shot at one of my deputies," Quinn said. "Right after they broke into the old Pritchard place back in December."

"Y'all never proved that."

"TJ took everything they stole up to a fence in Ripley," Quinn said. "By the time we got onto it, everything was long gone."

"Those Pritchard boys didn't need it," Holly said. "One of them's dead and the other over in Parchman."

"That doesn't make it free for the taking."

"TJ may be a thief," Holly said, "but she's not a killer."

Quinn nodded. The waitress refilled his cup of coffee as Holly ordered the All-Star Special. Two eggs, grits, toast, bacon, and a waffle on the side. Quinn's phone started to buzz, a call from Lillie that he sent straight to voicemail.

"Holly," Quinn said. "Where the hell are those kids headed?"

"I don't know if I should say."

"You should understand I'm the best chance of getting 'em back safe."

"Oh, yeah?"

"Yes, ma'am," Quinn said. "Some folks are sure TJ did this, especially with the history between her and her momma."

"I don't know."

"You have my word."

"Your word, huh," Holly said. "This is turning into some real Bonnie and Clyde shit out there, sheriff. Ain't it? That's why I run off like I did. I didn't want to stick around and see how the picture might end."

* * *

"You said you knew this girl's mother?" Charlie Hodge asked, he and Lillie halfway to Texarkana by now. The billboards and little roadside towns lit up in the dark night, whizzing past the windows, a little bit of rain tapping at their windshield.

"Yep," Lillie said. "She was a friend until she went and fucked herself up."

"How's that?"

"Mainly by a real piece of shit named Jerry Jeff Valentine who sported a mullet and drove a black Monte Carlo SS. Black with red racing stripes."

"Say no more," Hodge said. "That the kids' daddy?"

"The girl's," Lillie said. "Turned out to be a real hero himself. Drove himself off a bridge and into a creek when that girl was little. Her brother had a different daddy altogether, but don't ask me his name. They're just the Byrds, keeping that same family tradition going from a hundred years back."

"And what's that?"

"Town fuckups," Lillie said. "Gina could've been different. She wasn't like all the rest."

"And her daughter?"

"Meaner than a damn snake," Lillie said. "I can't recall how many times I had to make a call on their trailer after she and her momma got into it. One time, she beat up Gina pretty good, bloodied her momma's nose and left bruises all over that poor woman. TJ fought me, too. Kicking and scratching while I dragged her out by her damn ear. Something's wrong with that girl. So much meanness. I heard she and that boy Ladarius McCade sure made a pair. He got her into boosting cars and trucks, smash-and-grabs and house break-ins. He's been in and out of juvie most of his life. Jesus Christ, poor Gina. Did you see the photos of her body after they poured it from that barrel?"

"Wish I hadn't."

"Those kids ain't gonna go easy," Lillie said.

"You think they have some kind of plan?" Hodge said.

"What do you think?"

"Based on my years as a U.S. Marshal and immense wisdom tracking felons?"

"Yes, sir."

"I'd have to say, I've got no goddamn idea, Lillie," Hodge said. "Kids are like any other felons, making up the song as they go."

"Cowardly her bringing her little brother along."

"You got a real problem with this young girl," Hodge said.

"Gina Byrd deserved better than giving birth to that hellcat," Lillie said. "I can't quit thinking about what those damn kids might've done to her. It's not even human."

"Texarkana will give us four of their units," Hodge said. "We got six Marshals from the task force. How do you want to play this?"

"That's not up to us," she said, "now is it?"

"I got to go back with you?" Holly Harkins asked, her Huddle House plate completely cleaned. "Don't I?"

"Yes, ma'am," Quinn said.

"What am I being charged with?"

"Well," Quinn said, "that depends. Where do you think they went after leaving Hot Springs?"

"They talked about Texas," Holly said. "Maybe finding a way to get some money and head on to California."

"What's in California?" Quinn said.

"Swimming pools and movie stars," Holly said, offering a sad smile. "All that shit. That wasn't TJ's idea. That was that girl Chastity."

"And who's Chastity?"

"Spoiled little rich girl," Holly said. "Her daddy owns a Chevy dealership up in Fayetteville. She caught us squatting on her lake house. We thought the place was abandoned. Got weeds growing up all over the damn place. Didn't look like anyone had been there for a long while till that girl comes busting in pulling a gun on Ladarius while he was cooking up some steaks. She's the one who talked TJ into getting on Instagram and telling her story about what happened with Chester Pratt."

"I saw it."

"What'd you think?"

"I think I'd like TJ to drop the act and talk sense to me."

"She ain't gonna do it," Holly said. "She doesn't trust you. She says you're as crooked as everyone else and all you care about is throwing her ass in jail."

"That's not true and she knows it."

"She may take a few things that don't belong to her," Holly said. "My momma says that girl has sticky fingers. But she has a good heart. I promise you that."

"Where are they headed, Holly?"

"I don't know."

"But if you had to guess?"

"This ain't something I want to guess on," she said. "I'm too worried about what's gonna happen. Now they plan to pretend like TJ kidnapped Chastity. Chastity can convince TJ of damn near anything."

"Why would they do that?'

"More attention," Holly said. "More views. All that stuff."

Holly looked out the Huddle House window and stared to cry, wiping the tears away with the back of her hand. Quinn drank some black coffee and waited as someone plugged a nickel into the jukebox and an old Mac Davis song came on. "Baby Don't Get Hooked on Me." Their waitress began to slow dance with a pot-bellied trucker in all denim and pointed-toe boots.

"This sure is a weird place at night."

"Not much different in the day," Quinn said. "A rest stop for folks wanting to be somewhere else."

"Chastity's dad had this room downstairs," Holly said. "It was a secret room in the basement filled with more guns than I ever seen in my life. Chastity loaded a big bag full of them before we took that boat across the lake."

Quinn dropped his forehead into his right hand. Sleep wouldn't come anytime soon.

"She ain't going quietly," Holly said. "That's for damn sure."

Quinn reached for his phone and called Lillie Virgil's cell.

ACE ATKINS

"Atkins finds his natural-born storytellers everywhere. It's all music to these ears."

—Marilyn Stasio, *The New York Times Book Review*

For a complete list of titles and to sign up for our newsletter, please visit prh.com/AceAtkins